"WE MUST BOTH LIVE, OR BOTH DIE; THERE IS NO OTHER WAY."

Her green eyes were bright, and when she spoke, her words took Connal's breath away.

"I care nothing for the morrow. All I care for is tonight, Connal. Do not deny me this."

Fascinated, unable to tear his eyes away, he watched hands—surely they were his hands—pulling to untie the black robe that so loosely covered Maeve's silken skin and soon lay forgotten on the floor as he was confronted by the beauty of her, the golden bottomless mystery of a woman. Her pulse, a single jewel throbbing in the hollow of her throat, jumped and fluttered. A wild rose, a burning rose, a queen, a victim . . .

Her hands fastened on his body with a mastery all their own; her soft voice seemed to be part of the thunder in his mind. He was drowning; she had surrounded him like the storm that lashed the night outside these walls. . . .

FIRE
QUEEN

Deborah Grabien

BANTAM BOOKS
NEW YORK · TORONTO · LONDON · SYDNEY · AUCKLAND

FIRE QUEEN

A Bantam Book / January 1990

Map by Nicholas Grabien.

ISBN 0-553-27635-2

Published simultaneously in the United States and Canada

Bantam Books are published by Bantam Books, a division of
Bantam Doubleday Dell Publishing Group, Inc. Its trademark,
consisting of the words "Bantam Books" and the portrayal of a
rooster, is Registered in U.S. Patent and Trademark Office and
in other countries. Marca Registrada. Bantam Books, 666 Fifth
Avenue, New York, New York 10103.

PRINTED IN THE UNITED STATES OF AMERICA

OPM   0 9 8 7 6 5 4 3 2 1

To Linda Marrow,
who suggested it;
and Elizabeth Pomada,
who did everything else but write it.

Author's Note

Anyone who has read the Irish Cycles, either singly or collectively, will discover that I have taken some liberties with the original legends of Maeve and Connal. Although I have left each in charge of their original birthplace, they were never lovers in the original tales. Covac, while never an uncle to either queen or chieftain, should be immediately recognizable as the original Wicked Uncle of Irish legend. Even his name has remained the same.

What I have tried to do is to take these shades of that green and lovely place and clothe them in the sort of flesh both familiar and understandable to the reader. Therefore, I hope the purists in my audience—for whom I have the deepest admiration—will forgive the hand of the writer as it plays puppeteer instead, moving the strings to please them.

Glossary

allemeurach: Legal status, given to all citizens of Hibernia.

celi: The companions of the chieftain, usually comprised of noblemen.

Cernunnos: Irish deity, the Lord of the Beasts; he ruled animals and the hunt and was represented by his particular creature, the stag.

Crom Cruach: The Bowed One, Lord of the Mound (a very dark Celtic god of death); this deity can be safely equated with Baal.

dagda: The Irish concept of the "good god," whose club can both kill and restore life.

Danu: The moon goddess, ancestral mother of the ancient Celts.

druids: Great religious leaders of early Celtic society; their rituals were complex and sometimes very bloody, and their decisions were final. As the gods' earthly representatives, they held sacred the same creatures as did the gods; the snake, the stag, and the horse, in particular, were considered very holy. They placed great importance on the meaning of dreams.

fila:	Bard (musician, poet); although all druids were taught the arts of music and poetry, not all fili were practicing druids.
fomori:	The one-eyed Demons of the Night, similar to the Greek Furies.
forradh:	A meeting place, usually a flat-topped mound surrounded by open space.
Imbolc:	The festival of lovers and fertility, held in February.
Lugh:	The Sun God, probably the most important of the Celtic deities.
Lugnasadh:	Festival held in honor of Lugh on August 1.
ogham:	Early Celtic alphabet.
oinach:	The common assembly and citizenry, composed of free men and women.
rath:	A circular earthwork (fort), usually surrounded by a palisade; this served a dual purpose, being used both for meetings of the tuath and for defense against invasion.
rath-na-riogh:	The royal rath.
riogh:	King; the feminine, queen, is *rigu*.
Samhain:	This concept has lingered into modern times and corresponds to our Halloween: in Celtic society, the night in which the Sidh, spirits of the otherworld, have the full freedom of the earth.
sheela-na-gig:	Celtic goddess of creation and destruction; carvings of this image are still to be found throughout modern Ireland.

the Sidh:	Spirits, fairy folk; also the otherworld or place where these spirits dwell (pronounced "shee"). This is similar to the Christian concept of purgatory.
the Trinity:	This was comprised of three goddesses: Macha, Morrigan, and Boann. It is a Celtic version of the goddess Kali.
tuath:	Small states and the people who inhabited them; a clan.
tuatha de Danann	Literally, "children of Danu." The ancient Celts identified themselves very strongly with their gods, and saw themselves as the descendants of the goddess Danu or Annan.
vair:	Very soft, bluish-white squirrel fur, greatly prized for adornment.

ULSTER

• Emain

Iron
Hills

Cruachain •

TUAD-
CONNACHT GABAIR • Tara

Wicklow
Hills

forest

DES-GABAIR

MUMAN

HIBERNIA

(CIRCA 200 BC)

Prologue

Under a sky showing sunlight with ominous storm clouds behind, the hosts of Hibernia gathered on the vast plain to watch the kill.

Few among the watchers expected any surprises; the fight would surely last for as long as Maeve could lift a spear, and not a moment longer. Many of those present had fought against Connal's army, and a few had come to their present power because their fathers had fought Ulster's chieftain hand to hand. That a young girl, however potent a fighter, might best him was out of the question; that he might stand back and let her do it never entered their heads.

So they came slowly, singly or attended, each trying for the best vantage point from which to see. Of all the chieftains at Wicklow this day, the two most concerned had brought with them the smallest retinues; surrounded by the ruling classes of the five provinces and the hosts of sanctuary, the combined representatives of Ulster and Connacht numbered less than ten. Three of them—a captain, a celi, and a bard—stood shoulder to shoulder at the very front of the rest, watching and waiting.

To the east and west, clear paths had been left. Up each of these came the two chieftains, dressed for battle, holding their own weapons, alone and unattended. Heads swiveled to watch them, and a sudden buzz of excitement

rippled through the huge crowd, a hum of voices that
moved like wind through the clover.

Connal, the sleeves of his black jerkin stark against
the sheen of his breastplate, looked like a statue of the
lord of the beasts come to life. The copper and iron flashed
where the sun struck it, the black beneath accentuated his
enormous height. A sling was thrust through his belt; in
his left hand he carried the soft pouch that held the deadly
flints, and in his right was a short spear. The bronze
helmet, horned and ornamented with jewels, gave him the
look of some fantastic beast out of legend.

As impressive as he looked, however, few eyes followed
his progress. All attention was riveted on Maeve.

Many of those present were fila, brought by their
lords to record what was happening. Of all the songs that
were made that day, no one ever heard one that did not
include the young Queen of Connacht, so lasting, so great
was the impression she made.

Of all those watching, no one was harder hit than
Brihainn. He stared down, his eyes glazing suddenly, as a
wind from the past moved through him, heavy and irresistible. Connal was his lord, his lifelong friend, but he
had no eyes for Connal. It was Maeve, Maeve slender and
beautiful, Maeve who had suddenly pulled him back into
another time with her, a time where the young Brihainn,
fleeing from two men who would have spitted him on the
end of a spear, watched his warrior mother with a warhorse
between her knees bring them down, killing one, driving
the other as though he were no more than a stray sheep
that must be herded home.

Like Connal, she combined the ores of the warrior,
the gems of the royally born, and the black of the mendicant. But the effect, on Maeve, was precisely opposite that
of Connal; in the gleaming metals she seemed ethereal, a
faery, a spirit sent to guide the dying to the waiting Sidh;
against her white skin the black looked like widow's weeds.
The waterfall of flaming hair was completely hidden, bound
tight so as not to distract her eye, and covered by a helm.
Under the fitted bronze, her neck rose like a lily stem, so
fragile, so slender, so very beautiful; in each hand was a
short spear, the ends wrapped in doeskin.

The field of battle, a slight hollow surrounded by four gentle slopes, was of a size to give the two combatants enough room to maneuver. It ran a length of some fifty feet and came to a width of slightly less; most of it was flat, and all of it was muddy.

They met at its center, their faces a few inches apart, and waited for the master's signal. Through the banded helm Connal's eyes showed shadowed and hollow. His whisper could not have been heard by anyone but Maeve.

"When you begin to tire, my darling, I will know it and drop my guard. Remember what I told you, and kill me then."

Her lips curled into the smile he loved. "I can but wound you with damaged weapons, chieftain."

The black eyes suddenly blazed. As he opened his mouth to answer, the master stepped forward.

"It will begin," he said calmly, and the watching men closed in.

1

CHILDREN AND KILLERS

1

The Chieftain's Daughter

To the woman on the sheepskins, coiling and stretching in the long, continual dance of labor, the singing and the smell of blood were no more than distant shades of the mind.

She turned her body, allowing herself a grunt of pain; she resolutely ignored the desire to force the pain from her with the wild screams that waited deep in her belly. The sun, warming and somehow personal, fell across her cheek; she muttered a short thanksgiving to Lugh, her fists knotting convulsively as another contraction came and went. The warmth of the sunlight was all too brief; in spite of the sweat that coursed down her body, she was very cold.

The hide that protected the doorway of the hut was pushed aside; for a moment she lay in sunlight, blinking and dazzled. Then it fell back into place, and Flyn came softly across the clean straw to kneel at her side.

She looked up into his face, seeing the familiar and well-loved features through a red haze. The eyes that looked down at her were worried; she saw this, and managed a wan smile. He laid a hand across her brow.

"Is it any closer, then?"

"It is." She bit back a cry, shifting in the pool of sweat that had soaked the skins beneath her. "Soon; it will be soon. No worry, Flyn; the child fights me, but not with

anger. This will be a warrior, clean and sharp." The hand
that stroked her brow was tense, and the eyes did not
relax. She tried again, keeping her body as still as possible
to hide the pain. "It was kind of you, to leave the
Lugnasadh and come to me. All is well, Flyn. Trust me for
it."

He struggled with himself for a moment. At last he
burst out, in pain and anger, "I wish you would let me
summon the women to you. What use, to birth our child
alone?"

She closed her eyes against her own weariness. "You
may call the women when the sun is down, and not
before. I told you, I dreamed of this. The Bowed One
came to me, he told me that if I obeyed him in this, I
could keep the child. He would not take it from me, for
my strength in suffering alone in the birthing would
journey into the child and give it a warrior's spirit." She
saw his mouth set mutinously and said quietly, "Your
disbelief is hurtful to me, Flyn. If you cannot believe me,
then you grieve me, and if you grieve me, you cannot stay
here. Believe me or go."

Their eyes locked for a moment, the red haze that
seemed to obscure all clear vision deepening. Flyn's eyes
fell first, and he sighed.

"All right, Nieve. All right. I will leave you and obey
you too. It will be as you say; alone until nightfall."

He got to his feet. With the hide in one hand, he
turned and looked at her. "But the moment the last ray of
sun is vanished, I will send the women. You hear this?"

"I hear and agree. Go back to the festivities now,
chieftain, or you will be missed."

He dropped the hide behind him and went. On the
rank bed of skins Nieve listened to the sound of her own
body raised in protest, not hearing the voices of the men
outside as they lauded their ancestors, praised the gods of
sea and sun, called their sheep to fold.

The old woman came out to find Flyn pacing in tight,
concentric circles, his red hair washed with moonlight. He
jumped when he saw her, then took her shoulder in a hard
grip. "Well, mother? Is it over?"

"Over, and all is well. A daughter for you, young chieftain, a fine daughter, strong and healthy; she suckles even now, and her fists hold tight."

She chuckled suddenly; all the clan knew of Nieve's dream and her belief in it. "It is said that Crom of the Mound has some humor, and here is the proof of it. A warrior daughter for you, chieftain, and for your lady, many hours of lonely pain when she lay thinking of days yet to come. But Crom spoke the truth to her, though the truth be twisted, for she will indeed keep this firstborn. Crom does not demand the sacrifice of a firstborn warrior when the warrior is female." She saw the thin mouth quirk as he fought to suppress a smile, saw the single dimple on one cheek go long with amusement, and said cheerfully, "Go in to her now, young chieftain, else she will sleep before you see her, and that is bad luck. She is fretting to show you."

"Yes, I will go in. My thanks to you." Flyn's voice was husky with relief; despite the show of unconcern demanded by his position, Nieve was old for a first child, everyone knew that such a thing was chancy, and he had been worried sick. He turned on his heel and strode into the hut, leaving the moonlight to fall on the shadowed hills behind him.

The hut held only four people, yet to Flyn, who wished to see his wife alone, it seemed impossibly crowded. There was Tuannh, the fila, with his harp across his knees; he sat staring at the babe, lips moving soundlessly, obviously lost in the throes of an inspiration that would become a song to honor his chief's firstborn. At the foot of the bed sat Anu the midwife, watching Nieve's handling of the child with professional approval. And sitting up, sleepy but seemingly content, Nieve sat with the baby held lightly to one breast. Flyn, soft-footed, came to the bedside and stared down.

He had meant to speak only common words, words shaped by long years of custom, but they would not come. He looked down at the child and spoke from the soul.

"By high Danu! Nieve, is this illusion?"

She smiled up at him. "No illusion, chieftain. Here is the very picture of you." She bent down to nuzzle the child's head, which was covered with a thick layer of red down. The child, never stopping in her suckling, reached a tiny hand upward; the pearl-tinted fingers found the long strands of black hair and wound tight. On one cheek, soft as vair and undulant with drinking, was a long dimple, unmatched on the other side. She was, indeed, the mirror of her father.

"Honor to you, chieftain." Tuannh spoke formally, but his smile was wide and relaxed. "Does this girl please you?"

"She pleases me." Flyn, in the grip of a feeling of awe which was new to him, reached out a tentative hand and laid it on the child's cheek. "No son could have pleased me more. How often is it given to see one's every feature, and each lineament so small and fine? Yes, I am pleased. How not?" He met his wife's eye and, seeing the swell of relief there, suddenly threw his head back and shouted with laughter. "So tiny and pale, a wind would carry her with the seeds. Is this your warrior, Nieve?"

"It is." Nieve shifted the baby from her breast and held it out before her. The child, deprived, suddenly puckered her face into a tense knot and let out a wail of protest. Nieve chuckled, and old Anu laughed with her.

"A moment, and you will feed again. Maeve I name you, in the name of Danu I honor you, you are of the tuatha de Danann, child of light, child of water, welcome."

The baby's crying died abruptly, and with it her mother's laughter. She put the child back at her breast.

Nieve looked at Tuannh, who stared at the now silent infant with superstition clear in his eyes. She looked at Anu, and saw her hands move in a sign against magic. Swallowing hard, eyes wide, she gazed at her husband and said, "She knew my words, Flyn. By wind and water, she understood me."

2

Ulster: Autumn

"Now, young Connal, now! Try for the target!"

For a few moments the young boy and the older man stared at each other. The boy gripped the spear in one hand; the shaft, carved of the finest ash and rubbed to a soft sheen, felt alive to the touch. He was off balance, standing on a slight slope, and he met the eyes of his teacher. The dislike in them was plain for the boy to see; all his life he had been seeing that same inimical wariness in the faces of his people.

A surge of fury rose in his throat, choking him, and with an effort he fought it down. He had just passed his seventh birthday, but this rage was not new to him; he could no more control it than he could control the sharp and hurtful things he said when the anger was on him.

He looked at Mharbain and saw, very easily, what the old man was thinking. The old man, assigned by the chieftain to teach his son the arts of war, had deliberately placed him at a disadvantage, choosing the one side of the target that would make it harder to cast the spear; here was a slope, negligent but enough to put his aim off. And he was facing into the sun, the late afternoon dazzle making his eyes water and blurring his vision.

No, he would not lose his temper, not now. The old man thought to make him look a child, did he? Very well, then; Mharbain would see. Connal gauged the differences of height and balance from the flat ground and, with a sudden twist of his back which pulled sharply at the muscles of groin and thigh, he cast the spear.

There was a whistle as it cut the air, followed by the solid and satisfying sound of iron meeting wood. The dead tree stump, pocked and scarred with years of children and warriors alike casting their practice spears, vibrated momentarily and then settled once more. The shaft of the spear protruded, quivering, from its center.

"So, you learn to adjust, as I had planned. Well done, young Connal." Though the words were praise, the tone was grudging, and Connal knew he had been right. Mharbain had hoped that the chieftain's bad-tempered son would disgrace himself at practice. Connal took a step forward and pushed hard at the old man. Mharbain turned, looking down at him from his greater height with dislike apparent in every line.

Connal spoke through clenched teeth. "A fine teacher, old demon. You did not tell me to adjust; I learned it for myself, in spite of you. It would pleasure you, would it not, and all the tuath, too, were I to fail as a warrior? Well, I will not fail, and may the fomori find you all. I hate you." And, turning on his heel, he ran from the place of learning, away from Mharbain's dislike, making with shaking shoulders and compressed lips to the one place where he might find himself completely alone.

On purpose, on purpose, he did it on purpose . . . the words ran their cold cycle through Connal's mind. His nails dug into his palms, drawing blood. Why, why could he not control his rages? His people hated him for it, his father, his teachers, all of them. Then he reached the glen, blessedly empty, and throwing himself down in the long grass, he closed his eyes against the pain of his thoughts.

But the thoughts would not be stilled, nor would the mocking voice that whispered to him when he was weakest. I will spite them all, he thought, I will be chieftain one day, and a great warrior with it. But the voice waited, sly and suggesting; not if you let anger be your master. A warrior has no masters but the gods and his spirit, his strong arm and the will of his dagda, that god of the heart. . . .

The glen was quiet. Here in this empty stretch of meadow the very birdsong seemed muted and distant, and one could be alone, to wrestle with himself. Connal felt his anger ebb, and the hot tears that always followed anger streaked his face and wetted the daisies. Memories crowded him thick and fast, too many memories for a small boy, and all of them hurtful.

His uncle Fearghail, that huge pale man with his pinched smile and singsong voice, returning to the tuath from failed seasons spent among the druids, looking down at him and saying to his father in a disgusted voice, this puling and evil-tempered brat, was this the best you could make? Mhora, his mother, lying in agony; she was dying in an effort to bring forth another child, to meet his father's desire to supplant him, though the druids had told her to do so would kill her.

Another picture came: Connal himself, creeping close to touch her hand in farewell. He screwed his eyes tight in misery, for of all the bad memories, this was the worst. Once again, as though it had been yesterday, he felt her rebuff, heard her hard voice wracked with pain, and heard it bitter and clear. "Leave me. Do not touch me. I die for your faults, but I will not carry your anger and your bitterness with me when my spirit goes to the Sidh. . . ."

He clutched at the grass, scattering soft clouds of white dandelion seeds across the soft air. It was unjust; they hated him, all of them. His father, his tutor, all the other boys of the tuath. They were jealous, eaten up with their envy of his skill, hating that someday he must be chieftain; and he hated them, one and all, in return.

And what had he done to ask for that? Nothing but shown the high temper and spirit becoming to a warrior. It was not his fault he could not control his furies or hide his pride. Why blame him for what the gods had made him?

The tears had stopped. Connal, limp and exhausted, rolled over onto his back and stared into the bright sky. It was warm, too warm for October; soon it would be Samhain, that night when the ghosts of the Sidh would have the hour between night and morning to work their will on men, and yet here it still was as hot as the day of the midsummer festival. Even as the thought crossed his mind, a sudden gust of wind shook free some leaves, scarlet with the badge of autumn, from the rowan tree under which he lay. He picked them up, for rowans were highly prized and considered to hold magical properties; holding them gently and reverently in one hand, he drew the sign for portent with the other and muttered a short prayer to the Trinity, the three goddesses who ruled the water and the airy places. It was simple and straightforward, and had anyone heard it, they would have known it was but a child who spoke.

"Mother Macha, Mother Morrigan, Mother Boann of the rivers," he breathed, "show me the way to keep my anger deep, and make the people love me."

He repeated this three times, one time for each goddess in the holy trinity, and then once more for the dagda. Then, as the druids did, he threw the leaves from him as far as they would go. They landed close together, two of them touching at the stem, a good sign, a good omen. They heard my prayer, Connal thought jubilantly, and suddenly made an interesting discovery; he had been so absorbed in this casting of magic that his anger had vanished as the summer had. Standing quiet now, he felt the blessed calm rising in his veins like sap. If only I could forever feel as I do now, he thought clearly, the people would love me, my father would love me, and the gods too. . . .

"Connal! Connal, are you—ah, there you are."

Connal turned to meet his father's fila. Among the oinach, the freemen who comprised the Ulster tuath, Cormac alone seemed to honestly like him; the young poet, ten years older than Connal, often took the boy wandering through the hills, showed him which plants were good to eat and which were deadly, playing the bittersweet songs of love and death that the boy wanted most to hear. It was to Cormac alone that the chieftain's son had confided his love of this quiet, empty glen, and wonder of the gods, Cormac had immediately understood and kept his silence. The fila understood Connal's need for privacy, and this holy spot provided it; the glen was avoided by everyone else because of the cromlech, the sacred mound that squatted like a dark and brooding creature at its northern edge.

Now Cormac, his harp bouncing loosely against one leg, came panting into the clearing. "Connal, young Connal, your evening meal will grow cold with waiting for you. Will you come, young lord, or will we give your food to Brihainn?"

This was a long-standing joke between them. Brihainn, the bastard son of the tuath's most feared warrior woman, was a quiet boy some two years older than Connal. He was painfully thin; though healthy and active, he seemed to gain no flesh, in spite of habitually eating more meat than the rest of the tuath together.

Brihainn was a sensitive youth, contemplative and gentle, and Connal would have liked him for a friend. Brihainn's stoicism was a quality Connal did not possess, and seemed to him unusual and admirable. He had seen the older boy watching him sometimes, interest in his gaze; but Brihainn had once seen Connal in the grip of one of the murderous rages that often possessed him, and since that time had proved unapproachable, avoiding him.

As do the others, Connal thought bleakly, and climbed to his feet. Cormac, after one shrewd glance at the misery on the boy's face, dropped his arm across Connal's shoulder and drew him toward the town, chattering amiably.

As they approached, it became apparent that something had happened. The banqueting hall, used only for gatherings of the tuath or visitors from other places, was being lit by torches. Slaves ran to set trenchers at the great table, and the smell of roasting meat eddied on the evening breeze. Cormac stopped with Connal beside him, staring in bewilderment at the scene of frantic activity.

"Mother Danu, what is happening here? All was quiet enough when I left."

"I do not know." Connal's eyes were bright. "It must be visitors, for this is a celebration, and not word of war. Cormac, will you go to my father and ask what has happened?"

"No need for that," said a voice behind him. Brihainn was standing at Connal's shoulder; now, as their eyes met, Brihainn gave a smile as gentle as it was beautiful. "It is travelers from the south. They bring cattle to trade, at a fair price, and the chieftain has called for a high dinner. There will be song and feasting." He turned to Cormac. "The chieftain was asking after you, fila. I heard him."

"Then I suppose I must go and make my bow to him. They will want me to sing at supper." He squeezed Connal's shoulder and went quickly.

The two boys were left staring at one another. Connal, looking at the calm planes of the other's face and seeing the strength beneath it, felt a desire for this strange young man's friendship so strong as to nearly choke him. Yet he could not make the first move, for he feared a rebuff. If an overture was to be made, Brihainn must make it.

He did so. Once again flashing that beautiful smile, he said quite simply, "You look weary, chieftain's son. Is all well with you?"

Connal drew breath. "Yes, Brihainn, I thank you. I am weary from working with the spear, nothing more."

Brihainn looked surprised. "I have seen you at practice, and to me it seemed that the spear grew straight from your soul. Why weary?"

"To cast a spear is tiring," Connal told him dryly, "when your teacher has set you on a hillside, casting down."

"But that is unjust! We are not meant to learn such things so young; why, I can give you near two years, and they have not set me at such work." Abruptly Connal's tone registered. "Do you mean he did it to make you look a fool?"

"I do." Connal shook his head over it, and saw the sudden wariness on the other's face. He spoke wearily. "You have no need to worry, Brihainn; I feel no anger with it, only tiredness in my spirit, and a wishing that I could escape it. To learn from one who hates you is sorry work."

Brihainn reached out, tentatively, and touched the other's shoulder. "Well do I see this. Is there anything, anything at all, that I might do to help you?"

Connal shook his head and smiled. He did not smile often, and his face felt cracked with it. "No, Brihainn, though all my thanks to you." He saw awareness and sympathy, and thought, I will risk it. If he refuses me, what is one more rebuff in so many? Nothing at all. "Brihainn, will you sit with me at the feast tonight? I would be most honored."

Brihainn was very still for a long moment. Then he threw an arm across Connal's shoulders in the traditional gesture of friendship and acceptance.

"Choose your place, chieftain's son, and let us share a skin of drink together."

Through the haze of smoke and firelight, through his delight in having found a friend and his awareness of the speculative glances being cast at him, Connal was aware that the traders were villains.

It was nothing he could have put into words, nothing he could have justified or explained. He only knew that when his father had led the twelve men to table and introduced them to the free citizens gathered for the meal, he had looked at this band of traders and found them rotten.

The leader, a burly man with bad teeth, had given his father the wristshake of friendship. As they sat together, sharing the mead and talking with animation, Connal bent close to Brihainn and whispered softly in his ear.

"My friend, there is something wrong here. If these men are simple traders, then I am Great Crom."

The words were barely breathed; certainly no one but Brihainn could have heard them. Yet Brihainn, his shoulders stiff, spoke almost inaudibly in reply.

"Have a care, Connal. They are your father's guests, and your uncle is watching you. No love for you there."

Connal lifted his head and glanced down the long table. At his father's right hand was the traders' leader, and beside him was Fearghail, pale-skinned and husky, listening to the conversation around him. But for all his seeming air of absorption, his eyes were fixed directly on his nephew.

"He hates you. Now, why is that?"

The softly spoken words so closely echoed his own thought that Connal jumped in his seat. Brihainn, to anyone watching, was merely chatting as boys do; he was smiling, waving his arms around. But the words were in sharp contrast to the gestures, and Connal, with a surge of respect that bordered on awe, understood Brihainn's awareness of danger and his ability to present a face to the world far different from what he truly felt or thought. If I could do that, Connal thought. Sweet mother, if I only could . . .

"Follow my lead, chieftain's son, for now your father's eye is on you as well."

It was true. Connal felt the looks, speculative, chilly, and nearly flushed. But he pantomimed the casting of a spear and laughed aloud, and the eyes moved away.

"Well done, very well indeed." Brihainn's voice held approval. "They have lost interest. Now, my friend, why does your uncle hate you so? Is it envy? Does he wish to be chieftain when your father goes to join the Sidh?"

"Do you know, Brihainn, I have never stopped to wonder? Perhaps I have grown overused to the dislike of others, but I truly never stopped to consider it. I am a fool." He sat quiet a moment, remembering that he had never laid eyes on his uncle before his return from the druids, realizing that he had never given Fearghail a reason to hate him. Yet the first time his uncle had seen him, he had spoken words of chill cruelty and looked at him with distaste. "Brihainn, you are right. He has always hated me, always, and never did I give him any cause. Perhaps he does envy me, after all."

"Find out about it." Brihainn looked sideways at him, and Connal saw the intelligence there. "Be secret, be silent in the doing of it, but find out. You must find out."

Connal nodded and said slowly, "You are right. If he is indeed my enemy because he wants the high chair . . ."

"He may try and murder you, when your father dies? Yes, my friend. I have watched him, and I think he would not hesitate." Brihainn hesitated a moment and added very quietly, "Know your enemies. Always, always know them for who they are and what they are. They will kill you else."

Connal opened his mouth to reply but was forestalled. The chieftain had climbed to his feet, holding a hand out for quiet. "Oinach of Ulster, I would present my son to our guests. Connal, come up to me."

"Be silent, be careful," Brihainn whispered, and Connal walked the length of the great hall, his face calm. From the corner of his eye he saw Brihainn's mother, the warrior woman Sheilagh, watching him with some approval. When he reached the chieftain's chair, he knelt on one knee. His father pulled him to his feet.

"Stand. Machlan, I give you Connal mac Sibhainn, who will be chieftain after me." In a low voice harsh with warning, Sibhainn added, "You will not dishonor us with tantrums, Connal. Remember this."

Connal stood, smiling, and looked into Machlan's eyes. And he saw there what Brihainn had seen, and what his elders and betters seemed to have missed. The man was a renegade, his evil shining out of him. Connal felt his muscles tauten.

Be silent, be secret . . . Connal held out a hand, and for the first time since his infancy, smiled wide and charming. From the edge of his awareness he saw the surprise in the faces surrounding him, saw the startled look on Sibhainn's face and the spasm of hate that slid like moving water across his uncle's face. He glanced down the hall to where Brihainn sat, his face unreadable but his eyes amused, and thought, Goddesses, I thank you, for you have answered my prayer. You have shown me a way for my tomorrows. Be silent, be secret.

"All honor to you, Machlan, leader. With my father I greet you. Be welcome here, and safe traveling when you leave us." His duty done, hearing the rough mutter of thanks from the trader, he went back to his seat. Halfway down the hall his eyes found Cormac, his harp at the ready, nodding and grinning. More approval. Mother Boann, could it truly be this simple, this painless, to gain knowledge, and approval too? Why had he never known it?

"Wisely done." Brihainn's amusement was evident as Connal slipped into his seat. For a moment they grinned at each other. "What is he like close, this trader?"

"I have said it; a villain, no less. Did you see the cattle he brought to trade? Fat and healthy, but their legs too thin; they have seen a long march, those cows. I wonder where he stole them?"

"In the south, I would wager; they have indeed seen

a long march." Brihainn spoke with certainty; he had obviously given the question some thought and drawn his own conclusions. "Not traders, but raiders. Do you agree?"

"Yes. But what can we do, Brihainn? I cannot go to my father; he would dearly love the excuse to have me beaten for presumption, and he would tell me to keep my fingers from matters meant for men and not for children." His voice held an old, familiar note of bitterness. "Can my father be so blind that he cannot see what stares children in the face?"

"Oh, he sees. It is not expedient to admit to himself what his eyes tell him, that is all. This is what it is to be a chieftain, Connal, to mix expedience with courtesy, honeyed words with hard fact. I would not be chieftain for all the gold in Wicklow hills."

Sibhainn called for silence for the fila's singing then, and they finished their meal in silence. When the feasting was over, perhaps only the two boys took note of the fact that when the assembly had broken up, Fearghail went not to his own hearth, but to the shelter raised for Machlan.

To the surprise of the tuath, the friendship that had sprung up between Brihainn and Connal flourished.

Over the next days the two boys were constantly in one another's company. They hunted together, and together slipped from under their teacher's eye to go fish the waters of the great lake to the north; Connal, two years younger, was the better spear handler, but when they hunted the wild geese that flocked to the lakeside for fish and water, it was Brihainn who handled the sling, for he had a superb wrist to match an uncanny vision. They built fires and raced and wrestled one another; more than anything else, however, they talked, with the breathless relief of those who have been denied confidants their whole lives long.

Much of the talk was of fighting, some of ideas; other times they talked of the tuath, exchanging likes and dislikes. But in the end Connal always returned to the ruling of the tuath, for he had found in Brihainn a long eye and the wit to properly interpret what he saw.

Four days after the high supper, Machlan and his band of eleven left the tuath, leaving their cattle behind them and taking, instead, weapons and ornaments, so much easier to transport. It was Brihainn who quietly pointed out that Fearghail seemed to be in unusual spirits, his bitter tongue for once stilled. He kept one eye always on Sibhainn; indeed, for the moment he seemed to have forgotten his nephew's existence.

Early on the second day after Machlan's band had taken their departure, Connal heard Brihainn's familiar low whistle outside his hut and poked his head out. He was surprised to see that morning had not yet broken; small stars showed faintly overhead and a light frost lay across the land. The tuath slept in quiet; not a man or woman, not even an early slave, was to be seen.

"A new morning to you, Brihainn," he yawned. "Oh, my eyes are full of sleep still."

"Then rub them clear and come out quietly, chieftain's son, for there is mischief afoot. And keep your voice low." Brihainn's voice was grim enough to jerk Connal fully awake. He motioned for Brihainn to wait, dressed quickly and quietly, and went outside.

Brihainn took his arm in a firm grip. "Come with me, Connal, and quickly. I have seen something my eyes should not have seen. We must find out."

Connal, who was following close behind, grinned involuntarily. This was Brihainn's song, his motto, his creed: find out about it. But there was something in the set of Brihainn's shoulders, in the way his friend's head was held, that bespoke a tension beyond the normal.

"What did you see, Brihainn, and where are we going?"

"We go to the woods by the lake. As to what I saw—" He broke off and stopped, Connal bumping him hard. "You may not believe me. Yet I saw it, Connal, in truth I did."

Connal, trying to read his companion's face in the blue-black of the night sky, spoke in bewilderment. "Brihainn, I am willing to believe anything you would tell me, but I can believe nothing until it is told. Be clear for me now, cela; what did you see?"

"I saw Fearghail, your uncle Fearghail. I never sleep deep, and tonight I slept hardly at all; I heard a sound, as if someone moving through the tuath who did not wish to be heard. I looked through the hide and saw him."

"My uncle Fearghail? And what was he doing?"

Brihainn's voice was somber. "I saw him make for the forest track, the track to the lake. I saw him reach it handily, then stop to speak with the man who awaited him."

"What! What man was this?"

"Machlan. Machlan who led the travelers; Machlan whom we all saw take his leave of us two sunrises past. He stood in the trees, wearing a secret clear to my eye. Fearghail looked this way and that, fearing eyes on him; men with secrets, Connal, and secrets no good for us."

"Yes, I see." Not since the high dinner had Connal felt the stirrings of his old enemy, rage; now, vital and warming, it crept up along his back and warmed the frost of the dawn from him. His voice grew deeper.

"You did well to wake me, cela; we will find out. Have you any weapons?"

They had reached the forest track and stopped. In the hoarfrost before them two sets of footprints showed clear. Brihainn turned back to Connal and spoke softly.

"Weapons? What good are weapons against grown men? I did not say we must stop whatever villainy is afoot, Connal; I said only that we must find out. When we have the sum of it, we have all the weapons we need."

They stepped into the trees, following the path while never setting foot on it. As it curved out to meet the eastern shore of the great lake, the first rays of sun touched the cold ground, turning it to flame, and Connal halted suddenly, shivering. His voice held a tremor.

"Brihainn, wait. Tonight is Samhain; the evils will be out, hungry for us. It is only morning, and we have some hours to fullness, yet it is still Samhain, daylight or no, and I am uneasy. Are we safe, do you think?"

"Safe from the evil of spirits, yes. But we are not safe from the evil of men, my friend, so keep your voice well down and stay close to the trees. Is it understood?"

Brihainn spoke with authority, and Connal, merely

nodding, took him by one arm. Together they skirted the trees, following the footprints, until they had reached the edge of the woods beyond.

The stifled shriek, followed by the sound of a blow and the muted laughter of men, came from so close that Brihainn was forced to bite back hard on an exclamation. He recovered quickly, his face hardening, and slipping like a shadow between the trees, he motioned Connal to follow.

The three people were in a small copse of beech trees not more than fifteen paces in from the edge of the wood. Two were men, their clothes rumpled, their faces lit with a species of enjoyment unfamiliar and somehow terrible to the younger boy. Drunk with whatever was driving them, they stood shoulder to shoulder over the body of a woman.

She was undressed, trussed and gagged to keep her from crying out. As she shivered in the cold grass, trying feebly to twist her body free, Brihainn saw the bruises on her skin, and suddenly, nauseatingly, he understood what he was seeing.

He wrenched Connal back into the shadows of the trees and spoke unsteadily into his ear.

"Listen to me, chieftain's son. Go back to the tuath as quickly as you can. Wake my mother—you understand, not any of the men—and tell her there is a rape afoot, down by the lake. The woman is my cousin, Alhauna; tell her that. Tell her where I am, as well, but say nothing of Fearghail or his companion; tell her only that you think the men are renegades, trespassers; she will do the rest. Go quickly."

"I will obey you. What will you do?"

"Draw them off," Brihainn answered, and with shaking hands, bent to the ground to snatch up a good-sized stone. "Draw them off and hope I can outrun them. Go."

Running, not caring whether he was heard or not, Connal crashed through the trees toward the town as quickly as he could. As he went he heard the stone strike flesh and the shout of pain. Then Brihainn was gone, running in the opposite direction, leading the men away. He redoubled his pace and came to the hut that Brihainn shared with his widowed mother. The woman still slept.

"Sheilagh," he whispered, and shook her gently by the shoulder. "Sheilagh, I pray you to wake. Brihainn needs you, lady. Wake, wake, and that quickly."

She opened her eyes immediately. Like mother like son, Connal thought; she sleeps like a cat with one eye always on the waking world. Sitting up, pulling her clothing on quickly, she spoke softly. "What is the trouble, young Connal? What need has Brihainn of me, and where is he?"

"By the lake, lady. He sent me to get you and bade me tell you there is a rape afoot. There are two men down there, and a woman, and the woman is your niece Alhauna. He said you would do what must be done."

She was up before he could finish speaking, reaching for a spear with one hand and the bronze trumpet of alarm with the other. She moves like a cat as well, he thought, and was dimly aware of admiration. At the door she stopped, the spear in her hand, a dangerous warrior who would kill to protect her young; her red hair, still tousled from sleep, hung in a wild cloud that fell to her waist. She looked back at Connal and spoke tersely.

"Rouse your father; tell him what has happened, that I have gone to get Brihainn and Alhauna, too, if I can. Bid him bring weapons and company and follow, but say he must not sound the trumpets, for I wish them taken alive. Bid him keep his trumpet quiet and listen for mine and follow."

"It is done," Connal answered, but she was gone, vanished into the night like a shade of Samhain. Connal, following, saw her run like a deer for the forest track, her spear held high and dangerous. He went quickly to his father's house.

Sibhainn, unlike Sheilagh, was slow to wake. It was not until his son had reached out a furious hand and come away with a handful of his father's hair that the chieftain woke, snorting and furious.

"Wake, Sibhainn. There is rape by the lakeside, and Sheilagh and Brihainn have gone forth to save Alhauna's pride for her. Sheilagh bade me tell you to follow quietly, bring men and weapons, but make no sound and listen for her trumpets, for she wishes to take the men alive. Chieftain, cannot you wake!"

But he had underestimated his father's reflexes; Sibhainn had begun to wake with the first words and was reaching for his tunic and his great spear, eyeing his son with wary surprise, before Connal could finish his speech. "I am gone, and you will rouse my ten celi. Tell them they must bring spears and slings, and lead them to me. Who are the men, Connal? Did you see them clear?"

"No." The lie came smoothly and convincingly, though he had never lied before in all his life. "But Brihainn said he would both draw them and hold them for us, and he sent me to rouse his mother and you. It is the forest track and the east shore of the lake. Go quickly, Father, and I will bring your celi."

Connal had never asked his father for anything in all his life, but now, thinking of one young boy and two men who wanted him dead, he swallowed his pride. "Father, I beg you to make all speed. Even now Brihainn may be dead, or dying, and my—and the two men fled to the hills."

Sibhainn strode from the house with Connal stumbling behind him, trying to keep pace. As the chieftain vaulted lightly to his horse's back, Connal heard him chuckle.

"No fear, if Sheilagh is on the hunt," he said, and suddenly the black mare was gone, put at a dangerous speed to the narrow forest track overhung with boughs and branches. As the horse disappeared and the hoofbeats died, Connal thought he heard the three notes of triumph played on a distant trumpet, falling sweet and clear on the morning air. He went to rouse the ten companions of the chieftain.

The oinach of Emain stood in a tight circle around the fire and the council was called.

Brihainn, showing a deep gash at one corner of his mouth, stood shoulder to shoulder with Connal; behind them, protective and dominant, stood Sheilagh, arms akimbo. From her waist dangled a man's head, dried blood streaking the coarse ridges of its severed neck. The face

that had been Machlan's held a faint echo of surprise at his
own ending; the eyes were wide open, one of them
crushed to nothing and crusted with gore, where Sheilagh's
spear had taken him down.

It had been long years since such a meeting had been
held here. Rape was uncommon, for the despoiling of a
woman of one's own tuath brought forth the rage of the
gods and the tuath alike. Yet a rape had occurred; at the
fire, huddled close to Sibhainn with a blank and empty
face, sat Alhauna. She was very young, very frightened,
and Connal could not look long at her without a touch of
fear. He was too young to understand the meaning of what
had happened, yet whatever it was must have been bad
indeed, for it had taken her spirit from her, leaving her
empty.

"Bring my brother forth." Sibhainn, in the two days
since he and his celi had followed Sheilagh to the
lakeside, seemed to have aged. His voice was harsh; as
Fearghail, bound tight, was pushed forward and stumbled into the center of the gathering, the chieftain's
eyes showed no mercy or easiness. Here was a chieftain,
cold and austere, who would allow no personal consideration to sway him.

"Sheilagh na Alhainn, step up, and the boys too."

Brihainn, not waiting for the others, went immediately to the fire. Connal hesitated, confused; a council for
something other than trade or war was new to him.
Behind him, understanding, Sheilagh dropped a soft hand
on his shoulder, and he knew a disturbance in him,
unidentifiable and deep. He glanced up into her face, and
she smiled at him, her red hair gleaming in the glow of the
fire, the dancing shadows giving her steep-planed face an
unearthly look.

How fine she is to look at, he thought, and together
they moved up into the eye of the tuath.

Connal stood beside Brihainn, noting how the boy
watched the crowd around him. Here a face showed avid
curiosity, there an ugly, aimless lechery; the faces of the
women all bore an odd stamp, akin to pity and anger alike.
From the corner of his eye Connal saw Sheilagh drop to

her knees beside Alhauna and lay a comforting hand on her shoulder.

But Brihainn's eyes had found Fearghail's, and their gazes had locked into a consuming bar of hatred Brihainn would not break.

"Oinach of Emain's royal gates, hear me." Sibhainn's voice was cold; he had not even glanced at his brother. The clan turned in a concerted movement, watching and listening.

"On the morning before Samhain broke, Brihainn son of Sheilagh, cousin to Alhauna, saw my brother Fearghail meet with the man Machlan at the forest's edge. We all took our leave of Machlan and his band; therefore he had no business left with us. Brihainn, young warrior, roused my son and together they followed.

"Lest any of you not know what they found, listen and you shall learn." He turned to Brihainn. "Speak to them."

The boy stepped forward, his eyes still fixed on Fearghail. "I found a girl, my cousin Alhauna, stripped of her robes. She lay, tied and beaten, in the long grass. I found two men, two men who abused her as she lay."

"And you saw those men clearly?"

"I did, and Connal mac Sibhainn with me." Brihainn fingered the gash at the corner of his mouth; when it healed there would be a scar there, a mark of honor, and he would carry it with pride the length of his days. His voice rose. "I saw Machlan, leader of the traders, whose head hangs at my mother's girdle. And I saw Fearghail, who stands in chains of iron before us this night."

Fearghail's face twitched, a tiny spasm of hate coming and going like the shadows cast by the firelight. Connal saw his hands clench tight behind him as Sibhainn continued.

"Tell the tuath, Brihainn mac Alhainn, what you did."

The boy's voice came steady and clear. "I sent Connal, finest of all celi, to rouse my mother. I took a stone, heavy and sharp, and from the edge of the woods I threw it with all the strength of my arm. I had no weapons but my wits, and they had slings. The stone struck the chieftain's brother on the cheek; you can see the blue mark there.

They came after me and I ran." He stopped and touched his mouth with a ginger finger. "They left Alhauna to hunt me, and Machlan caught me with a sharp stone from his sling."

"And that is all, Brihainn? No more than that?"

"After that my mother came, with her horse and her arms, and she hunted them until the chieftain came up with his celi. She drove Fearghail into the arms of the tuath and slew Machlan handily; you see his head there."

"That is well said, young warrior. Our thanks to you, and our great admiration with it. Sheilagh!"

She gave her niece a final valedictory pat and stood to face the chieftain. All eyes were fixed on the ruined head that dangled, as casual as an amulet or a water skin, from her belt.

"Honor to you, chieftain. There are things you wish to know, and these I will tell you. I know you have tried to speak with Alhauna, to learn how she was lured from her bed to a rape in the morning; I know she has not spoken to you."

"This is true." Sibhainn's voice was heavy. "And this is something we must know, Sheilagh, for the way of doing will give us the judgment. If it was unplanned, a passing lust, Fearghail looks to a clean and honorable death. Can you learn the truth from her, warrior woman?"

"I have done so." The words were simple but charged with meaning, and a murmur of anticipation went through the people like wind in the river reeds, hungry, alive.

"Speak to us. Give us the truth of it."

"I slew Machlan, as is known. When Fearghail was taken, I came to the side of my dead brother's daughter and knelt beside her. She saw the head of her enemy in my hand, and she spoke to me, spoke in a rush of words without guile or pause. This is what was told.

"She said that near dawn Fearghail mac Bhoru came to her hut and told her of a druid, a druid who had traveled far, waiting in the woods with a message for her. She knew that Fearghail spent several seasons with the druids. She trusted him, she followed him. When they reached the woods, Machlan came out and laid his hands about her throat until she was near stifled. When she

could no longer struggle for lack of air, he struck her
down, and when she came back to her senses she was as
my son and yours, chieftain, found her."

"Lies," came the small whisper, and she turned to
face Fearghail, who watched her with a white face. Slowly,
sinuously, her hand moved down to her girdle.

Fearghail's voice shook, but the words came clear.
"She lies, and you lie, and this bad-tempered spawn of my
brother's lies too." His eyes fell on Connal, who had not
spoken. "Sometime I will cut your tongue out, devil's
brat, for this night's work. Wait for it."

He blames me, Connal thought, and remembered the
feast night, Brihainn's words, his own realization. Even I
did not know how much he hated me, but hate me he
does.

Beside him Sheilagh spoke. "No lies but your own,
betrayer, and well do we know it. Do you seek to lie to the
gods, to yourself, even as you would lie to your own
people?"

Machlan's head was in her hand, free of the girdle.
Sheilagh, her fingers twined in the coarse hair, threw it
with the full strength of her arm.

There was a hoarse shouting from the crowd as the
head struck Fearghail in the chest. Under the force of
impact he reeled and fell, sitting down hard. The head, a
strip of flesh that had caught the chains flapping free from
the livid cheek, rolled and came to a stop, the one
remaining eye fixed on Fearghail. He made a noise deep
in his throat.

The silence was absolute. Sibhainn, alone between
his brother and his people, raised his arms to the sky.

"The portent is given, the truth is spoken, the penalty clear. This was a planned rape, a betrayal of the tuath.
The judgment is given, and given within your hearing."

He turned to face his brother. "Outcast you are,
stripped of your name. Taken is your family, taken your
hearth, taken your celi. You are gone from us, banished
from us. May the night take you, may the fomori hound
you, may the demons of the next Samhain find you. The
forests are yours, and the hills. Taken is Ulster from you.

Banished, exiled, of the tuath no more, of the clan no more."

He turned to his own celi. "Take him to the borders of our land. Free him there; give him food and water, for he was my brother once and this chance I must give him. Send him into the hills. If he is ever seen in Ulster, blind him and castrate him, let him live sightless, less than a man. Tonight he sleeps in his own hut for the last time. See you guard him well, celi. At first light he is banished."

Through the roar of the people, Connal heard the harsh clank of chains falling. Then the celi had closed around Fearghail, spears arched in a lethal barrier, and they were gone, Fearghail pushed through the door of his hut to sleep for the last time among the people of Ulster.

"Connal? Connal!"

He had not come here, to lie on his back in the empty glen and stare at the heavens, since the morning of his uncle's banishment. He was ten years old now, and things that had once been the depressing mysteries of adults, muddled and terrible, were slowly coming clear to him. The solitude he had once needed, that silent substitute for friendship, was no longer so important to him; he had Brihainn and Cormac, and if the people of his tuath still did not like him, they at least respected him.

Yet today, when his father had gone out on the hunt and refused to take him, the old misery and bitter anger had welled up in him, cutting him with their familiar blades. He had stood shoulder to shoulder with Brihainn and watched the hunt move off to the north, the horses dancing with impatience, the shadows of the dogs behind them. When the hunters had disappeared in the distance, he had turned silently to his best, his truest friend, and seen sympathy in his eyes.

That sympathy, unexpectedly, had been more than he could bear. "Let me be awhile," he had said in a choked voice, and Brihainn, no longer fearing the violence of Connal's temper, had nodded his understanding and drifted away, leaving him to the solace of warmth and quiet.

The glen, silent and beautiful, deserted by man, seemed welcoming; he had a sense that it had missed him, waiting here, its flowers dying each autumn only to grow again when the warm rains returned to melt the winter away. The black stones of the ancient cromlech were streaked with bird droppings, the grass lush at their base. He flung himself down, the smell of the earth rich and potent in his lungs, and closed his eyes to think.

He remembered the morning of his uncle's banishment; that day was permanently etched in the boy's memory. He had stood with Sheilagh's hand on his shoulder and Cormac and Brihainn beside him, watching his uncle, a rope around his neck, stumble off to a life without honor. Sheilagh's touch had been unbearably soft against his skin; Sibhainn, looking like a man made of stone, had stood watching in silence as his only brother was sent into privation and shame. Alhauna, clutching his sleeve, huddled beside him; Connal saw the girl's trembling, and how Sibhainn had touched her hair, gently comforting, without ever glancing her way. There had been something, a strange mix of things, in that touch; it seemed suddenly possible to be tender and uncaring at the same time. . . .

Insight faded as memory moved forward. Eight years old, only just turned eight, the day that Manat, chieftain of Lagan Des-Gabair, had come in state with all his household and his only son in tow. The boy was called Cet and was just Connal's age; they had been formally introduced, sharing wrists, and had been told by both their fathers in sight of the tuath that they would be friends.

They had stood side by side, Connal and Cet, listening politely to the words of their sires, eyeing each other. Nothing to be done about it and no help for it; they had hated each other on first sight.

He had been fortunate, he knew, that Brihainn had been with them the day before the visit ended. They had gone walking, the three boys, down by the great lough. Cet had said casually, spitefully, "They say at my home that the men of your tuath rape their own women and are pardoned by their people, with no thought for justice done. Is that truth, Ulster crows?"

Connal had gone white, turning his face to this foreign whelp who, not knowing him as the tuath did, failed to read the signs of anger rising fast. "They lie, the people

of your home," he had told Cet. "The man who did so was
banished in chains, to flee the fomori his whole life long.
He was not pardoned, and justice was done."

Cet had snorted, a sound of unusual sophistication for
one so small. Then, as the Ulster boys stood staring their
disbelief, he had spat, grinding the spittle with deliberate
malice beneath his heel.

"They say your rapist was let live because he was the
chieftain's brother. They say the girl he raped lost her
wits, with no one to do her justice. They say your tuath
has no honor in it, Ulster scum."

Connal's voice was silkily dangerous. "Do they, then?"

"They do. And so do I."

Connal, his short knife flashing, was on him before he
had time to move. Yet Cet, too, was a warrior in the
making; Connal's own knife met the edge of Cet's blade.
Then Cet, seeing an advantage and knowing that the
larger boy would speedily outmatch him, put his teeth
into Connal's arm.

Connal's howl brought half the tuath and the visitors
too. Sibhainn, arriving with Manat and his celi in tow, had
leaped to separate the fighters, only to find Manat's hand
on his arm.

"Wait," the chieftain had said. "Wait. For days they
have been itching to be at it; and they will be fine warriors
both. We can stop it if need be. For now, Sibhainn, let
them fight it out."

It had ended soon after. Connal, frothing at the
mouth with fury, flipped Cet onto his back; the motion was
swift, oddly beautiful, and Cet had no chance at all. He lay
still, his eyes bulging, Connal's knife at his throat.

Connal spoke through his teeth, Brihainn close beside him with clenched fists at the ready. "Take back your
words, liar from the south. Take them back or, full sure, I
shall make you eat them."

Cet's voice was cracked and trembling, but the spite
was still there. "I take back nothing, for to say that truth is
a lie is to ask for dishonor."

"Then dine well on your false honor," Connal spat,
and raised his arm high for the killing.

The flint struck him on the hand, numbing it, knocking

the knife free. Then the men were there, pulling them apart, questioning, shouting, some laughing.

He remembered with bitterness how his father had assumed, without asking a question, that the fault had been his. Great fortune for him that Brihainn had been there to hear, then. They might well disbelieve the devil's spawn, but Brihainn was another matter.

Slapped for his discourtesy, forced by his father to make the Ulster tuath an offering from his birth gold, Cet had departed with his tuath's train. But the enmity was there, and sometime they would meet again with no one to stop them, no fathers to interfere.

The sun was high now, riding the sky's crest. They should be returning soon, the men of the hunt, with the kill. They had even taken Sheilagh with them, yet his father had refused to let him go. . . .

"Connal!"

He sat up, shading his eyes with one hand. It was Cormac, and even at this distance it was apparent that something was wrong. The fila was running, stumbling, leaping over obstacles, and he was not alone; Brihainn was with him, his face white. And, high Danu, there was Sheilagh, too, her red hair streaming behind her. She outpaced the others, running like water, and left them behind.

Connal met her at the edge of the glen. The look on her face, the whiteness of cold dread, almost dried the words in his throat. He gulped down on his fear. "Lady?"

"Connal." She was winded, her eyes wide. "Connal, you must come back with us. There has been an accident."

"An accident." He knew it now, knew the meaning of her look, her speed, her shaking hands. "The hunt?"

"He was thrown, Connal." There was no need to ask her whom she meant; the thin voice was terrible in its very expressiveness. "The boar charged his horse, and it stumbled and threw him. His head came down and struck a stone, a sharp stone."

"Dead?" Was that him speaking? he wondered, that voice grown suddenly deep and sharp. Was it truly his own voice? She was staring into his face, and he repeated himself. "Dead?"

The others had come up with her now. Through the fog of anger, of disbelief, of grief unrealized, he saw them kneel; Brihainn with grace, Cormac slowly, Sheilagh, all of them falling to their knees in veneration, the beautiful formal gestures for the oath of loyalty.

Sheilagh pressed his hands to her forehead and answered him. "Yes, chieftain. Sibhainn is dead."

3

The Iron Hills

Stumbling, trembling with exhaustion, Fearghail came to a clearing by a great lake.

Another man in his situation might well have panicked; Fearghail, his eyes fixed always on his own survival, had stayed calm. Seventeen sunsets had passed since the men of Ulster had thrust him across the border into Connacht, seventeen sunsets in which he had taken night and day, and all the surprises they had to offer in this strange territory, well in stride.

The men of the tuath had still been visible in the distance when he reached a hand into the tiny pouch hidden beneath his clothing. The five objects contained within, four of gold and one of copper, fell bright and shining into his palm and rested there.

He had stood·among the trees, weaponless, exiled, and smiled down at these things. Two clasps, two bracelets, a ring; this last he took up and studied carefully, the smile thinning to a nightmare grimace.

It was heavy, and very beautiful; as with the others, it bore the sign of the Ulster tuath, the twined snakes eating each other's tails, which only the chieftains of Ulster were allowed to wear. It had been his father's ring, kept in the coffers of his brother Sibhainn, and he had stolen it the night before the rape of Alhauna as a bribe for Machlan.

Well, Machlan would have no need of it now, and it might prove useful. He wrapped the pieces in leaves to stifle their musical clatter and stowed the pouch away once again.

Seventeen sunsets, he thought now, and stared at the hills on the horizon a few miles away. The Iron Hills, where Machlan's marauders would be found. Seventeen sunsets and, with no weapon but the knife I stole, I have come through whole and alive.

He fingered the heavy knife thrust through his belt, remembering with pleasure how he had come by it. The shepherd boy, no more than ten, on the third day of his exile; five sheep, an isolated village some three miles distant, the soil bare and infertile. No grazing there, it had been obvious, and the boy sent to feed the sheep of this poor place on the nearest green pasture.

He had watched the boy from the shadow of the woodland, wondering, planning. The boy must die, and that quietly; he had a good knife and a skin of water, and though his ragged cloak was far too small for Fearghail, it would do to wrap around his feet for some warmth at night.

But give the boy any chance, let him sound an alarm, and Fearghail would be worse off than before. He had hunted quietly for a likely rock.

It had been easy, in the end. Fearghail had a strong arm, and the rock, thrown hard and true, had taken the boy on the back of the head. Fearghail had watched him crumple up without a sound, waited a moment to make sure no one came, and stepped out to calmly finish his work.

He had left the shepherd lying with his throat slit, and four of the sheep too. The fifth, a young lamb, he killed and cut up, taking long strips of the fresh-killed meat with him for food. The knife he cleaned on the grass and took with him, and the boy's water skin too.

He had known from the moment sentence was passed where he would go. No doubt the men of the tuath expected him to wander the hills and valleys, coming at last to die in the jaws of some wild beast, or hounded to madness and emptiness by the fomori, the one-eyed demons of the night. But the fomori had so far let him be, and he was armed now, not well, but enough for the time being. Let a man help himself, he thought, and he will live, gods or no. . . .

He had only one true worry. The year was dying, autumn coming inexorably to winter. As he made his way to the south, he felt the air growing colder around him. The hoarfrost that lay on the grasses grew stiffer each morning, the ice on the streams and loughs from which he stopped to drink harder to break.

He had no trouble finding food, even with the wild berries growing ever more scanty; there were always hares and the birds of the ground, and the loughs teemed with fish, his for the catching. But his clothing would not protect him from the coming snows. His only way to obtain skins warm enough for protection would be to fight a bear or a wolf, and with no more than a knife to his hand, he stood no chance. If he did not find Machlan's stronghold, and that quickly, he would die of exposure.

Bending to the lough, Fearghail drank deeply, refilled his water skin, and sat down to rest. When his legs had stopped trembling, he stood and began to walk once again, his eyes fixed on the chilly mountains that waited, gray and watchful, in the distance.

In the end, Fearghail did not have to search for Machlan's raiders, for they found him instead.

Five days had passed since his rest at the lough. In that time he had walked toward the hills, avoiding the main road, keeping his eyes open for another shepherd or a solitary traveler who might be ambushed and killed.

But he had seen no one, and that in itself was odd. The lands to the north of the Iron Hills were fertile enough and well watered; why, then, were there no farms, no villages, no people? Fearghail remembered his time with the druids and thought, with a shudder, that perhaps these lands were accursed. He made the gesture against magic and kept his eyes from straying too far.

He entered the densely wooded lower slopes of the hills as the sun was setting. As he stopped, scanning the trees and bushes for a safe and warm place to sleep, he heard the call of a fox and another to answer it. His mind was occupied with the problem of rest, and he paid no attention.

In the end, though he disliked it, he opted for a tree. There was no comfort to be found there, but there was a small degree of safety; the great wolves that haunted the forests could not climb trees, and if he were still enough, it was unlikely that a bear would put itself to the trouble of dragging its great bulk after him.

Fearghail chose an oak, huge and ancient, its spreading limbs thrown high across the forest canopy. It was not the easiest tree within sight for climbing, for the first limb strong enough to bear a man's weight was a good twenty feet from the ground. But the bark was rough, showing the scratch marks of animals, and afforded him a good enough surface for a foothold.

It was very cold. Even as he threw his stolen hide across his shoulder and grasped the trunk to climb, a few flakes of snow drifted in silence through the green cover to melt on the leaf-covered earth. He straightened his back and, cursing softly under his breath, scaled the trunk to settle on a strong branch.

"Make no move, stranger, and keep silence."

Even as Fearghail stiffened, he felt the cold touch of iron against the nape of his neck. He was not alone in the tree; three men, their filthy and matted clothing a perfect camouflage to the greenery around them, moved like cats along the surrounding branches and closed him in.

He stayed perfectly still. The men looked half savage, and they were armed with weapons of lethal sharpness; all three held short spears, some three feet in length. In the deepening gloom Fearghail saw the glint of a copper badge on one man's shoulder and suddenly relaxed.

"Peace," he said calmly. "No worry; I will not run from you or raise any alarm. I think you are the men I have been searching for these many weeks past." The spear pressed suddenly harder, and Fearghail added quickly, "I knew your leader, Machlan. You need have no fear of me; no worry at all."

There was a brief muttering in a dialect Fearghail could only partially decipher. The spear's pressure eased fractionally. He added, "I bring you a small gift of gold, as a token of my good faith."

One of his captors drew closer, speaking in a low voice. "Machlan? You say you know Machlan? Where is he, then?"

"Dead. He and his men brought cattle to the Ulster tuath; we did some business together, Machlan and I, private business and not for the Ulster men."

They were watching him, stony-faced. The lie had been nourished and perfected during the weeks of wandering; it came with fluid ease, completely convincing.

"He sent the others, his celi, to go before him. The chieftain of that tuath took him and killed him; he carried the gold he had been given for his cattle, and Sibhainn the chieftain took it back from his body, and kept the cattle too. Sibhainn would have slain me, but I slipped through their ranks and came to find you."

"So Machlan is dead? We wondered." Once again they muttered, with much waving of hands and consultation. At last the leader turned back to Fearghail.

"The others returned two sunrises ago. They told us Machlan had stayed behind to do some private business with the brother of that tuath's chieftain, saying he would come within two days. When he did not come, they sent a spy back who saw Machlan's head on the village gate." He looked directly into Fearghail's eyes. "Are you that brother?"

"I was. But they acted with dishonor to kill a guest, and I am of them no longer, never again. I come to you."

"To what end? We are raiders, a small band of small numbers; we have only forty men. We cannot make war on the Ulster tuath."

Look after yourself and you will live. Fearghail bowed his head to the leader, a gesture both courtly and dignified, and spoke with confidence and ease.

"This I understand, for Machlan took me into his confidence and told me of your band. I come to join you. I can be useful to you, and aid you too."

The man behind him shifted the spear and spoke. "Aid us? How is that, chieftain's brother?"

Fearghail spoke smoothly. "I spent many months among the druids, hill people. From them I learned to read dreams, to find water where the eye sees none, to cure sickness in men and beasts. And as son to a chieftain, I learned the arts of war, both raiding and fighting. I was well taught. These things I offer you, if you will welcome me to your band."

The men were whispering, but not to each other. Fearghail caught signs for magic and felt awe in them. They looked at one another, their eyes showing white. At last the leader turned to Fearghail, subjecting him to a hard stare.

"Very well, chieftain's brother. It is decided. We will take you to the hills and offer the question to our men; among us nothing is decided by one man alone. You will be given a chance to prove yourself there." He turned to his two companions and spoke sharply; they edged back from Fearghail, sliding down the tree and standing, spears at the ready, at its base.

The leader gestured. "You will go down next. I am called Alchlaidd. And you?"

"Once I was Fearghail, of the Ulster tuath. Now I am tuath no longer and Fearghail no longer." He drew his breath deep and moved toward the body of the great oak. Over his shoulder he said, "Mark that, Alchlaidd; Fearghail no longer. From this time I am hidden." Using the druid's word, the word all men knew and used wherever they were, he smiled coldly into Alchlaidd's eyes. "I am Covac."

The bitter winter locked the Iron Hills with snow, cutting them off from the starvation and sickness in the lowlands to the south. On the first day of the new season, Covac woke to thin sunlight that fell, laughing and tempting, across his bed.

He opened his eyes, rubbing the sleep from them. If spring were indeed here, if the thaw had begun, there would be much to do.

He swung his legs to the ground and stood naked and shivering in the cold air. A sudden rush of wind raised gooseflesh. He turned to the door.

"A new day to you, Alchlaidd. Is it spring, then?"

The other nodded. "Yes, commander. Sunlight, and

cool water instead of ice on the land; Rachlam saw two cranes heading south not an hour ago."

"Two cranes toward Cruachain? A good portent for the business at hand, then. There are things to be done, cela; I grow weary of eating food better fitted to birds than to men, and the Connacht tribes will be ranging far in search of pasture."

Alchlaidd met his eye and grinned. "A raid, then?"

"My first as commander of the hill people." Covac dressed quickly. When he was ready, he threw over his shoulders the bear's pelt that had given him command of this wild band of marauders, fastened it with a gold clasp and accompanied his second in command out of doors.

The camp was a hive of activity. During the long nights of the winter months it had been quiet, the men cold and demoralized; hunger had made them edgy, leading to fights that flared up suddenly and had no root in reason. They were stripped of purpose, imprisoned in their mountain fastness behind a soft and impenetrable barrier of snow.

But other things ailed them. They had lost their leader, and without Machlan they were aimless, each man looking from the corner of his eyes at the others, wondering who would lead them if the long winter ever ended.

And then Covac had slain the bear.

Not for nothing had he spent that time among the seers; within two days of his arrival at the camp he had taken their measure. They came from different tuatha, these raiders; some were well-born, some slaves. But one thing they shared, and that was a boundless capacity for superstition. They saw omens in every star, every bird, every eddy of smoke from the cooking fires. Covac noted this and bided his time.

And then, one night, he had been given his chance. During the empty hours before the gray dawn broke, he had been wakened by a scream. It was not the harsh hooting that the raiders used to signal intruders; this was a scream of terror, gurgling into agony as it was lost in a chilling roar that came from no human throat.

Covac, a trained warrior, once a chieftain's son, had reached them, man and bear, before any of the others;

they were arched together at the very edge of the camp. He knew the man at once; Chlair, small and shifty, a good thief and a poor fighter. He had been set at the watching tonight, and the bear, perhaps maddened by hunger, perhaps with a litter to feed, had caught him here.

In one hand Covac held a sling, soft and flexible; in the other nestled a stone, carved from the shiny black rocks of the hills, polished to a glittering point. It seemed a poor weapon against such a thing as a bear, but he had hunted bears before.

Chlair's screaming had subsided; he was limp in the six-inch talons and bled from many wounds. The bear, upright and unearthly in the pallid winter moonlight, was huge and potent, a picture of death walking.

Covac threw his head back and shouted. The bear, howling, threw the limp body aside and charged; from behind him Covac heard the cries of terror and then, small and clear, "Take it."

The spear, four feet and heavy, slid into his hand; he dropped it, leaving it to glitter in the white blanket at his feet, and fitted the stone securely. His lips stretched into a hellish rictus, he pulled back with the strength of his arm and let fly.

The stone took the charging animal in the left eye, slicing through it to lodge in the skull behind. The bear made an unearthly noise and rolled frantically to one side, slashing with its powerful front legs.

Covac snatched the spear and leaped.

After that the end was certain. The spear, flashing in the dimness, did its lethal work. The beast rolled once, howled, and with a convulsive shudder lay still. The snow under the immense carcass was a sea of fresh blood running.

The men, who had watched without moving, suddenly burst into activity. Some gathered around the bear, to gesture and exclaim; others took hold of Chlair, carrying the maimed man to shelter. A little to one side, Alchlaidd and Covac faced one another in silence.

The raider spoke first. "That was done well. You have courage and quickness, with wits to match."

"Yes." The monosyllable was flat, uninterested; to

Alchlaidd, standing in a small pool of the bear's blood, the other seemed calm and unmoved by his own daring. But Alchlaidd was no skilled reader of men; he was not to know that behind the outer calm a melange of things too wild, too formless to be called feelings surged in a strangling dance. Hate, hope, amusement, all ranged and were gone again, swallowed by the larger pleasure.

It was the same pleasure he had felt those many months past, looking down at the young Alhauna, bruised and frightened at his feet; lust of a kind, but twisted and dark, with no light in it. He had felt this way, too, as the shepherd boy died under his own knife, as the lamb he had slaughtered for food and the sheep killed for pleasure had struggled in his grip, warm bodies growing cold and stiff.

At the raider's words, he almost laughed in Alchlaidd's face. If this fool would mistake pleasure for courage, so be it; this night's work would make him leader of the raiders, and was that not, after all, what he wanted? Was that not what he had planned from the moment he left Ulster?

The simple truth was that he enjoyed pain, the watching and the causing of it. He had found himself aroused when he first saw Chlair, screaming piteously in the bear's claws, and as his own spear slashed, he had felt the beast buck in agony below him and his own pleasure mounting to a white heat, running down his thighs, uncontainable. No need to tell Alchlaidd of this; let him call it courage, if he would, and admire as he wished.

It had all come to pass as he had believed it would. The seeds of his leadership were sown that night; they set their shoots out in the fertile soil of superstition and grew rapidly. The camp rang with whispers, and whispers became low speech, muttered in corners; *We have no leader, and here is one who has proven his skill, his daring, his lack of mercy. Who better, among us? Will he consent to lead us?*

Covac heard the whispers and the low-voiced conferences but he said nothing. If he was to be leader, they must call it; once it was done, he would take them down to Connacht, yes, and Ulster too, and there would be blood had in exchange for the sentence passed on him. There would be village girls, young and terrified, for the taking or the slaughter; cattle, well-fed, would feed the band. He would say nothing, for he had plans, and he would never have it said that he had stolen the leadership, for in the event of failure such could be used as a weapon against him. If they would follow him to whatever hell he could find, it must be of their own free will.

So he kept his own counsel, and wore the bearskin at all times, a visible reminder to his fellows. And before spring could come, Alchlaidd had come to him with word that the men wished him for war leader.

"Honor to you, leader."

The men led the stolen cattle, sixteen head of them, through the camp to the empty pens. Covac, at the head of the band, dismounted and turned to face Alchlaidd.

"And honor to you, celi. A good raid, my first; I call it a portent of prosperity and good things to come to us. I regret only the loss of the three men and the escape of the child. Still, we wore no badges to tell them who we are."

It had been a fairly successful raid. Leading the horses through the woodlands on the southern slopes, the band of forty men had come upon a band of Connacht oinach with a full complement of cattle, obviously in search of pasture.

Under Machlan they would have attacked in a single wild surge, fighting hand to hand, swooping down on the hapless strangers and counting on the advantage of surprise to carry the day for them. But Covac was not Machlan, and seeing the wariness of the men below, the way they kept one hand to their weapons even as they led their cattle, he decided on another way.

The men stood silent, their horses muffled, watching the travelers from the safety of the trees as Covac looked and considered. There were twenty of them, sixteen men, three women, and a child. The child, a little girl perhaps five years old, appeared to be the highest of the party; she sat her own horse and sat it well, her shoulders cloaked in the fine soft squirrel's fur men called vair. He noted with surprise that she carried a spear in her left hand while controlling her mount with her right; the spear was small enough to seem a toy, but the tip, its bright metal glinting in the sun, was no toy. She was a pretty child with an aureole of flaming hair; Covac considered her, briefly and coldly, then turned his attention to the young woman who rode beside her.

He stared down at her, perhaps fifteen years old, and felt the muscles of his groin tighten. High Danu, he would enjoy this; the girl was the spit of Sheilagh, and if he could not make the warrior woman pay, this one could pay quite well in her stead. He steadied his hands and turned to the band, waiting patiently behind him.

"Split into two bands," he said coldly, "one at head, one at rear. Alchlaidd, celi, you lead the frontal attack; go down first with your band and take them. If I guess aright, the child is a chieftain's daughter, or perhaps even a princess, and as such they must protect her, even above the cattle." He paused, marshaling his thoughts. "Cimhaill, lead the attack on the rear. Do not charge when the front goes; take your men to the trees, there, and watch me here. Wait for my signal. When it is given, you will go for the road and cut off a rear escape. Understood?"

Both men nodded curtly. "Good. And Alchlaidd, Cimhaill—leave none of them alive but the girl who rides beside the child. I do not want her killed. Bring her here to me, for I have a use for her."

He heard a coarse joke behind him. Ignoring it, he jerked his head at Alchlaidd in the signal to attack.

Within moments the road below was a running hell of screams and weapons flashing.

It was as he had surmised; at the first cries of attack and the thunder of hooves in front of them, the men ignored the cattle completely, instead forming a protective circle around the child and her companion. It could not last, of course, for the men of Connacht were outnumbered; though they fought like demons, the raiders began slowly to break through the defenses.

Suddenly the child shouted something Covac could not make out; her voice, curiously deep for one so small, carried on the cool air like water running over rocks. Her words must have been a command, for the men around her instantly broke and reformed, leaving a clean gap between herself and Drihaidd, the raider closest to her.

He should have suspected something. But no man can seriously imagine that a child may do him harm, and he merely pressed his advantage, thrusting forward, spear at the ready.

She stood straight up in the saddle, dropping the horse's reins, relying instead upon the warrior's technique of controlling his mount by the pressure of knees to flank. A second spear appeared in her right hand, seemingly out of nowhere, to match the one gripped cleanly in her left. Both hands occupied, her small body jerked viciously forward; Covac, staring incredulously, saw her push forward and down.

For a moment they stared at one another, the red-haired girl and the seasoned fighter. Then Drihaidd went down screaming, one hand flying to the place where shoulder meets throat, pulling vainly at the spear deep buried there. As he hit the ground, one of the Connacht men wrenched the spear; it came free with a sickening sound and an extrusion of blood. Without a second glance he tossed it back to the child. She caught it and whirled to face another attacker; this time the spear in her left hand, thrown with equally deadly skill, caught the raider deep in his throat.

Covac did not wait to see more. He thrust both hands to the sky, and Cimhaill's men broke cover to swarm across the road. Covac, watching tight-lipped, saw the pretty nurse taken in a firm grip and flung struggling across Cimhaill's horse.

He was so intent on the girl's struggles that the sound of hoofbeats diminishing in the distance took him unawares. Swinging around, he saw four horses vanishing to the south at high speed; three men and, yes, the child. None of the raiders seemed to have noticed, for the fighting was now hand to hand and there was no way Covac could raise the alarm without showing himself. He stared after the escaping horses, his face grim, a muscle jumping high on one cheek.

"Chieftain?"

He jumped and whirled, a hand to his knife. But it was only Cimhaill, filthy and disheveled, with a bloody gash down one cheek. Across his horse, bound tight, was the girl.

Covac went slowly through the ranks of his watchful men. On the road below, a small group of the raiders were roping the cattle together. The bodies of the dead, fifteen of the travelers and three raiders, were dragged to the roadside and heaped into a pile.

Covac come to a stop and faced the girl. She stared back at him, her face closed, her eyes narrowed. He reached out and from the shoulder of her robe tore the copper badge, the badge of a high house, shining and bright, with two cranes flying.

"So," he said smiling, and with that smile he saw the fear come up in her face. "The tuath of Flyn, High Chieftain, King of Connacht, and the child a princess, no doubt. Am I right, then?"

She said nothing, only staring at him. His voice was a snake, deadly and low, and the terrible smile never wavered.

"Three of my men dead, and only you left to pay forfeit. Time now to pay it, my pretty one."

He laced his fingers through her hair and wrenched her from the horse's back. As the raiders pressed tight around them, grinning and anticipatory, she saw the eyes of wolves dressed as men and began, at last, to scream.

"Druids?"

Covac laid down the sling he had been inspecting, to stare at his captain. The weather in the eight weeks since his first raid had warmed to comfort; the hills were green, lush with the coming summer, and the days were good for hunting.

Cimhaill, bringing news of a seer where none had been seen in long years, saw the heavy body go tense and wondered at it. Since the night Covac had killed the bear, his men had learned to fear a temper kept mostly hidden, yet dangerous and violent. Controlled though he was, Covac could be angered, and in a rage he was like one of the fomori; fierce, unpredictable, the pale hair bristling, the light eyes glazed with something akin to madness.

"Druids." Covac tilted his head, giving Cimhaill a look the captain found unnerving. Covac smiled, showing his teeth, and Cimhaill took an involuntary step backward. "Druids here, in the Iron Hills? Where had you this story, Cimhaill?"

The captain swallowed. "Sir, from Alchlaidd. He and three of the men were hunting the boar, in the forest by Lough Lein, and saw the druids there, two of them, by the lough. Alchlaidd says they look to be elders, by the robes and the gold. They travel on foot, no horses." Covac smiled wider, his eyes opening wide, and Cimhaill began to sweat. "They sent me to tell you."

"Yes. I will come and see in a moment. Where are they now, these elders?"

"Sir, I don't know. Alchlaidd set two of the men, Chlair and Padraic, to watch them from the trees. No more than that."

"Enough." Covac abruptly turned his back, a gesture of dismissal. Cimhaill was glad enough to go, and go he did, wondering why the mention of holy men should so upset the commander. Hadn't there been something, though, when he first came to them, something about having spent some seasons with the elders?

Alone once more, Covac did not relax. Druids, he thought, elders from the grove, men who would know him on sight. A trembling began, and a sweat creeping across his skin like a cold fog. Down by the lough? Then they could only go in one of two directions, north toward Ulster or south into the Iron Hills. If they went to Ulster and talked to Sibhainn, he would be cursed. If they came this way and saw him . . .

The trembling intensified as the idea took hold. No, he could not; no one could kill a druid, it was death without honor and the rest of time spent wailing in the hills, a spirit never at rest, always hurting. Yet what other choices were there? If they met with Sibhainn, he was cursed anyway; and should they by some chance be men he knew . . .

His decision made, he reached for the sling and several flints, sharp as spearheads. These he pocketed with wet hands. After a moment he reached for his knife and slid it down inside one boot.

He found Cimhaill waiting outside his door. The man spoke apologetically.

"Sir, Alchlaidd bade me bring you to where he waits."

"No need. You said the woods by the lough? Which end?"

"The south side, commander." There was something in Covac's stance, something in the set of his shoulders, the cold anticipation of his thin mouth, something familiar. It took Cimhaill a moment to place the look; when he did, his breath shortened. This was the death look, the look he had seen the night Covac rode the bear's back, the look that had suffused the commander's face when he had taken the red-haired wench by the hair all those weeks ago, taken her as she lay helpless at his feet and then slit her throat. The same smile, the same stance.

Cimhaill's throat dried. No. No, it was not possible, he could not be planning a kill this time. To kill a druid was the ultimate, the act that drove men into the arms of the demons; death might come or be given to man or woman or child, but to willfully give death to a seer, a walking shadow of the gods, was madness and ruin. To kill a druid was to be forsaken by man, hounded by the gods ever after. He knew dizziness, a terror too deep for understanding, and shut his eyes against it.

When he opened them, he was alone.

Covac, moving like a deer, had slipped through the camp and into the trees without being seen. Marooned by the season itself during the winter months, he had explored these paths enough to know every turn, every foothold, every bush and tree that looked to form solid barriers but in fact masked hidden ways to clear paths between the underbrush. Halfway down the mountain he stopped to listen; nothing, no one following, no one moving ahead. He slipped like a shade to the foot of the hills, to a hidden path shared only by the forest foxes, to a place for watching and waiting. . . .

He settled, his green clothes disappearing into the bushes and grasses, and slid the knife into his hand.

His wait was short. A spot of color to his left, far up the wooded slope among the dense trees, flickered a bright orange and disappeared. The wide eyes took approving note. Good. Chlair and Padraic, in their orange tunics, heading north up the hill, no doubt back toward the camp, seeking him, wondering why Cimhaill had not brought him back.

He slid from his hiding place and ran, swift and silent, to the wood's edge. Stopping just short of the open plain, hidden from sight, he stared out at the great lake.

Elders, both of them; Alchlaidd had been correct. The white robes were rich, and gold depended from wrist and neck. At the moment they were resting, perhaps meditating, sitting quietly on the grass by the charred remains of a small fire. It had doubtless been the smoke that had caught Alchlaidd's eye; from the scattered bones and rubbish beside them, it appeared they had caught a fish and had just finished their meal. Two sacks of fine leather lay on the ground behind them; as Covac watched, he saw the slight movement in one of them and knew what it must contain.

It came back to him, complete and vivid; the grove, the masked men, the altar of rowan with its kindling of holy oak piled high. A stag, sacred darling of the god Cernunnos, tethered to the altar, its legs bound securely with woven ropes. The voice of the master, high, toneless as insects seeking nectar on the summer wind: let the sword be of song, let the air be of breath, let he who would power have, power to the dagda give. The slowly mounting drone of the elders as they moved in for the kill. The roaring scream of the stag as its throat met the edge of the master's knife, the bright blood of the offering splashing. And, damning him, his own cry of pleasure at the beast's agony and terror, an affront to the gods, a sign of his own weakness which could not have been shown clearer had it been written in ogham. . . .

He swallowed hard, fighting back a sudden wash of superstitious terror, the knife slipping in his sweaty palm. Narrowing his eyes against the dazzle of the sun, he saw the older of the two men reach for it, drawing it into his lap, removing with care and love what it contained, bringing it forth into the warmth of the day.

It wriggled in its master's grasp, the dark scales shining. It was not oversized, as sacred snakes sometimes were, but stretched out to perhaps two feet; there was something slender and beautiful about it, a curve and a glow denied to creatures with warm blood and hair.

Covac stood motionless, lost in the flooding memories he had thought forever buried. Another brand of his failure at the self-abnegation a druid must possess; midsummer at the shrine, in the sacred grove. The Nine, high elders all, standing in a tight concentric circle, touching palm to palm. The acolytes, himself included, their nerves strung as taut as the killing noose on a hunter's snare. The Master, the adder held in the air, his own eyes piercing the hood until they looked very much like the snake's own. And his, Fearghail's, shrill cry of fear, of an unbounded terror at the shining scales and deadly fangs.

He came back to the present, knowing he had almost lost his nerve, and brought his gaze back to the scene before him. Though detail was denied him at so far a distance, he knew the words that would pour like molten honey, imagined how the snake would hang still and loose, its will gone into the man who had mastered it, its curving fangs with their lethal venom shining and sharp against its curled lip.

Then it was over, the snake vanished back into its leather bag. The younger druid, a fish in one hand, opened the sack and dropped it in. The bag heaved convulsively, settled, and was still once more.

As the younger man turned, his hair lifting in the breeze, Covac caught sight of his face. A noise broke from him, low and frightening, a sound compounded of recognition and decision. There was no mistake; he would have known that face anywhere. Ahnal, Ahnal who had shown him the first rituals, had bathed him for the dream ceremony. Ahnal, who would know Covac's face as he knew his own.

No choice, he thought. No choices left at all.

The sling, rubbed and new, felt like warm flesh in Covac's hand. He fondled it a moment, his palm learning its grooves and edges, finding the killing grip. The flints, polished to a deadly sharpness, slid into his other hand, the knife vanishing into his boot.

He looked around quickly. Too far from here; he was a

good hundred yards away, and besides, he needed the perfect spot, a place close enough for the quick strike, with two paths at least to choose from for the ambush. He must get closer or risk a miss.

His eyes on the earth at his feet, he began his slow edging toward the east. Here the forest encroached on the great plain surrounding Lough Lein; here he could stand at the crossroads of three hidden trails, no more than forty yards from the target, and make the kill quickly and cleanly. The bushes parted and let him through.

To Covac, his memory merging intolerably with his present need, things seemed to move with unnatural slowness. Ahnal stood facing the west, his arms thrown toward the embracing sky. The flint took him square in the back of the skull, with a sickening sound of bone splitting like paper, clearly audible on the soft air. Slowly, how slowly, the other got to his feet, reached out an arm toward Ahnal, cried out something, a question perhaps, which was lost. Slowly, too slowly for life, Ahnal crumpled to his knees, a long thin band of scarlet rushing from his ruined brain down the back of his robe, staining it, fouling it.

For the longest moment of Covac's life the elder who had taught him stayed on his knees, his shoulders twitching, his head moving from side to side like a man who seeks to shake sleep from his eyes. Then he fell forward, facedown in the grass, and was still.

Covac ran for the westward path. The other was coming; he heard the footsteps pounding on the soft earth. He whirled, dropping the sling, pulling the knife from his boot in one fluid motion, and doubled back quietly. He was unaware of his own shuddering. He stood behind an ancient oak, breathing through his nose, his eyes wide and dilated, watching, awaiting his chance.

A crunch of branches, the suspiration of heavy breath. A white back moved directly into his line of vision.

Covac moved a hand in the sign for luck, then jumped.

The knife, obedient and efficient, took the man at the base of the skull, just where it meets the neck. He had time for one spasmodic jerk, no more than that, before he was gone. Then Covac, jerking out the knife and flinging it down at his side, was rolling the body over, to keep the robe from the pool of blood that grew like an evil blossom on the forest floor.

He had stopped trembling; the thing was done, the day was his, the danger silenced. But there was more to do, and quickly; let any of his men find this, and their superstitions would ruin him as leader.

He stripped the robe from the dead man, rolling it, thrusting it deep within his own sack. Standing, he gave a considering look about him.

If he left the body here, the forest creatures would dispose of it cleanly for him. But if he left it here, it might be found too soon. Taking it by the feet, he dragged it through the underbrush, through the grass, until he and his macabre burden had reached the smoldering remains of the druids' campfire.

He could not bring himself to look at Ahnal; had the druids themselves not taught him that to look at the dead face of one slain dishonorably was to bring madness upon the killer? With his eyes kept away from the dead faces, he stripped both bodies of their gold and weighted their tunics and one of the sacks with stones. A good way, a clean way. . .

The bodies made a satisfying splash as the lough took them. They would sink now, sink to the bottom, feed the lake and the creatures that lived within its cool silence. He caught sight of the second sack, the lines of the sacred thing inside making long, sweet shadows in the pale leather, and sweat ran down his neck, blinding him.

This he could not kill; with the memory of a midsummer night long vanished into mist yet still so fresh in his mind, he could scarcely bring himself to touch the bag it slept in. Yet he could not leave it here; searchers after the truth would know it for what it was.

His eye, seeking inspiration, lit on a forked stick. He had taken it at first for a simple piece of firewood; now, calming, he saw the sharp prongs and the roughly carved hilt and recognized the tool of the snake handler.

Gingerly, cautiously, he lifted the sack, nearly dropping it as it moved in his hand. He kicked the remains of the fire into the lough, scattering the wood; it would take a sharp eye now to find any trace that men had been here. With his sack over one shoulder and the snake's bag held at stick's length in the other, he ran for the woods.

Silence, a velvet shroud, hung across the day like a breath held back. The trees were cool, offering blessed calm and shade from the accusing eye of the sun above him. Yet Covac was hot, his skin scalding, his eyes glazed. This one time he had not enjoyed his killing.

He dropped the druid's sack to the ground. With the extreme tip of one foot to hold down its bottom end, he reached out with the forked stick and wrenched the bag open.

It came out slowly, uncoiling its small length to rest like a jewel in the grass. He saw the forked tongue taste the air, seeking familiar smells, perhaps finding none. It inched forward, sensuous, dangerous, crawling for freedom.

As it reached the trees, it suddenly stopped. Covac could not move; hypnotized, helpless, in thrall, he looked down at the tiny face, so potent, so deep.

Its eyes found him. And then Covac did cry out at last, flinging up a hand, his fingers moving frantically against magic. For the eyes of the snake were the eyes of his nephew Connal and the eyes of the young princess as she stared at death in the dusty road of Connacht.

4

Connacht

When the four riders pulled their sweating horses to a halt before the house of Flyn, High Chieftain of Connacht, the people of the city of Cruachain knew at once that something had gone very wrong.

Three of the riders, all of them wounded and stumbling with tiredness, were men grown. They dismounted, throwing their horses' reins to the waiting stable slaves, and turned together to help the fourth rider, a little girl with wide, glazed eyes and trembling lips, from her saddle.

As she slid to the ground, her legs giving way beneath her, the hide door was pushed aside and a tall man came out.

He stood immobile, the weak sunlight behind him casting a wavering shadow that was bigger by far than he. His eyes moved from the three men who had dropped to their knees, to the child. He spoke quietly.

"You were attacked."

It was a statement, not a question, and the men made no answer. He knelt, opening his arms wide, and suddenly the child had launched herself at him, hurling herself into his arms and streaking him with tears. He felt her trembling, felt his own anger, molten and violent, but spoke softly.

"All is well now, Maeve, darling girl. You are safe

now." He looked up over her bent head, seeing the streaks of dust in her flaming hair, and said curtly, "Were the others slain, then?"

One of the men, seeing the upward flip of Flyn's hand, rose shakily to his feet. "Yes, chieftain. All the men but us and old Brigidh the healer. They speared her as she tried to make her way to the princess."

Flyn nodded, his face cold. In the years since his daughter's birth he had ascended the throne of Connacht, and the kingship had left its mark on him. Still young, still loving to his celi and family, he had grown formidable, a dangerous warrior and a ruler of renowned fairness in his dealings with people, oinach and slaves alike.

He studied the man before him and was pleased to see that the man's eyes held his. Good. That meant he had fought to his best teaching, for had he faltered or shown cowardice, he would have feared to meet his king's eye.

"My thanks for courage, Carhainn; you did your best, I know. What of my niece Ahnrach? Was she slain as well?"

He heard the outraged mutterings of the two men still kneeling and saw their sudden tenseness. His own shoulders stiffened and his grip on Maeve tightened. Carhainn's reply was grim, his eyes stony with hurt.

"Lord, we have no way of knowing. They took her alive, no doubt for their use." The man's face was working, and of a sudden, Flyn remembered that there had been something between those two, his ablest warrior and his child's companion. Carhainn burst out, unable to contain himself.

"I tried to get to her, to take her back from them. But they wanted the princess as well, and we could not allow that. We surrounded her and brought her back. . . ."

Flyn could feel the man's agony as a tangible thing. He gave his daughter a final hug and put her gently from him.

"My thanks to you. You have burdened me with a debt I cannot hope to repay. And what did Maeve do? Surely she did not sit quiet with her hands in her lap."

Carhainn glanced down at the child standing quietly at her father's side, and the misery on his face was swallowed by remembered awe. "Lord, she did not. Three raiders we left in their own blood, dead by the roadside." So small, he thought, so small and so young. He remembered her controlling her war pony with her knees alone, a weapon in each hand, and of a sudden she seemed unearthly, something of spirit, not flesh. He looked up, and seeing the pride in Flyn's face, swallowed hard. "She killed all three, lord. With a spear in each hand she killed them."

Flyn picked her up in both arms, planting a formal kiss on each cheek, the salute from warrior to warrior. "So," he said, and his voice held a deep satisfaction, "your weapons are blooded. An early beginning for Connacht's next chieftain, and an auspicious one. No, stop your trembling, darling girl; it was well done, and you have done your people a service. Carhainn, I grieve with you for Ahnrach; we will avenge her, never fear. What of the cattle?"

"Taken by the thieves, lord." He licked his lips and continued unwillingly. "Lord, I have given this some thought; I do not think these were men of another Connacht tuath. We will return and see to the bodies, I know, but I fought hand to hand with three of them, and I saw no badge to mark them, nothing to show us who they were."

"Raiders. Yes, I see. Well, rest yourselves now, for a deed well done. I will take thirty men to the place; no need for you to come, Carhainn, for my daughter will show us the way. Maeve, you ride with me. No, don't look so anguished, lamb, you need not sit a saddle again today. You will ride with me, on my horse's back."

She looked up into his face, the unhappiness gone in the radiance of a sudden wash of anticipation. Her lopsided dimple twitched into life, carving a long line in one cheek. For a moment they stood thus, uncanny echoes of each other.

"You will let me ride on Bhonal? You truly will?"

"I truly will. First I must call men and gather weapons; get you indoors and ask your mother for something to eat." He gave a gentle push. "Quickly, now."

"Maeve! What has happened?" The hide had opened once more, Nieve stepping quickly into the sunshine. She looked from her daughter to the men and dread came up in her face. "Sweet Lugh," she whispered, "were you attacked, then?"

"Mother," whispered Maeve and then, at last, burst into the tears her pride had kept from falling. She ran into her mother's arms, weeping and talking at once.

"They took Ahnrach and the cattle, they killed all but we four, and I killed them, I killed them, I took my spears and killed them, Mother, oh . . ."

Nieve, the child fast in her arms, turned on her heel and vanished indoors. Flyn, his face set and somehow older, gave the orders for men and horses. When the slaves had run to do his bidding, he followed his wife.

She was sitting on her bed, Maeve in her lap. The child was calmer now; one thumb was firmly in her mouth, a gesture her parents had thought long abandoned. Reaction had taken her and, already, she was dozing. Nieve looked up and met her husband's eye.

"Is it true, chieftain, what she says? Did she indeed use her spear on men?"

"Carhainn told me so himself; one spear to a hand, as she was taught." He looked down at his daughter, deep in slumber, her thumb in her mouth, and felt a surge of love so heavy as to almost choke him. "She will be chieftain after me, Nieve; already she has the respect of the people. Today she has taken the respect of the fighting men as well." He looked at his wife. "Do you remember, Nieve, the day she was born? How you would not let the women tend to you while the sun was in the sky, and the dream you had?"

"I remember it." She nuzzled her sleeping daughter's hair. "And do you remember, chieftain, how you looked down at her in laughter, to ask if she was Crom's warrior? We have learned it, Flyn, and learned well. Crom did not lie; here is a chieftain to rule from border to border and beyond." Maeve murmured something and nestled closer. Her mother looked up. "It would be good for her to sleep."

"True." He followed his wife's eyes and sighed deeply. "So small, and looking so peaceful; I hate waking her, yet I must. The men who came back are wounded and half dead with exhaustion; there is none other to lead us to the place of ambush, and I must get there. It cannot be far, Nieve; I will bring her back the moment we are done, and she may sleep tomorrow, well into the morning." Unexpectedly he grinned. "No need to rouse her early; her first duty of the day is to work with the spears. She has shown her teachings this day."

"A two-handed fighter, with a left arm as true as her right. Have you ever seen such a one, Flyn?"

"Never, in all my life." He bent and kissed Nieve's cheek. "It will be a while yet before the horses are ready; I shall come back and fetch her in an hour's time. Let her sleep awhile yet."

He turned and left the house. As he stepped outside, he stumbled over a dead hare and some fresh blossoms. Stooping to touch them, he saw the copper coin, the small gold pin, the ogham letters slashed in the hare's side, and he grinned to himself. Offerings for Maeve; already word had gone around Cruachain like wildfire in the dry summer brush.

A great worry, one that had lived unacknowledged within him since the druids told him Nieve would bear no more children, flickered and went out. Already she was a warrior the like of which the people had never seen; someday, in the great chieftain's house he now occupied here in Cruachain, Maeve would rule secure. When the time came, woman or no woman, they would accept her.

Flyn, with Maeve held fast between his knees, suddenly felt the tension in the great war stallion Bhonal; he wrapped one arm tight around his daughter and grasped the reins with a firm hand as Bhonal whinnied and reared, pawing the air with his forefeet, plunging in fear at the smell of death in the spring air.

Flyn brought the horse, a well-trained but nervous creature, under control. Glancing down at his daughter, he found no need for reassurance; her eyes were sparkling, her curving smile lighting her face. He swallowed one of those choking surges of tenderness that she always aroused in him and smiled back at her.

"You enjoy the horse dance, daughter?"

"I do that." There was no mistaking her delight; her pleasure in the feel of the great horse moving beneath her was evident. "I would love a horse like Bhonal. Father—"

"Yes, Maeve, you will have one of your own. The time is not yet, though; when you are bigger."

"But I could ride him now."

"Yes, I know you could. But a horse so strong and high in temper needs a hand always to his reins; he cannot be controlled with knees alone, unless the grip of your legs is as strong as your horse. And you will have a spear to each hand always. When you are grown, you will be able to lead him with your knees, but not yet. Your legs are too small."

She thought this over, oblivious now to the nervous movements of the stallion. At last she nodded.

"You speak truth. Father, we are close to it; the first troop came down the slope, there." She pointed a small finger. "You see where the grass is crushed. Why is Bhonal dancing? Why do all the horses fret and plunge?"

"They smell blood." Flyn spoke soberly. "I knew we must be near, from the horses." He turned his head to speak to the men behind him, who had been listening with unabashed interest to the interchange between Flyn and Maeve. "Around the next bend, then; we ride for it."

They cantered slowly, weapons at the ready, and so came upon the field of bodies.

The horses were pulled to an abrupt halt. Maeve, her stomach wrenched with sudden sickness, felt her father's hold tighten nearly to pain. The field before them was a scene from hell; bodies lay piled one upon the other, and the grass was laced with scarlet ribbons of gore.

Flyn waved a curt hand and, with a concerted movement, the entire company dismounted. He handed Maeve down to the nearest man, who set her on her feet with a gentle pat on the shoulder and turned to survey the carnage.

Off to one side, robes bloody and disarranged, the body of old Brigidh lay sprawling. Maeve looked at her, the beloved and sometimes frightening old healer, looked at her colorless face, her staring eyes, the broken shaft of spear that protruded obscenely from her throat, and began to shake. Trying to control it, she moved closer to her father.

At Flyn's feet was the body of one of the raiders, dead in his own gore, a slash that gaped like a smile severing the great vein in his neck. Flyn pushed at the body with one toe and felt Maeve's cold hand slide into his. He turned his face down to her, saw the mixture of fear and hate in her eyes, and with shocking unexpectedness, he laughed.

"Yes, Maeve; this is your doing, this is your honor, this is the honor of your tuath. This vermin, and two others also, they told me; no warrior grown could have done better." Very softly, unheard by anyone save his daughter, he added, "This day's work will make you chieftain after I have gone, little one. If you sicken at this sight, look at our slain warriors, at poor Brigidh, and remember it. You did nothing but what was right. The tuath honors you for it, and the gods give you their praise." He stooped and kissed her brow. "And I, too, honor you. No chieftain, no king, ever had a worthier daughter, no, nor son either."

She was quiet, her trembling stopped, her eyes moving now from the piled corpses to the trees on the hill, to fix suddenly on the hilltop. Flyn's eyes followed hers and saw nothing. "What is it?"

She broke away from him. "At the top, there, between the trees—there is something there, I saw it. A spot of color, blue among the trees. Father, come!"

"I see nothing," he said firmly, but she had grabbed for his hand and was pulling with all her strength for him to follow. He called for men and, with six men behind them, went up the hill on Maeve's heels, stopping at its crest to stare with pity and cold anger at what was there.

Ahnrach, or what was left of her, lay with her sightless gaze fixed on the sky. Her legs were streaked with blood, her face livid and bruised, her gown shredded and trampled in the grass; beneath her head was a pillow of blood, pooled and foul-smelling, which had streamed from her slit throat.

Maeve, unable to turn her eyes from her dearest companion, made a noise deep in her throat; turning her back with a violent, abortive gesture, she fell to her knees among the slender trees and was suddenly, violently ill, wracked with sorrow and sickness.

Flyn faced his celi. There was hate, clear in all their faces; there was pity, too, in the glances that moved between the dead girl and the living. The chieftain looked around him, a slow look of appraisal that took in the men, the dead, the living.

"Go down, two of you. Tell them to make a fire for the dead and pile the bodies high. The rest of you, search the hillside; I want stones, big and small. Ahnrach we will bury. She will lie here, poor broken flower, with the seasons to bear her company, and the hill will receive her into itself. Bring stones. Go now."

Maeve had stopped retching. She sat huddled, pallid and silent, a small child in the midst of desolation; Flyn, watching her, thought she looked more broken than the ruined body behind him, and pity stirred in him. He went to her and lifted her up. She lay in his arms limply.

"Will they go free, then?" It was a whisper, with no color of feeling to it; a whisper only. Flyn answered her, chieftain to warrior.

"I cannot tell you, Maeve. We will track these beasts, ask questions of the other tuatha, see what knowledge comes to us. There is little else we can do, if I read this aright; Carhainn is a seasoned warrior, a man with an eye, and he believed they were raiders, nameless, sons of no tuath. If he is correct, they will be hard to find. Such men live in no towns, speak with no druids, follow no laws."

He had her attention now, all of it; her face was pointed and somehow feral with the effort of concentration. Through her sickness, her anger, her childish sense of betrayal by the gods, she was dimly aware that her father's words would someday be useful to her, not as warrior, but as High Chieftain of the people of Connacht. She nodded at him and, satisfied, Flyn continued.

"They will have a fastness, in the hills most like; but the Iron Hills have many crags, many valleys, and these men are wily. Many such will attack all at once, you see, rushing down in a blind rage to kill, using the surprise of those they prey on as their best advantage. But Carhainn says, and you say, too, that these men split their ranks and attacked in two rushes, once before, once behind. And that means something I don't like the smell of, Maeve; these men have a leader who knows something of warfare."

His eyes looked past her, staring into the empty distance, seeming to speak more to himself than to her. "There have been attacks before now. Early last spring a party of traders carrying gold from Wicklow were slaughtered on the banks of Lough Lein, with all their treasure taken and their horses too. You remember that? We tracked the killers, tracked their horses as far as we could, but they crossed a stream still icy with winter and all trace of them was lost. What happened here," and he waved an arm around him, his eyes never shifting, "is not the same."

Maeve's eyes were fixed on his face. She spoke coldly. "Not the same? How not?"

He looked down at her. "This was an attack of trained men, not of men simply wanting blood and slaughter. The attack on two fronts tells me that."

His voice was harsh. "And Ahnrach. Men bent on theft and slaughter would not have taken the trouble to bring her up here; they would not waste their time in such a way. They saw you escape, Maeve, they would know that soon there would be pursuit and avengers hard on their heels. If they wanted Ahnrach, they would have taken her where she stood and left her to lie. You saw her thrown across a horse and brought up here; to go to such trouble should have meant one thing and one only—that they meant to take her with them. Yet they did not. This has a dark and chancy smell to me."

She opened her mouth to question him further. But Flyn, with a shock, had returned fully to the present and remembered that he spoke not to a fellow, but to a small child. However special she might be, however many men she had taken at spear's end, she was a small girl and these matters were not fit for her. He took her up in both arms.

"That is enough for now, darling girl. See, the men have lit the pyre down below and we must go down."

She turned her face to him, the red hair lifting

around her in the sudden breeze. "And Ahnrach? What of Ahnrach?"

"They will make her a tomb here at the top of the hill, and sun and moon will wash her with love. See, the men return with the stones for it. Say farewell to her, and a prayer to Danu in her honor. It is time you were in bed."

Maeve, sleepless and staring, lay in brilliant moonlight and waited for the night to end.

She was not an introspective child, but neither was she insensitive. The events of the previous day ran through her mind in a wretched circle, a snake that chased its own tail, and try though she would, she could not banish them.

The night was warm, with a light rain falling outside. As befit a princess, she had her own tiny house; most nights, she slept with her companion beside her and an armed man to guard her door. But Ahnrach was gone, broken and ruined, her body stretched beneath a cairn of stones, and Maeve would have no one yet to take her place. There was only herself left tonight, and her house was her own.

She heard the scrape of iron on stone, a distant, muffled sound, as the guard outside her door shifted from one foot to another, his spear scraping the earth. She spared a fleeting thought for him. Poor man, kept from his bed to keep watch over her sleep, and all for naught; there would be little sleep for her tonight, and all his work wasted. She wondered if he resented the duty Flyn imposed on him, and found no answer.

Unable to bear the stifling weight and warmth of the sheepskins any longer, Maeve rose to her feet. She could not remember ever having been awake this late before; darkness, something the other children feared, settled around her in a soft, enveloping blanket.

How quiet it is, she thought, and how clearly one hears things at night. The call of some night bird, perhaps an owl, rang out on the quiet air; with nothing to mask it, it sounded startlingly loud and close. She stood still, entranced by the purity of her senses, breathing in the stillness and the quietude of the small hours like a thick, velvet blanket of sweetness.

But the real world intruded; a distant scream, a fox on the hunt, drifted like smoke through the night. Suddenly she was lost in it once more, astride the war pony, a spear to her right hand, surrounded by her father's men. Her body trembling, she relived it yet again, as she had done without count since night fell, as she would do for years to come; Ahnrach, in the grip of two men, screaming, struggling, raking with her nails. Maeve saw, once again, her dearest companion, her cousin, trussed to a lean horse.

And here it was again, the thing that had hurt the most; her eyes meeting Ahnrach's, seeing the sudden realization in the girl's face of what must happen, the love and the frozen pride settling into the pointed features, turning the lovely face into a mask, a statue, like the perverted primal effigy of the mother goddess, the sheela-na-gig who squatted, eyes popping, sex held gaping, the symbol of all that was brutal in womanhood.

A joke, no more than a cruel jest. Maeve shut her eyes, reaching in desperation for the fading map of her cousin's face, knowing that Ahnrach's lovely, lightning changes of mood—humor to giggles to sudden sobriety— were lost to her forever. When she thought of Ahnrach now, she could only see that frozen face, the love in it etched and clean, knowing she would die so that Maeve, the chieftain's only child, might live. . . .

Maeve began to weep, the tears running silently down her thin face. It was wrong, unjust, not to be borne. How did she differ from Ahnrach, from the man at her door, from the raiders themselves, that she might live and others die for her sake? They had not hesitated, not Carhainn, not Ahnrach, none of them; they had believed, one and all, that her life was worth more than any of their own. Her father believed it, the tuath believed it, and Ahnrach's belief, as she was dragged to a horrible death, had shone from her eyes like sunlight. It seemed to Maeve that the only person who neither understood or believed was she herself.

Carhainn . . . Maeve, who had been wandering aimlessly about her tiny home, suddenly stopped. She had spared him no thought; any sympathy she might have felt had been swallowed up in the larger grief of Ahnrach's death, and the terrible, overwhelming reality of the man shuddering at the end of her spear.

But she thought about him now and her slow weeping changed to heavy sobs, bitten back and stifled so that she might not disgrace herself by allowing the man outside to hear. She had loved Ahnrach, but so, too, had Carhainn. She found her own grief insupportable; though only dimly aware of the passions of adulthood, she yet knew enough to wonder. If she felt this way for the loss of a friend, how must Carhainn be feeling now, with no one to comfort him?

Well, she thought, there is but one way to know. Barefoot, her nightrobe wrapped around her, she pushed the hide of her house aside and stepped out into the moonlight.

If the man at her door had been dozing, it did not show. At the first sound behind him he whirled, spear at the ready. As the hide fell behind her, so too did the spear. The guard dropped to his knees before her.

"Princess! Has something happened?"

He spoke in an urgent whisper. She shook her head at him; keeping her voice low, she asked her question.

"A fair night to you, Mharal. All is well, and no need for you to worry. But I cannot sleep as I am; there is something I must do. Will you help me, please?"

"Any way I can, princess." His answer was immediate and heartfelt, but she saw the curiosity come up in his face and continued in a rush.

"I am sick with grief, Mharal, for my cousin Ahnrach; truly, she was the best friend I had. I must live with my grief, I know. But what of Carhainn? Who is to comfort him in his loss, loving my cousin as he did?"

He stared down at her, staring and silent. Maeve, for an interminable moment, thought he would order her back to her bed, tell her to leave the affairs of grown men and women to those whose place it was to deal with them. The truth was that Mharal could not have spoken without weeping too. She bit back impatience and spoke pleadingly, touching his arm with one small hand.

"Please, Mharal. I must see Carhainn; there is no one

but me to understand, to share his grief with him. I will not worry him, I swear; I only wish to comfort, if I can."

His voice was unsteady. "Never has Connacht seen a child like this. Carhainn sleeps in a small hut over there, across Cruachain. Come with me; I will take you to him."

She slipped her hand in his and together they walked softly across the empty town.

They came to a halt before a small house, and Mharal spoke formally. "Princess, that is the house of Carhainn. I shall guard you from without."

"My thanks to you, warrior."

She left him standing, straight as an oak tree with his spear held between his hands, outside Carhainn's hut.

The hut was dark. For a moment she stood in silence, wondering if after all he had found sleep, wondering if after all she should turn and leave him to himself. Then a weary voice came out of the darkness, not from where his bed must be, but from the small room's far end.

"Who is it? What do you want, so late at night?"

She stepped forward, unable to see. "Carhainn? It is I, Princess Maeve." She stopped; now that she was here, she found that she did not know what to say to him. The voice that came so uncannily out of the gloom had held more than simple weariness; it had a deadness to it that frightened her, speaking to her of feelings she could not understand.

He spoke to her. "Princess! What brings you from your safe bed under moonlight?" The weariness suddenly sharpened into life. "Is something amiss?"

"No. Yes. Carhainn, please . . ."

She heard him moving, not toward her but away from her. She bit back a cry as the room flickered to life; he had lit a tallow, flooding her eyes with sudden light. She flung up a hand to protect her eyes and then dropped it.

They stood regarding each other in silence, the barefoot child and the naked warrior. He had always seemed splendid, almost godlike to her, in the way a strong man will to a child. But in the midnight chill he was somehow pathetic. I never noticed the lines on his face, she thought, and she knew with a shock that before Ahnrach's death they had not been there for her to see.

Tears welled up, the tears of a warrior who was, after all, only a little girl. She ran across the room to him, burying her face against his knees, sobbing.

"Carhainn, I beg your forgiveness, I beg you will forgive me, please . . . if I could have done something, anything, I would have, you must know that. . . ."

He stared down at her, astonished; the lethargy, the sense of death and exhaustion that had sat so heavy on him since the previous afternoon, ebbing a little. "Forgive you? What have I to forgive you for, princess? You did nothing wrong and nothing to injure me."

She raised a tearstained face to his. Sweet Lugh, he thought, but she looks like something from the other world and not flesh at all. The firelight cast deep, sweet shadows across her cheeks. She will be beautiful, he thought, the most beautiful woman in Hibernia, when she is grown. . . .

"Forgive me for today, Carhainn, I beg you. I loved Ahnrach, even as you did, and she should not have died for me." The small voice was vehement and fierce.

"Is this why you came, to tell me that?" Carhainn said very slowly. She knuckled her eyes, shaking her head.

"It is not. I came because I knew how you loved Ahnrach, and I thought . . . I thought . . ." Maeve's voice faltered at the look on his face.

"You thought what, princess?"

"I came to comfort you, if you would let me." Her voice was small. Suddenly she looked very young, one dirty foot rubbing at the other, standing off balance, staring at the earthen floor. "They know I loved Ahnrach, captain of Cruachain, and they give me what comfort they can. But who is to comfort you? They worry for me, but your loss is the greater." She had stopped crying, and held his gaze with her own. "You can share your grief with me, warrior." And she reached out to take one scarred and massive hand.

He stood immobile, lost in the strangeness of it, a cycle of odd, unrelated thoughts hitting him, making him dizzy. It is the dead hour of the night; Ahnrach lies beneath cold stones on a cold hillside; I am naked, yet I am not cold; this child, this child, a few weeks short of six summers, and she understands. . . .

He began to cry. The tears he had been unable to shed, the anger he had buried from need, that had eaten at him like a worm at a corpse since the only person he had ever loved was taken from him to die in agony while he was forced to turn his back for his king's sake, boiled to the surface and burst in a storm of sobs. He fought them a moment and then, battle lost, his knees buckled beneath him and he fell to lie in a huddled, tortured ball, wracked with sobbing.

Arms, small and cold and unbelievably soft, surrounded his bowed head and held him strongly. "I grieve with you," she whispered, and warm tears ran down his back. "I grieve with you, I grieve for you." She began to rock him, a slow rhythmic movement that was soothing, calming.

When he had stopped crying, the rage and furious agony was gone, transmuted to an aching sorrow that was so much easier to bear. He wiped an arm across his swollen face and brought his eyes to the calm, beautiful creature, the tiny miracle who had come to him with understanding.

"I am yours, princess." His voice was thick with tears, but it held the flat ring of truth. "Body and soul, from this day forward, I am yours. You have all my loyalty, you have my good arm and a spear with it. May the gods bring you all there is to have and grant me the honor of helping you keep it. When you are High Queen, I am your captain, lady." He took her hand in his and kissed it. "Yours, lady, your servant and your shield."

She smiled, a smile of transfiguring beauty. "I accept your loyalty and your strong arm too. You will sleep now."

5

High Chieftain of Ulster

The army, after months of war, came back to the fires and the celebrations that awaited them in Emain. Sheilagh, weary of her temporary leadership and fretting for freedom, was the first to see them come.

For Connal, known through the land as the Victorious, this homecoming had a certain sweetness. He had led the men of Ulster down the dangerous eastern coast road, through the mountains, straight into the stronghold of Lagan Des-Gabair. It had been a long war and a tiring one, capped off on Connal's eighteenth birthday by the final victory against his old enemy, Cet.

The seeds of war had been officially sowed some three years earlier. Sharing the waters off the coast, the two tuatha had found themselves in flat disagreement as to how much fish might be taken by each from the chilly sea, and when; it had dragged on, the boats of each province harrying those of the other, stopping just short of open hostility.

Then, seven years to the day after Sibhainn's death, a boat of each province had gone down off the coast. The handful of survivors, sick and furious, had straggled back to their respective tuatha and straight to their chieftains, each to lay blame for the sinking on the other side.

After that, war was inevitable. The death of the fishermen had given each chieftain an excuse to do what they had been spoiling to do for ten long years. The grudge was an old one, dormant yet strong, and if the people of Des-Gabair knew little of the north, Ulster remembered well enough. Connal, respected but never truly liked by his cold-tempered people, found the task of persuading them to war far easier than he had expected.

If their enthusiasm surprised him, he was astonished by the savage delight with which Brihainn, always more a man of thought than of action, threw himself into the preparations.

Connal, shocking the tuath by leaving Sheilagh in charge of Emain's defense in his absence, found himself cornered by his closest cela. Brihainn, in fact, was delighted with the honor done his formidable mother, and he wandered into Connal's house the night before their departure in a high state of glee. His good humor was mixed with trepidation, for in Connal's action he thought he saw the confirmation of an old suspicion. The time had come to ask Connal for the truth; he could only hope that the result would not be that deadly and mindless rage that had kept Connal his whole life long from the love of his people.

He found Connal checking his weapons. "Ho, my friend, that's a pretty thing you have there. Surely that is new? I don't believe I have seen it."

"The spear? New, yes. I crafted it myself." Connal hefted the slender weapon in one hand, testing its balance. "Note the thicker end, Brihainn; it affords me a better grip for holding and betters the aim and the striking strength alike when it is cast downward."

"Pretty, yes." Brihainn ran one finger absentmindedly down the edge. "Connal . . ."

The chieftain stood, smiling faintly. "You are not usually at a loss for words, cela. Speak out. Has it to do with Sheilagh?"

"My mother. Yes." Brihainn, though his face showed nothing, was vastly relieved that Connal had taken the burden of first speech from him. "I came to thank you for that. It was bravely done, to leave a woman as your shadow behind; you surprised the tuath, you know."

"Yes, I know. But she was the logical choice, the best choice, though I hated to do it."

"Hated to do it? Why is that, then?"

"Because," Connal replied flatly, "she is among the best of my warriors, and I would rather have taken her with us. Someone must guard Emain, though; it is not as if she will be wasted here."

He had begun to prowl, wandering restlessly throughout his house. Brihainn had a sudden intuition that Connal was trying to set each tiny thing, each personal belonging, into his memory, lest he not live to return. He spoke gently.

"I have something to ask, Victorious, something not easy, and if you will not answer, I will not take it amiss. But it touches me closely, and you too. May I speak?"

Connal paused to regard his friend over a shoulder. Brihainn saw one mobile eyebrow lift, and drew a deep breath.

"Dangerous ground, then? Speak, of course."

Brihainn, with a short prayer, fired his question point-blank. "You are in love with my mother, are you not?"

He watched Connal's color rise, saw the sudden tensing of muscles, the tic jump in the corner of the tight mouth, and closed his eyes against anger. He opened them again to absolute silence, and found Connal grinning.

"Brihainn, you devil's spawn, your eyes are too sharp for your own health. They will undo you one day." He shook his head at his startled friend. "Sheilagh. Your mother, wise eyes, is a remarkable woman. She took my respect and my adoration, too, the day she killed Machlan and took my uncle captive. She has the softest touch, the most beautiful eyes, the strongest face, of any woman I have known. And you know how I warm to hair the color of the sunrise. In love with her? No, Brihainn, not as you and I understand that word."

He turned his back abruptly. His next remark, sounding stifled, made Brihainn jump. "My own mother hated me, you know that. Yours does not. I count myself fortunate, for she is a bad enemy, and I am richer for her friendship and her tutelage. Regard your own luck, thinking man."

"Oh, I do." Brihainn, the dangerous moment past, could smile. "It worried me, not from jealousy, for any woman would be honored. But the tuath would never have agreed."

Connal's eyes lit with laughter. "The tuath! Who cares for what the tuath thinks? Sheilagh would never have consented even had I wanted it, which I promise you I did not." He laid a gentle hand on Brihainn's cheek. "Nor, lest you torture yourself with wondering, have we ever bedded. Put it from your mind, best of friends, and worry it no more. The honor I did your mother tonight was an honor due her for what she is, and not for what I think I see."

It was these sudden flashes of insight, Brihainn thought, that made Connal the man he was. Not the violence of temper, the skill at arms, the cold and absolute justice for which he was famed. It was this unexpected vision, this seeing through the subterfuge to the spirit within. . . .

He suddenly gave a snort of laughter, and the moment was broken. Connal dropped his hand and looked questioning.

"No, chieftain, you would have no need to bed with a woman who can give you fifteen years at the least. You have that little barbarian, do you not?"

"I have not." The words were snapped; the wall had come up once more. "I have finished with her, though it pleasured me once; no more. I freed her, in full sight of the tuath. She is not mine, only her own."

The barbarian, a tiny, dark-skinned daughter of the Belgae, had been taken in a clash between her traveling tribe and a small troop of Connal's men. The skirmish had been short and bloody, the surviving men of the raiders leaving their heads to adorn Connal's banqueting hall.

But he had not been able to bring himself to order Annak's execution. She had stood before him, tiny and dark, with defiance and a high pride in her eyes. Connal, staring now at Brihainn, did not see him; instead he saw the straight lines of Annak's body, outlined in the barbaric clothes she wore, as she confronted him in chains before the tuath.

"Raider woman," he had told her, "I offer you now a chance to save yourself. Tell me why I should spare you."

She had lifted her head, no easy task, for her neck was weighted with chains. With a heavy clanking that fell loud in the quiet hall, she had smiled and spat in his face.

There had been a stunned silence, then a rustling, as the watching tuath waited for the famous temper to explode. They had stared, chieftain and prisoner, into each other's faces for a long moment.

Connal had burst into laughter.

"Take her," he had told Brihainn, "take her, leave the chains on her, but take her to my house. Put her into my bed. This prize I will keep. I like the taste of pride, of spirit. The women of this tuath, with few exceptions, have little enough of either."

He had wiped the spittle away, staring after her as she was led off with her nose in the air, to await his pleasure. Seeing the amusement in the faces of the men, the envy and greed of the women, he had called after Brihainn, who was leading her from the hall down the ranks of the tuath, "Be careful, cela. She spits."

For a year she had slept in Connal's bed, teaching him to drown in the reality of things he had only dimly been aware of, learning slowly to enjoy the fact that she was held in honor by the tuath, so long as she shared the bed of the chieftain. He had grown slowly tired of her ceaseless demands, her self-serving shrewdness, and even the hot delights of their physical union ceased to compensate for the irritations. So he had let it be known that he no longer wanted her, and that was that.

Under any other chieftain she would have been killed, or perhaps thrown as a gift to another chieftain, or a man of the tuath deserving of special favor. But the sense of fairness that Brihainn had helped to nurture in Connal made him understand that she was helpless, in no way responsible for what had been done with her, not to blame. The treatment expected of him would be unjust, and he would not do it.

So he had installed her in a small house of her own, made a gift of gold to her, and told the startled clan that she was henceforth a free woman, a member of the tuath, and as such was entitled to the common justice, the allemeurach, granted only to citizens of Hibernia.

Now he remembered, and remembered well, and Brihainn remembered with him. But the memory was put aside for the coming war and the long trek south which would begin at first light; the war itself had occupied Connal's waking mind to the exclusion of all else. It was not until the army was within half a day's reach of home did Connal once again let his thoughts stray toward the body of the barbarian that, through his own generosity, he could never again possess unless she willed it so.

It had been a quiet season in Emain, and Sheilagh, anticipating trouble with those of the tuath left behind, had found little to test her. She knew full well that by leaving her in command, Connal had estranged many of his people still further; they had known eight generations of male chieftains, and though they obeyed Connal's orders, the grumbling had been widespread enough to reach Sheilagh's ears. Suppose an army comes upon us from the rear, can a woman deal with such a thing, has she the wit, the training? Suppose there are raids on the cattle? What was the Victorious thinking of, to be leaving a woman to defend us?

Mindful of Connal's words to her, remembering how he had laid upon her the order that peace must be kept, she could yet see only one way to still the disquiet in the people.

She had kept her ears well opened, waiting her chance, until the day she had heard one of Sibhainn's old cela—left behind, to his great resentment, to aid her—remark to another that hens were only fit to lead chicks. His listener, seeing her close by, had not warned Marak in time, and Sheilagh, taking the warrior by one shoulder, had spun him around to face her.

Her timing and her luck alike had been perfect. Catching him off balance, seeing the surprise in his eyes, she had dealt him a blow to the chin that lifted him off his feet and set him down in the mud. Then, with a few softly spoken and dangerous words of warning, she had turned on her heel and strode away.

As she had known must happen, word spread throughout the tuath; if the grumbling persisted, the malcontents had at least enough sense to keep her from hearing it. From that day she had no trouble in carrying out Connal's wishes.

It had been a tiresome thing, that temporary leadership of the people. The tuath might whisper that she had plotted for this power; high astride her stallion, her neck craned to the column of men moving like ants on the horizon, she recognized the colored banners in the distance as Connal and his army coming home, and felt a great weight go from her like snow in spring.

She turned her horse's head toward Emain, bringing the people of Ulster the good news, ordering the beacon fires to be lit, the sheep killed and cooked for the victory banquet.

Twelve heads, their sightless eyes seemingly fixed on the victory dinner, dangled in the flickering torchlight of the Ulster banqueting hall.

The army was home, the free folk gathered to feast. The men of the army moved on the streets of Emain, some drinking, some singing the rowdy songs of war that had sustained them on the long trek up the eastern coast and home. Many had vanished through the doorways of their homes, to lose themselves in the welcoming arms of their women.

Here in the banqueting hall the feast was at its height. The dozen slain warriors of Des-Gabair, twelve of Cet's best fighters, had not weathered their journey at the belts of the Ulster men well; impaled on the bronze spikes reserved for enemies of the chieftains, they had a surprised look, flesh livid, tongues limp between blue lips. Sheilagh, sitting at Connal's left hand, glanced up at them and quickly back to her plate again.

Though her gesture of repulsion was brief, quickly controlled, it did not escape Connal's eye. He looked at her sidelong, then up at the heads. Leaning toward her, he spoke under cover of the roar of laughter and conversation.

"You dislike our trophies, warrior woman?"

"You have quick eyes, chieftain. No, I do not dislike

them; they honor you, for sure. It is only that one directly above your head I dislike."

Connal, one brow lifting, turned his chair to follow her gaze of distaste. He broke into laughter.

"Oh, I see now. Brihainn!"

His cela, sitting deep in conversation with Cormac at Connal's right hand, turned smiling. "Chieftain?"

"Your mother is having a bad time with her food, wise eyes. No woman resents a wink from a man's eye in his lifetime; a lecherous look in death is another thing. See to that head up there, my friend, and let our warrior woman get on with her mutton."

Brihainn, grinning, rose to his feet. Connal tore a piece of mutton and, through a mouthful of the hot meat, resumed his conversation with Sheilagh.

"Tell me truth, lady. Had you any trouble here?"

She shrugged. "Only what I expected. It was a quiet season; a few traders, a visit or two. No trouble there."

He understood her immediately, his face hardening. "What, then? Trouble with the men of the tuath?"

"Not the men alone, chieftain; I frighten the women too." She set her knife down and contemplated him. "It is not to their blame, Connal. For generations they have known only chieftains who were men; we have had no warrior woman to rule in Ulster for uncounted years. They wondered what I could do, should the need arise for action, and grumbled over it. I feel no surprise at that."

There was no softening of the harsh face. "It is not for the tuath to grumble at what their chieftain does. I left you as shadow; they had no say in that."

She put her hand out, smiling. "Oh, I dealt with it, never fear. I made a slight example of one who grumbled close enough for me to hear; that was an end to it."

His thoughts had already passed hers. "Ah. Marak, no doubt; he was ever a complainer, why else would I leave him here? What did you do to teach him his duty?"

"A blow to the jaw and a few imprecations. That took care of the matter, and I heard no more of it. But you have all my honor, chieftain; may I speak?"

Connal sighed. "Like mother, like son. Speak, then."

She looked at him straightly. "The people have never

given you your due, Connal mac Sibhainn. Oh, they give you all respect, they know your prowess, but from childhood they have disliked you. Only my son and Cormac, there, had eyes to see what a cold temper hid. Yet you rule them with a strong hand, you have never yet known a defeat in war, they do what you tell them."

His face was unreadable. "And so?"

"I only—I wished to say that while you were gone, I must needs play the chieftain. The people were wary of me, and unwilling; sure, they would never choose such as me to guide them. And in that season I learned what it is to be a leader that the people do not love." She took his hand and laid her lips against it. "A weary thing, and you are graceful in your handling of it. All honor, chieftain."

He left his hand in hers a moment, saying nothing. Beside him, Brihainn stirred; though his friend's back was to him, Connal doubted not that Brihainn had heard every word, and suddenly Connal remembered the conversation they had held together so many months past. Letting go of Sheilagh's hand, he put his lips to Brihainn's ear.

"Be silent, be secret," he whispered mockingly, and Brihainn, his shoulders shaking with suppressed laughter, whispered back, "You could visit the barbarian, chieftain. But be silent, be secret. She spits."

Connal's laughter rang through the hall, turning heads his way the length of the table. But when his amusement had eased, he leaned back in his chair and thought about Annak.

She was not here; he had scanned each face in the hall and caught no sight of her. It had been months, days and nights spent forcing a tired body to fight, to march, to present the image of power to friends and enemies alike, and the truth could not be gainsaid; he wanted a woman.

But Annak was a free woman now and, though entitled to be present at such a feast as oinach of Ulster, she had elected to stay away. Anger, that old and unpredictable companion, shivered and was forced away.

Well, he was chieftain; he could do as he chose, and if she refused him, the problem took care of itself. He need make no excuses. Nodding to Sheilagh, he rose to his feet.

"Oinach of Ulster, I am for my bed. I pray you feast till dawn, if the desire takes you thus. A fair night."

The hour had grown late, the streets of Emain had emptied. Under a thin edge of moon Connal strode across the town, stopping in front of the tiny house he had gifted to Annak in sight of the tuath.

No light showed through the thick hide. Sleeping, and with a lover, perhaps? No matter; if another man lay there, the man could stay there. But try he would.

He pushed the hide aside and went in to darkness.

The hut was black, darker than death. Connal, holding his breath, heard the soft and regular breathing and moved carefully toward it. Only one person's breath, and he could be easy; nothing more to fear than refusal, after all. There would be a taper, he knew, a taper close to her hand. His hand, moving quiet across the floor, found it, and the flint.

The room flickered to soft life. With the taper in one hand, he turned to face the bed and cried out.

The woman who sat up, disheveled and frightened, was not Annak. Through his confusion he recognized her; the town midwife, an old woman, what was her name? Anis?

"Yes, chieftain," she whispered, and he realized he had spoken his thoughts aloud. He looked down at her, his eyes wide with shock, and suddenly saw her terror.

"Be not frightened," he said quietly, and knelt beside the bed. "I will not harm you, nor am I angry. Are you not Anis, our good midwife?"

She nodded, trembling, the skins clutched against her in protection with one veined hand. He kept his voice even.

"Where is Annak, midwife? What do you in her bed?"

With a sudden chill he saw the pity come into her eyes. Her voice, soft, comforting, seemed to come from miles away, muffled and unreal.

"I thought—they did not tell you, then? I grieve with you, chieftain. She refused to have you told before you left for the south lands that she was with child. Two months ago they brought her to me, but it was too far gone, I could do nothing. Great pain, and she and her daughter dead in my bed." Dazed, stupefied, he saw her hands move against magic. "I could not sleep in that bed, chieftain, and before she died she said I could come here after she was gone."

Connal spoke numbly. "She knew she was dying, then?"

Some of the fear had fallen from Anis. Wrapping her robes around her, she climbed from the bed to lay a gentle hand on his shoulder. "How not? The child was poorly conceived, and malformed with it." She saw something in his face that made her add hastily, "No blame to you, chieftain; Annak was malformed herself, the womb could hold nothing living. No blame to you, chieftain."

The sense of her words finally hit him. He got unsteadily to his feet and stared down at her.

"No blame to me? Was it not my child, then?"

"Yours, yes. No mistake there, the babe was the spit of your father. But no blame. You were not the cause of her misfortune. Had she stayed in her own country, to mate there with a man of her own choosing, she would have died of the same thing in a different time."

But Connal could listen no more. Turning his back on the rumpled bed, the luxurious room, he stumbled through the door with a head throbbing to bursting point and made his way to the clearing, the glen, the place where only Cormac or Brihainn would dare to disturb him.

The moon was almost down; in a few hours dawn would fall across the chilly ground, wetting the grass, bringing the rays of Lugh with it. He stood in the center of the glen, directly under the rowan tree, and turned his face toward the massive cromlech.

Hidden by darkness not a hundred yards away, two figures stood together. The wail of anguish floated across the night sky and settled sickly on them.

"Leave him," Sheilagh said quietly. "I have done wrong, I expect, in letting him find out this way. But I could not bring myself to tell him, Brihainn."

The tall figure at her side turned to her. Brihainn's voice was harsh. "But you might have told me, Mother.

You heard me urge him on, there in the hall, to seek out Annak for what he wanted. He will never forgive me for this, never, and it is your doing." His whisper was breathless. "Sweet Boann of the rivers, could you not have told me, let me tell him, spared us both this?"

Never since his birth had he used that tone of voice to her. She opened her mouth to speak in anger, but shut it again and sighed. "I beg your forgiveness, Brihainn. You are right, and I was weak and foolish. Yet I truly did not think he would take it this badly, for what he had for the girl was passion, and no love in it. He feels guilt, I expect, more than loss, and that is a sorry thing for a man. I will tell him tomorrow how I knew but could not find the courage to give him such bad news." She laid a gentle hand on his arm and spoke kindly. "Fair as he is, he will know there is no blame to you."

Brihainn, who knew that Sheilagh never apologized unless she meant it, was mollified. Shoulder to shoulder, mother and son pressed closer into the shadows, keeping their unseen vigil as night moved toward morning. In the glen Connal sat sleepless and hot-eyed, his arms wrapped around the ancient cromlech for comfort, waiting for the sun.

Anis had not kept silent about what had come about on the feast night; before another day had passed there was no one in the town who did not know how the chieftain had gone to ask his little barbarian for her favors, only to find her dead in childbed, and his deformed child with her.

It was whispered that he blamed himself; some, seeing his favorites stay carefully out of his path for some days, thought he laid the guilt for Annak's death on them.

The people, shrugging the matter off, were impatient with his mood. They had won their first war in many years with ease, their losses minimal, and Cet had been soundly punished for both the ancient insult and the present presumption; the prevailing mood was satisfaction, and they had no mind to sorrow. Their lack of understanding mingled with Connal's own guilty sorrow to produce a cold detachment that made even his closest companions uneasy.

For two weeks the discomfort of his silence held. Then, one bright morning, Brihainn went out riding for hare and came thundering back to Emain with a druid in tow.

It had been many years since one of the holy men had come this way. The people, clustered tight, watched with awe and reverence as the cela's horse, carrying both Brihainn and the druid, roared to a stop at the door of the chieftain's house. Panting and breathless, Brihainn slid from the horse and threw an order to a stable slave.

Connal, as it happened, was asleep. Since the feast night he had been sleeping poorly, suffering from dreams that lay like vultures across his shoulders; with Ulster at peace and the presence of the chieftain at all times unnecessary, he would sometimes fall exhausted to his bed in high daylight, to catch what rest he could.

He was awakened from an uneasy doze by Brihainn's hand closing tight on him and shaking hard. Sitting and stretching, his eyes blinking to adjust to the sunlight that streamed in through the open hide, he saw the faces outside, the two men by the door, and snapped, "Let the hide fall."

There was a tightness to Brihainn, a glow of white excitement that Connal had never seen in him before. He looked at the druid, a young man not yet an elder, and his eyebrows rose. "You have some news for me, it would seem. Wait, though; you must drink first."

The chieftain's slave, waiting his master's commands at the door, came running with wine. Connal poured in silence, wondering at his cela's tautness. When the druid set his empty cup down, Connal laid a hand on Brihainn's shoulder.

"Now. It has been too long since Ulster has been honored by a druid's presence. What brings a holy man to Emain, and how can her chieftain aid you?"

"Too long, yes." The man, his hood held lightly in one hand, regarded Connal with frank curiosity. He was indeed young, no more than Connal's age, with a high color and brown eyes well opened upon the world. His voice

was curious; light and raspy, almost affected. "What brings
me here are men gone missing, chieftain. As to your aid,
you can give me what information you have."

"Men gone missing? Holy men?"

"Two of them." The druid's face had hardened. "My
name, chieftain, is Neill. A season past, two of our elders,
Ahnal and Mahram, left sanctuary to travel north. They
had received disturbing news from a visitor of Des-Gabair;
news that concerned Fearghail, brother to Sibhainn. Did
this traveler speak truth, chieftain?"

"Truth, yes." How the past came back to haunt one;
the room had faded suddenly and they were children
again, he and Brihainn, standing in the shadow of the
woods while two men and a tortured girl acted out a
passion play in the wet grass a spear's cast away. . . . He
shook his head, willing the pictures away, and looked at
Neill.

"That was long in the past, wise man, ten years at
least. You were slow to hear of it."

"We do not receive visitors at sanctuary very often,"
the druid replied dryly. "The journey is hard, and most
fear to come; only in an extreme case will men seek us
out. This man came to ask us for a boon, that one of us
might travel to his chieftain and interpret an ugly dream
that came too often. He brought us news, the first news
from the outside we had in a long span." Neill lifted his
empty cup, moving it aimlessly between his fingers. "We
of the sanctuary care little for the moving world outside.
Chieftains are born and die; it does not touch us. The
news of Fearghail was not all we were told, you know.
We learned that your father had died, that Des-Gabair and
Ulster had warred. We learned of the man called Connal
the Victorious, and learned that in Connacht there is a
princess, a two-handed warrior, who is the best in Hibernia,
young though she may be. Much news, Victorious, but we
cared nothing for it."

Connal watched him, his face closed. "Yet you sent
men to seek the truth about my uncle."

"That. Yes." Neill set the cup down with a snap. "That
news we cared about; I have no memory of Fearghail
myself, for I was but a child when he left us." He looked

from Connal to Brihainn. "It is a thing of importance, men of Ulster, when one who knows the secrets of the grove turns from the light. It is akin to playing with the sky fires of summer, to abuse the knowledge and the power, and to do that you must learn to flame. The power turns in on itself in the end and destroys the possessor. But before that happens, much damage is done to the world along the way."

"So your elders came to seek Fearghail?" Connal, who had watched Brihainn's trembling and barely suppressed excitement with mystification, saw one hand move to rub the scar at the corner of his mouth. With light dawning, he dropped an arm across his friend's shoulder and faced Neill.

"We, too, were but boys when Fearghail was named as outcast from our tuath. It was Brihainn's doing, Brihainn's and mine, that he was caught and sent from us; the scar you see here is left to Brihainn for that morning's work. We have heard nothing of him since then, and to say truth, I have scarce given him a thought these ten years past. I had thought he must be dead."

Neill gazed steadily at him. "Yet two elders went to seek news of him and have vanished from the world."

Brihainn spoke impatiently. "If you are thinking that we of all men would shield Fearghail, your wits are gone. Vanished, yes. But there are many ways to vanish, wise man. If they came from sanctuary in the south, they must needs have come by one of two roads; the eastern coast, or the road that runs between Connacht and Ulster and through the Iron Hills. Had they come by the east, we must have met them on our way to Des-Gabair or home when we had finished there."

"And you did not."

"We did not. They must have come through Connacht, then, by the Iron Hills."

The druid's face was unreadable. "And so? Connacht is a civilized place; no man or woman born would harm a druid, for no worse crime can be committed in all of Hibernia. You know this as well as I."

Brihainn's face had taken on a dreamy cast. "I did not

mean those of the Connacht oinach who spend their lives
going about their lawful business. But the Iron Hills . . ."

"What, then?"

Connal answered for him. "The woods there are full
of beasts, bears and wolves. It is said that outlaws live in
the hills, and monsters in the depths of Lough Lein. I
have been there, once, and I found it an uncanny place,
full of silences that ring on the ear." He shuddered suddenly. "They could have drowned, or been taken by the
beasts of the woodland."

"Or murdered by outlaws for their gold. Yes, I see."
Neill looked thoughtful. "Tell me, Connal the Victorious.
Do the Iron Hills lie under the hand of Ulster?"

Connal was quick to catch his meaning. "They do not.
The lower slopes to the north are considered to be of
Ulster, and those to the south of Connacht. But, in truth,
no chieftain will claim them; they are equally far from
Emain and Cruachain, too hard to watch, too dangerous to
waste time and lives in the keeping of."

"Yes. You can give me no help, then?"

Brihainn bit back an impatient exclamation as Connal
raised a placatory hand. "A moment, cela. Neill, I will give
you whatever help I can render, but to what end? Even if
you found them lying in their blood, what could we do?
No man here knows those hills, and even a druid may
make a meal for a bear or a hungry wolf. What do you
want of us?"

Neill sighed; a long, mournful sound. "Your words are
true, to my sorrow. I can gain nothing by a search of an
unknown place. No, I will ask nothing of you, chieftain,
save one thing only, that you keep your ears well opened.
If you find anything, hear any news, that may lead us to
our vanished elders, send men to sanctuary to bring us the
word." He twinkled suddenly. "No fear, they will be
welcome."

They saw him off with ceremony. Watching his horse
disappear over the eastern horizon, Brihainn spoke idly.

"A two-handed warrior princess," he said. "Have you
ever heard of such a thing?"

"Never. And yet . . ."

Brihainn, aware of an odd quality in Connal's voice,

turned to face his chieftain. "And yet? By the gods, Connal, you have a hungry look! What is it, then?"

Connal shrugged suddenly and turned back toward Emain. "Oh, nothing, nothing very much. A fit of pique, to keep me humble. I thought I was the greatest warrior in Hibernia, but I cannot fight two-handed. A warrior woman in the making; that would be Flyn's daughter— Maeve, I think she is called. A princess of Connacht who kills with two hands; I would be curious to see her."

6

Murder and a Throne

Maeve, fifteen years old, stood at Carhainn's side and watched the bustle of the royal party preparing for departure to greener pastures.

The cattle, several head of the tuath's best tethered together, waited patiently to be moving in the search for food. The ground below them was warm, but that was deceptive; it was still March, the true thaw of spring had not yet come, and the fodder cut before the long winter had set in was nearly exhausted. Nothing would grow awhile yet in this hard ground, and the cattle must be fed; nothing could even be sown until the iron hold of the cold months had melted away. Maeve, shivering a little, wrapped her arms tight around her fur-edged cloak and watched her parents.

She remembered her shattering argument with Flyn, his refusal to allow her to accompany them. Though the quarrel was days past, the memory could still cloud her brow and make her seethe with resentment. A marriageable fifteen, by her father's own estimation the best warrior in Connacht, and she must stay at home like a stupid child, chained to her hearth in Cruachain while even her mother was permitted the pleasure of leaving the town for a space. She was at an age where many girls were already mothers and many boys had already fallen in battle, and she must sit alone wasting in her empty house, all for her father's fears. . . .

It had been the worst quarrel she had ever had, that fight, and she remembered it with no pleasure. Her father had been flat in his refusal; thinking back over it, she had come to realize that since the day of the raiders' attack so many years ago, he had barely let her leave the confines of the town.

Maeve, fearless, restless, a ruthless and well-trained warrior as well as warm-blooded girl, was coming to hate the very sight of Cruachain, its thin streets, its barking hounds, its people. The uneventfulness of her life had set up a canker in her, gnawing and seeking, a desire to move, to wander, to be away from here, even for a short while.

But Flyn had refused to take her. Her lips set into a thin line as her mind's eye brought that confrontation back in painfully vivid colors; Flyn purple-faced, herself furious, the two of them shouting at each other while half the tuath cowered in an unattractive combination of fear and avidity and Nieve was cast in the unenviable role of trying to make peace between her two angry warriors. . . .

Carhainn, standing quiet beside her, felt the tension in her. His own feelings were an odd mixture of sorrow that she should be so unhappy and his own elation at being left here alone with her to be her bodyguard, her right arm. He looked down at her red head, seeing the set of her jaw and the slump of her shoulders, and knew a yearning to touch her, if only in comfort, so strong as to hurt him.

I have hidden it well, he thought wryly; I think too well, from her and perhaps from the gods as well. Since the day of Ahnrach's death, when the barefoot, frightened child had come, unsure of her welcome, to comfort him under the moon, he had loved her with an intensity and an unswerving concentration that sometimes frightened him. Yet she was princess, destined to rule, perhaps to marry a man of high estate, and there was nothing to be done about it.

During the years in which Maeve came to adulthood, he had settled into an aching acceptance of his situation. She was completely out of his ken, as distant from his reach as the midsummer moon. He knew it, accepted it, understood it, yet none of that mitigated the simple fact of his love for her. It was like a wound that would never heal, like putting one's tongue over and over into a rotten tooth; painful yet compelling, and in the end impossible to resist. . . .

As though sensing something of his mood, she lifted her head to smile at him. The stiff wind that blew in from the west lifted the heavy red hair and fanned it out around her face. Carhainn felt his heart turn over.

There was an effect about her, something about the high bones, the pointed chin, the coloring, that was somehow feral. It was not her air of alertness, for that came from an inner strength and the teaching given to a warrior; it was a purely physical resemblance. She looked like a very beautiful forest creature, a fox perhaps, or a cat. The green eyes tilting upward at the corners, the lips that would fold back over small white teeth when she flashed a smile, enhanced the impression.

Now she gave him that bewitching smile, the thin lips folding and the single dimple curving into being. Her voice, for such a slim creature, was surprisingly husky.

"Your pardon, dear captain; my mood blows over us like winter wind. I must try and overcome it."

"You are disappointed and restless, princess." He spoke to her, as always, with a blend of understanding and diffidence that, had he but known, she found attractive and intriguing. "A hard life, to be a wild mare tethered at a village gate; who among us could blame you for your mood?"

Flyn had swung a leg over Bhonal, old now, but still the greatest horse in a tuath that prided itself on its breeding stock. He had not glanced at her; for him, too, then, the quarrel had gone deep. Nieve, her horse waiting, cast a hesitant, worried look at her tight-lipped husband. Then coming to a decision, she straightened her head and came to Maeve's side.

For a moment they regarded each other, the two women; there was bitterness in the daughter's eyes, compassion and understanding in the mother's. Nieve, taking

Maeve's face between her hands, squeezed the girl's chin and kissed her lightly on the brow.

Maeve's mood eased. She could not be angry with Nieve; in the heat of the fight with her father, when such hard things were said, Nieve had risked her lord's anger by taking Maeve's side, not an easy thing to do, and Maeve could not but value it. She kissed her mother once on each cheek.

"Safe going," she said quietly. "Good finding. Danu go with you on your travels."

"We shall not be gone above four days," Nieve answered mildly. "No great journey, that, and no excitement to be missed. But I thank you for your blessing." She looked up at Carhainn, saw the helpless love he thought was hid so deep, and touched him tentatively on the shoulder. "Guard our daughter well, captain."

"I will that, lady," he said formally, and bowed low.

They stood together, Maeve reaching no higher than Carhainn's shoulder, as the last of the mounted men swung into position. Maeve, the habit of long years coming to the fore, found herself counting. Ten, fifteen, eighteen . . . twenty armed men, plus four as personal guard of honor for the king and queen. It should be enough.

"Move out," Flyn said. His voice was curt; he had not once glanced her way. Maeve, unused to the sensation of her father's displeasure, felt her own will hardening. She had never let him go before without a farewell, but this time it would be different. She had gone to him with a reasonable request and he had responded with an explosive anger; she would make no move toward him. Let him do it. The quarrel was of his making, not hers, and she would offer nothing unless he did.

It did not occur to her, standing stiff and proud with her eyes fixed on nothing, that since the day he had almost lost her, he could not bear to let her go into danger; it did not occur to her that his anger had been no more than a distorted reflection of his all-consuming love for her.

The party moved slowly to the north. As they reached the gates of Cruachain, Maeve saw her mother turn on her horse's back and caught the surreptitious kiss blown from the palm of one hand. Maeve lifted a hand and let it fall.

"Princess?"

She turned to Carhainn, raising her brows. "You sound very worried, brave captain. What, then?"

"Oh, nothing, nothing very much. It is only. . ." He struggled with himself a moment. "I hate to see you unhappy, or bored, or fretting. What can I do to ease you?"

Maeve turned to watch the horses, almost gone now from sight, and sighed deeply. Then, to his intense surprise, for she had never done such a thing before, she tucked one slim arm through his and pressed her cheek against his sleeve.

"What I need most I am forbidden from the asking of," she said quietly. There was something in her face that brought his heart into his throat; a hunger, a desire, that might have meant everything, or nothing at all. Freedom, love, he himself perhaps? She looked up at him, her eyes fixing his in helpless thrall.

"Forbidden to a princess," she said bitterly. "Yes. Therefore I will not shock you by the asking of it. I wish to be alone awhile, dear one. Leave me by myself for a time. Will you do that for me, dear Carhainn, kind captain?"

A muscle began to jump high on one cheekbone, its rhythm a dreadful counterpoint to the sudden throb that took his loins in a tight hold. Forbidden thoughts, thoughts to dishonor her, and for what? A wish, a dream? He said tightly, "I will do anything you want, princess, anything at all. You have only to name it."

Her mouth twitched. Amusement, he thought dizzily, she has seen what I want and is playing with me, and suddenly he saw the pain in her face and understood. I misjudged her, she did not mean what she seemed to mean, she could not . . .

Her words came with deliberation. "Comes the time, Carhainn, I will name it. Be sure of it." The green eyes were slits now, emeralds set in ivory, and her mouth was pursed to a bow that held back sorrow. There was something new in the look, an awareness of herself and her own power. He saw the glimmer of tears clustering in translucent radiance on her lashes, and suddenly he could bear no more.

"I will be in my own house, princess, and will not disturb your privacy," he said harshly, and turned on his heel. The soft touch on his back stopped him in his tracks.

Her voice was even, calm, the voice of a woman who has met a bridge and crossed it, a woman who has faced herself and acted with conscious will, not a girl's voice at all.

"My name, Carhainn. Princess, princess, and it means nothing in the dust of time passing. It is not enough, dear captain, not for me, not anymore, not now. You asked what I wished you to do? I will tell you, then."

The street was empty but for them. He stood shuddering. She spoke in a husky whisper that was the most sensual thing he had ever heard. By Danu, this must stop, he could bear no more of it, if she did not take that soft hand from his back he would not be responsible...

She spoke. "Turn back to me."

The words were a command, impossible to deny. Carhainn, turning slowly back to stare at her, saw her through a scarlet mist that was all the blood in his body.

She held his eyes. "My name, captain. I want to hear you say it, this once. What is my name?"

She was beauty walking, something out of the hills, not human at all; the green eyes widened, the sun fell on her red hair. His voice was gone; he could only stand, lost in her, one hand stretching out to touch the one thing he wanted, the one thing he had thought he could never have.

"Say it, Carhainn. I will hear you say it."

"Maeve," he whispered. "Maeve. Maeve. Maeve."

In the privacy of her own house Maeve waited for the night to fall.

She was young, very young, sheltered but not unaware. In the darkened house, in the movement of blood through her veins, she felt the memory of Carhainn and Ahnrach together, the changes, the differences in them when they were together. She sensed, however dimly, that she stood on the edge of something new, something different, something important.

So, terrified and generous and gleeful all together, she paced her quiet room until the moon rose.

It would be a simple thing; with her parents gone her word was law, and the tuath obeyed her to the letter. Washed and dressed with care, her nerves stretched, she had only to order the guard at her door to stay there and then to walk calmly to Carhainn's house, as she had done one time before. . . .

She was to remember how the full moon seemed to hold as much warmth as the noonday sun, falling on her shoulders, carving her shadow in the chilled ground behind her. The call of a dog fox echoed around her and she smiled at it, hugging her secrets to herself. This pleasure, this joy of power in hand and a secret kept, was new to her, and she savored it like wine on the tongue.

She came to the door of his house, drew a deep breath to steady herself, and pushed the hide aside.

"Who is it? Who comes?"

Awake, she thought, he could not sleep for thinking of me, and a sense of jubilation took her. Would the gods make it easy for her after all? "It is I, Carhainn. Maeve."

"Sweet Lugh," he whispered, and she heard the noise of covers being pushed aside, lost in his breathless whisper.

His voice came from the darkness only inches away from her. Through the velvet air she felt the heat of his body, the tension moving in electric waves. "Maeve, no. No. If Flyn learns of this—"

"If Flyn learns of it, I will answer for us." She spoke low, disdaining to whisper. "I am chieftain in his absence, it is not for you to refuse me. He cannot blame you, only me, and I will risk it." She added fiercely under her breath, so low he could barely hear her, "By every shade of the waiting Sidh, I will risk it."

He was quiet for so long that she was taken in a sudden panic, a sudden loss of confidence. Then he spoke at last, and she realized he was laughing. The confidence she had momentarily lost he had found, and it draped his amused voice like a silken mantle. She knew an odd resentment, a sudden fury at her own inexperience.

"And is that what you will say to your father, lady?"

"If I must."

She stood trembling, the meaning of what she was doing coming slowly clear to her. His hand on her neck was cool and comforting in spite of the heat she thought she felt, his voice clear against her ear; his breath, raggedly uneven, ran like a soft breeze across her straining eyes. She stood in total darkness, a prey to uncontrollable shivering that seemed to come from nowhere and everywhere; with nothing to guide him but her shuddering, he read her fear and, in the darkness, smiled to himself.

For an interminable moment the tableau held. Then she had lost herself, reaching for him, and he smiled no longer. The soft hands were searching, encouraging, flaming against him; with her body scalding against him, he knew he could hold back no longer, and managed to whisper, "I won't hurt you; I will go easy, no fear."

He heard her laugh, thought she answered, was unable to be certain that she truly spoke; it seemed he could read her mind, so close were they, and flesh and fantasy blended in a blissful confusion as she sank on weak knees to the hard floor, pulling him with her. "I do not care whether you hurt me or not," was what he thought she said, and then rational thought danced and flickered and was gone in the hot flush of claiming the prize that for ten endless years he had believed he could never take.

Later, much later, she pulled herself from the sweaty sheepskins and stood naked, her face turned toward the dawn. She was sore and bruised, and her feeling of elation was like seeing a new land that she had heard tell of but never believed she might see. A thin gray light crept around the edges of the hide, to fall at her feet.

Carhainn, lying back against the warm bed, watched her. He felt drugged with contentment and the feeling frightened him, for he had never known contentment before. She has bewitched me, he thought, enchanted me, and I am willing, ready for it, I would die if need be. . . .

As the thought came and went, the gray turned to rose. Maeve sighed, a deep sound from a frail body, and turned back to him once more. How different she is, he

thought; unlike any woman I have known; she stands
there, beauty walking, unconscious of her body.

And, indeed, Maeve was unaware of her own nakedness. She reached for her torn robes, wincing, and fastened
her girdle around her once more. With the donning of her
clothing, she had of a sudden become a princess again,
and Carhainn's face darkened.

She smiled across at him, reading his thoughts, re-
peating the words that had led her to his bed. "Princess,
princess, only trappings. They count for nothing; forget
them, and see only the girl you had in the wild darkness."
She bent to kiss his chin. "Do you remember how I came
here once before, a child in grief walking in moonlight,
and we cried sorrow at one another? Do you remember
that?"

He looked at her, trying to picture the small girl who
had cradled him in her soft arms as he wept for his lost
love. The picture would not come; here was no child but a
woman, beautiful, powerful, with his life and death held in
her hands. His lips trembled. "I remember."

She kissed him again, this time on the mouth. "Good
man, kind man. I must get me back to my empty house.
Wait upon me later."

Carhainn threw back his head and suddenly laughed
in supreme enjoyment. "I waited upon you long years,
lady, and I shall wait some more, be sure." He sobered
suddenly, the light dying from his face. "Never have I
taken such pleasure in anything as I did tonight. If the
king learns of this, he will hang my head upon his wall,
yet for what I had tonight he can take my head, and
welcome. I regret nothing."

She looked down into his face, her eyes gentle yet
oddly distant. He swallowed hard and took her wrist in a
hard grip. "I think I have run mad, princess."

"We are both mad. No worry, Carhainn; your head
shall stay on your shoulders awhile yet." She let him go
then, turning for the door; grinning over her shoulder
with a saucy twist of the lips and a flash of the vagrant
dimple, she let the hide fall behind her.

Carhainn did not move for a long time after she had
gone. His muscles were limp and uncooperative, each

sinew that had rested unused since Ahnrach's death protesting as they were rediscovered under the ruthless vitality of Maeve's youth. Gods, he thought ruefully, but I never thought to feel an old man so soon! Then the first trumpets of the day, summoning the guard to change, echoed across the clear morning air.

Running a hand across his belly in wistful reminiscence, he rose to his feet and grabbed his clothing. The night with its secrets and pleasures was over, and the rigors of day were waiting.

Within a week all of Cruachain knew that the princess had taken the captain of the guard to her bed. It was there for all eyes to see, there in the glint of Maeve's green eyes, the peace and good humor that sat on Carhainn where it had never sat before. But as the next week began, any worry Maeve felt about her father's reaction was rapidly being swallowed by a larger fear.

Ten days had passed since the royal party, locked in Flyn's anger, had taken leave of Cruachain. On the tenth night Maeve paced sleepless, perambulating the confines of Carhainn's tiny house like a caged animal.

To Carhainn, also wakeful, her voice came from the darkness as if from another place. "Something has happened to them. Four days, my mother said; you heard her, as clearly as did I. Nearly a fortnight now and nothing, no word, no message, and they have not returned." She turned sharply on her heel and walked back the way she had come. "Something has gone amiss, Carhainn. I know it."

Carhainn, as he had been forced to do more and more often as the days followed one another, tried gentle reason. "Darling girl, we have spoken of this. There were near thirty of them, and all armed; led by Flyn, that is enough to defeat any who might be fool enough to attack them. No doubt they found they must travel farther than they had planned, no more than that." He added, very quietly, "It hurts me to see you in such a fret."

This blackmail, so often used as part of the language of love, should have proved successful against so inexperienced a lover as Maeve; it had succeeded, in fact, in calming her for three nights past. Each time he had spoken thus to her, she had responded satisfactorily, with kisses and her quick remorse. But tonight the lover was submerged, the princess was uppermost, and Maeve snapped out her reply.

"I am sorry for it, Carhainn, but I can do nothing for it. Fretting I am; my mother promised me that within four days they would return, and never in my life had Nieve failed in her word to me. Do you think they do not know how I would worry for them? They are not insensitive, and they are not fools either." She swung around once more in the darkness, and her voice sounded grimly. "Nor am I."

"I never said you were, lady." Unable to bear her tension any longer, Carhainn pulled himself from bed and, naked and shivering, took her into his arms. "A promise for you, princess; if no word comes tomorrow, we will ride out, just you and I, and see what we can learn." He felt the sudden relaxation of the silken body in his arms, and dropped a gentle kiss on her hair. "Will that content you?"

He heard her sigh. "That, yes. Carhainn—I beg your forgiveness for playing the queen. But you must find it in you to understand me; I know something has happened." She trembled, and quickly controlled it. "It comes like a voice from Crom, a warning, a word of disaster, and it has never yet played me false."

The flat certainty he felt in her chilled him. "What is it you fear, darling girl—an attack, raiders?"

"No. Yes. Oh, sweet Macha, I have no words for it. Can you not understand? It is feeling, not sense, and to fight it is a kind of sickness. Raiders, an attack, I cannot say. How can I know? It has rained these four days gone; they might have been taken short by flooding, or a mountain coming down on them, or even something so small as the road home washing away. They went toward the north, then eastward; you saw the messenger, bringing us news of war between Ulster and that spider Cet, sitting in his web in Des-Gabair. Perhaps—"

"No," He spoke his reassurance quickly and strongly. "Your father spoke privately with the messenger, Maeve; he knew that the Ulster men would take the coast road.

For sure, he'd not be such a fool as to bring his band that way."

She straightened in his arms. "I heard nothing of this private meeting! I should have been present, not only at the public announcement of their hostilities, but at the private meeting too! We have all heard of this Ulster chieftain, of his evil humor and his prowess at war, and suppose he took it into his mind to come this way? Why did my father tell me no more than what every oinach in Cruachain knew?"

Carhainn's reply was short and to the point. "When Flyn saw him privately, you had already fought."

The silence spun out. Carhainn, never loosing his hold on the thin shoulders, felt warm tears streak his chest. Maeve, he thought, my poor love, is it guilt that makes the bite of your worry so sharp? He knelt to her, rubbing his cheek against her brow.

"Tomorrow we ride out, you and I. If word comes while we are gone, why, then, we come home to rejoicing. No loss in the doing of it, and you will know no peace unless we do."

"Truth." He felt her lips, pressed against him, curve into the smile that had become so familiar to him. "My thanks, Carhainn. I will sleep now, I think. Besides, you are likely right, and they will come home tomorrow."

But when the next day's mist was still thick on the ground, Maeve, taking care not to disturb Carhainn, pulled herself from sleep and walked by herself to the edge of Cruachain. The town still slept; she stood, her furs wrapped tight around her, staring into the distance. She could not have said what she hoped to see; the most obvious choice, her parents in the distance, flashed across her mind and was dismissed. Were the royal party this near to home, they would scarcely ride through the night; no, she knew perfectly well that whatever she might see, it was not her parents in the flesh. Yet she stood rigidly against the morning wind, eyes fixed on the horizon, where not even a wisp of distant smoke disturbed the dawn.

When Carhainn, heavy-eyed from lack of sleep, presented himself for his princess' pleasure, he found her in an odd state of mind; she seemed to vibrate, though she did not move, except to look up as he entered.

"Have you called for our horses?"

"They are waiting, lady; your war stallion and mine." He looked at her, trying to find the subtle difference he could sense but not see. "Will we take weapons? Do you desire any of the men to accompany us?"

"Spears for me, two of them; call for two of my father's, just in case, and a short knife for each of us. For you, captain, slings; that is your weapon, and I have never truly learned it. As to the men, I do not want them. We will go alone, you and I, and follow the road awhile."

"I am ready." He looked at her, worried. "Maeve—if we go with no companions, things will be whispered. Already the people know, or guess."

"I do not care what they guess or what they whisper." Her voice, too, held that curious vibration that so disturbed him. "My father is chieftain, and I will be chieftain after him, and if they have things to say, they can say them to me. It is not their place to dispute my wishes. What is it, Carhainn? Why do you stare at me in that way?"

He replied slowly, his eyes never leaving her. "Was I staring, then? Yes, mayhap I was. You look . . . different to me, of a sudden. Your face, and your voice. Something . . ."

"I feel different, so be not surprised." She got to her feet in an abrupt movement. "We must be away."

They took the road north at a brisk canter, hearing the gates of Cruachain clash shut behind them.

For the first hour neither rider spoke. Maeve, her uneasy certainty that something had happened lost in the sheer pleasure of the horse beneath her, the wind in her hair, the simple freedom of being someplace not Cruachain, held the stallion Ghan at a steady, easy pace. Carhainn, as befit a bodyguard, held his horse a pace behind her. Knowing how well she rode, he nonetheless kept a wary eye on her mount, the other fixed on the road ahead, one hand never resting far from his weapons.

She slowed suddenly, allowing him to catch her. As he pulled abreast, he saw a faraway look come up in her face.

"Carhainn, do you know where we are?"

He looked around him, placing the trees, the sharp

curve of the road a hundred yards ahead, the high crest of
a wooded hill around the turn. Memory took him in a
dizzying rush. The cattle, lowing and patient, and the
small child sitting atop a war pony, with an old woman and
a red-haired woman beside her. . .

"You remember, then." Maeve was watching him,
seeing the old pain burn its way into him, bubbling to the
surface like a pool where the fish swim high. She reached
out a hand and laid it, very lightly, on his arm.

"All behind us now," she said gently. "The days march,
and time carries us with it. There are tracks, old tracks, in
the road ahead, I can see them. They show where the
party went, most likely. Let us ride on."

She spurred Ghan forward, leaving him to follow.

To Carhainn, with the tortured past so fresh in his
mind, what happened had a nightmare feel of recurrence.
A dark haze seemed to lie across the land, turning Maeve's
figure into a shape of imagination. He saw the ghostly
riders, ten years dead now, superimposed across the road
like flickering shadows from the underworld of the Sidh.
In an odd way, he was almost expecting something to
happen.

She had almost reached the turn in the road, where
the broad fields beyond lay hidden by the dense trees,
when Ghan suddenly shied and reared. For a moment
Maeve, taken by surprise and nearly pitched off his back,
fought to control him. Then the horse subsided, balking,
sweating, refusing to move.

Carhainn came up to hear her urging the stallion
forward, and laid a hard hand on the reins. He was finding
speech difficult.

"Wait, Maeve. Wait."

She turned to him, bewildered. "You too? Both my
war stallions, shivering in fright?"

"I told you to wait." He was shaking now, picking up
what the horses had smelled on the stiff breeze, what
Maeve seemed to have missed. Then he saw her head go
up, her face wrinkling in a blend of distaste and shock,
and her hands wrenched the reins free. "Princess, please,
stay here. No need for you to go, I will do it—"

He grabbed for her reins again, a moment too late.

Her heels dug with vicious strength into Ghan's flanks and the stallion shot forward at a gallop.

At the turn in the road where the raiders had ambushed them so many years ago, he saw her pull Ghan to a stop.

He watched her dismount, the reins dangling loosely in one steady hand.

He thought he heard the shallow breath of shock, thought the sickening smell of stale blood was stronger now.

Everything seemed to be moving slowly, too slowly. He slid to the road, leaving his horse behind him, and came up behind her. She stared straight ahead of her, unaware of his presence, her green eyes impossibly wide, blank, dead.

The bodies, hacked nearly beyond recognition, lay strewn across the wide field in hideous confusion. Human and, in a few cases, equine corpses lay rotting under clouds of enormous flies, their droning a chaotic pulse in the air. Ghan whinnied once and was silent. Still Maeve did not move. She did not even blink.

"Maeve," he whispered. "Maeve."

A tic began to pulse in the corner of one eye. It was the only sign she gave that she still lived; she stood like a woman carved of stone. Silence, an empty, ominous pall broken only by the nervous breathing of the horses and the satiated hum of flies feeding, hung across the land. His lips trembling, Carhainn dropped a hand to her shoulder.

She shook him off, never glancing his way. Then, at last, she took a step forward, toward the carnage, the scene of hell waiting in the field.

"No," he said, "do not." But she was moving, lifting her skirts and running, a blind mad run not away from the horror but toward it. As she reached the field, he saw her stumble over a severed hand and kick it from her path.

He followed slowly, fighting back nausea and memory.

Near the center of the field she stopped and knelt. Coming up behind her he saw the rusty streak of dried blood on her skirt and nearly sickened on the reek of flesh dead a week or more. A hand to his mouth, trying to drive the foul stench from his lungs, he looked down at what she held and at the ruined thing that lay beside her.

The body was headless, lying on its stomach. But Carhainn knew the cloak, muddied and torn now, but still edged in the rich fur of the chieftain. The back was gashed in a dozen places, and on the stump of neck were marks of the fight. The High King of Connacht had not died easily.

Flyn's head, cradled in his daughter's lap, stared up at him. The eyes, open and staring, fixed on Carhainn and held him; on the ground at Maeve's knees was the thin circlet of red gold that was the crown of Connacht.

He said nothing, for he had no words and the power of speech was past him. Maeve, her face white and still, sat on the torn ground and nestled her dreadful burden closer in a terrible parody of motherhood. Suddenly sickened past all bearing, he turned away and found himself staring at what was left of the queen.

She, too, had died fighting. Carhainn took a swift look and knew that she, at least, had not met Ahnrach's fate; the stab wound to the heart, coupled with the jeweled knife still held in her hand, told its own tale. Unlike her husband, Nieve's eyes were closed, and for this small mercy Carhainn breathed thanks.

"Help me with him."

She had been so silent, so stunned, that her voice made him jump. He turned back to face her and found her steady on her feet, her father's head still in her arms.

"Help me. He was a king; he should not be lying this way." Her lips began to tremble. "I let him go without my blessing, in anger, sent him off and sent no love with him. I will never forgive myself, never. He should not be lying this way, I tell you. Help me turn him to Lugh's eye."

"You sent a blessing with your mother and it counted for nothing. No blame to you, Maeve. If he is to be turned, let me do it." He spoke curtly, his eyes averted from the head in her arms, and bent to the task. Flyn's body, lying in the changing weather, was limp to the touch. Carhainn took his lower lip between his teeth and, as quickly as possible, turned the body over. As it settled back against the ground, he heard a sharp exclamation from Maeve.

A ring, dislodged from its safe haven under Flyn's

corpse, rolled free of it to lie glittering in the sun. Carhainn moved toward it, but Maeve was before him.

She took it up, holding it to the sun. Two snakes, carved deep into the gold, chased each other in an endless dance; each had the tail of its counterpart gripped tight between its teeth. On the inner band, ogham letters showed.

"They were taking the eastern road, the Ulster warriors." Carhainn was whispering, not knowing why. "They would not travel through the Iron Hills; the messenger told us. The coast road, he said. You heard him, I heard him." His voice rose. "This is something I do not believe."

Maeve's eyes, cold, shadowed, the eyes of a stranger, lifted to his. "Connal of Ulster," she said, and smiled, a smile that turned Carhainn cold. "Connal of Ulster."

7

In Stolen Robes

At the height of the victory feast, when the men of the hills were loudest in their drunken celebrations, Covac sat silent at the head of the table, drinking, thinking.

Even after the passage of ten years he had changed little. The lines surrounding mouth and eyes were more deeply set, and his body, always large and muscular, had taken just enough extra weight through the passage of time to give his bulk an even more impressive presence. But in the blond hair glinting now in the torchlight, no silver showed among the flax, and the pale skin had weathered time well.

He leaned back in his chair, his face unreadable, and thought about this most recent ambush.

They would eat well this summer; that much, at least, this latest raid had given them. The men of Connacht bred fine cattle and the best horses in the south; a goodly store of both now filled the raiders' pens. The Iron Hills band now numbered close to sixty, and they had been more than a match for the Connacht riders, only half their number.

Covac, oblivious to the wary glances cast at him from time to time, turned a jeweled cup over and over in his hands and thought back to the raid.

It should have gone off perfectly, that attack; his men had the advantages of surprise, of hunger, of planning, of sheer weight of numbers. Moreover, Covac had done his research well; during the cold months he had sent his spies down to the lowlands of the south. They had brought back word of hunger and a land locked in ice. The reports had never varied, and all added up to the same simple fact: come spring, and the breeders of Connacht would be on the move, looking for pastures where the grass grew long and sweet.

He had laid his plans. At the first signs of the spring thaw, he was ready.

The golden cup, taken from the pack of Flyn himself, turned in his hand. An enormous ruby caught the light, glittering balefully, bathing Covac's face in blood.

Yes, it should have been perfect. Who would have thought that Flyn would be so dangerous a fighter, so fine in the moving of his men? Never dreaming that they might be attacked so close to home, outnumbered two to one, the men who fought under the King of Connacht had left twelve of Covac's best fighters to rot in their own blood.

His hand tightened around the cup, denting the gold. He had been denied even the satisfaction of bringing Flyn's head home to adorn his walls; the man detailed to take it had come back frightened, saying that a snake had wrapped around it, and after that no one was willing to touch it.

There was the matter of the horses too; of the nearly thirty beasts, trained war stallions every one, that Covac had hoped to bring back to the hills with him, they had managed only half that number. He thought back to the scene, a white line tightening around his nostrils. A Connachtman, wounded to the death, turning with what strength he had left to slash his horse's throat; sure, they would rather let the beasts die than see the attackers take them. Mother Macha, you would think the creatures were women, not horses. . . .

The final disappointment, souring him though he himself was only dimly aware of his own expectations, rose in his throat like bile. Two women only, the queen and her maid; the queen, still beautiful, had died by her own hand when her husband fell, and the maid was old, toothless,

dead of fright, and useless to him. He had stood on the
high ground before the attack, scanning the approaching
riders in furious disbelief, wracked with the disappointment of not seeing what he wanted to see.

She had been a child that first time, a wisp of a thing,
and even so small, she had defeated him, escaped him,
killed three of his men. He knew her name now; there was
no one in Hibernia who had not heard of her. His own
spies had seen her, always guarded, never more than a
spear's cast from the gates of Cruachain. Chlair, in fact,
had seen her at work with her tutor in arms; the fool had
come back prating of a woman beautiful past all earthly
women, with death poised in each hand.

Maeve, her name was. Maeve who, even as they sat
here swilling, might be standing straight at her own
forradh, her place of meeting, with her people around her,
raising high the new Queen of Connacht. . . .

She would be fifteen now. He remembered the red
hair, the still, pointed face, the concentration and strength
and perfect balance of her as she speared his men. Fifteen,
a warrior, old enough to travel. And, like his nephew
Connal, a chieftain of her people.

Connal . . . the memory of his nephew, the boy whose
birth had kept him from the throne of Ulster, whose
interference had banished him, still raised a hot sickness
in his belly. Well, the young chieftain of Ulster might find
ill fortune and trouble coming his way. One thing, at least,
Covac had managed to do, one seed sown, one gold ring
with the snakes of the north planted carefully under Flyn's
headless body for his people to find . . .

He set the cup down with a controlled violence that
silenced the revelers nearest to him. Bidding them a curt
good night, Covac hitched the tattered bearskin close
around him and strode from the hall into the chilly
darkness.

The stifling walls of his house would not do; there was
a restlessness in him that demanded the freedom of the
open air. With his knife dangling at one hip, he passed the
night guard without a word and strode into the woods.
The air was clear here and smelling of pines. Climbing

one of the great trees, he settled himself and thought toward the future.

Yes, the seed had been carefully sown. Covac was a master at the correlation of facts, and the reports of his spies had been gathered into his own capable hands, looked at, examined, mulled over, and woven finally to form a spider's web that would put an end to the two people who had thwarted him, two chieftains who had likely never even met.

Well, and they would meet shortly. He leaned back against the pine's rough bark, smiling with cold satisfaction into the night, remembering with pleasure the stroke that had taken Flyn's head from his body, the wail of anguish from Nieve, the stiffening limbs of a king who had gone to the Sidh as he was rolled onto his stomach as if he had been a bundle of old rags, useless and unwanted.

He remembered, too, his own feelings as he stood at the top of the hill, the ring of Bhoru warm in his hand, waiting for the fight to end, for Flyn to die, so that he might set in motion the events that would lead to war between the north and the south. He remembered his pleasure that none of his men seemed able to defeat Flyn in hand-to-hand combat.

The scene was vivid against the spring darkness. Flyn disarmed, held in the grasp of four men. Their eyes meeting, his and the king's, and the single slash across the throat. The sound of Flyn's head, falling with a gentle thud to the bloodied field, was a memory he would savor a long time yet.

But the girl was not with them. Wild red hair, the small face grown to beauty, the thin body to nubility. All the time he had laid his plans for the attack, he had been sure that the girl would be with them. He had smiled at the irony of it, had nearly drowned in the picture of taking her, as he had taken her companion so many years gone; he had planned on it, counted on it, and the thought of enjoying her and slitting her throat with the dead stare of her father's head on her all the while had raised a furor in his loins.

And she had thwarted him. By the simple fact of her absence, she had thwarted him yet again.

The moon was down now, the night drawing in. Covac, coming back to the present, realized that he had grown chilly and slithered down the tree. Some day soon, if all went as planned, he would be face to face with the only two people to ever best him and live. And when that came to pass, they would both pay.

He passed the guard, humming tunelessly under his breath, and betook himself to his empty bed.

"Alchlaidd, to the left. Cut it away from its mother, if you can. Cimhaill, cover the right."

The three men, with long spears and knives honed to killing point, circled cautiously. The hind, with the fawn cowering at her side, backed away, her head twisting wildly from side to side, scenting the air, seeking cover.

Alchlaidd moved in closer, a looming and unearthly figure in the white fog that blanketed the woods. Behind the cornered creature was a wall of trees; surrounding her, the men and the spears. She hesitated fractionally. Then, as Cimhaill jumped, she abandoned the fawn to its fate in a sudden, desperate leap for safety, clearing Covac and landing at the wood's edge beyond. They heard the soft thud of her hooves on the springy turf as she fled across the great clearing, circling the western shore of Lough Lein and disappearing in the fog.

The fawn, nostrils flaring, wobbled unsteadily on its thin legs. The wide brown eyes moved in panic from one man to another; bleating, it crouched back against the trees. Cimhaill, spear at the ready, moved in for the kill.

"Wait. Silence a moment."

Covac, a hand held up in warning, had whispered. The others froze, waiting, and the fawn slipped unnoticed through the trees and away.

Alchlaidd's reply was barely audible. "What, then?"

"Footsteps." Covac tilted his head, his eyes narrowing. "Only one person. Not one of our men; they had orders to wait in the camp." His head jerked up. "Listen."

There it was, a single footfall, hastily arrested. Someone, then, unsure of his way, someone who did not know these woods and was moving warily, stepping on dead branches in the mist, cursing in his mind, waiting, walking again. . . .

Covac's knife slid into his hand as the spear was thrust into Alchlaidd's. "Follow," he said softly, and in near silence made for the path out of the woods.

The capture, in the end, was easy. The man stepped carefully from the sheltering trees; he had barely time to orient himself to the open before Covac and Cimhaill together were on him, one holding him down, the other holding a knife to his throat. The man lay still, passive, sensing that a false move would result in his own ending.

Covac held the tip of the knife against his captive's neck. "What do you do here, in the Iron Hills?"

"I—I meant no trespass, lord." The stranger, near Covac's own age, was well-spoken and comfortably dressed. He cleared his throat, a look of confusion in his face, and spoke again. "I was going north, toward Ulster, and lost my way in the mist. I mean no harm."

"Ulster?" Alchlaidd, coming up fast, had caught the end of the reply. "And what do you do in Ulster?"

"I— We are seeking a druid, lord."

"Seeking a druid?" Covac pressed a little harder and felt the man wince. "To tell your dreams, perhaps?"

"No, lord. No. I seek a seer on a matter of grave importance for my queen. She wants truth." He looked in bewilderment from face to face. "No need for threats, lord; there is no secret to this, and I will be full glad to tell you my business."

"Your queen, you say." Covac's voice was a silken whisper, nearly a purr. The knife did not waver. "Not Queen Maeve of Connacht?"

"Yes, lord."

"And what does your high lady need of the druids?"

The stranger was silent, brows furrowed, fear at the rough treatment he had received battling with obstinacy in his face. Covac smiled down at him and shifted the knife from neck to face, leaving a thin trail of blood and a deep cut four inches long. The man gave a stifled cry.

"You will answer me, queen's messenger, or I will take an eye out. If you still refuse, the other eye; after that, the knife moves lower. You understand me? Yes, I see you do. Good. I will ask you again: her need?"

Fear won out. "Why do you treat me thusly? I mean no harm to you and will answer your questions without force. Have I not said it?" The knife held steady, and he continued with desperation in his voice. "Lord, our king was slain and a ring of the Ulster chieftain, he they call the Victorious, was under his body. She seeks the truth of it."

The seed had sprouted, then, and so soon, so soon. . . .

"And if the druid affirms, what then? A war?"

"Yes, lord. War with Ulster, and five thousand men of the south at the ready. Please—"

"And what of you, little man? Are you to bring the druid back, to claim your queen's favor?"

"I am to travel north, to learn what I can of the Victorious, what manner of man he is, how he moves his men and his weapons. That is all, lord, truth. Please . . ."

Covac stood, the smile stamped deep, and slid his knife back into his belt. "Kill him," he told Cimhaill, and turned for the woods. Striding into the mist, he did not hear the short, choked scream and the rasp of metal on flesh.

The time was come, then, his plans moving forward to their end. Dense air, thick and stifling, filled his lungs; the white, wet blanket cloaked him as he made for the camp. There was a trembling in him, a silvered pulse of excitement, and his mind worked furiously.

So Queen Maeve wanted a druid? Well, she should have one, to tell her precisely what she must do. His mind, still active, moved backward in time to one memory he tried to keep away; through the eddying mist he saw, fresh in his mind's eye, the glittering black jewels that were the eyes of the sacred snake, sliding for freedom with its master dead. Once again they watched him, knew him, accused him.

He wrenched himself loose of it. One had to take the moment as it was offered; the fact that Ahnal had been his friend in those halcyon days long gone counted for nothing in the face of life or death. Ahnal and the unknown other lay deep in the lough, their bodies sleeping eternity away while their souls disported among the Sidh. The fishing in

Lough Lein had been good since that time, the great bass were plump and tasted well. But Covac ate no fish now, not taken from Lough Lein. . . .

Something rustled in the bushes. The sound, coming on the heels of his memory, was sly and suggestive; there were snakes in the forest, real snakes, not the shadows of the dreams that slipped through him in remembrance of the times now lost to him.

He felt the cold sweat break out in the hollows of his body and ran toward the village. Phantom or flesh, he wanted nothing to do with snakes.

The guard who watched at the edge of the camp night or day avoided looking into his leader's face with well-trained discipline. For his part, Covac was barely aware of the man; the muddy lanes that ran through the camp seemed distant and unimportant, the faces of his fellow outlaws unreal.

In the privacy of his house he let the bearskin drop to the floor. The hide was shut, his men under orders never to enter without his permission; his privacy was complete.

Slowly, carefully, he went to his knees at the foot of his bed. With hands that shook, he pushed the rushes there aside, revealing a small cavity under a thin layer of soil. Reaching into the gap, he pulled out the small oaken chest, its edges green with mold, which rested there.

He opened the lid and sat a long time, gazing in.

The druid's robe had weathered well. Wrapped carefully in soft cloth, the white showed unnaturally bright in the dim room, the gold bands on hem and sleeve glimmering with a hard sheen. A bundle within a bundle, the heavy gold cuffs and necklets that were the honor badge of an elder lay cool in his palm. He had studied to wear these things, wasted the prime months of his life to earn the right to wear them, and he had failed in that.

Well, all things came full circle; he would wear them now, by the right not of the acolyte, but of the victor.

Bathed in the golden light and liquid birdsong of high summer, Covac stood atop a hill he knew and looked down the winding road toward the royal city of Cruachain.

Twice before he had stood beneath these shadowing

trees, hidden from his victims, directing his band of killers
in their rendezvous with murder and theft. His first visit
to this hill, he had stood and watched a child get the
better of him; on this very hill he had wrenched a young
red-haired girl from her captor's horse, taking her as she
lay and leaving her body to rot in the soft grass. The
memory, both sweet and bitter, returned now with uncanny clarity as he rested his hand on the small cairn of gray
stones beside him.

He knew who lay buried under this sad mound of
stones. They had come, the men of Connacht, to take
their fallen warriors; no doubt they had found the girl up
here and, rather than give her to the flames of the dead in
the field below, had piled the stones around her, leaving
her to sleep.

He stroked the tomb almost fondly. Few things in his
life had pleasured him like the girl's ruin and death; he
remembered her facing him, supine across Cimhaill's horse,
her lips obstinately closed despite the fear in her eyes. He
remembered her body twisting frantically as four of his
men held her down, remembered how, when he had done
with her, she had lain there, blood streaking her legs, her
face a flower bruised from his blows. The final memory
tightened his lips; she had looked him in the eye and spat
into his face.

Then the short, choked scream as his knife came
down—

Jerking himself back to the present, he realized that
he had broken out in a sweat, his body coming alive. Well,
that pleasure was past; there would be other times just as
sweet. The stones felt warm with the summer sun; giving
the cairn a last, comradely pat of his hand, he dropped his
sack beside him and began to strip the robes of the bandit
from his body, changing them for the white splendor of
druid garb.

When the transformation was complete, Covac stuffed
the sack with his own clothes and went to the stream that
burbled in constant song across the hillside. The moving
water made an unsteady mirror but it was clear and he
could see himself as the red-haired bitch would see him.

He stood for a long time, the noise of summer settling around him, and regarded the man in the stream.

It was fortunate, the hand of the gods perhaps, that he and Ahnal had been of a size. He was broader through the body than the dead elder had been, and the white robes strained a bit across the shoulders; the hood, smelling of cedar, settled over his face. Through the eyeholes two pale beacons glittered oddly.

Watching his own reflection, he clipped the gold to wrist and neck. For a moment, as he moved his arms, the glittering snakes with the eyes of chipped rubies seemed to take on a strange life of their own, climbing his arms, twisting, reaching for his throat. In his mind's eye he could almost see forked tongues dart from between the golden fangs, tasting what rode the summer breeze—

Covac turned his back abruptly. Enough of this; it would serve. He made a convincing druid, in body at least, and he had spent time enough among them to convince Maeve. He knew the mysteries; there was no way she could and no reason for her to disbelieve him.

He reached for the sack, holding it loosely in one hand and considering. Then, with a small shrug of decision, he reached a hand in and pulled his knife out, slipping it deep inside one soft boot.

He glanced around the hillside. The sack must be hid, and that securely; he was taking no chance on some stray wanderer finding it. But he could see nowhere to put it in the verdant expanse of flat grass, the green dusted with primrose and speedwell. He held the sack, his eyes moving, and his back brushed against Ahnrach's tomb.

Well, and why not? For sure, no one would think to look inside; it was as safe a place as he could wish. No need to disturb the stones at the top; he needed only a small hole to push the bag through. Dropping the sack, he began to pull away a few of the bottom stones, piling them to one side as he burrowed deeper. When the hole was a foot across, he took the sack and, with the full strength of his arm, pushed it deep inside the cairn.

It happened so quickly that he had time only for instinct. Later he would tell himself that he had heard rustling and moved his hand from reach; perhaps, on some level of hearing or knowledge just below the surface, he did hear it. Whatever the source, his instant reaction saved his life. He heard a soft whistling hiss, the sound of something hard striking a hard surface. And then something moved across his hand as it lay within that dark place, something cool, something warm, something living.

He cried out, not loudly but with ultimate terror. Wrenching his arm free, he jumped to one side, his eyes wide and mindless as he stared at the black hole. What had he awakened in that place of shadow, what sleeping demon, what guardian of the dead?

The adder, released from its enforced hibernation, slithered into the sunlight. As another of its kind had done so many years ago, it stopped a few feet from where he cowered, the hard gems of its eyes regarding him with a snake's terrible impassivity. Then it was gone, disappearing like a shade between two stones, into a clump of wild daisies and away down the hill.

Covac did not know how long he stood, his chest heaving, leaning against the desecrated cairn with hot sweat pouring into his eyes. Eventually his knees could no longer bear the weight of his fear and gave way; he sank down in the grass, his breath coming in short, sobbing gasps, his eyes closed against the snake's return. When he opened them, he found himself staring through the hole he had made, into the interior of the cairn.

Something shone in the darkness, catching stray beams of sunlight; something glimmered, pale and ghostly. Not his sack, for sure; that was made of the brown hide of a goat. Treasure, something buried with the girl he had killed?

The snake was gone, and he was a man grown. The unreasoning terror of superstition swallowed by his greed, he cautiously slid his hand through the hole, closed on whatever shone in the darkness and pulled it free.

It lay in his palm, the delicate bones glinting. On what had been Ahnrach's hand before time transformed it, three fingers and the thumb were laxly straight, lying in his larger palm; the index finger was curled inward. Where the hand had fallen from the ossified wrist, the bones had gone into powder, dusting the gold band on his sleeve.

His muscles turned to water. The buzzing of the insects on the sweet-scented air seemed intolerably loud, and the birds suddenly quiet. "No," he whispered, "no," and his grip loosened. The bones dropped with a soft thump at his feet; staring down, a deathly grin like the rictus that must have been stamped across the face of she who slept under those gray stones plastered across his face, he saw one of the fingers snap loose and roll away, to lay shining in the sun.

He was shuddering now, harsh spasms wracking his body. Drawing his foot back, hardly knowing what he did, he kicked the hand with all the strength of his leg back through the dark tunnel he had made, and the lone finger after it. On his knees in the grass, he reached for the stones and began to pile them back in place with frantic speed. Sleep, he thought madly, stay in your dark bed. You will not have me, and nothing of you will see the sun again. With fingers that bled, he rammed the stones home, muttering under his breath, the empty sky watching him.

Then he ran, his heels kicking up loose dirt as he fled down the hill.

By the time he reached the road, his fear had eased. She could not follow him, not now; her tomb was intact, he would make no apology to the gods for her, and in any case, he had a job to do. Brushing the dust and the powdered bone from his robes, he waited for his breathing to settle to normal and began the long walk south to Cruachain.

"So soon?"

Maeve, surrounded by maps of Ulster and the litter of a war in its planning stages, stared up at Carhainn. "Mharal has been quick; he must have come across a traveling druid this side of the border. Is it an elder, Carhainn?"

"An elder, yes." He stood before her, looking down with an impassive face that concealed his feelings.

No one knew how bitterly they had fought on that

endless night following their dreadful discovery; no one had heard the battle waged behind the fastened hide of the queen's house. It was not that no one had been interested, not that they had kept their voices low; Cruachain, at the news of the slaughter of their king and queen, had gone into a state of shock. The streets had been bare, those people who had not been sent to bring the bodies home sitting indoors, staring numbly at their own walls, unable to believe.

Nothing Carhainn had ever seen in Maeve had prepared him for the storm that broke when the shock at last wore off. She had been inhuman, a bansidh, a screaming monster with gaping mouth and bulging eyes, whirling and frenzied, throwing herself against the walls of her house until Carhainn, terrified that she would do herself an injury, tried to restrain her.

He remembered with sickness how she had screamed the name of Connal the Victorious over and over again, her small fists beating against Carhainn's chest. He remembered her violent vows of revenge, dreadful in their fluency. Most bitter, most cherished, he remembered how she had at last collapsed against him, hot tears streaking down her face, soaking him as he supported her helplessly.

He had calmed her at last, at least enough to make her listen. The thing was too pat; it had a rotten smell to it, and Carhainn found himself disbelieving it. None of it made sense. Ulster was at war with Des-Gabair, and why would the High Chieftain of Ulster add an extra ten days to his march? Was one to believe that he had come, by sheer chance, to a place he could not possibly have known existed, to lie in wait for the King of Connacht? And how would Connal, with no reason to wish Flyn ill, have known that the King of Connacht would pass that way, that day?

He had pleaded with Maeve, who in her grief would have mustered an army and attacked Emain without preparation or confirmation of the truth, trying to make her see what seemed so plain to him.

He had succeeded, after that dreadful fight, in persuading her to a compromise. The people of Connacht, once the first shock wore off, were wild in their grief-stricken fury; they wanted to smash the whole province of Ulster to the ground as much as their new queen did. Maeve, summoning men to war, found Connacht solidly behind her. In the days since Flyn's murder, Cruachain had filled to bursting point with men at arms, each wanting nothing better than a chance to personally slay the man who had killed their king.

But Maeve, with her new power and its attendant self-discipline settling around her thin shoulders as easily as her own cloak, had finally seen the sense of Carhainn's words. For herself, she had no doubt of Connal's guilt; to have that guilt confirmed by a seer, however, would serve more than one purpose. It would silence Carhainn and the few who agreed with him. It would act, too, as an additional spur for a heterogeneous army that was coming together as a well-trained killing machine with astonishing speed. In the end she sent Mharal, her long-standing and trusted bodyguard, over the Iron Hills in search of a druid.

And he had done what he promised. Good, faithful Mharal; gone less than a fortnight, and here was the druid already, and an elder with it. Against the muffled ring of metal on metal as the army practiced its arts, she stared at Carhainn and truly saw him for the first time since the day they had gone out riding together.

The love was there in his eyes, plain for her to see; it hurt her and comforted her, and she could do nothing about it. Something had happened to her on that blood-soaked field; when she took her father's head in her lap, she had lost all desire for Carhainn.

But Carhainn had not changed. He had seen the change come to her and grief had taken his face, lining it, giving it a weight of years. She was lost to him now, lost; the beautiful woman was untouchable, sacrosanct, forever beyond his reach. He met the green eyes, and the sudden desire to take her in his arms, to murmur lover's words, to have the girl he had loved and lost cling to him once again, almost choked him. To stand here and look into those bottomless eyes was to hurt beyond bearing, and he could stand no more of it. Turning on his heel, he made for the door and spoke coldly.

"Give me leave, madam, and I will fetch the elder."

"Carhainn."

He had not heard that tone of voice from her since the day she had first reached out to him, demanding that he speak her name. The voice was the same spider's web it had been then, and it held him in the same thrall. Shoulders slumped, fists knotted with frustration, he stopped and waited

"Carhainn, I am sorry. I am so sorry. This is not what I wanted, what I intended."

Carhainn stood immobile, clenching his teeth against the words that he must not say. Her voice, almost as soft as her touch, bespoke her own sadness.

"I never meant to bring you hurt. But something that lived in me those few short days lives no longer. I cannot bear to see you like this. Can you not forget?"

Forget. At the word, something in Carhainn snapped. He whipped around with the speed of a hunting dog and took her wrists in a tight grip.

"Forget? You ask me this, to forget what we had, to forget the only sweetness my life has given me? May Crom take you for a fool for those words. Forget?" The grip on her arm tightened; he laughed harshly.

"No, my queen, I cannot forget. Can you possibly know, can you even begin to guess, what it does to me to have you so near and so far from me? May the gods pardon me, I want nothing more this moment than to throw you down and teach you precisely what my sufferings are." His lips thinned to a painful travesty of a smile. "My body aches for you, my spirit dies for you, I am a man chained and thirsting in fragrant water I can never again drink, and you ask me to forget." He dropped her arm suddenly and closed his eyes, suddenly dizzy and nauseous.

"Go send me the elder," she said quietly. She began to rub the wrist where, in the white skin, the livid marks of his hold showed plainly.

Tears began to seep from under his tight-pressed lids. Without another word he turned his back to her and stumbled from the house. Maeve, empty and exhausted, stood in a pool of sun to await the seer who would tell her the truth.

He came in quietly, unescorted, a man in white with a white hood hiding his face, and stood just beside her door. Maeve, lost in her own thoughts, was for a moment unaware of his presence. Suddenly her attention was caught, perhaps by his even breathing, and she looked up. For a long moment they studied each other.

Covac, behind his hood, was conscious of a sense of triumph both deep and painful. This was the child he had sworn revenge on so many years ago; she was a woman now, a queen, and she was in his hands, though she knew nothing of it. Maeve, her eyes fixed on the hood, thought how strangely the pale eyes glittered. But holy men were not the same as other men; no doubt he had special powers, this elder, and the shine of his eyes was the color of holiness.

They stood in silence, Maeve unwilling to speak until the holy man spoke, giving Covac time to look his fill. Yes, she was beautiful; the promise implicit in the watchful, still beauty of the little girl had been fulfilled. She was slender, a wild rose that burned. It would give him great pleasure to see her die, however it was done, though it seemed a shame to leave her to Connal's spears. . . .

She was growing edgy, and it was no part of his plan to overawe her. He saw the twisting of her fingers, one upon the other, and judged it time to speak.

"You asked for a druid, great queen."

He sensed, rather than heard, the sudden relief as she let her breath out. "I did, holy man, and I thank you for coming to me with such haste. Come, will you not sit with me and partake of refreshment? Your throat must be parched; dry work, to journey in such heat. I am both thankful and amazed that you came to me with such speed. Where did you find my man Mharal?"

A marvelous voice, low and husky, and a beautiful smile along with it; that lopsided dimple was, in itself, an enticement to sensuality. He felt his lips curl and was glad for the concealing hood. He kept his voice hollow, neutral.

"Many thanks, queen, but I want no refreshment. Your man found me as I wandered in the north; he had found a tame horse roaming the foothills, and so by the gods was his errand made easier." He felt the beginnings of enjoyment rise in him as his lies poured forth with convincing fluency.

She leaned forward, laying one hand on his arm. The touch, even through the soft sleeve, was like a whip of lightning; his jaw tightened, his flesh warming to her. By all the watching gods of the world, it would be like nothing else to take this one, this regal beauty, to throw her down and listen to her plead with him. . . .

Maeve, not understanding his sudden stillness, pulled her hand away and blushed. "Your great pardon, holy man, I meant no disrespect to your robes. We of Connacht are sometimes overly familiar. Your pardon."

"I give it freely." Covac spoke harshly, swallowing a confusion of raging sensations. "I believe I can save us time and worry, queen; your man having told me why you needed my presence here so urgently, I performed the snake dance for you at full moon, two nights ago."

She stared at him, the green eyes blazing. "Already? Oh, sir, you can indeed save us trouble. Please . . . what was the meaning of it? Have I the truth of the matter, or do I risk my army and my honor, and all for naught?"

He was gone from her, his mind traveling back to the grove that smelled of blood and pine intermingled. Ahnal, his spirit gone from his body to join with the sacred snake, the symbols, the slow chanting drifting like currents of their own through the holy smoke, the rhythmic weaving of bodies as elders and acolytes alike came together and met as one in the spirit of the snake. . . .

He got to his feet. This he had not rehearsed; his performance came from memory, the stored knowledge and feelings he had taken and misused. His arms raised high, his voice dropped to the toneless chant of the soothsayer.

"New moon, full moon, rain; this the snake showed to me, a true picture, the only picture. Men on horses, men in hunger. A chieftain, a stallion, spears glittering like sloe plums among the trees. A gray cairn on a lonely hilltop."

Maeve began to tremble, backing away from the raw power in his voice, believing as she had believed nothing before. His voice had thickened, the latent power in it coming to the surface, holding her where she stood. From behind the hood the pale eyes impaled her. She could not move; she could only stand in terror, mesmerized by the oddly musical voice.

"Snakes, sacred snakes, snakes of Crom Cruach. A badge, a token, a ring. Two snakes dancing, two snakes chasing, a circle unbroken. Snakes. Snakes."

His voice had soared now. She backed away from him, her fists pressed against her shaking lips. Covac, lost in his memories and his own performance of an act he had been forbidden when he failed the druid's final test, took off his hood and stared into her face: Hulking and enormous, he stood towering over her, the essence of domination.

"Snakes, and a token. Show it to me."

Unblinking, caught in the snare of his eyes like a rabbit who falls to the poacher, she reached a nerveless hand between her breasts. On a thin strip of leather dangled the ring with the two snakes, the ring of Bhoru, the ring of the chieftains of Emain that Covac had put beneath her father's body for her to find.

They stood staring at one another, each unable to turn away. Covac was breathing hard, his light eyes staring and mad; under the white robes his legs trembled and his groin clenched in the hard grip of the pleasures of deceit. He felt dizzy, almost drunk, and as the green eyes blurred under his own, his sense of power reached its peak and pleasure spilled in a warm rush down his legs. His voice was husky, compelling.

"You have your truth, queen. Do what you must."

II

THE CHIEFTAINS

8

Invasion

On the morning before Samhain, just as it had happened so many years before, Connal woke from a profound slumber to a familiar voice whispering his name.

For a moment, as the sleeping and waking worlds touched and eddied, the chieftain of Ulster was aware of a chill, an eerie feeling that the years had dropped away and he was, indeed, a small boy despised by all but his father's fila and his only friend. Then the early morning mist seeped through the open hide, wreathing him in cold and dampness, and he opened his eyes to darkness.

"Chieftain. Chieftain, wake."

Like Sheilagh, like Brihainn, Connal had learned the art of waking immediately. He sat up, the skins falling away to leave his bare chest cold with gooseflesh, and spoke quietly.

"Cormac?"

"Yes, lord. It is Cormac. Please, you must come."

The sense of familiarity, instead of fading with sleep, had intensified. He thought, oddly, I have no uncles left to surprise me, and then shook his head, sending the long black hair, unbound for sleep, whipping across his face. Pulling himself out of bed, he fumbled for taper and flint. The room was still dark; morning had not come yet, though it waited on the horizon.

"I am awake. What has happened, fila, to bring you here so early in the day?"

"Ten men, lord, from our borders with the south. They bring urgent news and must speak with you."

The flint rasped harshly, and suddenly the room sprang to flickering life. Connal stood, naked and cold, and reached for his robes. "From the south. Odd. What is it, then?"

"I do not know, lord. They are with Brihainn now; he woke me and sent me to fetch you. Urgent, he said, and indeed the men are blown with journeying; they say they left three horses behind them, lamed by their haste."

"Very well. I will come." But Connal, in spite of his words and the urgency in his fila's voice, did not move. He stood, his flesh rippling with the cold, his clothing dangling from one hand, the taper held in the other.

Cormac watched him in silence and knew a surge of pride. Sure, the boy had grown to a manhood blatant and well-favored enough for envy. He had watched the thin child grow from skinny infancy to awkward adolescence. Connal at eighteen was perfection, and awe too. The naked body towered, Connal's great height accentuated by broad shoulders and long legs; the sinews, each trained and obedient to its purpose, stood out on chest and limbs. The fingers that held the taper were long and sensitive, the fingers of a musician or a midwife; in the dim wash of candlelight the black-diamond eyes and massive cheekbones stood out in sharp relief, giving him the look of something from the Sidh, nót earthly, unreal.

There was something in Connal's eyes that made Cormac obscurely uneasy. It was not anger; in recent years the anger had come more under Connal's control, taking the form of sudden harsh words and black silences during which the people avoided him. It only happened when something of magnitude, some stupidity or failure touched the chieftain wrong; for the most part anger was kept deep and was apparent only in the brevity of his speech and the nervous movement of his fingers always moving, never still. He was as angry a man as he had been a boy, and his people knew it; now, however, rage was a looming threat, rarely a burning fire.

But this was not anger. He hesitated, swallowed, and spoke quietly.

"What is it, lord?"

The black eyes lost their disquieting glaze. "Cormac. Oh, sweet Lugh, a heavy feeling on me; do you remember the morning that my uncle and his bandit took Alhauna, and Brihainn and I found them at it? This is very like."

"Oh, I see it." Cormac understood perfectly. "A bad memory that will not die is indeed a heavy feeling. Will you come, then?"

"I will." Connal threw his robes on and stretched a hand out for the gold circlet that hung above his head when he slept. "Where are they, fila?"

"Lord, shivering at the forradh, with a slave to bring them hot wine. Brihainn's house was too small to hold them, and he would not go to the banqueting hall without you."

"My thanks. Cormac—is the town awake?"

The fila, looking oddly undressed without his harp, stopped in the doorway to glance over his shoulder. His eyes, the color of the sky at midsummer, met the glittering black ones with perfect comprehension.

"No, chieftain. Emain sleeps still, and no one saw them come but the night guard."

"That is best." Connal slipped his knife in one boot and with a practiced flick of the wrist, adjusted the heavy wolf's pelt that served as his cloak. "Take me there."

Emain was, indeed, still sleeping. A word from Connal to his bodyguard held the man to his post at Connal's door; as they quickly traversed the stone-paved streets by the light of the chieftain's torch, the two men saw not a single freeman. Here and there a slave, yawning and incurious, went about his business, but the town was quiet, and even the hens stayed curled together in warm unconsciousness.

The forradh, Emain's place for high or public meetings, was a high, flat-topped mound; it stood on a solitary hill a quarter mile west of the village. Those situations that called for the participation of the free citizens of Ulster were held on the slopes surrounding the forradh; rarely, very rarely, was the structure at the top of the hill used.

This was the rath-na-riogh, the place of the king. It was an earthwork surrounded by small palisades; in the very center of the ancient hill was a solitary stone, a sentinel that had watched over Emain before the gods gave the hill to men. To enter the rath-na-riogh without the chieftain's consent was to invite death.

But they were there. Even in the distance Connal could make out the flickering torches at the forradh, and knew they came not from the hillside, but from the circle that faced the sky. Cormac, laboring through the mud ahead of him, heard the sudden breath, the muttered words of disbelief. He stopped and turned, facing Connal.

"Urgent, they said. A high matter, a matter of state." He looked into Connal's face and, with a mounting dismay, saw rage burn into it like a lambent flame, coloring the heavy bones with a dark, ominous sheen. "Lord, you know Brihainn. He would not bring them up there unless it was a high matter, to do with the safety of the kingdom."

The olive flush on the cheekbones eased. "Truth. I wonder what has happened to upset Brihainn so. If anyone had done what he has done, he would take their eyes out."

"Also truth." The torches were dancing pinpoints of light in the air, growing steadily closer. As they reached the field surrounding the forradh, the mutter of distant speech became gradually audible. Connal, stopping to draw breath and wrap his cloak tighter before taking the mud of the field, heard a phrase float clear and discernible across the still air.

For a moment he stood in shocked silence, not believing he had heard correctly. Then, as the meaning of the words came clear, he ran past Cormac, snapping for the bard to follow, his flying heels sending showers of cold mud behind him as he ran.

Brihainn had obviously been watching for him; as he reached the hill and threw one leg across the first of the palisades, he heard his best friend's voice ring out. "Praise to Danu, the chieftain comes. A moment, warriors, and all will be dealt with. I pray you, patience."

Connal, looking for footholds on the treacherous hillside, called up to him. "A hand up, cela. My thanks." With a sharp effort he pulled himself into the heart of the rath-na-riogh and stood surveying the kneeling men, with Cormac, panting, scrambling up behind him.

He needed no more than a single glance at Brihainn to confirm his fears. Something had happened, something of great import; Brihainn's face wore a look that Connal had not seen there since the morning of Alhauna's rape, a tight, sickened awareness of trouble. The puckered scar at his mouth, a visible reminder of that morning's work, showed livid against lips compressed with worry. Connal turned to the men who had fallen to their knees at his feet.

"Get up; the ground is wet and cold. A moment back I heard words I had no liking for; I will have those words explained, and that at once. Which of you is the leader?"

A burly man, his huge chest covered with a breast-plate of bronze, stepped forward. "I lead, lord."

"Yes, you would." Brihainn, hearing faint amusement in the deep voice, bit back on surprise; sure, and this was no time for jest. Connal shot his cela an unreadable look and turned away once more. "And your name, leader?"

"Mennat, lord. My mother was sister to the chieftain of Cluad, far to the north."

"Yes; my father was friend to your family. What news from the south brings you to me in such haste that you must needs lame your mounts beneath you?"

"Invasion."

The single word, spoken flatly and without inflection, fell like a stone into a silent pool. It seemed to echo, its implications sending reverberations of itself across the slowly lightening sky. Connal's eyebrows snapped together.

"As I came up I heard that word, and yet it is hard to believe. Invasion from the south?"

"From the south, yes."

"The coast road? An invasion from Des-Gabair?"

"No, lord." Mennat spoke with absolute certainty. "It is Connacht; they have crossed the border to the east, skirting the Iron Hills. A sunrise ago we left the border to bring you the news; even then they were pouring through, and I saw their banners. Connacht, lord, not Des-Gabair."

"But that cannot be true!" The black eyes were

stretched to impossible limits. "Have they gone moon-struck, the men of Connacht? We have had no trouble with them, we have not invaded or even raided. Why, when our men moved to take Cet, I went to the trouble of sending them a man with the news so that they might not take alarm. They have no reason to invade Ulster, none, none at all." His hand shot out to take Mennat by one shoulder and grip hard. "Are you certain of this? And how many of them?"

Mennat had paled, but his eyes held Connal's. "Lord, I am certain. As to numbers, it is difficult to say. At a guess, perhaps five thousand men, with more following."

There was a stunned silence. Obviously they had held back this bit of information for the chieftain's ears; Brihainn stood in shock, jaws dropped, hands lax. Connal's face had gone very tight and he spoke softly.

"An invasion, indeed. Five thousand men, and more to follow. There must be a reason, unless Flyn has lost his wits; Ulster has no quarrel with Connacht, none at all. What is it, Mennat? Why do you look like that?"

Mennat replied, stammering. "Lord, I ask pardon, but I thought you knew. Flyn is dead, and his queen with him; I know little of what happened, for the borders have been closely guarded since then. There is a new queen in Connacht, the princess Maeve. It is she who leads them."

"Maeve?" Brihainn swung around to face Connal and saw his own bewilderment mirrored on the chieftain's face. "The two-handed warrior lady the druid told us of? By all the gods of the world, Connal, why would she do this?"

"That I do not know." The bewilderment had faded to a look of concentration. "Flyn dead, and Queen Nieve with him; a heavy thing, for Flyn was a good king, just and beloved of his people. As I say, I had no quarrel with him; not since before he met with my father, when I was newborn, have there been hostilities between our tuatha. We have kept the borders whole and traded to both our benefit. I cannot understand this, Brihainn, not at all."

"One other thing, chieftain, seems strange to me." Brihainn, who had been thinking, spoke slowly. But Connal, mind racing, was ahead of him.

"I know it; in its way it is yet more puzzling than the rest. Even if this warrior girl thinks she has a reason for this madness, what has driven an army some five thousand strong to follow her lead? Connacht is prosperous and the citizens of that province are canny, with an eye toward preserving their chattels and their skins alike. They are fine warriors, but rarely do they seek to battle. And at this season, with the snows coming! One would say they have all run mad. What could have happened that they risk all they have to follow her?"

But there were no answers, not to any of it. The fact remained; an army, huge and well-trained, was even now moving across the fertile southlands of Connacht toward Emain. And Connal, a chieftain from childhood and a vicious and dangerous fighter who had never yet been bested, shook his head slowly and turned his gaze toward Emain.

To the east the sky lit suddenly with the harsh carmine of an October dawn. At their feet the rime glittered with touches of early sun. Spread out in the distance, a world of its own contained within its gates and earthworks, Emain was waking. The first oinach, languid and not yet free of sleep, had come out of their homes and seen the pale flares of dying torches that lit the sky from the rath-na-riogh. Connal saw groups forming, small clusters of worried life huddling, frightened, pointing toward them.

Already, then, it had begun. Even as they avoided him, remembering their own dislike in times of peace, they would now turn to him like the frightened sheep they truly were, crying for safety, for protection, for the Victorious, honored lord, to beat the invaders back. . . .

For a moment, staring down at his city and his people, Connal hated them. Those whose looks when times were prosperous held the most caution and dislike would be the first to cry for succor when the wars came. Ironic, yes; Brihainn had told him time and again that in irony was some humor and a way to ease the heart. Yet Connal, though he trusted the other's instinct and knowledge, could find pleasure in irony only very rarely.

But he was chieftain, and there was no help for

it—love them or no, he must lead them. With a tiny shrug that only Brihainn and Cormac caught, he turned to the others.

"Sound the trumpets, Cormac. Sound the five notes. We will have a council of all the oinach, here, at this moment. The people must be warned, and plans laid quickly; I want the life and strength of Emain here, and now. Their breakfasts can wait."

Maeve, with Carhainn at her side and her ten celi close behind, cantered at the head of an army that, even to her warriors' experienced eyes, was a wonder of efficiency and obedience unlike any they had ever before seen.

From the day the druid had taken his departure from Cruachain, the gods seemed to vie with one another for the pleasure of making Maeve's task easy. Uncanny good fortune had blessed the invasion of Ulster every step of the way; Maeve, wondering where she might find gold enough to outfit this vast body of fighters, had forgotten that word of her ascension to Connacht's throne would have reached the other leaders.

The chieftains of Hibernia's tuatha, large and small, had sent gifts of whatever luxury they could afford; to Maeve, sitting in her tent lost in worry, the arrival of that first messenger from the kings of Wicklow with a huge gift of raw gold, of carved weaponry, of cattle that would feed the men on the long march northward, had seemed like a portent straight from the gods. Every weapon that arrived as a gift of homage seemed to bear the approval of Crom Cruach, every head of cattle a sign of approval straight from Cernunnos, the Horned One.

And now, breaching Ulster and moving ever closer to Emain, even Lugh of the skies seemed to smile upon them. The year had narrowed, Samhain had been and gone; at any moment it should begin to snow, blocking out the roads, making travel difficult if not impossible, delaying them. Yet the clear skies held; as they crossed the border, Carhainn had looked back toward Connacht and seen the snowcaps, purple and gray, sitting like vultures across the crest of the Iron Hills, blowing toward the southlands they had just left. Yet another gift from the gods, then; the bad weather had waited for them to depart, and the north stayed clear.

Now, within three days of Emain itself, Maeve had found herself settling into a kind of serenity. This far the gods had taken her; surely they would not abandon her now. And always between her breasts, a cold and constant reminder, the ring of royal Emain dangled.

Ghan snorted and blew. Maeve, jerked from her reflections, reached a hand out and scratched the war stallion between the ears. "Peace, warrior. Not much longer and we will rest. The night draws in, Carhainn; I believe we should make camp."

"Yes." His voice was flat, dull, and Maeve was aware of a flicker of familiar irritation. Even in the face of the druid's words, he obstinately refused to believe. Since their confrontation in Maeve's tent, he had addressed her only formally, his voice never wavering from this uninflected deadness. She sighed, and waved a hand in signal. Behind her, a living snake of humanity trailing out of sight to the south, the army came gradually to a halt.

Maeve slid off Ghan's back, throwing the reins to a slave, and stretched. "Oh, I am stiff and sore. To ride is a pleasure, but to rest afterward is even better. Carhainn, tell the men to raise the tents. The wind will not be a bother to us tonight; have the fires built and set a meal to cook. The men must be fed, and so must I."

Carhainn, with a stiff salute, turned unsmiling and disappeared into the milling throng of men. The bearers, already experienced in raising tents, took very little time to go about their task. Maeve, after seeing Ghan tethered and watered, climbed gratefully through the flap of the royal tent and lay down to rest before dinner.

The meal was hearty and nourishing, for six sheep had been slaughtered and roasted over the open fires. The hot mutton gave the royal party an inner warmth; and even the foot fighters dined well, for Maeve had decreed that an army held its loyalty best and performed most efficiently in the face of hardship if the men were well-fed.

The policy was not only wise, but expedient, and had in truth cost her very little. This was no army conscripted

from unwilling oinach, but men who had offered themselves to her, wanting vengeance against the murderers of
their king. They had come to Cruachain from the corners
of her province in a steady stream, and among them only a
very few had not brought rations to see them fed for a
time, weapons their fathers had given them, sheep and
goats.

So while Maeve and her closest companions ate freshly
killed sheep roasted over an open spit, the humbler ranks
of her army dined on goat or on the pheasant or wild hare
brought down along the line by those men highly skilled
with slings. And there was drink for all; this Maeve had
insisted on providing, commanding only that drunkenness
be kept to the tents. The memory of her parents' bodies
was still fresh enough to wake her with the nightmare, and
she wanted no atrocities committed under her reign. She
had, with this in mind, issued an edict promising a slow
and hideous death to any who killed unnecessarily or
raped on the march.

So the army ate well, and at the royal fire the talk ran
on strategy, on whether or not the Victorious would have
got word of the army's approach and what he might do.
Maeve sat and listened, saying very little; these men had
seen war, she had not, and she wanted to learn.

Carhainn was the first to retire. With a curt nod and a
formal bow to Maeve, he hoisted cloak and spear and went
silently from the roaring warmth of the fire to disappear
into the darkness. Eyes slid to follow him and exchanged
knowing glances; the celi, rather too carefully, avoided
their queen's eye.

They all knew why Carhainn suffered, knew, too, that
in spite of the scores of men set at sentry duty, Carhainn
had taken it upon himself to spend a portion of each night
to watch the queen's tent from outside his own. Of a
sudden unable to bear the cheerful conversation, Maeve
rose to her feet. The men immediately rose with her,
ready, expectant, awaiting her command. She waved a
hand.

"Warriors, celi, I give you a fair night. Pray stay by
the fire until you desire to do else; I am for my bed."

Nodding at the man who guarded her tent, she

slipped indoors and stripped for bed. It was cold, the bitterness of the November night permeating even the thick skins that covered her, and Maeve lay sleepless for many hours, her green eyes spots of color in the blackness.

It had become commonplace since her the discovery of her parents' deaths, this inability to sleep; even when exhaustion finally claimed her each night, she would fall only as far as an uneasy doze, always at the edge of the waking world, dark dreams making her wretched. She had come to dread sleep, hating the hours between sunset and cockcrow, for the night was infested with demons that took the shape of memories, and they would not let her be.

So she lay stiff, willing her muscles to relax, unable to ease the steady commotion in her mind. The pictures painted themselves against the darkness, vivid and painful. Some nights she saw herself sitting in a field gone tacky with dried blood, her father's staring head in her lap like some dreadful animal she did not want yet could not put down. At other times she was a child again, a prize for raiders too precious to be left to her fate, and Ahnrach's look of acceptance as she was dragged to dishonor and death pierced her once more, the intensity of her expression undimmed by the years. The bed was stifling, and there was no escape.

Tonight, her stomach settling on mutton and wine, the memory that hurt least, yet made her feel worst, stole into the tent to haunt her. Another tent, a different darkness, a strong body against hers as they spoke in whispers. A man's warm breath, stirring her hair. The feel of hands, callused yet soft, brushing gentle as a mother's touch against breast, shoulder, thigh. . . .

Maeve rolled over on one side, biting her lip. This she would never forgive herself. She had taken Carhainn, Carhainn the faithful, Carhainn who had adored her her whole life long, taken him in a fit of pique against her father. She had him in thrall and had used her power over him, never thinking beyond her own pleasure, her own spite, her own desire. She had destroyed him, ruined him for any other woman, and all for nothing.

The memory, sentient and insinuating, nuzzled against her sleeplessness. She could not fix what she had done to

him; well, then, this much she could do, bear these
memories that were made of equal parts of guilt and
desire, even if they scalded her soul halfway to the Sidh.
The goose-feather pillow, sodden with tears she did not
knew she shed, was pulled against her cheek. As the hours
moved in their inexorable course, she clenched her fists
and suffered. The feel of skin, her finger tracing the ridge
of bone and muscle that ran from shoulder to groin,
learning each of them like a map, a living thing . . .

"Queen Maeve."

For a moment, lost in torment, she thought she had
reached a level of suffering so close to madness as to
produce a living voice in an empty room. Then she sat up,
the fine hairs on her arms standing straight in the cold.

"Carhainn?"

"Get up." It was Carhainn, yes, but what had happened
to the stony voice, the shades of a dead spirit, a spirit she
had killed? This voice came from the old Carhainn, it held
life, urgency, color.

"You have visitors, queen."

She struck a taper, sitting naked in her bed. Carhainn
was not alone; with him were two men, strangers to her.

Her cry was sharp and quickly bitten back. With a
hand that trembled and eyes that flamed, she pulled the
skins to cover her breasts. Her voice was steely with rage.

"Visitors. Do you know no better, captain, than to
bring strangers to the queen's tent with no warning, no
permission, no word from me? And my bodyguard, what
is he about, to thus allow it?"

Carhainn, with a sharp exclamation, swung around.
One of the two men behind him stepped forward and
spoke, a voice deep and echoing, fine and beautiful,
completely male. "Your pardon, lady. The fault is ours; he
told us to wait. No blame to your captain. As for the man
who keeps watch on you, your captain sent him off."

Well, the damage was done, and she was a queen; she
would show no shame at her nakedness. "I see. Your
pardon, Carhainn, I meant no injustice; let us see if your
reason justifies my clemency. My robes?"

He stepped forward and, with a ceremony uncommon
to him, draped her bare shoulders. She pulled herself out

of bed and came forward to stand staring at the two strangers who had invaded her tent and her waking misery.

She looked first at the smaller man, saw the puckered scar that pulled at one corner of his mouth and the startled admiration in his eyes, and nodded at him. As she turned away her eye brushed Carhainn's and she saw a message there, a message that puzzled her. Urgency it held, and warning, and something else she could not read.

With brows raised high, she turned to face the other.

For Maeve, this first picture would stay forever, a bright shade shouting down all the memories, good and bad, that were yet to be made. He towered over her, dressed in fine robes with a wolfskin across his shoulders, looming like a god. She studied him, from the long legs to the impossibly broad chest and upward. Then her eyes, green and wide, found the black ones and they stood looking at one another, faces impassive, neither showing the shock of heat, of their immediate mutual recognition of what was to come. On the high brow Maeve saw the circlet of gold, shining against the pale skin and black hair.

They stood, three men and a queen, and the silence ran into itself and held. No one moved, no one spoke; each was busy with private thoughts.

Brihainn, his arms crossed against his body, stared at this creature who was already becoming legend, and was lost in a confusion of feelings. There was something of Sheilagh in her, yet something of Alhauna too; she was a warrior woman, a queen, yet vulnerable and so very young. He remembered how she had sat up in bed, her hair tousled, her breasts of palest ivory stiff with the cold, and swallowed hard.

And Carhainn, looking at a face he knew and loved, saw what came up in Maeve's eyes. As he saw it he knew it for what it was, and the pain he had lived with since Flyn's death sharpened to agony. It was all there for him to read, clear, sharp, shining, every feeling that ate at him like a worm in death, never to be ousted. Love, and hunger, and none of it for him. He had never seen her look like this.

"Queen Maeve." Connal went to one knee and took her hand to kiss. "Forgive this intrusion, but the matter is urgent. We came alone, armed only against the beasts of night; do not fear us. We must have speech with you."

"Get up." Carhainn closed his eyes as the pain bit deeper. She was whispering, her hands trembling, her heart in her eyes, even as she fought to hide it. Sweet Lugh, Carhainn thought, I have lost her, and that for good now. If he was less of a man, less royal, not so easy to admire, I could bear this better. . . .

The stranger rose. Maeve gazed into those black eyes and saw her own reflected there. Her voice took on color and strength, Who is he, this man, this god, who stands here looking down at me so soberly? Who . . . but I am a queen, she thought dazedly, a queen and not a village wench to fall in love on first meeting. She suddenly resented him, whoever he was, resented him and Carhainn, too, for putting her at such a disadvantage. Her voice was sharp and strong.

"I will decide whether to forgive the intrusion when I better know your business with me. You wear a crown, yet no badge; are you then ashamed of the tuath you rule, that you must hide your crest?"

Was that warmth, anger, desire, understanding? What was it that had come up so quickly in the black eyes holding her? And why did she find him so unnerving, this tall stranger? She saw Carhainn's face, and a sudden suspicion that she refused to acknowledge rose in her. "Who are you?"

"I am Connal of Ulster, lady. I am the one they call the Victorious, chieftain since my tenth year, never defeated in battle. Three days past, my men at the southern borders came to tell me that Connacht's new queen was even then marching on Emain with an army of size and training. I am here to learn why."

The ring of Bhoru, never taken off, bumped coldly between her breasts as she suddenly sucked in breath. "You? You are Connal?"

"I have said it. As to hiding my crest, the reason should be clear; would your men have let us into the camp had they seen the two snakes?"

"Let you in?" Her lips were shaking now, the skin of her face pulled taut against her cheekbones. "They would have brought me your head, chieftain of Ulster." This man, this beautiful giant who was exercising such a fascination, holding her like a snake held its food . . . no, it could not be, it could not. This was a dream, another of those demons come to haunt her, unjust and unwanted—

"My lady!" Carhainn jumped and caught her as she swayed. Gods have mercy on me, he thought, and saw the tragedy in her eyes. He had walked into her tent, her enemy, and without a word had claimed her, body and soul, never lifting a hand to do it. And he himself had loved her so long, so long. Could the gods truly be this cruel?

She stared at Connal blindly. "You come to me and ask me why? By the waking gods, but you have nerve."

For the first time the planes of his face shifted. Carhainn, watching, saw the honest bewilderment there. Well, and he had never believed in that ring; Connal's puzzlement, his very presence here, was the proof of innocence.

"I do not understand you, Queen Maeve. My men rode from the southlands with word that all Connacht had banded against me. They could not tell me why, and I want to know why." He reached out a hand and laid it hard on her shoulder, feeling the jumping heat of her flesh. "You have come into my lands, swearing you would bring my head back to hang on the gates of Cruachain. Oh yes, lady, I have heard that." His grip tightened. "Well, I am here, and my head with me. I will know why."

She moved so quickly that Brihainn jumped backward. Wrenching herself free of Connal, she pulled the ring out from between her breasts and, wrenching it over her head, flung it straight in Connal's face. It struck him on one cheek and rolled away. As she watched him, seeing his confusion, realizing that he had come to her alone and unarmed, she knew that she stood on the brink of some truth that would change everything, for good or bad. Words broke from her, panting, breathless.

"You will know why? That is why, oh Victorious. Murder is why, foul ambush is why. I sat in my father's blood and held his mutilated head in my arms, and I swore a fate on you, Connal of Ulster, and every man of

Connacht has followed me, wanting no better than the honor of killing you." She was whispering now, her hands clenching and unclenching. "You dare to ask me why? You dare to say you do not know why I have come?" She pointed a shaking finger. "That ring gives you the lie, chieftain."

He spoke quietly, one long finger rubbing the angry red weal the ring had left there, never taking his eyes from her. "Brihainn. Get me the ring."

Brihainn, the working muscles of his jaw making the scar dance, retrieved it. As he took it up, holding it to the light, an exclamation broke from him. Connal, his head snapping sideways, did not see Maeve's exhalation of relief as the lock of eyes was broken.

"What is it, cela?"

"Lord, it is the ring! The ring of Bhoru, stolen those many years ago, when we were children! Do you remember your father's rage when he found it gone?"

Connal's hand shot out, snatching the golden token from Brihainn's hand. The two snakes gleamed dully against his palm. And Maeve, at the edge of the abyss, looked at their faces, saw Connal's black brows snap into a frowning bar and knew they had spoken the truth. She had been lied to, the druid had been mistaken, Carhainn had been in the right of it all along. She had raised an army, taken the best of Connacht and brought them here on a quest for revenge, a quest based on nothing.

Connal turned his head back and captured her eyes once more. Carhainn heard the danger in the quiet voice. "It is as Brihainn says; this ring, with some other pieces, were taken from my father Sibhainn's tent many years ago." His lips were thin, the black eyes capturing hers once more, rooting her in place. He said, very softly, "Where had you this ring, lady?"

She could not speak, and after a moment Carhainn answered for her. "We found it in the mud beneath Flyn's murdered body, chieftain. I—I did not believe in it, it made no sense to me that you would do this thing. You had no quarrel with Flyn or his people, after all, and your name is spoken cheek by jowl with justice, even in

Cruachain. But we had a druid, and he told us of your guilt."

Connal moved very slowly. Reaching out, he dropped the ring on its leather chain over Maeve's head once more. His hands, seeming to have a life of their own, slowly drew his spear; it lay, a glittering and deadly toy, across his outstretched palms.

Through a haze Maeve saw him drop to his knees before her on the cold floor. His words were clear, calm.

"I am innocent, lady. I had no reason to wish Flyn ill; all of my army can swear before you that I personally led them to victory against Des-Gabair, never leaving them, not even for a day or a night. I do not know why this druid told you what he did, but it is false, lady. I even sent my man to your father so that he might not lose any men by sending them into my path as I marched against Des-Gabair.

"I am known for my fairness, lady. I never laid a hand to your father, did not know until a few days ago Flyn had gone to the Sidh, never had the ring of Bhoru in my possession; my father raged like a wild thing when he found it gone. I do not know who took it, but I swear to you I have not seen it since that time."

His hands moved forward. "Take the spear, queen."

She took it up, her eyes wide, dead lakes rimmed in tears. She seemed unable to disobey that steady, quiet tone of command. Connal's voice never faltered.

"I grieve with you for your father's death. I grieve with you for the way of doing it, cold and cowardly. I tell you I am innocent; I came to you with no men but my closest cela, no arms but a spear for wolves and bears. Yet the ring of Bhoru speaks with a voice of its own, that a man of Ulster did this bitter thing. I am chieftain of Ulster, chieftain to the man that did this thing, and I will pay the forfeit."

"No," she whispered, but the even voice continued.

"You have my only weapon, lady. I give it to you of my own free will. Strike me dead with it, lady, and I pay the debt my people owe you. Blood for blood, and your quest for vengeance will be satisfied, and the innocent of your people and mine will be spared. Brihainn, you will wear the crown of Emain from the moment of my death.

Do not grieve for me, cela; I am innocent of this thing, and I go to the Sidh unstained. Take the crown from my head."

Brihainn's sinews had turned to water; he took the golden circlet and stood in stunned silence, unable to believe, the crown of Ulster dangling in his hands. Beside him Carhainn made a noise deep in his throat.

The spear trembled in Maeve's hands as she stood staring down at the man she had sworn to kill. He knelt before her, his black braid pushed to one side, baring his neck for the final strike. He did not look up at her; his eyes fixed on her bare feet, he waited for his death in kingly dignity.

Slowly, how slowly, the hand holding the spear lifted high. Brihainn was weeping silently, tears streaking his face to gather in the small hollow made by the scar at his mouth. Carhainn had closed his eyes, silently willing her to stop, unable to interfere.

Her left hand closed over the right, to get a better grip. The spear moved up, up, back over her head. "I cannot," she said quietly. "I cannot. I believe you." To Connal, his head bowed, his mind emptied of all feeling as he waited to die, her voice was the softest, sweetest thing he had ever heard.

The spear clattered to the earth. Carhainn, moving first, was just in time to catch her as she fainted.

"What are we to do? High Danu, what are we to do?"

Outside the royal tent the army was going about its business. Sounds of activity, muffled and unreal, came through to the four people within as a constant, uneven counterpoint to the desperate conversation that had continued since Maeve, coming to her senses so many hours ago, had found herself held like a baby in Connal's arms.

In that short time she had lost the ability for decision; the knowledge that she had brought five thousand men across Hibernia, raised them to a dangerous pitch with her desire for revenge, and must now, somehow, tell them that they would go home empty-handed, their spears unblooded, her father unavenged, had melted all the steel from her.

The royal party knew that something was in the wind;

Maeve's celi, excepting Carhainn, had been forbidden from entering her tent, and the slaves who brought food were told by their white-faced queen that a single word to the curious about the strangers closeted with her would mean their lives.

The army, told only that they would camp here yet another day, had merely shrugged in relief, glad enough to rest a day from the grueling march to the north. Closed up together in Maeve's tent, the four of them had discussed the situation, seeing no way out of the snare.

Connal, through a mouthful of breakfast, took impatient command of a conversation that had run in circles too long. "All right. What we have is just this; five thousand men outside these walls who know what the druid told you. Five thousand men who believe me guilty of this thing. Five thousand men who have lived day and night since your father's death with a single thought, the thought of taking my head from my body. You cannot hope to cool their fires by saying to them, I was wrong, we are going home, the druid was wrong. They will go mad if you do."

"Truth." Maeve, pacing the length of the tent, swung around to face him. "And there is more than that at stake here, chieftain, at least for me. I am but newly made as Queen of Connacht; I must earn my people's loyalty. In their first flush of anguish they flocked to me, for my own grief and my vows of vengeance suited the mood of their hearts. But if I do this thing..." Her voice died.

Brihainn laid a gentle hand on her arm. "If you do this thing, lady, you will lose them. You are as yet untried, and their loyalty could be shaken. A bitter thing, to rule a people who hate you, who disbelieve in you."

Connal looked at his cela. "As who should know if not I? A hard thing, a bitter thing. Maeve, my poor girl, well do I see the problems that lie in wait for you. And not only for you; I have much at stake here, as much as you."

She looked at him, noting his "my poor girl" and biting back on a sudden smile. Never in all her life had she found any man so easy to deal with; they seemed at first meeting to understand each other in a way new to her. Through the worry of this critical situation, through her own confusion as to what she must do, she was aware of a delight in him, a joy in his company, a wondering happiness in his very existence, that ran through her blood like sweet wine.

"Yes, you do have much to lose, dear chieftain. You are not called Victorious for naught; even as my people expect revenge and will settle for nothing less, your people sit waiting, confident that their leader, who has never been beaten, will punish my presumption in daring to challenge him." She smiled into his troubled eyes. "Truth?"

"Truth." He sighed deeply, washing down his meat with a gulp of wine, and turned affectionate eyes to Carhainn. He had taken an immediate liking to this Connachtman, seeing something of himself in the still face that contained so many passions. "I am to thank you, captain. We gambled with our lives last night, Brihainn and I, trusting them to the honesty I saw writ large across your brow. Had you seized the moment and revealed to the guard our names, we would have died with the truth untold, and many hundreds, perhaps thousands, would have weltered in the blood of their own innocence." He laid a strong hand on Carhainn's shoulder. "You are a true son of Lugh, Carhainn, a man of the light, and the people of our tuatha owe you a great debt."

"You speak too soon." Carhainn spoke harshly, for he found himself tangled in emotions as confused as they were contradictory. He, too, had been aware of the immediate pull between them; looking into the chieftain's face, he had seen there the qualities he most admired in a man. Pride, honor, a disdain for falsehood, and above all a cold sense of what was fair; to Carhainn, a man of war who was not afraid of his own heart, these things were to be admired above all else, and they were rare blooms.

But there was Maeve... she stood now, intolerably close to him, looking at him with soft eyes. By Crom, if she followed Connal's lead and put a hand on him, he would weep like a babe. There was a golden flush to her, a glowing newness that was beautiful and disturbing. With her future, perhaps her life, at stake, she was shining like a rose, happy to be alive. And all of that because of Connal's presence. Carhainn, in his abject love for her, would have given his life to have caused that glow. And in had walked this stranger. . .

He cleared his throat and turned his back on them, to walk to the far end of the tent. "Yes, chieftain, you speak too soon. They owe me nothing yet. The fact is that we have tumbled, through an unknown design, into a pit from which I can see no release. The people will not disbelieve the words of a holy man; to them your guilt can never be in question."

He forced his eyes back, to meet the watching chieftain. "They want you dead, Connal, and will accept nothing less. Maeve must ride to Cruachain with your head at her girdle or lose her crown. Nor is your burden any lighter, for your people have grown complacent, knowing that you must triumph because the gods have never given you failure. So what are we to do?"

They had come full circle. Brihainn, silent in his corner, spoke up quietly.

"You could put the question to council."

There was a sudden, breathless hush. Three faces turned toward him with questions in their eyes. He did not move, but lifted his head and let his gaze move between them.

"You could do that. When there is a question of guilt, and the crime is murder of a chieftain, the new chieftains can do this, send messengers to sanctuary, call for druids and kings alike. A high council."

"At Tara?" Maeve, wondering and cold, dropped her voice on the name. "Brihainn, this frightens me. No council has been held at Tara of the Kings in my lifetime; I thought it was a heavy thing, final and terrible, to do this."

"Terrible? No, lady, not terrible. But very serious, and once the council heard your case and gave you their answer, there would be no turning back. You would have to abide by their decision, whatever it was, however cold."

"Tara . . ." Connal stood, tall and stiff; even the black braid hanging down his back seemed to bristle, so tense was he. "A heavy thing, cela, heavy and drastic."

Brihainn met his chieftain's eyes and spoke quietly. "What other choices do we have?"

Into the quiet room came the muted conversation of

the guards outside, the clanking of weaponry, the sounds
of an army five thousand strong poised for war. Maeve, her
face pale, faced the others. She saw the question in
Connal's eyes, the sympathy in Brihainn's, the anguish in
Carhainn's.

"It is decided," she said calmly. "Carhainn, sound the
five notes for the meeting. I have no rath of my own here,
no forradh, but I will speak to my people and tell them
what has happened. Ten men ride for sanctuary today;
give them good weapons and the best horses. They will
take the coast road, for the way through the Iron Hills will
be shrouded with snow. Brihainn, if Connal agrees to it,
you will ride to Emain and give your people the story;
someone must be left as shadow for Ulster, and as Connal
told his people what he meant to do, they will be awaiting
word. Carhainn, one hundred men, in parties of four or
more, will ride to every chieftain in Hibernia and bring
them the news. A council at Tara of the Kings."

Connal reached out and took her hands. "Are you
certain, my girl? I will abide by your decision, and that
freely. But the council's ruling may be too hard for either
of us to bear. Are you certain?"

She looked up at Connal a moment, her face calm and
still. Then she slid her hand into his.

"What the council will decide is with the gods. Yes, I
am certain, my friend. There is no other way."

9

The Council

On the wide plain known as Bregia, below the hill called Tara of the Kings, the leaders of Hibernia, both religious and secular, gathered for the judgment.

It was February, the time for celebrating Imbolc, the festival of lovers, a time for snow and rain together. To those encamped on the fields of Wicklow, the melting snow, turned into rivers of icy mud by the first torrential rains of the new season, were a constant misery.

Each chieftain had come with his celi, and in most cases a sizable escort of armed men; the plains of Tara, filled to capacity with the best of Hibernia's tuatha, rang day and night with the sneezing and coughing of thousands of men sick with the ague.

But mitigating the physical discomforts was a sense of excitement, barely repressed. Few of the leaders gathered to cast a judgment upon two of their fellows had been born when the last such meeting had been held; few had ever dealt with the druids, knowing them only as shadowy figures, legends, seeing them only when one was needed. The murder of Flyn of Connacht and his queen was known throughout the land, and for the most part a certain sympathy for the new queen was very evident. The discovery of the ring of Bhoru beneath Flyn's headless body was

147

also common knowledge, and not a single chieftain felt her invasion of Ulster was unjust.

Yet she had called this council, and Connal the Victorious had agreed to it; they seemed, astonishingly, to be on the best of terms, each sitting at one hand of the druid master in the great banqueting hall. The reasons for this extraordinary meeting were a close-guarded secret, and rumor, fed by the lack of hard fact and the air of mystery resulting from so many druids gathered in one place, ran wild among the expectant chieftains.

So it rained, day after dreary day, and the people waited for the weather to clear. The druids kept to themselves; the gravity of what was to occur enforced a good deal of meditating, and they were rarely to be seen in groups larger than two or three. Indeed, many stayed in solitary contemplation, seeing no one, speaking not even to the other druids, never lifting the heavy white hoods to reveal their faces to the curious.

In a tiny tent at the edge of the druids' circle, Covac kept his hood on and smiled, waiting for the sun.

The meeting with Maeve had fallen out precisely as he had known it must. She had no reason to disbelieve the words of an elder, and she had not done so; watching from one of his familiar spying posts in the lowlands, he had seen the army of Connacht ride out to the north. Detailing two of his men to follow behind and report the result of the invasion back to him, Covac had hunted and fished, drinking heavily to dull the edge of his inner fret, waiting for news.

The news, when it came at last, was unexpected. He had been at first unable to believe what Chlair, panting back to camp, had told him; Maeve and Connal had met, Connal had denied the druid's words, and somehow, somehow, had given Maeve such proof of his words that she had believed him. Neither Connacht nor Ulster would accept their decision, and it seemed the two young chieftains had known it. . . .

Chlair, small and inconsequential, merely another face lost in an army five thousand men strong, had stood to the rear of Maeve's troops and listened to the pronouncement. Connal of Ulster, she had told them, had brought her proof of his innocence. Yet he was chieftain of his people, and one of his people had done this thing; she could not make war on a man she believed innocent, for honor would not allow it. Yet something must be done, and Flyn's death avenged.

Men were to ride to sanctuary, summoning the druids; others were to ride to every tuath in the land. In default of a better answer, Maeve had told her stunned army, she was taking the extraordinary step of calling for a council at Tara of the Kings. The chieftain of Ulster had agreed to it, she added calmly, to her mind a further proof of innocence. They would put their cases to the decision of their peers, and by that decision they would both abide. . . .

Druids, thought Covac, hundreds of druids, all to pass judgment fair and just. He had stood in the outlaw camp, his light eyes blurred, seeing not the exhausted man who knelt at his feet but a slender face, beautiful and full of purpose in its frame of hair that was the color of sunrise. . . .

She would not thwart him, not this time, not again. He had known what this council would entail; let him but keep his hood close around him, and none would know of the masquerade.

Leaving Cimhaill and Alchlaidd to rule the band in his absence, he set out for Wicklow and the southern hills.

On the fifth day of his journey, reaching the standing stone and ancient cromlech that marked the joining of his path to the coast road, he suddenly remembered something that turned him cold. He was going among the men who would have been his brethren had things chanced differently, going among them in the guise of an elder. And an elder, with a hood or without one, must have a snake. A sacred snake . . .

The standing stone, looming over him in its endless silent vigil, enveloped him in its shadow. He stood at the joining of the roads, sweating and shivering. By all the gods, he wanted nothing to do with snakes. Even as a boy he had been nervous of them; since the day he had killed the two elders and found himself held by the look of a creature whose gaze was stronger than his, nervousness had been transmuted to a superstitious terror that sucked the marrow from his bones. That terror, enhanced by the

fact of its being the only thing that could raise a fear in
Covac, took him in a clammy grip and held him.

I must have one, he thought concretely, and leaned
his back against the stone. I must have one, or risk
exposure and a terrible death. The sack that had once
been the home of a holy creature was stuffed into his pack;
squatting on the wet earth, he rummaged through his
meager belongings until he found it. It dangled, loose and
empty, in his hand.

Soon it would hold a snake once more, an adder,
slender and shining, its fangs hoarding the precious venom, its black eyes holding glitter and fire.... The fear
rose in him again, and he swallowed hard on it, willing it
back and away. The thing must be done; what use, then,
to sit and shiver like a maiden at a lover's touch? The grass
here was long and the sea was close; there would be
snakes here, if he could but capture one, for snakes liked
the warm and the wet.

Covac climbed to the top of the cromlech, scanning
the distance until he saw a thick stand of trees a few miles
to the south. The edge of a woodland; good. There would
be wood there, a suitable stick that could be carved into
the fork. And in the woods there would be stones, under
which a creature whose blood ran cold might sleep the
winter months away. Snakes could rest there, their heartbeats slowed, sluggish with the long nights of enforced
rest.

Setting his lips in a thin line, he thrust the empty
sack through his belt and set off toward the trees, a knife
ready in his hand.

He came to the wood a half hour short of sunset and
stood scanning it with a new fear; this was no natural
woodland, but a grove planted by the hand of man.
Rowan, ash, birch, willow, oak, apple... yes, there at the
back of the wood, the other two, alder and hazel, the
sacred eight. No doubt there would be a clearing, a grove
for the worship of Nemet, and then an identical thicket on
the far side.

Instead of unsettling him further, the knowledge that
he had come by chance to a holy spot, that he must in this
place of true worship use whatever came to hand for his

own purposes, steadied him. He cast a calculating glance at the surrounding trees, weighing the virtues of ash against oak, willow against alder.

Covac decided, in the end, on birch; not ten paces from where he stood grew a healthy sapling, its springy branches perfect for his needs. A snake handler's tool should be flexible and easy to bend; the wood of the birch tree was well-known for its elasticity. Reaching a hand up, he caught a thin limb in one hand and slashed it free of the trunk with a hard flick of the knife.

As he sat and whittled, he felt a sudden chill that raised the fine hairs at the base of his skull. How silent this grove was; no birdsong, no hum of insects living in the bark, not even the rustle of the wind in the boughs. It might have been a waiting place during the journey between this world and the Sidh, so quiet was it. Turning his face to the green canopy above him, Covac saw that the sun was lower in the sky, the dense and quiet blanket of air growing thicker with darkness as the light went.

He broke into a cold sweat and climbed to his feet. There was a fear in him, one he would not admit to himself; he did not want to be caught among these thick trees when darkness fell. A holy grove, the sacred eight towering above him in the black and starless night, with whatever held watch here, perhaps the fomori, taking strength from his fear. . .

He began to run suddenly, the birch limb in one hand and his knife, trembling, streaked with the sweat that poured down his arm, in the other. He had a sense of eyes on his back, of something watching him, inimical, amused. . . .

He burst through the trees, his breath coming in dry sobs that tore at his chest. No, he had not imagined it; behind him, hidden by the long trees and the encroaching shadows, something had moved, rustling. With a single motion he flipped the knife to fighting grip and dropped to a knee, his eyes fixed on the trees, awaiting whatever might emerge.

Another rustle, gentle and suggestive; on the hard edge of the sky the new moon showed as a thin line of gold in the late winter twilight. Then he saw it, the long grass parting smoothly in its wake, and with a strangled noise in his throat he got slowly to his feet to stand staring, unable to believe his good fortune.

It was young, the adder, perhaps eighteen inches in length; the thin light that was all that remained of the dying day fell on it as it rippled toward him, giving the pale scales a reddish cast. Covac looked down at the rough tines of birch in his left hand and then back at the snake. It was motionless now, scenting the air, its body arched for vision and smell. He saw the eyes fix on him and he stepped forward, the knife slipping into his belt, the sack replacing it. The adder had found him now, darting its beautiful, deadly head toward him, Then, to Covac's complete astonishment, it began to move, not away from him, but straight toward him. As it came he saw its eyes, dark, understanding, eyes that knew, seeing straight through the man to the reasons behind, accepting. . . .

Darkness grew deeper, drowning the tense and motionless man with memories. The pictures, in a succession too quick for denial, ran through him. Two dead men, white robes, blood pouring down the legs of a red-haired girl, a cairn, a snake. A snake. The fortune of the gods, blessing him, coming to his hand. A snake. . . .

It was only a few feet away now, and the moon was rising fast. The light was almost gone, the snake no more than a dim shining line in the grass at his feet. His fingers opened numbly and the sack fell open at his feet.

Gracefully, quietly, the snake crawled in. He saw the sack move as the creature settled itself into this new place of warmth. Then it was still, a gift of the moon.

He picked it up carefully, drawing the golden cords tight. Hunger had gone from him, fear had gone from him, both replaced by an exhaustion deep and impossible to deny. He dropped his cloak on the ground where he stood and then eased his body down on it. Within moments he was deeply, dreamlessly sleeping. Two feet from his head, warm and safe in its soft white prison, the adder slept too.

After nine days of rain Maeve woke to a new warmth in the air and pale sunshine falling.

She lay awhile, waking slowly, growing conscious as she had every morning since the chieftain of Ulster handed her his spear of that odd mixture of feelings that had become her constant companion. She stretched, glad for the warmth on her naked arms, and let her thoughts take her.

Doubtless, she thought, there are a thousand men who will wake this day and be glad of this same sun that falls so gently on me. Doubtless there will be mutterings and short prayers, all in gratitude that the council can be held, that they can go home soon.

She closed her eyes, letting the visions come.

Connal would be waking in his stark tent, a quarter mile from her own, separated by the tents of ten chieftains. She stretched luxuriously, imagining how he would wake and enjoy the pull of flesh that was the body's first greeting to the new morning. That long body, she thought, so easy to see; the long legs would pull taut, the arms would ripple. She could see, a picture of heat in her mind's eye, how the veins would cord in his brow, his shoulders bunching, the lines at mouth and eyes deepening in the way she had come to love. . . .

The single dimple quivered. So much to worry me, she thought, so much, why can I not feel it? We have never touched, he and I, never come flesh to flesh, shared only our minds and our hearts, and our troubles too, and for those few moments we shared the truth. Yet desire, a hot flooding expectancy that lived with her waking and dreaming, was more real to her now than anything else.

And he felt the same. He had said so.

Mother Macha, Mother Morrigan, she thought, and pressed her eyes tight. That night, that cold wet night when the army had been told, when the men of Connacht had retired muttering to their beds. Carhainn and Brihainn, dismissed to await them elsewhere. Alone, alone, no one to watch them, no one to interfere, only man and woman under the gods . . .

She could have had him then; Connal, shining with his own desire for her, seemed to have been born without the ability to lie or hide his feelings. She remembered now, how clearly she remembered, the sound of the flap falling behind a troubled Brihainn, an expressionless Carhainn.

Alone with him. None but them, a violent generation of love—his for the taking, and he knew it.

She lay in her bed now, her palms itching. They had faced each other; Maeve was tall for a woman, yet her head only just reached his shoulder. She had looked into his eyes, feeling her own smile, oh sweet Danu, all the world could die and she would care nothing for it, if only...

The conversation, seared into her memory like a chant in the druid's language, came back to her now. "We are for each other. You know that, then, darling girl?"

"I know it."

One hand moving, lying lightly against her cheek; even now the memory of that touch could tighten each separate muscle in her body. "I could take you now, and you would do nothing to stop me. You know that, too, I think."

Where had she gone, that queen, that new woman grown cold and angry, in whom she thought the lover was forever lost? Her answer, soft as vair. "I know it."

"Yes. And one other thing we both know." The hand had moved down, brushing cheek to shoulder to breast, to lie there as a living symbol of love, of dominance. So many weeks gone, and still it was hard to breathe when remembrance was on her. The hand had rested peacefully, owning the soft skin it touched, and her heartbeat was wild and uncontrolled under Connal's fingers.

He had moved suddenly to take her chin in a harsh hold, wrenching her face up to his, their eyes meeting, seeing white heat in his and feeling the fire come up in her own... Mother, Mother, where had her backbone gone?

Breathless she had been, so breathless, her heart grown too large for her body, risen up into her throat, choking her. "Yes, you could take me. Tell me to lay myself down, tell me this is the hour for begetting a king on a queen, and I will tell you do as you choose. I could not kill you, but I could live for you, Victorious, live for you and with you, and you for me. What else do we both know, then?"

Gently, callused hands whose touch was impossibly light for anything so ruthlessly male had opened to lie flat against her cheeks. The black braid had fallen across his shoulder to brush her face as he bent to her.

In all the nights with Carhainn, nights of pure enjoyment, nights when she had become the sum and total of her own body, she had never felt anything like this. The kiss was not long, nor was it passionate; it held a sorrow and a pleasure, too, a mating of feelings that lifted her out of her flesh and set her, a spirit that hungered and thirsted in its own incompleteness, into him. It was the sealing of a bargain, that kiss, and an apology too. More than that, it was a translation of flesh to spirit and a promise of things yet to come.

He did not release her when the kiss was done. They stood as before, in total understanding of each other, lost in the knowledge that had been there from the moment she had sat up in her bed to see him towering in her doorway. Her skin had lifted in a rush of gooseflesh to meet the touch of lips against her ear. He had sounded sad.

"What else do we know, my only one? We know that the time is not yet, for us. Not yet. Not now."

"Yes." She had spoken absolutely flatly, suddenly chilled and sick with disappointment and want denied, but he was right, she knew that, and the black eyes that held her saw into her and knew her agreement. "Yes. But a time there will be, Connal. When this is done, when the council has met, when I learn the truth."

"When we learn the truth." His lips had thinned out, his hands moving back down to her shoulders. The touch turned her, queen and young woman, to water, the arms that held her so tightly made of her a child again. A man, the only man, who knew her, and with that knowing, would help her carry the weight that lay so hard on her uneasy shoulders. . . . "I will know the truth of this as well, Maeve. It is hidden to us, yet we both suffer and the crime is against us both."

Truth. Truth, truth, then and now. But they had

parted, they had gone back to their own tuatha, they had
waited across the miles for the summons to Wicklow.
Soon, now. Soon it would be done, and then, please,
Danu . . .

Suddenly her warm bed was hot, the sheets clammy,
the skins a shroud to stifle her. Unable to bear any more,
Maeve wrenched the covers free and got to her feet, to
stand naked and panting in the room's center. She was
unaware that all her body was covered in a sheen of sweat,
lying like film over a pale blush that covered her from
head to foot.

At the scratching from without, she closed her eyes
once more. "Who goes?"

"It is Brihainn, lady, Brihainn mac Alhainn. I bring
you word. May I enter?"

"Yes." She spoke idly, forgetting that she stood in her
flesh. Realization hit her, but it was too late. Well, her
father had never wasted his time in teaching her modesty,
and she would not be caught flustered and shrieking like a
village wench ashamed of her femininity. She waited for
the hide to fall, standing poised and naked.

Brihainn came in, dressed in formal black and silver;
without looking at her, he dropped a low bow. Then, as he
kissed her hand, he realized that the arm he held was
bare, and got to his feet, his face turning scarlet.

She burst out laughing. "Your pardon, Brihainn; I was
lost in thought when you called my name and had forgot I
was undressed." The flush on his face, the tension obvious
in every line, told its own story. Sure, and what is so
special about me, she thought, that men behave this way?
She kept her voice even and cheerful. "No need to turn
colors, Ulster man; sure, and you have seen this all before.
You are no babe, and one woman's body is very like
another."

Brihainn swallowed and forced his clenched fists open.
"Your pardon for any discourtesy, lady, but you are talking
nonsense. I have seen this all before, that is truth; never
have I seen any to approach such beauty."

Her eyes flew to his, startled, and she spoke in a rush
of penitence. "Oh, Brihainn, dear friend, I am sorry. I ask
your forgiveness; I am a shameless little fool to torment

you so. See, here are my robes, and we can start fresh.
You say you bring word; what word is this, then?"

He had recovered his complexion. Brihainn, fatherless son with a warrior mother, had grown up under a
discipline both harsh and demanding; to keep control of
feelings was the duty of all men, and he would not
disgrace himself now.

But under the facade, now calm once again, was a
sorrow too deep for self-denial. He was a normal man,
with the same wants that haunted his fellows; a man of
thought before action, however, he had rarely felt drawn
to the easy exchange of pleasure available to him, a
well-favored warrior and the favorite of the chieftain.

He could have had near any woman in his tuath for
the asking, for he was higher in favor than anyone else
and, had he but known it, the scar that he himself saw as a
physical disadvantage was almost hypnotically attractive to
the women of Ulster. To Brihainn, accustomed to the
sheer physical magnificence of his chieftain, the red weal
that puckered his mouth was ugly, disfiguring; he could
not know that to the women of his people, it was a badge
of his masculinity.

The scar, the lack of a sire, the close friendship with a
man he considered physical perfection, all these things
had combined to imbue him with a shyness of women that
he barely acknowledged to himself. And now, after a whole
life spent in avoiding his own needs, he had taken one
look at the Queen of Connacht, the enemy, the woman
prized by Connal the Victorious even above his own life,
and fallen deeply and helplessly in love.

And she knew it. Lugh have pity, she saw it in his face
and was sorry for it. He could not let this matter weigh on
him, for if he gave in to his feelings, took her in his arms,
took her breath away with kisses to drown them both, it
would avail him nothing but a momentary respite and the
loss of everything he held dear. He forced his tight jaw to
relax, and replied in his normal impassive tones.

"Why, word from my chieftain, lady, and from the
master of the druids. The rain has stopped, our business
must be done by Beltane; when the sun is at zenith, we
are all to meet at the rath-na-riogh, where the kings and

druids await us, there to hear our case." He saw her face change suddenly. "Lady! Lady, what troubles you?"

She turned blindly to him. Her eyes were enormous, the green almost entirely swallowed by pupils that had blurred and expanded. "A feeling, my friend. A feeling of cold across my skin, that something heavy and sorrowful is waiting to fall on me. A fate, a doom perhaps." She began to shudder, long tremors that shook her body. "I am afraid," she whispered. "I am afraid, Brihainn, afraid..."

Love and desire alike forgotten, he caught her and shook her hard. Her head snapped back with the force of it; with a muffled cry she threw a hand out to right herself. He saw, with deep relief, that her eyes had cleared.

"I thank you, my friend. It was cold, but it has passed now." She looked around the small room. "I must dress and prepare myself. Will you call Carhainn?"

"Indeed." At the door he turned back to her. "Lady. My chieftain bade me bring you a message, separate from whatever else I must needs say. I have not yet given it."

The indrawn breath, the sudden flame in her eyes, were scourges against him. Well, Connal deserved this, and none better; had the chieftain of Ulster never been born, this prize would still be beyond his own reach. He was seized with a sudden dislike of himself and an unwillingness to be here any longer. Before she could answer him, he hurried once more into speech.

"Not a long message, lady, but he said you would know the meaning of it. Time will be soon, he said to tell you. No more than that."

She pulled her crown from the wall. As it settled into the flaming hair, she turned back to him, her eyes glowing, her face lit from within.

"I understand it," she said, and contradicting the glow and the smile, he saw a glaze of tears across the green eyes. "I only pray he is right."

His hood fastened securely in place, the snake held fast in the white sack, Covac took his place among the druids gathered on the rath-na-riogh.

The hill of Tara, a rounded mound thrusting five hundred feet into the air, provided a spectacular view of the countryside for miles around. Covac, sitting behind rows of white robes and hoods that rendered their wearers as anonymous as they were impressive, found that shifting his head slightly to one side gave him a clear line of vision to the two people he hated most in the world.

Any lingering fears he had that the stolen robes might be recognized and himself unmasked had long been set to rest. None had questioned him or demanded to see his face; he thought, with a quirk of his thin lips, that the druids themselves fell as much a prey to respect for their own garb as did any superstitious slave from the outside world.

Well, that was all to the good. He would sit here, taking note of every word said; when the time came for counsel, he might well be able to turn it to yet better use.

The five trumpets, a clarion call silvery yet clear on the warm air, brought him out of his private thoughts. Around him were rustlings, mutterings quickly suppressed; craning his neck, he looked down the side of the hill to where two people, dressed in the black of the mendicant, walked slowly to Tara's mounded crest.

For Covac, who had not seen his nephew since the days of childhood, the first sight of Connal was a shock. By Mannannan, high lord of illusion, could this truly be his brother's son? The skinny brat with the evil temper, could he have grown to a manhood such as this? Maeve, her pale skin against the black cloth giving her a frail look, he clearly recognized. But Connal? Was it possible?

Covac was not alone in startled incredulity; to many of the watchers, both royal and holy, the man and woman who walked with humility to place their hands on the king stone at Tara's summit were the stuff of legend. The Victorious, a chieftain at ten and never yet beaten, and the princess who fought with a spear to each hand, bearing the name of the queen of the faeries; they were names, stories, a tale told by a roaring fire on a winter night. Yet here they were; a man built like a god with black hair streaming in the wind, and a woman with skin of ivory and eyes like the hills of summer.

Covac tore his fascinated gaze from the boy whose birth had kept him from the throne and let it wander, taking note of the faces in the chieftains' trains. A large man, his face white, his eyes expressive, unknown to Covac; a fighter, no doubt, but with a wretchedness in every line of him. Covac looked farther and suddenly went stiff.

A face, two faces close together, and he knew both of them. The hair, the set of the shoulders, most of all the harp; never doubt it, he thought savagely, it is indeed Cormac, my virtuous brother's prying little bard. His face taut with excitement and hatred, he looked to the man who stood beside Cormac.

The snake, sleeping in his lap, squirmed against his cloth bed at Covac's convulsive movement. Brihainn, fatherless brat of the witch Sheilagh; a nice scar he had grown, a fine memento of his own intrusion into things that hadn't concerned him. He heard the sound of the stone as it hit the boy's mouth, nearly felling him, as if it happened now, before his eyes, before the druids, the chieftains . . .

The druid master climbed to his feet, holding his arms wide. "Oinach, seers and rulers all! The council is met, the cases to be stated here, within our sight and hearing. We know who called us here; let them speak. Queen Maeve!"

With a quick look at Connal behind her, she stepped forward, kneeling at the master's feet. His hood, unlike the elders' concealment, was not white. It was stretched across the ivory antlers of a stag, the creature which among all others is sacred to Cernunnos, Lord of the Beasts; the great rack of horns pierced the fabric. The painted face, in disturbing variance to the towering horns, was the replica of the master's own sacred snake, the creature sacred to the worship of every god, all gods. His voice, through this frightening facade, was oddly clear.

"Rise up, woman of Connacht. Rise up and face your people." The clear voice rose, lilted, became a chant, a nasal singsong both monotonous and compelling. "Sword of a song, song of the truth, speak it, speak out."

Maeve's voice rang out, carrying across the hill to reach the vast multitude gathered in the fields below. "Rulers and holy ones all. We come before you, Ulster and

Connacht, to seek a judgment. Months past was my father slain, taken in ambush, and my mother with him. I sat in a river of blood with Flyn's murdered head in my arms and swore a fate on his killer."

"Tell us." The druids had spoken together, in a single voice that rumbled like distant thunder across the uneasy faces surrounding them.

"A ring I found, the ring of Bhoru, the ring of Emain. I knew that Connal called the Victorious came south to punish Cet of Des-Gabair; I knew that none but Connal, none but the lord of Ulster, may wear this ring. I took up the ring, rulers, took up the ring, druids. I took up the ring and swore a fate on him."

"Tell us." It was louder this time, a terrifying hum of voices. Maeve was shivering but her voice held firm, and she continued in the formal, beautiful phrases of the seers.

"An army I gathered, and counsel I took. My captains reasoned with me, seeing me in all my fury and grief. They reasoned with me, wise men, chieftains all, and in their wisdom they prevailed upon me that I should send for a druid, a druid to tell me the truth of my father's death." Her voice raised. "An elder came to Cruachain."

There was movement now, the unending line of white backs in front of Covac moving in a ceaseless, uneasy dance. Maeve let her eyes sweep across them and brought them back to face the people once more.

"An elder came, golden-banded, to my house. The snake dance had been done for me, he told me this. The ring spoke true, he said, the tale was true, that Connal of Ulster had lain in wait to send my father to the Sidh. In grief, in belief, an army I gathered."

"Tell us! Tell us!"

The crowd was chanting now, taking the druids' words and sending them like the wind rippling across the muddy fields. The master held a hand up for silence, and Maeve, her chin straight, went on steadily.

"We crossed from Connacht to Ulster. Three days from the gates of Emain two men came to me, alone they were, unarmed they were, save only for a single spear. They came to me to ask why I had come."

Her voice began to lift, growing louder with each

word. "Connal of Ulster and his handman Brihainn they were. They swore innocence to me, right loudly they swore it; Connal knelt before me, saying the ring of Bhoru was taken from his father's house when he was but a child."

The master raised both hands, an order for silence, and came to the edge of the hill. "Men of Ulster, did your chieftain speak the truth? Step forward and say it."

Halfway down the hillside a body of men moved and muttered. At length one of them stepped uneasily forward. "Master, he spoke the truth; well do I remember the day Sibhainn found it gone, how he shouted and swore. Ten years ago, perhaps more, and the ring gone missing since."

"Note that, seers and rulers." He turned back to Maeve. "Give us the rest."

For the first time her voice faltered on the high phrases of the tribunal. "There is little more to tell, gentle seer. He knelt at my feet and offered his life to me; he said that though he was guiltless, yet a man of Ulster had given my father the death strike, and as he was chieftain, the debt was his to pay." She turned suddenly, blotting out the faceless thousands waiting on her every word, and spoke softly to the snake's mask. "I believe him, Father."

The painted mask, flat, inexpressive, gave nothing away. "We have your story, Queen of Connacht. Chieftain of Ulster, speak your case to your people."

"Tell us," rang the druids' chant, and Connal moved, easily and gracefully, to stand beside Maeve.

"I have little to say, seers and rulers, for I am sore bewildered. All my army can speak for me, that all the time we were in the southlands, I never left their head. The Queen of Connacht can speak for me, that I took the trouble to send to her father a messenger, so that he might not mistake an invasion of Cet's lands for intrusion on Connacht. Carhainn of Connacht and Brihainn of Ulster can speak for me, that I offered my life as forfeit for an Ulster man's crime, though the crime was none of my own."

He looked the master directly in the eye, pitching his deep voice so that every man straining in the distance might hear him. "I am called the Victorious, father. The name was given for courage, for skill, for prowess in war. I have never yet refused a challenge, and those who invade my lands most often leave their heads on the gates of Emain. My courage cannot be called in question.

"I will not fight Connacht. Queen Maeve, in her grief for her father, in her anger for the cowardly way of his death, did the only thing she could do. I will not fight Connacht, not now, not ever."

He finished on an absolute silence. Covac, staring at his nephew, saw the black eyes rest on Maeve. So, not an enemy, but a lover. How stupid, he thought grimly, that among all the possibilities, I never thought on this one. It must be stopped. . . .

The druid master spoke quietly. "You have called this council, chieftain of Ulster. Why? If there is agreement between you, what do we do here?"

Connal opened his mouth, but Maeve forestalled him. Laying a hand on Connal's arm, she stepped to his side and spoke out urgently, pleadingly.

"We are in agreement, yes, but our people are not. In Connacht they are devoured by their memories; they will have vengeance, and in my ignorance I swore to give it them. In Ulster they are eaten with their pride, for Connal has never yet refused a challenge, his people do not love him, and if he refuses to war with me, he will lose them. We are in a snare, father, as sharp and tight as any wolf trap. We come to you for a word, a sign. Tell us what to do."

"It is understood." The calm voice had thickened. "Well do I see what has brought you to this pass. Well, we will do what we can. We will do what we must."

He turned to the ranks of druids, silent now; he looked at the chieftains, come from every corner of the land, sitting close together below the holy circle. Dark clouds had formed in the sky overhead and a few drops of rain fell on the king stone, darkening it.

"The cases have been given, seers, chieftains. Rain is coming, and darkness with it; we will move to the hall of feasting, there to confer, there to decide."

He turned to the two chieftains who had called him.

What he saw, they could not tell; the mask was a blank, telling nothing. Connal, with a sudden feeling of fear he could not have explained, reached out and pulled Maeve back up against his body, holding her there in a pose both tender and protective. From the shelter of his arms she stared with hollow eyes at the master.

"Go now," he said quietly. "Each to your tent, and not together. Send for food, if you wish, and someone to bear you company. I am sorry for it, but you must not be in each other's company while the fates are working. The elders will pray and take counsel of each other; in such a way is the will of the gods made known. When it is time for you, the five notes will sound; listen for it. Now go."

10

One on One

Connal, an imposing figure robed in black, paced the length of his tent, as he had done without pause since the council convened.

He was not alone for the waiting; Cormac and Carhainn sat close together, watching the stormy rhythm of his worry, casting an occasional knowing glance at one another. The sun, present for so brief a time, had been replaced by a driving storm of the kind so common on the Wicklow plains; night was gathering fast, and the heavy sides of the tent rattled and shook as rain lashed against them.

Connal had been silent. Fists clenched, eyes hooded, he strode from one end of the tent to the other, never looking up. Neither of his companions had dared to speak to him in this mood; except for the muttered exchange in which Brihainn had requested his permission to bear Queen Maeve company, nothing had been said.

Now, as if he had been elsewhere and had only just come back to himself, Connal glanced up and for the first time noticed Brihainn's absence. He jerked his head up, to stare at his fili.

"Where is my cela, Cormac?"

"Lord, he has gone to wait with Queen Maeve. Carhainn begged her that he might stay with you, and she granted that. But Brihainn..." The words tailed away.

Connal finished for him. "Brihainn would not have her left to pace her tent with no one to bear her company. Yes." An odd expression, fleeting and unreadable, crossed his face. "He admires your queen greatly, Carhainn."

"As we all do." The words were curt, too abrupt for the courtesy due from a mere fighting man to a chieftain. Yet Carhainn barely seemed to realize what he had said; he was lost in some hell of his own, and his mind was elsewhere.

Connal stopped his angry walking and turned to watch him. He noted the lax hands, the tortured eyes, and into his mind came a bitter memory of an old woman in Annak's bed. He said, very softly, "Carhainn."

The other looked up. "Chieftain?"

"You were lovers." It was a statement, not a question; the man's torment was too deep, too obvious, to be merely that of a man who worshipped what he had never had. And Carhainn, unresentful, replied just as simply.

"We were. Only a few nights, and never to be had again. Yet it was enough, chieftain, or so I thought."

Connal was quick to understand. "I am sorry, my friend. I am sure she never intended pain to you." He saw the full lips thin to a straight line and added, very gently, "She is very young."

Carhainn replied with a pathetic attempt at lightness. "I have said it was enough. It was not to be, and for what I was given, I thank Lugh. She honored me, and if the honor was brief, why, it was yet an honor and will stay with me always." He saw sympathy in the eyes of both men, and his attempt at coolness died. "You are fortunate, chieftain, very fortunate. At first seeing, you took each other, flesh and spirit, and this is as it should be. She must wed a chieftain, not an oinach. I begrudge you nothing."

"Nor I you." The sincerity in Connal's voice was so evident that Carhainn's pain was insensibly eased. He rose to his feet and laid a hand on Connal's shoulder.

"I wondered, chieftain. Do you not mind that you are not the first?"

"Mind?" Connal spoke with an odd intensity; to Cormac, in the peculiar state of passivity that presaged a burst of creativity, the words had a certain rhythm. A song would come from this, whatever else happened, a song for legend, to be passed through the land, mouth to ear. "Why should I mind, captain of Cruachain? I commend her choice and rejoice that she should have taken so fine a man to her bed." He saw the surprise come up in Carhainn's eyes and smiled suddenly. "She is no chattel, no man's possession; she is a queen unto herself, higher in rank than me. Her body is her own, her spirit is her people's. She belongs first to her dagda and the gods, next to her people, and only last to me. It is not my place to mind what she does, and I would not so insult her."

"Yes, I see." Carhainn hesitated, made up his mind, and spoke out. "Nor are we the only ones to love her, chieftain; our queen draws strong feeling from others as the flame draws the moth from the darkness."

Connal shot him a sidelong glance, and spoke somberly. "Brihainn? Yes, I saw it. Some of it I understand; Maeve looks much as Sheilagh did when she was younger."

Something in Connal's voice made Carhainn lift an eyebrow. "Sheilagh, lord?"

"His mother. I left her as shadow for Emain; a woman of beauty and wit, and among my people a warrior second only to myself. Maeve has a look of her; in coloring they are very like, and they are warriors both." He shook his head. "My poor Brihainn. There are things I could tell him, had Sheilagh not sworn me to silence after my father died. Yet though I know his secrets and he does not, they are not mine to tell. Not now."

"Whatever his reasons, he wears his adoration of our queen like a flower; it shines from him." Hesitatingly, Carhainn put the question. "Will it be a trouble to you?"

"I think not. Whatever his feelings, he is loyal to me. More than that, he is no fool, Carhainn. As you saw that Maeve and I were for each other only, so must he have seen it. His eyes see far, his eyes see deep."

Carhainn opened his mouth to answer, but he was forestalled. Clear and sweet over the mounting voice of the storm, five silver notes rang out. They echoed across the distance for an interminable moment and died.

"It is the summons." Cormac, rising to his feet with

both hands clutching his harp, spoke through stiff lips. "The summons to council. They have decided."

"Yes." Connal threw his fur across his back and fastened it with hands that shook slightly. "An answer for all of us, cela. To the banqueting hall, then. Attend me."

They ran through the rain toward the torches. Maeve, with Brihainn at her elbow, was there before him; as Connal entered the great room and stood blinking in the firelight, it seemed that every living thing in Hibernia was gathered to watch him. He looked sideways at Maeve, standing proud and silent before the master, and approached the high chair.

"We will have silence."

The snake's mask moved in the shadows, the stag's horns were glinting and burnished with copper. Men crowded against the rough walls, shoulder to shoulder in the vast throng. All faces were turned toward the head of the hall, where that uncanny figure stood, hands raised, voice poised.

"Ulster and Connacht, meet before me."

Side by side they stood, faces expectant. From under the cloak of Maeve's hood there had escaped a few curling tendrils of hair. Connal saw the raindrops glisten.

The master's voice was even, measured, emotionless.

"You came to us with a problem, Maeve of Connacht, Connal of Ulster, a problem not your own, but of your tuatha. An answer was needed, and an answer begged. The council is met, the answer is given."

Silence, a well of quiet. All that waiting body of humanity seemed to be holding its breath.

"For yourselves, you have shown honor. For your people, it is not enough. More you shall give them, and give them what waits now in the hand of the god."

Behind him, waiting, watching, the faceless horde of druids moved up closer.

"Tomorrow, if it rains or if it suns on us, you will fight for your people. Each will have two weapons, choose what you will. Rain or sun, when the trumpet sounds, to the great plain Bregia you will go. None but you, chieftains, each to represent your people, north and south, Ulster and Connacht. In the sight of your people, in the sight of the gods, there you will fight. Men will not wait for you, the gods will not wait for you. Fight you will, until one of you is dead and honor satisfied, vengeance claimed."

"No," said Maeve thinly. Her face was lifted, tilted, as though to some uncanny music none but she could hear. "You cannot do this. No."

"The name of the victor is with the gods, the life of the loser the prize for the taking. One of you will kill the other, and when that is done, there will be no war between your people. Should both of you still live when the fight is done, two new chieftains will sit in your place."

"To the death." Connal's face was blank, an empty slate, blind and barren. "To the death."

"The council has spoken, and honor will be met. Tomorrow, when the trumpets sound. There is no more to say."

And then there was movement, voices raised in shock, in exclamation, bodies released from their tension to twist for the doors of the hall. The druid master, with his train behind him, swept past them and out into the night. Men went behind them, pouring out into the rain, talking, whispering.

The hall emptied out, until only five remained.

Brihainn was weeping, letting the tears pour down his face, unaware and unashamed. Carhainn had turned from the others to stand, eyes closed, his face to the wall. Cormac had dropped to his knees, his lips moving in prayer.

They faced each other, the chieftains. Maeve lifted her eyes to Connal's face. They held no tragedy, no sorrow, for the look was that of one who had already died.

"Don't leave me," she said quietly. "I beg you."

He reached out for her, caught by those dead eyes, that still body. "Never, Maeve. Never."

Oblivious to the excitement that ran through the camp like a firestorm, oblivious to the agony of those who loved them, Connal and Maeve faced each other on what, for one of them, must be the last night of life.

They had sent the others away, three men weeping and choked with agony, to wait out the night together in

Maeve's tent. Now they stood alone, where only an hour before Connal had paced, awaiting the council's decision, and for too long a time neither could find any words for the other. Silence, bewildered and desperate, hung over the cold room like a pall of unshed tears.

To the death. Whatever they had expected, of anything the council might have decided, this was something that had occurred to neither of them. There was little doubt as to who must win; though Maeve was a deadly fighter with the advantages of speed and weapons, she could not hope to outlast a man who had been warring since his tenth year. The same thought was in both their minds.

"The council must have known that." Maeve, realizing that she had spoken aloud, jumped a little. Her voice was hollow, empty. "Even if I was so minded, I could not have hoped to defeat you in hand-to-hand combat. They must have known that, Connal. How not?"

"Yes, they knew. May Crom curse them all!"

The violence in his voice brought Maeve a little way out of the terrible numbness of mind that had taken hold of her. She took one of his hands in both of hers.

"We should not be together, I suppose."

Connal laughed, a sharp, bitter bark. "What will they do to us in their displeasure, Maeve? Kill us?"

Her hands gripped tighter. "Connal, what can we do?"

"I don't know." The words were flat; he had not raised his eyes from the floor. "I don't know, my beautiful one. I know only that of any fate they might have chosen for us, this is the cruelest. I know only that death, madness, an eternity spent howling in the hills as the fomori took me, would have been better than this."

"Better, and easier to bear." It was still remote, still so far from her; why cannot I weep? she wondered. Why will the easy tears not come? "Tomorrow, he said, whether it be wet or fair."

Connal sounded savage. "On the wide plain, with all the world to watch this travesty." He gave a short, hollow laugh. "May the gods pity me, I never thought to find myself fighting as a mummery show for others."

"You must win tomorrow."

She was still detached, and said only what seemed, to her, to be a simple fact. But the words acted on Connal like a stroke of lightning. Whipping round, he caught a handful of the red hair and wrenched her close. He spoke through clenched teeth, his face inches from her own.

"Win? Have you run mad, queen of the southlands? We can neither of us win. Do you think I could do this thing and live afterward?" The grip on her hair tightened painfully. "Could you? Think, Maeve. Supposing you best me, you two-handed warrior, supposing you drive me to my knees in the mud tomorrow. Can you see it?"

It was closer now, reality moving ever nearer, the thin shell of deathly calm perilously close to collapsing. As if he saw it, wanted it, his other hand moved with the full strength of his arm behind it. As he had done once before, he took her chin and pulled her face upward. Under the long fingers the pale skin showed livid.

"Vision that, my queen, vision it as you love me. My body stretched, awaiting the death strike. The crowd cheering. My face in the mud. You stand above me, you straddle me, a spear to each hand. Your arms will lift—"

With a shattering stab of pain, the unnatural calm broke. Maeve made a single sound deep in her throat, the sound of a creature in mortal pain. Suddenly the stiff body was a moving whirlwind and she was crying with a muffled screaming terrible to hear, thrashing, unmindful of anything but the pain she had refused to acknowledge, returning to devour her. Both hands lashed out, leaving long scratches; Connal, releasing her only to gather her in, saw that tufts of red hair had come away in his hands.

He pulled her close and held her there.

As suddenly as the storm had broken, it was gone. The choked wailing became plain tears, the clenched fists opened to fall, limp and compliant, on the folds of his robe. Under her fingernails were shreds of skin; blood, straight thin trickles of it, moved sluggishly from the scratches on his face and ebbed away to nothing.

"Forgive me." He bent to lay his bleeding cheek against her hair, his voice no more than a husky whisper. "I ask your pardon. We must both live or both die; there is no other way. There is no honor in their solution, none, but to the council's voice there can be no appeal."

She raised her face. The green eyes were bright, burning from some source he could not see; they held knowledge, desperation; so many things. He stared down at her, watching, waiting. When she spoke again, her words took his breath away.

"I care nothing for the morrow, whether I live or die. All I care for is tonight, Connal. We will have tonight." The pale hands reached out to him, tracing the passage of drying blood down one cheek. "Will you take me, then?"

Memories, moving and dancing, jumbled and clear. He saw her as he had seen her first. Red hair tousled from sleep, green eyes blinking in the onslaught of unexpected light, soft white arms reaching to cover her nakedness, perfect pale breasts gleaming like ivory, like the snow that dressed the hills in winter...

"Connal. I beg you, chieftain. Do not deny me this."

He seemed to have lost control of his hands. Unsure of themselves, fumbling like babies trying to catch the wind, they fell tentatively on the rounded shoulders, curled a strand of hair around one finger, dropped it, moved down to untie the black robe that so loosely covered the silken skin, the pale breasts that he remembered.

Fascinated, unable to tear his eyes away, he watched the hands—surely they were his hands—pulling at the rough cord, tensing as the knot resisted and then surrendered to his twitching fingers. He saw the waterfall of black cloth sliding like shadows over light, to drop to the floor and lay forgotten as he was confronted by the beauty of her, the long legs, the small waist, the play of red on white, the golden bottomless mystery of a woman. Her pulse, a single jewel throbbing in the hollow of her throat, jumped and fluttered. A wild rose, a burning rose, a queen, a victim...

The hands, still not a part of him, moved without his direction. They stroked her shoulders and lightly, so lightly, slid across her breasts; one slid down to cup the curve of her waist, the other moving up to rest, palm open, where neck met shoulder. So slender a throat, he thought; if I close my hand, I believe the fingers will meet. On an impulse, a sudden inexplicable need to see if he was right, he tightened his grip. Around the alabaster curve his fingertips touched, a necklace of living flesh.

She arched under it, her backbone rippling. Her head fell back, as though of a sudden too heavy for the slender neck to support, and a sudden tremor ran through her like wind on lake water. Her lips trembled up into a smile, joyous and complete.

The small hands were moving, pulling at his robes, winding painfully tight in his hair, fastening on his body with a mastery all their own; her teeth buried deep in the lobe of one ear, and a soft voice whispered incomprehensible endearments that seemed to be part of the thunder in his mind. He was drowning, she had surrounded him like the storm that lashed the night outside these walls. . . .

Connal would not remember lowering her to the floor, when his senses were his own again. He would find a painful bite on one ear and long scratches down his back, and he would have no memory, none at all, as to how they came there. He would remember nothing but the body below him, the coming together, spirit, flesh, laughter, endless tears falling. He was lost in it, lost in her, believing through the roaring furnace in his blood that this perfect lovemaking, in which every moment of his life merged with everything he had ever wanted, would somehow keep the morning back.

Across the plain Covac waited through the dark hours for the day to come with its gifts and benisons.

His face had frozen into a smile that had not altered since the scene in the banquet hall. It had taken all his courage, that speech to the druid master, but he had never lacked courage, after all, and for an enemy's blood, for the sweet taste of revenge, he would dare much. Whether Connal's blood or Maeve's, it mattered not at all.

The wind, carrying a taste of cold and wet, seeped into the tent and brushed his ankles. Covac noticed nothing of it; he sat smiling, his hands twined together, in a state of dark amusement that was almost glee.

Had he really feared these druids? He thought back to the banqueting hall, chieftains ranging first this way and then another, arguing about honor, debating what to do. And the druids, those holy men renowned for their wisdom, they had been no better. Some had meditated, some had been silent, others had brought forth suggestions as nebulous as they were unsatisfactory.

All but the master. He was disturbing, this high seer; it was not merely the frightening facade of the horned snake, the mask of Cernunnos, Lord of the Beasts. There was a depth to him, a stillness, that Covac recognized as someone who possessed that same quality could do. He had sat quietly, listening to the debate rage around him, saying nothing at all. The horned head had turned this way and that, but the voice behind the mask was silent. Waiting . . .

Covac closed his eyes now and laughed in silent ecstasy, laughed until he rocked to and fro, his arms wrapped around himself, tears of pure enjoyment streaking his face.

Sure, and the gods took care of those who dared. How simple it had been to lean over, to drop his suggestion into that painted ear, in tones of reason and sober judgment. And how very readily the master had accepted it!

Well, no matter who died on the morrow, he would savor every moment of this time. He remembered the frozen misery on Maeve's face as sentence was pronounced, and the disbelief on Connal's. Tears had swollen Brihainn's scar; let the tears choke all of them, let the salty water seep deep into Cormac's harp and swell it past use, past redemption.

The nightmare smile widened under the hood. Lovers, and one must slay the other or both would die. And this in the name of honor, a snare from which there was no escape, no salvation.

Oh, what a jest, a jest for all the gods who watched in the world! A lover to die under a lover's spear, at a lover's hand; he could not have dreamed of a better revenge on them, the red-haired whelp who had escaped him and left three of his men dead in the road, the little rat grown to manhood, whom he would have killed at birth had he been there to do it.

Like a black cloud over his amusement, he suddenly remembered the look of the master, the unearthly stillness of those golden horns, that snake's face. Carelessness was a bad enemy, and it would not do to believe oneself beyond failure; sure, and the man would be no fool, not a man chosen to the highest seat of power in the land. He had not liked the watchful feel of the master, not liked the way the snake had turned slowly to meet his own mask, dark, considering. What had he been thinking about, that hidden man?

Had it, in fact, been too easy? Sure, and it had been a simple enough thing to quietly drop the seeds of his own deadly suggestion here and there among the ruminating elders; enough of them had taken it up, set the idea of a personal combat before the master, to make the casting of portents the obvious course of action. The master had done so, but in secret; no man had seen those auguries, and there had been none to interpret them but the master. He had consented, true, but to what end? What had he seen there, and what darkness or light had moved through that subtle mind?

As if in answer to his musings, the white sack at his feet abruptly moved. The snake, disobedient to the instinct of its kind, had woken in the chilly night; it must be fed, let out of its darkness awhile. Covac turned to the small woven cage in the room's far corner. Inside, sleeping and quiet now, was a young linnet.

Carefully, using the pronged fork of birch, he lifted the snake bag and loosened the ties. Though the snake had been dropped into his hand as though straight from the gods, though it had made no attempt to bite him, the old terror remained. He would never be easy with the creatures; let him once put some distance between himself and the necessity for these white robes, and he would kill the thing.

For now, however, he needed the snake. Holding the bag at arm's length, he opened the cage door. Quickly, before the linnet could come to itself and escape, he dropped the half-opened bag into the cage and closed the door once more.

It emerged slowly, a sensuous twist of shining scales,

its flat head lifting, looking for food. It found the linnet at once, for the bird, its instincts tuned toward survival, had sensed the snake immediately and was shrilling piteously, beating its wings against its prison, desperate for freedom.

Covac, smiling, sat and prepared to enjoy himself.

The linnet had no chance. Its plumage, which had not yet changed to spring camouflage from winter white, ruffled madly as it forced its small body against the unyielding roof of the cage. The snake, interested and hungry, darted its head from side to side as it began its graceful pursuit. Covac heard the frenzied trilling suddenly muffle as the snake, its versatile jaws opening wide, caught it by its back end and began, in the way of snakes feeding, to suck it in.

Covac sat, one booted leg slung over the other, listening to the bird die and thinking of what he must do.

Almost certainly Connal would take the contest; a young chit of a girl could not hope to match the endurance and strength of a seasoned fighter, however agile she was, however many hands she used. Yes, Maeve would certainly die. And then?

There was no one to succeed her on the throne of Connacht, no other children, no kin. Flyn had had no brothers and sisters, he knew that much, and among all the talk flying on the plains this last week was one thing that had interested him greatly. Nieve once had a sister, a sister who had died in childbed. The child, a girl named Ahnrach, had been killed in an ambush some years back, when Queen Maeve was but a child. A pretty child, it was said, with the red hair of the royal family. . . .

So her name had been Ahnrach, that heap of bone and dust who slept now under a gray cairn on a windy hilltop. It was something to know that, something he would remember when next he stood and rested his hands on those dark stones.

With Maeve dead at Connal's hands, the throne of Cruachain would stand empty awhile. Not for long, for the druids would never allow it, but for a little time, at least, all the rich lands to the south of the Iron Hills would be leaderless, ripe for forays, ripe for the taking.

He tucked the information away at the back of his

mind and considered what would be the outcome if, by some stroke of the gods, Maeve somehow triumphed.

Well, should that happen, there would be some reward. In terms of raids, of death to be given, it would not be nearly so satisfactory, for Ulster with its chieftain dead yet had better defenses than Connacht ever could. Of course, there was a question here, too, as to who would reign as chieftain with Connal dead.

Covac laughed aloud, in genuine amusement. He had long suspected what his brother had fondly imagined to be a secret known to no one; that secret, if Connal should die, might suddenly take on importance to the north. . . .

Like his counterpart in Cruachain, Sibhainn had only the one child that the world knew of. The old fury rose in Covac, a bitter bile, as if at an insult freshly given. Sibhainn had a brother, of course, but that brother, though entitled by birth, could never come at the throne of Emain. Still, if one could have neither power nor birthright, one could at least take the solace offered by a sweet revenge.

Covac thought back to a love affair before Connal was born, a love affair broken by the woman, and to the child born to her. A half sibling for the filthy brat Mhora had at last succeeded in bearing two years later? Perhaps. Certainly the bitch's brat looked upon the world with the long dark eyes of the royal line.

If his suspicions were true, if Connal knew the truth, then the choice of new chieftain on Connal's death should be obvious. And, if that happened, the new chieftain of Emain should Maeve emerge the victor on the morrow would find himself with an enemy both deadly and secret.

No, should Maeve take the day, the material rewards would not be nearly so great. Yet, in a way, it would be even sweeter to see his nephew's blood running free to mingle with the trampled mud of Wicklow.

The snake was sated now, curled up, the shining scales pulsing in a slow, contented rhythm. Around the floor of the cage a few white feathers lay scattered. Covac rose slowly, languidly, to his feet and crossed the room. Reaching a careful hand through the bars, he prodded the creature lightly with the birch fork; sluggish but obedient, it inched its way back into the bag, replete, ready for sleep.

Well, tomorrow would bring the answers. No point to sit and wonder who would win and who would die; whatever happened, one thing was certain. Covac would be watching.

"Connal?"

Deep in the arms of sleep, troubled by fleeting dreams of love and death that had come and gone across his spirit the whole night through, he heard the soft voice call him.

"Wake, my man. Morning has come."

By the gods, what a lovely voice; purity it had, and clarity, and the sweetness of the lark at daybreak. Yet he did not want to wake; something waited, a doom he could not remember, and to sleep was to keep it off from him. . . .

"Connal."

He opened his eyes to gray light and a shower of red hair falling across his bare shoulders.

Maeve, yes. Maeve's voice calling him back to the waking world, Maeve's fiery hair a veil across his vision, Maeve's flesh, warm and vital, pressed up against the curve of his back like two spoons fitting together, like the two snakes of the crest of Emain, entwined, entangled, devouring each other, impossible to split.

It came back to him in a rush, the night, the perfect exchange of body and spirit, salt and oil. Morning now, cold morning, bitter morning, the sun lying across the plains of Tara, and he must rise, dress, choose a weapon.

A groan broke from him, a harsh, tortured sound. Soft white arms encircled as much of him as they could, tears fell against his back. For a while they lay together, silent and cold. After a while he could bear no more of it.

"What weapons will you take, darling girl?"

She sounded calm to the point of indifference. "Spears, I suppose, or slings. What does it matter? Were I twice your girth and possessor of ten times your skill, I could not kill you. It is all charade." She rubbed her cheek against his neck. "What does it matter?"

"You speak the truth." He spoke dully. Staring out across the room, he caught the gleam of gold where two crowns lay; in the heat of the previous night's discovery they had been discarded, dropped and forgotten. *As we will be,* he thought, *when this wicked day is done. Discarded, dropped, forgotten. . . .*

He began to cry. He had not wept this way, not ever, and the tears produced choking sobs that wracked his body and sent the bed shuddering under them. Maeve held him, whispering what comfort she could, soothing and warm.

When the fit had passed, he rolled over on his back and regarded her. "Your courage shames me."

"Courage?" He saw her lips lift. "No courage here, Connal; if I die, why then, I die content, for I take what we had last night with me. Whatever happens, we had last night, and I regret nothing."

He reached out to her, his fingers tracing that curving smile, and was conscious of wonderment. "And you say that is not courage? Yes, love, you shame me indeed." He sat up and pulled her into his lap. "Well, I will take a lesson from you; when we meet on the plain today, I will carry last night with me as a buckle and a shield."

She tilted her head at him. "A shield against me?"

"A shield against the curiosity of others. A shield against what can happen, what may happen." He kissed her and set her gently from him. "You must go and dress for the meeting, as must I. Go now."

She bent to retrieve her black cloak, and set the crown of Connacht on her hair in silence. When she was dressed, she made for the door without another look.

As she reached the hide and put a hand out to lift it, she heard his voice behind her, speaking in tones that were almost conversational. "My left leg is slightly longer than my right. No one knows that. No one knows, either, that my balance from the left is not so good as the other way. If an opponent knew that when battling me, they might find some advantage in it. Remember it; I am weaker, more vulnerable, from the left."

She was very still, only the sudden clenching of her

small fists betraying that she had heard. After a long pause
she, too, spoke matter-of-factly.

"I, too, have one or two weaknesses as a fighter,
though I would tell no one else. Though I see a spear
coming with the vision of the gods, I am not near so quick
at dodging stones and flints from a sling. And a word of
advice for those I battle: keep your head straight, and
never bare your neck to either of my spears, for both
hands are deadly. Some advice, an exchange among warriors only."

"Among warriors only," he repeated, but she was
gone, the hide falling with a dull thud into place behind
her. Thoughtful, an idea taking shape slowly in his mind,
he thrust his head through the door and called for Brihainn
to come and help him prepare.

Brihainn answered the summons so promptly that
Connal, tight-lipped and preoccupied, realized that his
best friend must have been waiting outside. Waiting all
night, perhaps; Brihainn was wet, his eyes red-rimmed
and exhausted. He had the look of a man who had not
slept.

"A spear, Brihainn, a spear and a sling. If we are to
make a show for the amusement of the oinach, we will do
it with dignity and do it well. There are some practice
stones in my pack; find them for me."

Into the hollow eyes came a spark of life. "Practice
stones, chieftain? Not sharpened flints?"

"Help me with my boots. Sharpened flints? Have you
run mad? Do you really think I would use true weapons of
war against the other half of my soul? It would be two
crimes, not one, murder and suicide alike." He jerked his
head sideways and found Brihainn staring at him open-
mouthed. The tight lips slid into a mocking smile.

"Yes, Brihainn, you understood me aright. Practice
flints; they may cause pain and some convincing bruises,
but never death. Now. Take my spear; I saw some heavy
stones behind my tent. One of them should be the right
shape and size, heavy enough to dull a spearpoint with."

Brihainn's eyes closed, his whole body slumping in
relief. "I will do that quickly, for the day is coming to the
full and the trumpets must sound soon."

"Go."

In her tent across the field, Maeve had finished struggling into her battle clothes. She had never worn the heavy leather leggings before, save in practice during her childhood, and they felt strange. When she had finished dressing, she stared down at herself with some amusement. Odd, the things men wore; yet there was a freedom to them, an easiness of movement, that was pleasing. She laced the soft, heavy boots and reached for her copper breastplate.

Carhainn, fastening it from behind, had turned overnight from a man in his prime to an old man. He had attended his lady in silence, so deep in his misery that the strange lightness of her face and speech had escaped him.

"Where are my two spears, Carhainn?"

"Here, lady, against the wall." He brought them dangling loosely from hands limp and trembling. As he made to lay them across her hands, he was arrested by the smile, the light in her eyes. "Lady?"

"Find me a stone, beloved captain, a heavy stone, and bring it here quickly. The trumpets will sound at any moment, and I have much to do."

"High Danu," he whispered, and ran from the tent on weak legs. Within a few minutes he had returned, a solid rock in his hands.

She took it from him and sat on her bed, the spear held tight between her knees. Bending her head in concentration, she began to pound the point of the spear, working quickly and steadily, until the lethal edge had dulled and the point had rounded, not enough to be detected by the hordes who would watch the fight, not enough to render it useless. It was sharp enough still to cause a bloody scratch, but it was no longer deadly.

"You mean to wound but not to kill."

Carhainn, staring at her, had whispered. She tested the spear against the side of her hand, nodded in satisfaction and laid it to one side.

"Truth." She smiled and reached for the second spear. "How not? I was lied to, betrayed by a druid who must have had some reason to wish me ill, forced into this travesty of honor by the lust of the crowd. Wound, perhaps, but kill? Never, Carhainn."

"But if the master learns of it . . ."

"Yes? And what will he do, Carhainn? Kill us?"

Her voice was scathing. Whistling, her bent neck looking unnaturally long without the cascade of hair to hide it, she bent to the second spear. As she once again began the methodical hammering that would disable her second weapon, a peculiar noise made her lift her head and regard the man who had once been her lover. He was laughing.

11

Spear and Sling

Under a sky showing sunlight with ominous storm clouds behind, the hosts of Hibernia gathered on the vast plain to watch the kill.

Few among the watchers expected any surprises; the fight would surely last for as long as Maeve could lift a spear, and not a moment longer. Many of those present had fought against Connal's army, and a few had come to their present power because their fathers had fought Ulster's chieftain hand to hand. That a young girl, however potent a fighter, might best him was out of the question; that he might stand back and let her do it never entered their heads.

So they came slowly, singly or attended, each trying for the best vantage point from which to see. Of all the chieftains at Wicklow this day, the two most concerned had brought with them the smallest retinues; surrounded by the ruling classes of the five provinces and the hosts of sanctuary, the combined representatives of Ulster and Connacht numbered less than ten. Three of them, a captain, a cela, and a bard, stood shoulder to shoulder at the very front of the rest, watching and waiting.

To the east and west clear paths had been left. Up each of these came the two chieftains, dressed for battle, holding their own weapons, alone and unattended. Heads swiveled to watch them, and the sudden buzz of excitement rippled through the huge crowd, a hum of voices that moved like wind through the clover.

Connal, the sleeves of his black jerkin stark against the sheen of his breastplate, looked like a statue of the lord of the beasts come to life. The copper and iron flashed where the sun struck it, the black beneath accentuated his enormous height. A sling was thrust through his belt; in his left hand he carried the soft pouch that held the deadly flints, and in his right was a short spear. The bronze helmet, horned and ornamented with jewels, gave him the look of some fantastic beast out of legend. As impressive as he looked, however, few eyes followed his progress. All attention was riveted on Maeve.

Many of those present were fili, brought by their lords to record what was happening. Of all the songs that were made that day, no one ever heard one that did not include the young Queen of Connacht, so lasting, so great was the impression she made.

Of all those watching, no one was harder hit than Brihainn. He stared down, his eyes glazing suddenly as a wind from the past moved through him, heavy and irresistible. Connal was his lord, his lifelong friend, but he had no eyes for Connal. It was Maeve, Maeve slender and beautiful, Maeve who had suddenly pulled him back into another time with her, a time where the young Brihainn, fleeing from two men who would have spitted him on the end of a spear, watched his warrior mother with a warhorse between her knees bring them down, killing one, driving the other as though he were no more than a stray sheep that must be herded home.

Like Connal, she combined the ores of the warrior, the gems of the royally born, and the black of the mendicant. But the effect on Maeve was precisely opposite that of Connal; in the gleaming metals she seemed ethereal, a faery, a spirit sent to guide the dying to the waiting Sidh; against her white skin the black looked like widow's weeds. The waterfall of flaming hair was completely hidden, bound tight so as not to distract her eye, and covered by a helm. Under the fitted bronze her neck rose like a lily stem, so fragile, so slender, so very beautiful; in each hand was a short spear, the ends wrapped in doeskin.

The field of battle, a slight hollow surrounded by four gentle slopes, was of a size to give the two combatants enough room to maneuver. It ran a length of some fifty feet and came to a width of slightly less; most of it was flat, and all of it was muddy.

They met at its center, their faces a few inches apart, and waited for the master's signal. Through the banded helm Connal's eyes showed shadowed and hollow. His whisper could not have been heard by anyone but Maeve.

"When you begin to tire, my darling, I will know it and drop my guard. Remember what I told you, and kill me then."

Her lips curled into the smile he loved. "I can but wound you with damaged weapons, chieftain."

The black eyes suddenly blazed. As he opened his mouth to answer, the master stepped forward.

"It will begin," he said calmly, and the watching men closed in.

For Maeve, her mind oddly empty, time dropped away. She was a child again, the precious treasure of the King of Connacht, learning to use every inch of her body under the tutelage of the finest teacher of arms that Flyn could procure. The noise of the crowd, an intolerable hum, faded and was gone as the years closed in and took her, to be replaced by her father's beloved voice, terse, encouraging.

Drop to the left, Maeve, you must learn that. Your guard is weak, suppose you fight an adversary who can give you three hand spans in height and reach, what will you do then? Good, well and good. Turn to the left . . .

Her left shoulder came up, tense and stiff, compensating for her slower reflexes in the way she had been taught yet had never been completely comfortable with. Flyn was here, surely he was here, an invisible presence behind her, pointing, placing, whispering suggestions. *Cast first from the left, Maeve, and put the enemy on his guard on that side. It will leave the right open to your wishes, well done, very well done, princess, darling girl. . . .*

Had someone else not called her darling girl, someone with as much right, someone recently? She raised her left arm, leaping backward in a crouch, her right foot finding a momentary footing in the treacherous mud.

Something seemed to be happening to her memory; who were all these people, these unfriendly faces that ringed her like hungry wolves, watching her, admiring, considering? Those three up there at the very edge, surely she had known them, and why were they watching her with anguish clear to see? Who was this tall warrior in the black and gold, circling to her right?

There was sweat on her face, tiny droplets gathering where helm met flesh, beading to fall into her eyes. She shook her head, circling sideways, and with the full strength of her left arm cast the short spear.

Unlike Maeve, Connal had done this many times before. The motions of hand-to-hand combat were easy, second nature to him. Unlike Maeve, no blankness came across his mind to relieve him, and no friendly voice from a loved one long gone spoke at his shoulder. He was captured in the present, hating the watching crowd, anguished and torn.

But he saw the stiffening of her arm, the beautiful precision of her drop, and his head jerked up to her face. The green eyes were no longer wide, no longer beautiful; they were slits behind the thin bands, and they held madness.

His mouth went dry. Was it terror, then, that had come to unhinge her, terror, or something else he could not name? He did not know. He knew only that the girl he had taken, the soft body that had pressed against him in the empty hours, the lips that had smiled to tell him she had crippled her weapons for him, were for this moment no longer Maeve.

Crippled weapons . . .

At that moment, as understanding came to him, she cast the spear. The crowd was roaring, fists waving, feet stamping; at the edge of the arena he caught a flying glimpse of Carhainn, mouth agape, shouting something that was swept away in the larger noise of the watchers.

Instinct and knowledge came together. He leaped to one side, but not far enough; the spear, cast with deadly accuracy, grazed his left shoulder a bare inch beneath where the protective armor ended. Bright blood welled up from the gash and ran in a cold flood down his arm. The spear, with a scrap of black jerkin caught on its tip, fell to the mud a few feet behind him.

Crippled indeed, he thought, and wrenched the sling free of his belt. Had the spear been whole, it would have taken flesh three inches deep from my arm and crippled me instead. She was moving now, running like a deer, quick and close to the earth. With a somersault that sent up a spray of mud, she hit the ground behind him and came up with the spear held once again in her left hand.

Flints, said her father's voice in her ear, *he is reaching for his flints. Keep your neck down, the muscles loose enough to move your head quickly.* She dropped once more, and as suddenly as it had come, the madness fell from her, and she was on her feet, a spear to each hand, and the man who towered like a black god some twenty feet away was Connal; Connal, her lover, all that mattered, and there was blood on his arm, a gash, what had she done?

He was too far away to see the change in her. He had but one thought in his mind, and that was to hit her hard enough to bring her mind back, yet not hard enough to do more than cause a bruise. The long body arched itself, shoulders straight, back tensed. Taking careful aim, not knowing whether she might cast again if he waited too long, he slipped the blunted flint backward into its place and let it fly, not at the exposed neck, but at her left hand.

Connal, she thought, oh Connal, no, and then she moved, legs together, feet pointed, leaping to one side. But she had not moved quickly enough, and she had no way of knowing the strength of his arm, no way of judging how fast the flint would travel. From her position on the ground she did not realize that he stood in the hollow while she lay at the first gentle curve of the slope, slightly above him.

The flint struck her squarely on the neck. Even blunted, it knocked her to the ground; had the missile been for war and not for practice, it would have severed the great vein, sent her lifeblood pumping out to turn the trampled earth scarlet.

She fell with a smothered cry, and the spear dropped from her left hand as her reflexes sent it flying to the place where the flint had struck, stroking, rubbing, clutching hard. The first shock to her neck and jaw gave way to a flood of pain down her left side and a sudden numbness in the fingers of her left hand. Her own hasty movement had deflected the weapon; instead of harmlessly striking clenched fingers, it had found one of those mysterious nerve links, disabling it, damaging it.

Frozen in place, horrified, Connal saw her bend once more for her second spear, saw the fingers scrabble aimlessly for the hilt, saw them come up empty. Her armor splattered with mud, she got to her feet, her left arm dangling limp and useless. The fingers of her right hand closed tightly over the second spear.

On the scree above them Carhainn closed his eyes. "Her left arm is gone," he said flatly, and Brihainn, who stood at his shoulder, took Carhainn's shoulder in a tight grasp. "She has no chance if she cannot use her left arm; without the second hand she is only another warrior, and no one-handed warrior in the five provinces can withstand Connal."

"He will not kill her." Cormac, pressed close against them, spoke desperately. "He will not. He cannot."

"He must." Brihainn could not tear his eyes from the scene in the hollow below him. So young, so beautiful; could Connal truly bring himself to do it? "I pray only that he makes it clean, and quick."

Maeve had gone from madness to sanity. Now, with one side of her upper body dead, she moved into an unthinking calm that was a blend of both. Flyn's voice was with her once again, a shade from the Sidh, consoling and welcoming. *Soon, darling girl, you will be with me. A hard thing, a bitter thing, but you will accept it with the courage and grace you showed to Carhainn when Ahnrach died. Yes, he told me all, how good you were to him....*

She planted herself once again, measuring the distance between herself and her lover with eyes blurred by tears. Her strength, along with whatever durability she possessed, seemed to have vanished like summer rain with the blow to the neck; her legs were beginning the sporadic trembling that meant exhaustion and frustration. Flyn's voice faded, and Nieve spoke now, spoke not to her but to Carhainn on that last day. Guard our daughter well, captain. . . .

She raised her head, seeing the encircling faces that kept her here as open mouths, staring eyes, washed by the red mist across her vision. Carhainn stood at the edge of the hollow, staring down at her. She lifted her head and spoke quietly to him, as though he stood alone, as though he could hear her through the screaming men surrounding him.

"I am sorry," she said. "But I am not worth very much, truth to tell; their death was proof of that. I sent my blessing with my mother, and the gods laughed to hear me. For what I have done to you, I am sorry. Forgive me."

Across the distance that separated them, lost in the odd mist of unreality once again, she thought she saw him nod. Then she forgot him utterly, forgot his very existence as she turned back once more to face Connal, a black and glittering doom. A fate on me, she thought. My fate is on me. Well, I would rather die this way; better at his hand than a lifetime spent empty, knowing I sent him to the Sidh and had not the courage to follow him there. She saw the stance, saw him fit another flint, and set herself up for the spear cast. She saw the thin flash of his helm as he turned to follow her motion, and knew he had spoken the truth to her before the master's signal.

She was tiring, and he saw it; if she cast the spear now, cast it straight for his throat, he would drop his guard and let her do it.

Courage, she thought, and the sly, insinuating voices from the world of light agreed mockingly in her mind. Such courage demands a like courage of me. Will I slay him, then, knowing that I kill the only thing worth living for, for fear of what these ravening beasts above us may do to me? By all the gods, waiting for the death strike, I will not.

Strength was coming back now, flooding into her. Planting her legs as best she could, she turned her face to Connal and nodded. To the crowd above, it might have been no more than a tremble of exhaustion. But Connal, his face creased into a nightmare grimace, saw it and understood.

The flint sailed past her head, a good six inches to the right. Unflinching, she hurled her second spear; the voices of her parents had become different voices, her own, perhaps, pushing at her, agreeing, disagreeing. Throw wide right, then, and let it land, too far beyond him to retrieve it. You still have one spear, and he must have only a few more flints. After that it will be spear to spear, and whatever happens then is with the gods. . . .

Her spear fell fifteen feet beyond him, its blunted point buried in the soft mud. Macha, Morrigan, Boann of the rivers, she thought calmly, it is with you now.

She reached for her remaining spear and took it up.

Connal, his fingers closing around his last flint, saw her stride forward with the spear held tight to one shoulder. His hand dropping, he raised his head and met her eyes.

It was all there, written across her face under the banded helm for him to see. She had thrown the spear away, far enough so that no one believed he would let her take it up again; she had only the one spear remaining, only one weapon to her hand, and only one hand to use it.

The pouch that held his last flint fell at his feet. Bringing one foot up, never taking his eyes from her face, he kicked the pouch away. It soared in a graceful arc, turning over and over. Falling some twenty feet away, it sank and was lost in the soggy ground. Gasps went up, cries from the watching crowd. With a single motion he pulled his own spear free of its shoulder sheath. Those he had fought recognized the clean, easy way it nestled in those long fingers, and their eyes turned in a collective rush to Maeve.

She was smiling, not the smile of madness, but the smile of the girl who had pulled him tight up against her, the girl who had stood above him in her tent on the road to Emain, the girl who had held his spear above his bared neck and refused to kill him for what he had not done. She spoke to him, gently and easily, for his ears alone, and the words went through him as no weapon she could have hurled at him could have done, sharp and clean.

"An end to it, my chieftain," she said. "The first to lose a spear will die."

"No," he said harshly, "you cannot do this."

"Make it a clean death, as you love me," she whispered, and turned her back to him.

It happened too quickly for him to see what she meant to do. He had heard the garbled tales of her speed with her chosen weapons, but he had not truly seen it. Now he did. One moment she was inches from him, exposing her back, every movement telling him in the language of the body that she meant to walk away. The next she had dropped to one knee, in the fastest and best coordinated motion he had ever seen, and thrown her last remaining weapon. It sailed over his head, hit a stone half buried in the mud and snapped in half.

Silence fell, a silence like nightfall, heavy and thick. She crouched before him, her face turned upward, the livid bruise on her neck already blackening. As the crowd watched, she put her hands out before her, the palms open to him in the traditional supplication of a defeated warrior. Calm, composed, she knelt at his feet and bared her neck for the death strike.

The world, for a few endless heartbeats, seemed to cease its endless spinning, to come to a standstill; the ground below him, the darkening sky above his head, seemed to hold their breath.

He looked down at her, at the long neck, the muddied armor, the white hands still and submissive. He lifted his head to stare at the ring of faces and at the uneasy clouds tumbling behind them. He brought his eyes around to where the druid master waited, his face and thoughts hidden behind the snake mask.

The spear hung poised above Connal's head. Then, shocking and unexpected, he threw his head back and wailed. It was a howl of pain, the howl of the wolf, and it rang across the plain like the cry of the bansidh.

He fastened his left hand around the shaft and brought the spear down over one knee. It cracked and snapped, the two ends falling at his feet. Panting, exhausted, he kicked the pieces away.

No sound, no voices, no movement. The universe was still, awaiting his pleasure. He stretched his arms out, lifted Maeve to her feet and spoke.

"Once I knelt before you," he said quietly to the bent head. "Once I knelt, offering my life to you, and you would not kill me for a crime I was clean of. Your honor would not let you. You gave me back my life. Now I give yours back to you. I cannot kill you, not for our people, not for the gods. My honor forbids."

The limp body he held began to shake, a slow tremor that started in her weary shoulders and ran through her like a current. "Connal," she whispered. "Connal."

"I will not kill you." And with that he pulled her into his arms and turned his face to the stunned multitude, to the druid master, to the tight knot of their three friends who watched in silent hope and disbelief. He began to shout, a roaring that echoed across the quiet plain like the thunder in the distance.

"I will not kill her! Do you hear this, druids, oinach, chieftains all? Listen and listen well, for I mean what I say. You set us at each other to appease your honor. Well, we have honor of our own, honor stronger than any of you can hope to know, and I will not murder innocence for your entertainment. To kill her would be to kill my own honor, and the fomori would follow me to the end of my days. The Queen of Connacht was lied to, lied to by a false druid, and together we will find this man and prove what we say."

The words ran through Maeve like fresh blood. She pulled herself up in his arms, raising her head proudly, pulling the helm away to let her hair fall free. Connal looked down at her for a moment. Unexpectedly, he let her go. He strode to the foot of the hill where the elders gathered and threw his head back once more. She saw the corded muscles ripple in his throat.

"Are you listening, wolves, ravens, serpents all? I tell you, I will not. Druid master!"

The snake mask moved, the glittering horns shifted. "I am listening, chieftain of Ulster. Tell us."

"We have fought for you, each of us under the hand of the gods. This is the outcome, fair and just. I say to you that one of your holy men is not so holy, that with some purpose as yet unknown to us he came to her with a false tale, hoping to cause grief and death. Give us permission, gentle seer, that we may find him, that we may bring him back to Tara in chains and prove the truth."

The painted snake tilted down to regard him. When the master spoke, his voice carried to all who listened.

"I have already taken thought on this, chieftain. There is some cold sense in what you say; the men of Connacht tell me the same, that a druid came to Cruachain and swore to your guilt. Yet no druid here admits to it. If an elder has turned to darkness, he must be found and cleansed. This is what the portents showed me, the ending to this fight, no death to either but a quest for both.

"Yet it is forbidden to defy the council's decision. You know it as well as I, and for that you must pay."

The small hands moved straight above his head. Even and uninflected, the massed elders began to chant. Against the toneless droning of his seers, the master continued.

"The decision of the council will stand this far. As of this moment you are both banished, queen no more, chieftain no more. Each will name a shadow to rule in their stead. Together you will go, taking no gold and no horses, with a weapon for each hand. On foot you will wander the hills, by sun you will search for food and shelter, by starlight you will sleep by the oceans and the loughs. When one year has passed, this council will come to Tara once more. Mark me well, son of Sibhainn, daughter of Flyn; you have until the dawning of the next Imbolc in which to prove your words. With no army at your command you must prove them, with no friends to your hand you must prove them, on foot and alone you must prove them. Free you are still, but royal no longer."

The silence was ghastly, a living, breathing thing. To the men who covered the plain, this was a sentence to equal death. But in the eyes of three men, looking down at their friends and leaders standing together in the trampled hollow, there was hope and gladness.

From between the ranks of chanting druids a single

white-robed body detached itself and disappeared quickly toward the tents. No one saw him go. And when, halfway between the council and the safety of his tent, he fell to his knees and was violently sick, no one was watching.

"Here, lord, this is as much as I could find. It cost me a jeweled pin and the promise of a song the man did not know for himself. Does it please you?"

Cormac staggered into Connal's tent under an enormous sack of smoked meat and found himself the cynosure of four pairs of eyes. Realizing that he had walked into an argument of some kind, he dropped the sack at Connal's feet, one mobile brow flying upward.

Connal himself sounded not angry, but preoccupied. "My thanks, Cormac. And I am your lord no longer; I am naught but Connal, a wandering man, with Maeve his wandering lady by his right hand. What have you in the sack, then?"

"A whole side of pig, lord, and much mutton; it should see you through awhile. New weapons, too, for you and for the Lady Maeve. As for the rest, you are lord to me, and it will take something more than a voice behind a mask to change that. Lady, that mark on your neck will swell and stiffen if it is not tended to. Bríhainn, what are you about, then? Can you not see to it?"

Maeve raised a hand and smiled. "He will tend to it after the crowd disperses and not before, fíla. There are plants he must have to make a salve; spikenard from the river, and too many men about to gather it. It shall do me no lasting harm. Let be."

Bríhainn, standing with clenched fists and angry eyes fixed on his friend, seemed not to have noticed a word Cormac said. Cormac, made wise by long experience, looked from his chieftain to Bríhainn and discreetly retired to one corner. If these two were in dispute, it was not for a prudent man to interfere; better, far better, to wait out the storm until one of them prevailed.

"You do not seem to understand me, Connal, that I mean what I say. I have no wish to be ruler of Emain, and I will not be ruler of Emain, not even for love of you."

The words were harsh to the point of rudeness. Sure,

and the boy was crazed; what had come to him to provoke the famous temper? Cormac closed his eyes and waited.

Astonishingly, Connal showed no temper; his mouth fell into a smile of genuine amusement, not unmixed with sympathy. "Well, and I cannot dispute with you on that, cela, for I have no real wish to be ruler of Emain myself! Yet it is something you must do. Do not argue with me any longer, cela; my word on it, you must do this."

"Connal, your wits are addled. What do you think the men of Ulster will say when they learn all that came to pass here? Bad enough that the Victorious is sent in disgrace to the hills, stripped of his throne, and their pride gone with him; if I tell them you have proclaimed me shadow—"

"They will fall on your neck with tears of joy." The easy voice was easy no longer; it had flattened out, not with anger, but with weight and meaning. So, Cormac, thought, time has come for both of them. A hand in a jeweled gauntlet flashed out and took Brihainn's arm. Connal spoke to the others over his shoulder.

"Cormac and Carhainn, give us leave awhile. Things must be said here, things which you cannot be hearing without Brihainn's leave. Later, if he gives me leave, you will be told; for now, it is between us." He saw his cela's face close tight, saw the quick glance at the silent woman in the corner, and added, "I will not ask Maeve to go, Brihainn, for I am Maeve and Maeve is me."

She got to her feet and came to stand face to face with Brihainn. They were almost of a height, Brihainn being only an inch or two taller.

"Connal will not ask me to go, but go I will; if you wish me to know, why then, I will."

She leaned forward and kissed him, softly and without passion, full on the mouth. "Our brother, our friend," she said quietly, and left the tent without a backward glance.

They stood silently, Connal watching his friend steadily, Brihainn staring at the hide where Maeve had disappeared. One long finger rubbed at his lips.

"She spoke truer than she knew," Connal murmured. "I wonder, now. I wonder..."

Brihainn, jerked from his reflections, let the hand

drop and turned back to Connal. "I have no wish to
quarrel with you, Connal, not now and not ever. Say what
you want to say to me; if it is truth, I shall hear it. What
do you wonder?"

Connal moved to the edge of the bed and sat. "I
wonder if she has not already guessed what I must say to
you. She has sharp eyes, my woman, and no mistake."

"Sharp eyes and blunted spears. Speak now."

Connal sat up straight. "Very well; what I tell you
now was told to me in confidence by your mother after
Sibhainn died, and Cormac and Anis the midwife confirmed it. It is why you must return to Emain, why the
crown of Ulster must rest easy on your brow, with me
banished." He saw something come into Brihainn's eyes, a
flare of light, of disbelieving hope, and with a deep breath
spoke simply. "We share a father, cela. Two years before I
was born, when the druids thought my mother Mhora
could never carry, Sibhainn got you on Sheilagh, with her
full consent. They were lovers then; he would have put
Mhora aside for her, but she refused. We are half brothers, you and I."

"Is this true?" Brihainn was whispering, his eyes wide
and blind. At the corner of his mouth the scar twitched.

"Truth," Connal told him gently. "By all the gods,
cela, have you never wondered why no one ever taunted
you, why you lived without the stigma of bastard shame?
You are Sibhainn's son, brother, and if I am stripped of my
crown, then you are chieftain by right." He looked in
puzzlement at the man, stunned and silent, across the
room. "I would have told you when first I knew, but
Sheilagh made me swear an oath to Crom Cruach that I
would never tell you unless the need came on us. The
need has come. Brihainn, did you truly never guess,
never wonder, never think to question Sheilagh?"

"My mother is not an easy woman to ask questions
of," Brihainn said ruefully. "Yes, I asked her once; I asked
why I bore her father's name and not mine. I ate naught
but soft foods for three days afterward." It was sinking in
now, memories that had troubled him for so long coalesc-
ing, making sense. He burst out, "Why could she not tell

me this? Why did Sibhainn not tell me? Were they so ashamed?"

"Not shame, cela. Pride." He met his brother's eyes. "Among our people not a man or woman born has more pride than Sheilagh. She has the gift of self-sufficiency, your mother; she wanted no part of the burdens that would come from sitting on the throne, and she wanted no one to be able to say that she was the chieftain's whore, that she had taken him to her bed, not for love but for the power it would bring her. It is hard for us, as men, to understand her, but I think we must accept it. For myself, I can only admire."

"Yes, I see. I see now." He was thinking it out, finding out, taking the myriad pieces and setting them into their proper places. "And there are many men she has bested in combat, and many who resented it when you left her as shadow when you marched on Cet."

"A high pride, and a fierce independence." Connal got to his feet and pulled Brihainn close. "You have them, too, cela, brother, chieftain. It is what I love you for."

"I am glad you told me." The words were patently sincere, a sharp contrast to the unyielding voice. "But chieftain's son or no, I still do not wish to rule Ulster!"

Exasperated, Connal shook him. "Brihainn, you would send the very moonlight mad. Who then, if not you?"

"Why, my mother, of course. Sheilagh."

Connal blinked at him. "Sheilagh? Not as shadow, but as chieftain?"

"Why not?" The words poured from Brihainn, eager and hasty. "Who better? She has been shadow, she has the respect of the tuath if not their love, she is a better warrior than I could ever be. She knows what it is to rule, and has a light eye for justice. Please, Connal."

"Sheilagh." The black brows had straightened into a thoughtful bar. "All right, cela. I will name Sheilagh as chieftain if you will meet a condition I put to you."

Brihainn's thin face was aglow. "Name it, then."

"You will return to Emain for a month, a month only, to see that the people accept her, to settle her on the throne, to explain to the tuath and to Sheilagh, too, what has really happened here. For one month only you will act as my voice and as your mother's eyes among the tuath. Then you may step down, go where you wish, do what you wish. Is it agreed?"

"Agreed, yes. I only wish I could come with you."

The hide was pushed open and Maeve's voice sounded plaintively. "My lords, it is wet and chill. May I not come back into the warmth, and Carhainn and Cormac too?"

"Indeed." Connal went quickly to the hide and drew her indoors. "Sweet, you are chilled to the bone. Carhainn, will you go across to my lady's tent and bring her dry robes to wear and a cloak for warmth?"

"No need, I have them here." Carhainn, not meeting Maeve's eye, set the pack down and unlaced it. "Shall we take ourselves back to the rain while you change, lady?"

"You shall not," she replied crisply. "I would send nothing and no one out of doors tonight. Besides, do you think I could feel so naked, even without my skin, as I did today before those many eyes? That is true nakedness; the rest is false modesty and fuss, nothing more. If you would turn your backs a moment? My thanks."

Connal, while the others stood with their backs turned, stood and watched her. The frown settled on his face once again as she dropped her sodden robes and stood, naked and shivering, before him. He saw the purple bruises that peppered both thighs, obscene against the white skin; he noted, too, the stiffness of her neck and shoulders, and how she used only her right hand to dress, leaving the left to dangle lip at her side.

"What is it, Maeve? Cannot you use your left hand?"

She struggled with the silken robe. "Not yet; when Brihainn has laid his magical salve across my shoulder, it will be better. Connal, please, can you help me with this?"

He crossed the room quickly and dropped the gown carefully over her shoulders. Kneeling before her, he began to twitch the creases out, settling it properly in soft folds over breast and hip. Suddenly aware of an odd quality to her silence, a sudden heat that brushed him like firelight through the silken folds of the gown, he pulled his head back to look at her. There were tears on her face.

She reached out to him, hunger and urgency in every move; fastening her arms tight around his head, she pulled his face against her belly and held it there, feeling the warmth of him, the tension of the vein throbbing in his brow, oblivious to the embarrassed silence of the others.

"What is it, my only one? Are you hurting, then?"

She smiled through tears at the muffled question. "I could be wounded in every part of me and I would notice naught. I am happy, no more; I care nothing for exile, I care nothing for shame, I care nothing for loss of my throne. I thought to die today. I thought I would never more see you, save only as pale and sorry shades moving through the halls of the Sidh. Yet I am alive and you are alive, and we go to the hills together. How can I not be happy?"

He freed his face from the suffocating folds of her robes and, still on his knees, took her hands. "Is this truth, Maeve? You do not regret?"

Her laugh rang out, joyous and clear. It startled the others into turning back again, and lifted a weight of black dread that since the master's words had sat like death, like feathered things that waited for stinking carrion, on Connal's heart. She laughed, and as she laughed, she wept.

"Regret? I have never been so happy, never, not in all my life." She turned her radiant face to the silent onlookers. "Some business to settle, celi. Carhainn, take my crown. I will come back a year hence, never doubt it, but until I do you will watch the throne of Cruachain for me."

She saw his nostrils flare and ran across to him. "My dearest, my truest friend, do you remember the day my parents rode away to their deaths? Do you remember how Nieve came to me and thanked me for my blessing, and how my father died while I was in anger with him?" She clutched his shoulders with fingers that trembled. "Do you remember?"

His lips were pinched. "I remember."

"You stood behind me that day, stood behind me as you had stood behind me since the day Ahnrach was slain. And she saw you, my mother. She spoke to you. Do you remember what she said to you, Carhainn, my true friend?"

He stared down at her, not seeing her. It was clear, the images vivid; he could almost smell the first days of spring, the scent of the horses ready for the road. In the space of a few moments he lived that day again, remembered the young girl whispering in his arms after darkness fell, and heard, across the months and the distance, Nieve's quiet voice as she spoke to him. *Guard our daughter well,* she had told him, and ridden, calm and serene, to a horrible death. . . .

His mouth was working. "I remember."

Maeve put her arms around his stiff body. "Down there on the field today, Carhainn, I spoke to you and only to you. I thought you heard me, over the shouting and the stamping and the chants of the druids. I asked you to forgive me, for whatever harm I have done to you." She smiled mistily into his face. "Do this for me, Carhainn. Forgive me, and rule for me. A year only; I swear it."

"Very well." *Guard our daughter well, captain.* . . . She would walk away, walk off into the dark hills to the north, into the wet forests of the southwest, and he could guard her no longer, he could keep that trust no more. It was for Connal now. For the first time in many months he remembered Ahnrach, her mouth wide and screaming as she was thrown across a raider's horse.

With that memory something stirred in his mind, some connection of facts. Was it possible? No, surely it could not be; ten years apart, how could it be the same men? The hill made a fine vantage point for anyone in ambush; the thing was a coincidence, no more than that. He was still struggling with the elusive thought as the others served food, talked, made plans, as the two chieftains who were chieftains no more sent a fila home to Emain, a bastard brother back to see his mother enthroned, and gave their final orders. He barely heard the conversation ebb and flow around him, scarcely noticed Brihainn's departure in search of plants for his healing salve, did not taste the roast mutton or the sour wine.

A coincidence, nothing more. Still, it was odd that no one had thought of it before.

III

THE WANDERERS

12

The Plains of Munster

"I never thought to miss Ghan as I do right now."

The words were so heartfelt that Connal, halfway up the narrow mountain path in his search for solid footing, turned his head to stare back at her. Clothes muddy, red hair streaked with clay and mud, she looked absurdly young, and Connal felt his heart turn over with the mixture of affection and desire that, however often it might wash over him, always seemed new.

He raised an eyebrow. "Who," he enquired, "is Ghan?"

"My war stallion, one of Connacht's finest, and a wizard at finding paths where I had thought to find none." She sighed deeply. "He will grow fat and lazy in my absence, with no exercise and no one to let him run free."

Connal, hearing the wistful undertone, abandoned his search for a shortcut up the hillside and slid back down to the path where Maeve waited. "Cannot Carhainn do this?"

"Ghan will allow none but me to mount him," she replied simply. "You must have heard the stories of the horses of Connacht, Connal; a warrior will slay his own mount in battle rather than let him be taken by an enemy. The horses of Connacht are legendary for their fierceness, and they are swift as the wind, but above all they are loyal. He will pine without me." She saw something come into his face, something that might have been disbelief, and added, "Ghan was mine, love, broken by me and therefore mine forever."

There was a distant rumble of thunder. Connal dropped his arm across her shoulders and pulled her close.

"I believe you, sweeting, for we of the north feel the same about our horses. But Lhiam will not pine for me, for he will not live long enough; Brihainn will offer him to Crom as a sacrifice for our safety."

"A good notion. Connal, is this rain I feel?"

"It is, and we must find shelter. Here, darling, follow me; I thought I saw a cleft in the hill, a little way up the slope; we can shelter there, and if it is big enough, we may build a fire against the wet and the chill." Scrabbling for a hold, grimacing at how her skirts impeded her climb, Maeve struggled up the hillside behind him, her eyes alert for the dark gash in the rock he swore was there.

It was, as it chanced, better than a cleft; it was a cave, not large, but spacious enough for two people and a fire. The thunder was coming with increasing volume and frequency now; Connal lifted Maeve over the last boulders and set her down under the high roof.

"Wrap yourself warm, Maeve, while I gather wood for the fire. We shall warm our supper and ourselves too."

"I stay here warm and dry while you soak for both of us? What nonsense! Two can gather more wood than one." She saw the mulishness in his face and added, demurely, "Besides, I should be frightened, waiting alone. What if a bear or a wolf should come home to its cave and take offense at me?"

He tilted his head sideways, looking pointedly at the two deadly spears that hung at her back. Suddenly he flashed the grin that to Maeve seemed to bring the sun into his face. "Then there would be much blood and we would have new cloaks. Are you teasing me, allana?"

"I am. But I am coming with you, so no arguments, for if we waste more time, the rain will come and we will have no fire at all. Wet sticks cannot be set alight."

"Truth. So why do you delay? Come, then."

It was already sprinkling as they gathered the loose kindling, the heavy branches, and carried them between them back to the cave. The sky, with day fading to evening, had an electrical feel to it; Connal felt his nerves jumping, and the beginning of a small headache that meant lightning coming. In the twilight Maeve's face had a pearly glow.

As they dropped the last of the wood in a heap just inside the cave's entrance, the skies opened. There was a roar of thunder, a sudden blinding crack of light, and the world outside turned gray. Maeve, speedily reducing the heavy tree limbs to a more manageable size, shivered.

"A storm, a true storm. I am glad we found shelter here, for to be caught out in this wet would be misery."

Connal had set the kindling alight. "By the gods, but misery is too light a word; a hillside whipped by sky fire is no place for you or me. Here, allana, come up by the fire and warm yourself. Where is—What are you doing?"

Naked, her white skin turned a pale rose by the dancing firelight, Maeve was laying her gown out to dry. "Well, and would you have me take my death, sitting here in wet robes?" She reached for her cloak, which during the warmth of the day had been bundled into her pack. Pulling it close, she dropped to the fireside and held her hands out to it.

Connal had found some strips of dried mutton, smoked to perfection over the campfire of some soldier at Tara two weeks ago. Passing a chunk to Maeve, he spoke through a mouthful of the tasty meat.

"The storm is violent and will blow the night through. But it should be over tomorrow, and then we can hunt."

The glowing wood was reflected in Maeve's eyes. "Oh, yes," she said dreamily. "I would dearly love a roast hare, or perhaps a bird, after nothing but mutton."

He was sitting opposite her, his legs crossed. At her words he lifted his head, to stare at her in surprise. "A bird or a hare? Why have you not gone for one, then?"

She blew him a kiss across the flames. "Hunt a hare or something that flies? With spears? Shame, Connal, and you a huntsman! They are for the strong arm and the sling. Have you ever tried to bring a bird down with a spear?"

He chuckled. "I have not, but I take your meaning. Well, and I have my sling and good sharp flints to go with it. Tomorrow, lady, you shall sup on the fattest bird that this benighted province can offer me."

"I will eat with thanks, and pleasure too. Connal, where are we? I have followed you these past weeks, not asking, for truth to tell, I care nothing for where we may be, so long as we are both there. But it seems to me that we have moving to the southwest all the time we traveled. I do not think we are in Connacht. Are we in Muman, then?"

"We are. And yes, I chose this way for a purpose, more than one." He saw the queen in her suddenly as she turned his possible strategies over in her mind. "Shall I tell you, allana, or would you rather see if you can reason it out without help from me?"

"Muman..." She mused, and suddenly smiled at him. "Ah. King Kieran rules here, and he is well disposed toward both our peoples. I had a gift of a thousand head of cattle from him when my father died, and I know he spoke kindly of you to the master, praising your courage and your honesty, back there at Tara. Is that it?"

"In part." He finished the mutton and wiped his mouth. "There is another purpose. Can you guess it?"

"You are teasing me. No, I cannot guess, and I have no mind to. Tell me, then."

Connal answered her slowly, his mind working back to the lessons of state he had been given as a newly made chieftain. "Muman has many tuatha. Yes, I know there is nothing odd in that, I know it is true of all this land. But the tuatha here are made up of peoples with different blood. Some came here from the continent to the south, some not; there is some competition between them for grazing lands. Oh, not open wars; Kieran would never stand for that. But skirmishing, petty and sly, between the smaller chieftains who rule their own tuatha under Kieran's hand." He saw she was looking at him in some bewilderment, and added gently, "There will be work there, for you and I."

"Work?" His meaning suddenly sank in, and she burst out laughing. "Connal, are we to be mercenaries? Hired arms?"

He let his breath out in relief; in truth, he had not

broached the subject to her earlier, not knowing how a High Queen would stomach the idea of hiring her spear out to an unknown tuath. "You have it. Maeve, do you mind?"

She was rocking back and forth in an ecstasy of laughter. "Mind? Oh, sweet Lugh, I have not been this amused in a long time, too long. That is the funniest thing I have ever heard." She wiped the tears of laughter from her face. "What a lovely notion. Do we tell them who we are?"

"We do not. Can you see yourself announcing to some fool in a dirty sheepskin that Connal the Victorious and the High Queen of Connacht would like to hire their spears to his service? The poor man would swoon from the shock."

She was laughing again. "Yes, you speak truth. But oh, Connal, I would dearly love to do it, if only to see the look on his face!" She sobered. "Do we do this to survive?"

"In part." He reached for another branch, watching the shower of sparks as he dropped it on the crackling fire. "But not all. We must keep in touch with the world of men, my darling. Do not forget, we have a quest to fulfill."

Hearing her sudden intake of breath, he knew she had forgotten. He came to her side and pulled her into his arms.

"Somewhere out there, Maeve, is a man. We know nothing of who he may be; we know nothing of why he wishes us ill. He has all the advantages and we have none; we move in the light, he moves in the darkness. Yet we must find him, and only through the world of men can we do this. Someday, somehow, we will learn what we must know, we will find what we seek. No man lives alone, without fellows; in some tuatha of this land this man has left traces of himself. And we will find them, my queen, make no mistake."

"Yes, I see." She had nestled close against him, the soft curves of her body automatically adjusting themselves to fit against him at chest, thigh, arm. She rested her cheek against his shoulder, ignoring the pain of the hard mail. "You speak truth, chieftain, and I agree with all you say. But I have a question to put to you."

He dropped a hand to the shining hair. "Ask, then."

"I told Carhainn nothing of where we would go, for at the time I did not know myself. But you knew. Did you tell Brihainn, then, that we would make for Muman?"

"I did." The fire cast a slumberous light around them; the steady, even sound of the rain falling outside had a rhythm to it. He held her, not moving, feeling how warm she was, how soft, and his body grew slowly aware of her.

She twisted in his arms, her hands coming up to his face. Slowly she traced the lines around mouth and eyes, moved across cheekbones, her hands slipping behind his head. She wrapped her fingers in his hair with painful urgency, and he saw the hunger, bright and beautiful, in her face. He looked down at her, wondering if he would burst, wondering if she was truly everything a man wanted and almost never got, wondering if he would die of his love for her.

"None here but us and the gods," she whispered, and with a sudden shrug of the shoulders, the cloak slid to a soft heap at her feet. Standing on tiptoe, the length of her body pressed so tight against him that his light armor left small imprints of itself in her skin, she fastened her mouth against him and pulled him down.

As Connal had predicted, the morning broke fair and warm. Maeve, slowly coming to consciousness before the sun was up, missed Connal's comforting warmth beside her as she opened her eyes to a rosy dawn.

She sat up, reaching for her clothing and wincing as she stretched. May Danu protect us, she thought ruefully, but the floor of a mountain cave is a harsh place for love and sleep! She was stiff and sore; above all, she was hungry, and curious as to where Connal had gone. Getting to her feet, reveling in the surprising warmth of the morning, she pulled her clothing on as quickly as she could. Deciding that her tangled hair must wait, she went quickly through the mouth of the cave and out of doors.

There was a soft breeze blowing, carrying with it the sweet smell of clover and pine. Clambering to the highest boulder within reach, she stretched her neck, seeking him.

A crashing in the undergrowth of the hill below them, followed by a frenzied squawking and a shout of triumph, told their own story. A bird for breakfast, then; well, he had done his part, and it was for her to do hers. She slid down the rocky scree, holding her skirts above her knees, and began to speedily gather enough wood for a small fire.

He came back to the cave just as she succeeded in blowing the small flame into life. She turned to greet him, her hair still tangled from sleep, the hem of her gown puckered with a rich edging of brambles and gorse she had picked up while gathering the wood. Smiling, her eyes found the two fat quail dangling from his right hand. The smile suddenly died and she ran forward.

"Connal! What you have done to your arm?"

He tossed the birds aside and his sling after them. The left sleeve of his tunic was torn and a dark stain showed against the pale fabric; Maeve came to his side to examine the ugly gash high on one bicep.

Her eyes were wide. "What happened, love?"

He shrugged, grimacing. "Nothing very much, lady; a lesson to me, not to be so careless and cocksure. The hillside above is rocky, and some of the smaller rocks must have been loosened by the heavy rain in the night. I was giving chase when a small boulder and a shower of sharp stones came down on me. One of them caught my arm." He gently put her questing fingers aside. "No worry, allana; it looks bad, I know, but truth to tell, it is little more than a scratch. Have you any of Brihainn's 'nard left?"

She was already rummaging in her pack. "It must be cleansed first, else it will fester. Ah, here is the salve. You stay here and pluck those birds while I fill our skins from the stream. I need more water to wash that wound."

He had pulled the bloodied tunic off and thrown it to one side. Sitting down, he blew the little blaze higher and reached for a bird. "Do you know, I have never plucked a fowl in all my life? Well, and if you find yourself with a mouthful of feathers, it will be no blame to any but you for leaving a helpless man to clean your breakfast." She turned at the door, the water skins in one hand, and shot him an enchanting grin. His own smile died. "Be careful, girl; you need not come back with a wound to match mine."

"I will be careful," she told him. "But you had best look to yourself when I return. A wound will not save you from vengeance from teasing me!"

She vanished through the cave's entrance, slithering down toward the stream that danced and burbled at the foot of the hill. Connal, whistling, began to pull feathers with a speed that belied his claim of inexperience.

She came back before he had finished the second bird, holding skins that now bulged with their weight of water. Dropping her burden beside the fire, she calmly tore a strip of clean cloth from the bodice of her dress and soaked it with the water. Connal made a protesting noise in his throat, and she looked up questioningly.

"Maeve, you have only two gowns. Why did you do that?"

She crouched beside him, the wetted cloth in one hand and the precious 'nard in the other. "I did some thinking, down at the stream, and an idea came to me." She probed gently at the swollen arm and continued decisively. "We are to be warriors, hired spears, fighters. It would be folly for me to travel in women's garb; the gown slows me down, gets in my way. I have my armor from Tara, with breeches and mail; I shall wear it from this time on." The look on his face made her add hastily, "Besides, the gowns will be lighter to carry than the mail."

"Truth." He spoke reluctantly. "I cannot dispute with you, but to tell truth, this does not please me."

Her voice held some asperity. "If you are thinking that it is unseemly for a woman to walk abroad in man's clothing, I can only point out to you that it is no more unseemly than a queen wandering the hills in the first place."

He looked startled. "Sweet Lugh, what a shrew! That never crossed my mind. It is only that your accursed armor will remind me to the end of my days of that dreadful day at Tara when we faced death at each other's hand."

Her face softened suddenly. "Oh, Connal, I ask pardon for my thoughtlessness. But to say truth, love, you have worn the same armor you wore that day since we left Tara. I, too, am reminded, but I have learned to live with it. One grows accustomed." She blew softly on the puckering wound. "Yes, you were right. This is barely more than a bad scratch, and with the 'nard to aid it, it will soon heal. A mercy it was your left arm and not your right."

He waited silently as she tore another strip of cloth from her gown and tied it with professional expertise around his upper arm. When she had finished, he swung it experimentally to and fro and nodded his approval.

"You have a healer's touch, my lady. A day, perhaps two, and this will be right again. Give me that stick, will you, the one with the pointed end? My thanks."

He spitted one of the birds and thrust it into the heart of the fire. As it cooked, the smell of roasting quail drifting tantalizingly across the still air of the cave, Maeve changed her clothing from woman to warrior.

"Shall we stay another night here or do we travel on?"

He turned the spit, inhaling the smell. "We travel, I think. The land on the other side of these hills is fine for grazing; there will be people there, a dry bed and perhaps some work for us." He smiled to himself. "Who knows, if we can but earn some gold, we may be able to afford the price of a decent horse for you."

"Why for me?" Her voice came muffled from the folds of the black tunic. "Why not a strong beast to bear us both?"

"Perhaps we can. But Muman is not Connacht, nor yet Ulster; Kieran's realm is famed for its fine cattle, not its horses, and we can scarcely ride a cow or a sheep. I fear we would have to search all day and night to find a horse here that would bear our weight together."

"Oh, am I so fat, then? No, don't throw that skin at my head, for I am only teasing. Well, and you may be right. We will see what is to be found here. I know little of Muman, you know; I came here on a visit of state, but that was many years ago, when I was scarcely more than a babe, and to say truth, my memories are cloudy. Is this province bountiful?"

The first bird done, Connal pulled it quickly from the spit. Blowing on his singed fingers, he wetted the stick with spring water from the nearest skin and slid the second quail in place for roasting. "Bountiful? Oh, in parts. There are wide plains here for the grazing, but not nearly enough, for the hills and the woodlands encroach, and these people are known far and wide for the numbers of cattle they keep. It is bountiful in water and game, certainly."

"Ah." She had pulled the breeches on and was busily fastening the ornamented leg plates. "Then as we wander the hills here, we will not starve?"

"No fear of that. There is plenty of game, and more birds here than Ulster can boast." He pulled the second bird from the fire and laid it down beside its fellow, watching her with a slight frown as she reached for the breastplate. "Must you wear that, lady?"

"Well," she said reasonably, "it is easier to wear than to carry. Will you help me with the back, then?"

He stood behind her, deftly working the copper hooks. "Yes, we will eat well. That is not what I fear in Muman."

She looked at him over her shoulder, disturbed by a grim note in his voice. "What do you fear, then?"

"Wolves and bears." Brushing the hair aside, he bent and placed a soft, lingering kiss on the nape of her neck. Maeve felt her legs go limp and sagged against him, hearing his amusement through a mist. "You are as wanton as you are beautiful. Come sit with me, and I will comb out your hair; you cannot walk abroad with this tangled mess flying behind you, armor or no."

She steadied her breath. "I am only wanton when you do things like that. If you think the moment unsuitable for covering a woman, you must keep your lips to yourself." She added, suddenly and shockingly, "It is most cruel of you to take advantage of my weakness and then tease me for it. You bring me to this state, and this is the result."

He was grinning. Maeve, her back still turned to him, did not see it; had she done so, she would have been startled at the sudden face of control and power he wore, might have felt a momentary fright at the pride, a completely male thing, her words had raised in him. As it was, she reached for the leg of a bird and sat cross-legged before him as he drew the silver comb through her hair.

"I wonder what is happening, back there in the true world," Connal said musingly. "I wonder what your people said and did when Carhainn came home with the crown of Cruachain on his head. And I would give much to see my people react to the knowledge that Sheilagh will rule them." He laughed softly, with supreme enjoyment. "And rule them she will, make no mistake, with justice and an iron fist. She is not a woman to bear insults or be patient with men's resentment of her position. Yes, I would give much." He laughed again.

She twisted around to gaze at him. "Do you know, darling, I am curious about this Sheilagh, this warrior woman who refused to be queen. Is she truly so formidable?"

"Such a word scarcely does her justice. After myself, she is the finest warrior in Ulster; I left her as shadow, that time I punished the worm Cet for his insolence, and she taught the people a few things."

"I would like to meet such a woman." She spoke thoughtfully, her head jerking back gently with Connal's rhythmic strokes. "In Connacht such women are rare."

"They are rare everywhere." There was passion in his voice. "How fortunate for me, then, that I know two."

Two days later Maeve and Connal crested a rocky slope and emerged on the outskirts of a small village.

Maeve, despite the two spears in the quiver over her shoulder and a strong knife tucked deep within a nearly invisible sheath in her armor, was nervous. She followed Connal, noting the thick flocks of cattle grazing and the curious gaze of the two shepherds, and decided to let Connal speak for both of them.

He stepped forward and, seeing the wariness in the eyes of the two strangers, spoke easily. "A fine day to you, guardians. Can you put us right for your village and the house of your chieftain?"

One of the shepherds, a boy of perhaps eleven, merely stood with his head ducked shyly down. The other, an old man, looked first Connal and then Maeve over from head to toe. There was a shrewd twinkle in his eye.

"Warriors, are you? Perhaps looking for work? Aye, I see you are." He lifted a hand and pointed. "Our tuath is that way, perhaps a mile down the road. Our chieftain is called Mhul, a fierce man, but always in need of a strong arm. He has just come home from the great council at Tara, and those savages from across the hill raided us all the time he was gone." There was indignation in the old man's raspy voice, an indignation doubtless felt often enough over the span of his life. "Fifty head of cattle we lost to them."

"Fifty head!" Maeve, listening carefully, thought that Connal might have been doing this all his life, so easily did he handle it. "Well, and that is a goodly lot. Perhaps we can help this Mhul take them home again."

"Perhaps." The old man, who had been giving his full attention to Connal, suddenly truly noticed Maeve. He looked in admiration at her, a faint smile playing across his lips. Suddenly his eyes lit on the two spears at her back, and a look of terror and superstition took the place of lechery. He opened his mouth to say something, closed it again, and brought his eyes back to Connal. This time they held fear and awareness. He spoke carefully.

"A half mile, I say. And you, gentle lord? Have you been to the council at Tara?"

"Perhaps, perhaps not." Maeve, glancing involuntarily at her lover, saw the amusement in the deep black eyes. "I am obliged to you, as is my lady. We will visit this Mhul."

He shouldered both packs and set off toward the tuath, Maeve hard at his heels. When they had put a fair distance between them and the shepherds, she risked a look behind her.

They were still staring, the older bent over in an earnest monologue. Though she could not see their faces clearly, she felt herself flushing, as though caught out in some rudeness. And Connal still grinned.

"Connal, what was all that about? Why did he look at us that way, and ask about Tara, and speak so strange?"

He stopped to shift the packs, and smiled down into her worried face. "Why, that is easily answered, allana. He mentioned Tara and then saw your spears; how many two-handed warrior women are there in this fair land?"

She blinked up at him. "By the gods, do you mean that the old man recognized us?"

"I do. At least he believes he has; he cannot be sure." He chuckled suddenly. "Well, and we will reach this Mhul before he can send the boy running to the chieftain's house with his suspicions. A pity, in a way."

She had pulled her pack from his hands and fastened it across her own back. "Here, let me carry my own goods awhile; you have made your back sore long enough. Why a pity? Did you not tell me we would do better disguised?"

They began to walk once more. Had they spared a backward glance, they would have noted a small figure running through the crops on a parallel track, and the old man alone with his cows and sheep. Connal was still amused.

"I did, darling. But what cannot be mended must be accepted, and we may well fare even better this way. After all, we need not tell these people who we are; let them but assume it and we will rate a higher wage for our spear arms, and more courtesy to go along with it." As they came to a slight rise in the road, he looked back at last, and then toward the tuath. "Ah. I underestimated the old man, my love; the boy is before us with the news, and even now he has entered the village gates. I can see him from up here; he is pelting toward the heart of the place." He watched a moment and continued with great satisfaction. "And he has just shown me where I might find Mhul. My thanks to you, old man, you have saved me some work."

The boy had, indeed, reached the chieftain before them. Maeve was conscious of an odd thumping in her throat, a constriction of nerves. But she had no time to be nervous, for as they came abreast of the gates, a chubby figure came sweeping out to greet them.

Mhul was a rotund little man. He looked, thought Maeve, like a child's toy, for his cheeks were clean-shaven and fat, and redder than apples fresh off the tree. He was richly dressed, as were the nine celi waiting respectfully behind him; bringing up the rear was the shepherd boy who, as he met Connal's eye, suddenly wriggled and was gone, vanishing into the crowd.

"Greetings, a fine day to you, welcome to our tuath, gentle strangers." The voice matched the outward man; it was thick as drippings, and unctuous with it. "I am Mhul, chieftain of this tuath, and I am told you are warriors, come to help us take our stolen cattle home from the accursed Coromi across the hill?"

"Why, your shepherd has told us of your trouble, and we would be pleased to offer you our good arms." Connal, towering over the chieftain, looked down into the small, narrow eyes and read the man perfectly. There was wariness there, and avarice; this was a man who would hesitate to anger his High King Kieran, a man impressed by his betters. Connal allowed his voice to deepen.

"We have much to offer you, chieftain; indeed, if you will tell us how we may recognize your cattle, we can get it back for you with no help from your people but a guide to lead us there." He saw smugness, and added coldly, "Our price is high, but you give us nothing until your cows and your sheep are safe in their own pens once more."

"I see." Mhul's head came midway to Connal's chest; even Maeve was taller. He looked at Connal a moment, nodding his head in silent satisfaction, and turned to Maeve.

He recognized her. It was obvious to Connal, to Maeve herself, to everyone standing behind him; his eyes, like the eyes of the old shepherd, went from the twin spears to the armor to the tendrils of red hair that had escaped their binding and blew in the spring wind around her face. Then he bowed low and stood once again, waving them into the heart of the milling throng, apologizing, explaining, shouting for the people to make way for the warriors who had come to give them back their flocks again. . . .

After they had run the gauntlet of the tuath's curiosity, Mhul led them into his own house and pulled the hide fast behind him.

As soon as they were alone, an astonishing change came over the little man. He sank to his chair, sweating profusely, and waved them to do the same. He stammered apologies for this rough accommodation, but he understood from his shepherd boy, a clever boy indeed, that they did not wish their names and ranks given out. He was sure they would understand, and please, would the high ones not sit?

Maeve, declining Connal's offer of the only other seat the room contained, sat at his feet, watching and wondering. The chieftain seemed to understand her scrutiny, for he flushed again and spoke apologetically.

"Your pardon, great queen, lord of Ulster. If you did not wish me to know you, I am sorry; I stood some three lines back at Tara a fortnight past and saw it all. I could not but help to recognize you. I will respect your wishes."

Connal inclined his head and laid a casual hand on Maeve's shoulder. "Our thanks to you, chieftain. Your offer of secrecy is welcome, but surely without point? Even the old man who tends your flocks to the northeast of here seemed to know us at first sighting."

"No, lord. He did not know that he spoke in flesh to the Victorious and the Faery Queen; he only guessed, I believe, from the queen's two spears. My lady?"

Maeve had gotten to her feet and stood staring down at him. "What was that you called me?"

The red face turned purple. "Your pardon, queen, I meant not to anger you. It is the name given you among those who watched the fight at Tara. No disrespect was intended."

Connal was struggling with laughter. "Because she looked like something from the world of light, so frail in her deadly armor, and I so dangerous and strong? Great Crom, Maeve, but the name suits you, and suits you well."

She bent and kissed his cheek. "You would not dare!"

"Only when you annoy me, allana. When you push me past any endurance I may have, I shall call you Queen of the Faeries, and you will know you have gone too far." He dodged the playful blow at his head, laughing, and realized that Mhul was watching them, pop-eyed with astonishment. "All right, enough; I fear we shock good Mhul. Sir, you need have no fear of us; let rumor fly, if you like, and we will not mind that. But we are neither chieftain nor queen today, and will not be until we find the man who brought us to this pass. Now. To the business at hand?"

"Indeed." The little man, at Connal's speech, had eased considerably. "But first, some wine with me. Lady, may the gods keep you safe. Gentle lord, your health." He drained his wine at a single gulp, dashed a hand across his mouth, and spoke earnestly.

"What the old man told you is true. The Coromi, those who live a day's ride to the southwest, sent no one to Tara; I went myself, as was the chieftain's duty, and while I was gone those miserable barbarians raided us some five times and took at least fifty head from us." He lifted his eyes to Connal's face and spoke simply. "If you can get them back for me, my people will be pleased with me, and I will pay whatever price you name. Can you do this?"

"Easily. We will need someone to show us the way and point out your cattle, perhaps the boy that ran to bring you the news? Also, a good night's sleep in a true bed, for while a cave is convenient in poor weather, it cannot be called comfortable."

"It is my honor to provide you both with quarters, and tonight you shall dine on a fresh-killed hind. The boy can lead you, and he is dependable. Your price?"

"High, as I said, but not unduly so. Enough smoked lamb for us to carry, and my lady's choice in a new knife."

Mhul's relief was evident. "Not so high, lord; why, the boy himself would ask me for more than that."

"There is one other thing." Maeve, sitting comfortably on the floor at Connal's feet, spoke persuasively. "We require a horse, chieftain. I know that Muman is weak in its horse-breeding, even as it is surpassed by no other province in the quality of its cattle. But we cannot ride cattle, Mhul. We ask for the largest horse you can provide that it might bear both of us for short distances. Can it be done?"

To their extreme surprise, Mhul threw his back and laughed in relief. "Nothing could be easier, gentle lord and lady. Our horses do not compare with those of Connacht but it so happens I have a fine horse, not swift, but gentle and strong, bred within your own borders, lady. One of

my celi did some gaming with the horse's owner, back
there at Tara, and took the horse in payment of debt. My
cela presented him to me, and I cannot ride him."

"Can you not?" Maeve was surprised. "Is he so
fierce?"

"Not fierce, but huge; he would tower even over your
head, lord of Ulster, and he has odd bands of hair about
his ankles. So small and unimpressive as I am, I fear I
would look ridiculous on his back. Come and see him, and
then you will sup with us and rest. The boy will be ready
to take you on the morrow."

The next day, under a soft blanket of heavy mist, they
followed the boy Lan through a seemingly solid wall of
tree and shrub, across the hills to the southwest and into
the territory of the Coromi.

Maeve, climbing with silent ease in Lan's footsteps,
was enjoying herself. Sheltered and protected all through
her childhood, forbidden the freedom of Connacht's woods
and hillsides from the day she was attacked, the scrambling that had begun at Tara still held the delicious taste of
forbidden fruit, of adventure she had never thought to
have. She was young, and supple with it; her slender body
twisted itself flat to slip through trees and between rocks,
and never once did she have the slightest difficulty in
keeping up with Lan's steady pace.

As for Connal, who like all small boys had spent his
youth clambering up hillsides and shinnying up trees, he
kept one eye on his footing and the other on Maeve. He
knew better than to offer her any aid unless she requested
it; to do so would be to offer an intolerable insult. As the
realization, the understanding, of her self-sufficiency, came
to him, he was suddenly visited by a memory of Annak,
lovely Annak, tiny and hot-tempered, imperious; she had
been every bit as high-couraged as Maeve, yet how different the two women were! Annak, who had insisted on
being lifted over every obstacle, big or small, and took his
occasional lapses as personal insults to her femininity...

He followed handily, some part of his attention always
on the slender legs that flashed through the undergrowth
before him, and put Annak from his mind.

They had set out at first light. Several hours had passed, and Maeve had become aware of hunger and thirst, when Lan suddenly stopped. "So please you, we will eat here."

Maeve sank thankfully to the mossy forest floor. Connal, pulling meat and water from his pack, followed suit.

"A good morning's journey, young shepherd, and we have to thank you for guiding us. How far have we come, then?"

The boy tore off a strip of cold mutton with his teeth. "Near the whole way, lord. In perhaps an hour we shall reach the Coromi grazing land."

"Ah." Connal cocked his head. "Some questions."

"Ask me, then." The boy, still eating, met his eyes.

"Questions, yes. Your tuath's cattle; are they like to be found so far from the village? Will the Coromi have so little regard for any revenge Mhul might take?"

The boy shook his head. "Lord, the cattle will be there. They think our chieftain of small account and know that we have no true warriors to punish them; we are a people of peace, not fighting. Once or twice they attacked our tuath outright, but Mhul sent to the High King—Kieran, that is—and he ordered them never to do so again under penalty of his deepest displeasure. But when the chieftain went off to Tara with all his celi . . ."

"The Coromi felt a sneak attack would be safe. Yes, I see. Now, if you are certain your cattle will be kept so far from their village gates, how many will guard the herd?"

"I cannot say for certain, lord; two, or perhaps three? Their richest pastures are on a straight line between their tuath and ours, and there are none to attack them from this direction save for us." He added, simply and without shame, "And they would never believe we might attack them."

Connal was smiling, a thin curl of the lips. Maeve had never before seen this expression, and it frightened her; she stared into the strong face gone suddenly cold and distant, not knowing the visage of outraged justice for which Connal was famed and feared, and wondered at him.

"They are smug little cowards, these Coromi of yours.

Well, and I for one shall enjoy giving them a rude surprise. Maeve, have you finished? Listen, then, both of you, and I will tell you what to do..."

Less than an hour later the three of them pressed tight under the shadowing canopy of woodland and stared out at a wide green field, at rich flocks, at two men watching them with no more than a thin pack of dogs to aid them.

Through his whisper, Connal's enjoyment was clearly audible. "Maeve, get your knife ready. Remember, do not hurt them; I want them distracted, no more. Go."

So it was that one of the shepherds, with a sudden exclamation, looked up to see a thin figure in armor, obviously female, staggering down the narrow road that led from the hills. This woman, whoever she was, was plainly in distress, or exhausted; as he ran toward the road, shouting at his startled companion to stay with the flock, he saw her stop, lift a hand to her head as though with a sudden dizziness, and crumple slowly to the ground.

The two shepherds, when they staggered back to their village long after moonrise, had similar tales of woe to tell; both of them spoke, very vehemently, of how quickly it had all happened.

The man in the field, standing and staring over the fifty head of stolen cattle, was taken around the throat, dropped to his knees, gagged and trussed so suddenly that he had no time to raise a hand in self-defense, or even to see the face of his attacker. One moment he was free, the next he was securely tied and blindfolded, with a rough cloth thrust between his teeth to keep him from calling for help.

As for the man who ran to help a warrior woman collapsed in the road, he insisted to his furious chieftain that he had bent down to see if the poor lady still breathed when something hit him on the back of the skull and knocked him out. When he came to his senses, he was lying in an empty field beside his companion, with the stars overhead and not a single sheep in sight. While his companion had been trussed tight, their attackers had done a less thorough job on him; it was almost, he insisted, as though these mysterious thieves had meant for him to get free in the end.

The chieftain of the Coromi, a fierce and bad-tempered man, had them whipped for their carelessness. Of course, he sent a party out the next day, charging them to return with all the cattle taken and the thieves as well.

It never occurred to him that the invaders, with a sure-footed and knowledgeable guide, would travel quickly and all night. His scouting party did not set out until the next day, and by that time the flock and the people who took them had vanished without a trace.

So Mhul got his cattle back with no lives lost on either side, and Connal and Maeve got their horse. And from the green pastures of the southwest came the beginnings of a legend, a legend of a man and a woman who could vanish at will and best any enemy.

13

Friends Bearing Gifts

"Connal, I can smell the sea!"

Connal, who had been whispering endearments and encouragement to Huil, pulled the enormous beast to a halt. The horse, who for all his vast size was gentle as a lamb, stopped obediently and shook his great head. Connal turned to look over his shoulder at Maeve, perched high on the horse's rump behind him, and smiled.

"Why so excited, allana? Have you never smelt the sea?"

"No, never, or at least not that I can remember; if I ever came this close to the wide waters, I must have been no more than a babe. Oh, what a lovely smell! Salt, and such a freshness to it—it tingles on the skin." She licked her lips experimentally and added, "On the tongue, as well."

"It does that. You will see it shortly, for we have come very near to the coast. And you will see it at its finest, what is more, for nothing can compare to the sea in summer." He thought back to journeys along the eastern coast of the island, and spoke more to himself than to her. "I remember the march to Des-Gabair, how I remember it; but that was an autumn march, and the seas were rough. The waves broke high against the land, and the wind howled like spirits from the Sidh. Few of my men had ever gone that way before, and they were frightened, for it was near to Samhain and the voice of the wind came dark and terrible."

"Well, and I shall not be frightened, for I am not such a fool." She spoke with bright determination, her voice charged and designed to distract him, for in the months they had wandered alone together, she had become aware of a danger in him she had never suspected, and had sworn to herself to keep him from it, however she could.

It was not that he was fretting for his lost kingdom; even less was he dissatisfied with having no company but herself. Indeed, he had never much cared to have great hordes of people in his life, and had never been truly happy as ruler of his tuath. But she had come to believe, all myths and popular beliefs about the softness of women's hearts aside, that men were more sensitive to the bittersweet delights of memory than women. I am stronger than he is, she thought, as she had thought so often in recent weeks, stronger not in body or mind, but only because I mind things less. Carhainn was the same, and Flyn too; only look at our last quarrel, she thought, how much my father minded, and how quickly I grew accustomed. And what of gentle Brihainn and his fierce mother? A sensitive man and a fine warrior, yet his mother sits on Emain's throne. . . .

She, too, traveled the thorny paths of memory. With her sixteenth birthday just behind her, things that she had taken for granted in the self-absorbed years of her childhood were coming clear to her; with Connal as a constantly present example, she found herself remembering her parents more and more. And it was true, true; Nieve had been the stronger of the two, and tougher by far. Flyn might rage for a week over a slight or an insult, while Nieve would speak sharply, deal with the problem, and shrug it off when it was done.

She would never tell Connal of that belief, but it was strong in her nonetheless. It did not sadden her, nor did it give her any sense of power over him. Rather, it seemed to bring him even closer to her, and if he did not understand how she was able to know when a black mood threatened, he was certainly grateful for the soft arms that would wrap around him in a tight hug, or the sudden wild mood of desire that would lead her to tease him, tantalize him past all bearing, and pull him down into dark sweet waters to drown all thought and memory in the depths of blood thundering until he thought his head would burst from it.

And she had succeeded once again. He looked down at the soft hands with their long fingers, hands that should have been coarsened and roughened by the long months of chopping firewood and wielding weapons and yet were miraculously still silken and beautiful, and felt that uprush of wonder and gratitude she could always rouse in him. The darkness faded from his face, the taut cheekbones relaxing as he smiled back at her. His voice was gay.

"Well, let us water poor Huil; he has carried us since sunup without a balk or a whimper, and the day has grown hot indeed." He rubbed the long hair of Huil's mane. "A gift from the gods, this beast; I had hoped for a single poor horse that might be up to your weight when we struck our bargain with Muhl, and resigned myself to a long walk. Who could have hoped for such a benison?"

"Why, myself," she answered demurely, and slid from Huil's back. "No sooner did Mhul say the horse had been bred in Connacht than I knew he must be a wonder."

This teasing about the superiority of Connacht's horses had become a long-standing and familiar joke between them. Connal laughed down at her; reaching out to swipe at her head, he missed, overbalanced, and slid with a graceless thump from Huil's back. He landed on his rump in the road with a howl of dignity surprised, and shook his fist with mock menace at Maeve, who was leaning against Huil's broad hindquarters, convulsed with helpless laughter. He shook his head at her, just as Huil bent and nuzzled into his hair. Maeve, holding her sides, collapsed in tears of delight.

Connal pulled himself to his feet, trying to rub the soreness away. "If you were not a queen," he told her balefully, "I would beat you."

She was choking with giggles. "It is not my high estate that must keep you from that pleasure, my love, but rather my superior running speed. Oh, Connal, how silly you looked!"

"And that," he told her, "is the final straw. Queen or no queen—come back here!"

She had dodged round to Huil's other side, using the horse as a shield. "What, and be tickled for discourtesy? I am too wise for that! Oh no—Connal, put me down!"

Much to her surprise, he did. Lost in laughter, it took her a moment to notice the sudden tension, the upflung hand, the head cocked to listen, as Huil cocked his ears and whinnied suddenly. She straightened her back and twisted her head to listen. "What is it?"

"Someone comes." Connal pulled her quickly to her feet, then put his ear to the ground. "A mile down the road, perhaps less; only a single horse, I think, or perhaps two, no more than that. Walking, not cantering. Quickly, love, loose a spear and lead Huil from the main road." He jerked his head, scouting the broad and shining valleys for cover, and swore. "No, we cannot make the woods from here. Mount."

She pulled herself quickly onto Huil's back, and Connal followed. To her surprise, he mounted behind her. He saw her surprise and explained tersely. "You lead; I can throw a spear farther if need be, and this way your back is not exposed. Now turn Huil to face whoever comes, and keep that spear ready."

Mystified, she did as he ordered. "Connal, what is this? This is not the first time we have met some stray traveler on the roads of Muman. Why so worried, then?"

"I don't know. Just a feeling . . ." He kicked his heels lightly against the horse's flanks, spurring him to a light canter. Maeve hung on for dear life, for when Huil moved with any speed at all, the motion was great and tumultuous and merely to keep one's seat was a challenge.

She could hear it now, even above Huil's hoofbeats; two horses or so, coming toward them. It was a steady rhythm, clip-clop, clip-clop, of horses walking, not cantering, and her bewilderment at Connal's reaction increased; surely, moving at such a leisurely speed, these riders could hardly be desperate, or planning to lie in ambush?

They were closer now, the unseen horsemen, just around the next bend in the road. Obedient to Connal's whisper, she pulled Huil to a halt in the dead center of the empty road and waited. He tightened a hand on her shoulder.

Cormac, sitting on a roan mare with his harp dangling over his shoulder, rounded the bend. Right behind him came Brihainn, leading a beautiful black stallion. Together they turned the corner and pulled to a stop.

"A year, I thought it must be. A year, never to see you, my dearest companions but one. And here you are after but five months."

The rocky beach was lit with streaks of dancing firelight. Connal, a small pile of bones at his elbow, had stretched his long legs out before him; Maeve, who over the past months had discovered in herself a surprising talent for cookery in the wild, had been too busy skinning the two fat hares and mixing them with the barley stew to pay much heed to the ebb and flow of conversation.

Now, as the others were finishing their meal, she was just sitting down to begin. She heard the note of relaxation in his voice and smiled to herself. Pleasure she had come to know, and tension, and anger too; this was the first time she had seen Connal purely and simply relaxed. He had eaten and drunk, all the time exchanging eager snippets of news with the others, and any worry she might have nursed that this incursion from his past might upset him was laid to rest. She tore off a small chunk of hare and ate rapidly.

Brihainn, too, seemed to radiate calm. "A year. Yes. Did you really think I would fold my hands behind my mother's chair, back there in Emain? You told me to remain at Sheilagh's side for a month, and I followed your word to the letter. We got back to Emain at the new moon, Cormac and I, and broke the news. It was a good month before all the mutterings had died down. At the rising of the next new moon, Cormac mounted Fila and I took Lhiam from your private pen and away we went, in search of you." As Connal cast an involuntary glance at the great stallion, Brihainn's voice grew even softer. "Shame, chieftain. Did you truly think I would allow a hair of his hide to come to harm? As long as you live, he is yours. I have brought him to you, no more."

"You have indeed, and truth to tell, my heart is full at seeing him. But it leaves us with a problem; three horses, four riders. Either you must ride Lhiam yourself, cela, or else you must share Huil with Maeve."

Brihainn raised himself to one elbow to stare at the three horses. "What, sit astride that monster? You jest with me. By sweet Morrigan herself, where had you such a horse as that? Sure, and you didn't possess such a thing when you left Tara!"

"He was payment for services rendered; a petty chieftain called Muhl, in Kieran's lands. A neighboring tribe had raided his cattle, and we got it back for him." He heard a deep chuckle from Maeve, and pulled her close. "We did it very well, my lady and I; a small boy to guide us, a bit of trickery, and fifty head of prime cattle led over a hidden mountain road for a sunset. No blood shed, either."

Cormac, who was tuning his harp, looked up. "What, none hurt and all the cattle taken? That is truly well done. But why did you do it? Did you know this Muhl?"

Maeve finished the last of her supper and answered the question. "No, gentle bard. But we must eat, and sleep sometimes in a true bed when the nights are rough. Too, what better way to keep abreast of the news, and perhaps learn some scraps of information to lead us where we must go?"

"Ah." The bard ran his hands over the instrument, and the thin, sad notes echoed fitfully across the hushing sough of the waves. "The false druid."

"Yes." Maeve's mouth thinned. She remembered him, but not well enough; often had she cursed herself for not paying better attention to him for those few short moments when his hood dangled from his hand and his face was revealed to her. Her own anguish, the fact that she had been half out of her mind with grief and worry, did not serve to excuse her in her own mind. Many times as she lay sleepless beside Connal in a small cave or an open field, she had tried to reconstruct a map of the man's features, straining every faculty to recreate what had not come completely into focus at the vital time. And it was no good; she knew she would recognize him on sight, but she could not properly describe him. All she truly remembered was a hulking, muscular figure, and paleness. And, of course, the voice, the oddly beautiful voice, musical, with a strange lilt to it. Yes, she would know the voice. . . .

Connal locked his fingers, stretching the joints. "Well, Huil is a fine horse, for all his outlandish looks. He has carried both of us nobly, and I will hear no word against him." He cast a roguish look at Maeve. "How could he not look odd, being Connacht bred?"

Maeve, pulled from her reverie, opened her mouth to reply in kind but was forestalled by Brihainn. "That reminds me, lady; we bring you greetings, and news, from Cruachain."

Her eyes sparkled. "Oh, Brihainn, you are a dear man! How does Carhainn? How did my people react?"

He grimaced. "Not very well, lady; there are those among your loyal tuath, among your personal celi, who want nothing more than to rend this island from mountains to sea to find this false druid." He saw the flash of alarm, and added hastily, "They have accepted Carhainn as your chosen shadow, no fear, but they want you back again. No surprise there, for Carhainn himself would have you back in your own chair; where your shadow leads, your people will follow. They have forgiven Ulster, too, forgave them readily as being past blame, and truth to tell, that surprised me. It is good for men to show such sense; they see themselves, and Emain too, as innocent victims to some deep-laid plot."

"Well, they are surely right." Cormac spoke directly to Maeve, even while his hands ran scales across the strings of the harp. "I had speech with Carhainn, lady; he would not confide too deep in me, or in anyone, but he says he has some few ideas about all this. He sent a message with me to you, knowing that a bard would remember it aright."

Something, a breath of intuition or the ghost of a memory too long buried, moved over Maeve's shoulders like a cold hand. "Tell me, then. What said my shadow?"

Cormac placed the harp gently on the pebbled ground at his feet. Then he folded his hands and closed his eyes. His voice dropped to a flat singsong, an uncanny echo of the tones of chivalry Maeve had used in pleading her case to the master at Tara.

"He bids you call your memory to aid, lady. He bids you remember Ahnrach and her day of dying, to remember three men left to sleep in their blood at the end of your spear. He bids you remember an attack when you were scarce more than a babe, an attack of raiders so perfect that a general might have led them. He bids you to think on the same field, steeped in the blood of your father the High Chieftain, and a ring left there for you to find. He bids you remember that the servant you sent in search of a holy man never came home again. Lastly, he bids you to think on the druid who came to you, alone and unescorted."

The beautiful, tired voice stopped. Cormac reached for Connal's flask and, without apology, helped himself to a long draught. When he spoke again, his voice was normal.

"There was no more than that, lady. It was little enough, I thought. But he bade me give you those words, and said you would understand."

"Yes. Yes, I understand." The emerald eyes were wide and glazed, fixed sightlessly on the pulse of the surf. Her cousin, thrown across a horse, suddenly calm, understanding, accepting. Raiders split into flanks. What had her father said to her that day so many years ago? The words suddenly came back to her, so clear that it seemed Fly stood at her shoulder and spoke. *This means something don't like the smell of, Maeve. These men have a leader who knows something of warfare. . . .*

Suddenly dizzy, she shook her head, and as the dizziness faded, the memory faded as well. A connection. Carhainn believed there to be a connection between those two attacks, so many years apart. But surely he was wrong; they had been raiders, and raiders were savages, not organized men to keep a leader at their head for ten long years! And even if he were right, what had those raiders to do with druids?

"Maeve."

Connal's voice was very gentle. She jerked herself away from contemplation, and found all eyes on her.

"No worry, chieftain mine; I was merely doing what my shadow bade me do. No harm in that."

The pounding of the surf, the softness of the summer night, were making themselves felt. Brihainn suddenly yawned, wide and huge, his muscles as he stretched rippling like a cat in the moonlight. "Oh, I am weary. Tell me, before sleep takes me, what else have you been doing these months, while we scoured the southwest in search of you?"

Connal rose to his feet and began to spread a warm sheepskin for Maeve to sleep on. "You will laugh to hear it, my brother, but we have been hiring ourselves out as mercenaries. Do you see me as a paid arm?"

"Sure, and why not? You have near the best arm in all the five provinces; it is said only the arm of the Faery Queen is more sure, and no one disputes your stronger muscles or superior strength." He turned to stare at Maeve. "Why did you make that noise, lady?"

"May Crom protect me, not you too! Am I never to be rid of this Faery Queen nonsense? Was all the world at Tara?"

Brihainn grinned. "No, lady. I did not hear the name at Tara; I heard it at Kieran's court, from one of his celi, Kas by name. A big barbaric fellow; do you know him?"

Maeve found Connal's eyes and burst into laughter. "Know him? Not in himself, Brihainn, but if he is who I think he is, we did a small service to his kinsman on a hilly road a half day's ride from Kieran's tuath."

Connal saw Brihainn's mystification and explained. "We stopped to see Kieran, not giving our names; you know he is favorably disposed toward us and spoke for us to the master? Well, we had some converse with him; a small campfire we had made in the wild had got out of control, and Maeve was a little burned. We sorely needed a dry bed and someone to tend my lady's hurts. Kieran helped us and told us he would send this Kas after us if he could learn anything about this druid we seek. He made us very welcome, gave us a fine meal and a warm bed, and let it be known to the oinach that we were ambassadors from another province. Whether they believed that tale I leave to your imagination. We took him up on his hospitality right gratefully and left court the next day, taking the road south."

Maeve took up the tale. "We had not yet gone out of sight when we came upon a warrior in the road, being set upon by four big bruisers, raiders perhaps; this warrior was a big fellow but, truth to tell, he was sore overmatched. We thought this most unfair and set about his attackers."

Maeve giggled suddenly, her eyes gleaming at the memory. "They must have thought we were shades of the Sidh, for no sooner did we kick Huil to a gallop than they shrieked and began to run off in all directions. The warrior was wounded, but not badly; Connal and I chased these fellows down, trussed them up like so many chickens, and left them by the side of the road to wait for Kieran's justice. The warrior was most thankful, gave us each a gold piece, and told us very proudly that he was younger brother to one of Kieran's personal celi, Kas the Strong-Shouldered."

Cormac was grinning. "I think it was your horse they shrieked at, lady, not you."

Brihainn shot him an amused look and spoke before Maeve could protest. "Yes, that is the same man." He glanced over at the massive beast, beside whom even the great war stallion Lhiam was dwarfed. He caught Cormac's eye and found himself unable to resist. "Cormac is right, lady. It is no wonder the raiders fled at your approach; truth to tell, had I been in their shoes and seen that horse of yours, I should have fled myself. Well, should Kas the Strong-Shouldered suddenly stumble into our midst, I pray you will not kill him; if he comes, it will be because Kieran has sent him with word for us. And I suspect, lady, that this overmatched warrior of yours guessed who you were and told his brother. I am sorry if it upsets you, but you are called the Faery Queen in every tuath in Hibernia right now, and I see no way around it."

"I suppose I must learn to live with it, then." She lay down on the soft skins and pulled them close. "Cormac, as you love us, give me some music to send me to sleep."

"I would like to ask a question of you, lady, if I may."
Maeve, immersed in a cluster of thorny bushes

pulled herself free and stood. Her war helmet, lying on the ground beside her, was full of berries, her lips stained with the juice of those fatter prizes she had been unable to resist. She took up her spears, set aside as she scrambled through bramble and thicket, and slid them back in their slings.

Cormac watched and waited. Since the night before he had been curious, yet he had not wanted to ask his question within earshot of the others, and had been wondering how he might get her by herself. It had been Maeve herself who, after breakfast, had cast a shrewd glance from Connal's face to Brihainn's and announced that she had seen some splendid blackberries, fat and glossy with the bloom of summer on them, halfway back to the road. She had patted Brihainn gently on the arm, kissed Connal, told them to have a nice talk together, and swept Cormac off in her wake before the others could say a word about it.

Now, looking down at Maeve, he saw the same understanding in her face. Lugh cover me, he thought, but she sees a long way for one so young. Well, and he had asked permission; it was for her to grant it.

She was smiling. "Ask what you will, Cormac."

He reached for the helmet full of berries, his thin fingers moving randomly among them as he ordered his thoughts. I will be direct, he thought. She has no guile to her and would see through tact. He drew a deep breath and asked his question straight out.

"That message, from Carhainn. It puzzled me. What did it mean, lady? Will you tell me?"

"Ah." The smile died. "I am sure you delivered it true in every word." She reached for her breastplate and shrugged it over her arms. "You wish to know more of it, then?"

Be silent, be secret, he thought; even Brihainn might have trouble keeping to that path with one so open as this girl. He stared at her, puzzled and frowning. He had been all his life used to women who understood shadow better than they would ever understand light, who balanced the two as easily as the gods balanced the seasons. It was, in Cormac's eyes, their greatest strength and the single most fascinating thing about them. Maeve was different; she stood in the light all the time, looking at the world through clear eyes as a child might, never worrying about the darkness that waited behind every corner, in every man's eye.

"It is rude to stare." Thus jerked back to reality, he began to stammer an apology, but words and embarrassment alike were stilled as she turned her face to him and he saw the faint smile there.

"I ask your pardon, lady. Yes, I would like very much to know more of it. It set something in me moving, and a bard who ignores what moves in him is a failed bard."

"True." She linked her arm through his. Together they began to walk slowly back toward the beach. "What puzzled you most, fila? The mention of three men sleeping?"

"Who was Ahnrach, lady? Who was she and why did Carhainn enjoin you to remember her day of dying?"

Perhaps, he thought suddenly, perhaps I was wrong. The green eyes were hooded now, shadowed and dark with memory; she looked, of a sudden, much older than her years. Her voice was a peculiar blend of flatness and softness. Something trickled down his back, something that would in time distill itself from the dark waters of conscious memory and the understanding that ran through the veins and not the brain, and become song. Maeve's voice came hollow and enormous, too big for the small body, and it washed him as the language of his own hands on the harp might. Music, he thought, this voice I hear is music from the Sidh, flowing dark and enticing. . . .

"Ahnrach. Ahnrach was my cousin, fila, my cousin and my dearest companion, my nurse, the daughter of my mother's sister. I was young then, so young. She was older than me, perhaps ten years older." They walked steadily, Maeve as sure-footed as a cat, and he noted with fascination that she never looked at the road, did not, in fact, seem to blink.

"You must vision me, you man of Ulster, vision me as I was then. Some five years old, destined for the high chair of Cruachain, my father's pride and best delight; they knew I could use either hand to good advantage, and already I was the stuff of legend, though I thank all the gods I did not know it then. Prized I was, kept like a rare flower, with no one to tell me why it should be so. My people held me in awe, the children of the celi and the oinach were afraid of me, too careful."

He could see her, the small girl, self-contained, lonely perhaps. She stopped beside him, her hands hanging limp at her sides, and the compelling voice continued.

"But I cared for none of that, for I had Ahnrach. She was gay, gay and good, always laughing, always knowing how to bring me out of myself and taking me into joy and laughter with her. She was very beautiful, too, red and gold and white, slender as a reed."

Something rippled across her face, and Cormac took an involuntary step closer to her, instinctively protective. "Carhainn loved her, as did we all. They would have bonded had she lived long enough."

"That is pain, and sorrow too." Cormac's voice had slid, without his knowledge, closer to the formal cadences of poetry. "Yet Carhainn bade you remember her day of dying."

"We had ridden out." She had begun to breathe heavily. "A party of, oh, I don't remember, twenty, I think. An armed troop . . . Ahnrach, myself, our old healer. We had gone perhaps an hour from the gates of Cruachain. We were attacked."

"And Ahnrach was slain."

She turned to look at him, staring from wide dead eyes that were blind with remembered anguish. "Slain? Yes, but not immediately. Carhainn rode with us that day; he led my personal guard, you see, and Ahnrach came because of that. She was not fond of riding, but she rode that day. She had tried to cry off, but I held it out to her as a bribe, that Carhainn would come. I bade her think on how fine he looked in the saddle, so tall, so proud, leading my guard."

Her eyes were the color of the pine forest now, muddy and mysterious. "We were outnumbered. I knew, even so young, that they wanted to take me hostage, and Carhainn would not let it happen. Ahnrach was taken, thrown across a raider's horse. We found her later at the top of the hill."

It was all there in her voice, the specter of an ancient guilt never, across the years, completely laid. He felt for a terrible moment what Carhainn must have felt, the utter helplessness of watching his lady taken, his knowledge that his duty to the deadly child with the two spears must come ahead of any other consideration. In the bright summer sunlight he felt suddenly cold and laid a gentle hand on Maeve's rigid arm. Her small hands had balled into fists, the pearly nails marking the skin of her palms.

They resumed their walk toward the beach, each silent awhile, busy with their own thoughts. Suddenly Maeve spoke.

"My father was worried by the attack, worried by the way it had been planned and executed. I remember that he spoke to me about it as we stood near my cousin's ruined body."

"And that is what Carhainn would have you remember?"

"I think so, yes." They turned from the path to clamber across the rocky bluff that led down to the beach. High above the cliffs towered, their sides scummed with the droppings of sea birds. Cormac stopped suddenly, his ears cocked to sound; a crackling, quickly stilled. Could there be a beast of some kind up there, watching down on them? Connal and Brihainn, close together, were small, inexpressive figures far below them. The sound did not come again, and Maeve seemed not to have heard it. She spoke slowly.

"Those raiders—they split into two flanks, one to cut us off from the rear. It was well planned, planned like an act of war, and yet of the four of us who survived, no one could remember seeing anyone who might have been a leader of both factions. He—or she—must have been watching out of sight, at the top of the hill, perhaps. It worried my father; he said it looked like an attack led by one with some true knowledge of warfare."

Cormac opened his mouth to speak, but the chance never came. There was a sudden slither of loose shale, a shower of small stones, and then Cormac was moving faster than he had ever moved in his life. He threw himself at Maeve, hurling her to one side, smothering her with his own body as an enormous boulder roared within inches of them as they lay pressed into the cliffside.

Over the confused sound of his own heart and the enormous noise of the boulder crashing below them, he heard a shout from Connal and the terrified neighing of the horses. Then the boulder came to rest on the beach, perhaps ten feet from where Connal and Brihainn had been sitting. A small cloud of pulverized sand rose and settled, and quiet fell once more, broken only by the soft hushing of the tide and the squealing of the horses.

Cormac, releasing Maeve, pulled himself slowly to his feet. He was scratched, his clothing torn slightly, but other than that he was unharmed. He helped Maeve to her feet with hands that shook, barely noticing the long cut on one cheek that trickled blood down her neck. There was a small pock in her armor where something in the hailstorm of loose stones had gone home.

"It is over, lady. Are you safe?"

"Unharmed, yes." Her eyes, fixed on the soaring peaks above them, suddenly widened. She whipped her head around to look wildly at the sand below, just as Connal and Brihainn, who had flung themselves away from the onslaught, got to their feet and began to move in different directions, Connal racing toward the path that led to where Maeve and Cormac stood, and Brihainn toward the rearing horses. She let out a deep sigh and slumped suddenly.

Connal reached them moments later, his face an odd mixture of fury and concern. "All well, allana?"

"Indeed." Leaning back against him, reaction set in; she began to shudder, long tearing spasms that shook both of them, and became aware of the blood on her face.

Connal was staring upward, his brows drawn into a straight bar of concentration, his onyx eyes glittering. "Did either of you hear anything before that thing fell? Maeve?" He felt the tiny shake of her head, and tightened his grip around her. "Cormac?"

"Yes." His breathing had steadied. "Lady Maeve was telling me about an attack on her people, and I stopped. I heard . . . something, I don't know. It was ill-defined, a rustling, a crackling, not too near and quickly gone. I stopped for a moment, and then the first stones came down."

Connal put Maeve from him, his eyes still fixed on the clifftops, and spoke curtly. "Maeve. Go down to the beach; Brihainn will need help with Huil, for the horses were sore frightened. Cormac, to me; let us see where— and how—this mysterious boulder fell."

Since it was Cormac who had taught Connal how to climb his first tree, it was not surprising that the bard reached the crest first. He stood waiting, listening to Connal come carefully up the scree behind him, and stared at the roughened patch of earth on the very edge of the hill. As Connal pulled his leg over the rock and came up behind him, Cormac pointed.

"See. There it sat, the great stone; the earth below it was strewn with loose stuff, shale, slate." He glanced at Connal, who had dropped to his knees and was carefully examining the ground, and spoke doubtfully. "It could have slipped, I suppose; there is some wind up here." And, indeed, this was the truth. Though the lower reaches of the shoreline were calm enough, the breeze at the top was stiff enough to lift Connal's black hair, as yet unbraided for riding, into a standing corona around his head.

"Perhaps." Connal sounded preoccupied. He ran a finger across the earth. "This rocky stuff will take no imprint; even if it had, all would have been brushed away by the dust the boulder raised as it fell." He tilted his head toward Cormac. "I have trouble, fila, in believing that this great stone fell with no help. Sure, and it must have sat in this patch long years. If it was undisturbed, what would send it crashing down at precisely the moment to do Maeve, or myself, an injury?" He shook his head. Cormac bent to help him to his feet. Shoulder to shoulder they scanned the rocky bluff. They saw a few small openings in the cliff nearby, which might have been caves or only cracks, a few thickets of sparse trees, their height and majesty stunted by long exposure to the sandy winds and the salt air; no true place to hide.

"We might look a lifetime, lord, and find nothing at all." Cormac was measuring the distance to the edge of the cliff and taking note of the additional paths that led down the back of the rocks. "If anyone were up here, he is long gone now; see how the paths all lead different ways." He saw the thin mouth, pressed tight against thought and rage, and spoke quietly. "The Lady Maeve was bleeding; should we not go down and see that she is well?"

Connal, hitching his cloak over one shoulder, turned toward the path that led back down to the beach. As they started their descent, he spoke thoughtfully. "It could have fallen alone. But I do not believe in this coincidence."

Cormac, planting one foot and swinging his body onto the jutting rocks with easy grace, spoke reasonably. "But lord, who would do such a thing to you, and in so stealthy a way?"

Connal stopped so suddenly that Cormac stumbled against him and nearly fell. He thought of another boulder falling on him, a boulder he had thought loosened by the night's storming, and thought of a dying campfire, both of them falling into light sleep, and how Maeve had woken screaming because her sheepskin was afire. "Stealthy? No stealthier, fila, than leaving a stolen ring under a father's body for his daughter to find." He heard Cormac suck in breath, and smiled grimly. "No more stealthy than that."

Higher up the hillside, his big body pressed as small as possible against the walls of the tiny cave, Covac heard them come and go.

When the voices and the footsteps had died away, he slid from the cave and stood gazing down. Something had happened to his face in the months since Tara; the pale eyes seemed to blink less than ever, and the thin mouth had seemingly frozen into a perpetual purse-lipped grin that carved deep grooves in his cheeks. A small tic leaped where his lips met, a small trapped flutter of tension.

The druid's robes, rolled into a tight ball, were crammed into the fine pack he carried. He was dressed in nondescript clothing, his feet swaddled in soft sheepskin boots; judging the sacred robes too risky in light of Connal's and Maeve's sworn intent, he had stolen his present garb not two days away from Tara.

The death's head rictus that passed for a smile deepened as he remembered the theft. Of all his robberies, all his killings, that had been the easiest, for what man would argue with a holy man? So easy to stop in the isolated cottage, to beg food as a wandering seer. So lucky, surely such luck was the blessing of the gods, that the man had been of a size with him. And fine, so fine, to leave the man and his wretched family in their blood and walk out with their money, their weapons, a fine leather pack, and clothing too—

His pleasurable thoughts were interrupted by the distant whinny of a horse. Keeping low to the ground lest one of them glance up and see him, he made for the edge of the cliff and looked down. Saddled and leaving once again; even at this distance he could tell his nephew from the others, sitting with the red-haired bitch on that outlandish horse of theirs. Brihainn, the king's bastard, astride the war stallion. That meddlesome bard on the roan.

He went back to the tiny cave and retrieved his pack. It shivered slightly as he lifted it; the snake, its jeweled eyes open in the darkness of its home and prison, no doubt wanting to stretch itself in the sun. Well, it would have to wait. Where those four went, he must follow. Five long months had passed since Tara, and five long months he had followed them. One year, the master had said, one year to bring the false druid back in chains.

The tic jumped and stilled. Whatever would happen at the gathering for the next festival of Imbolc, it would not be that. He had come close, very close indeed, to killing them; the first, tentative try, the morning after the storm in Muman, when he had caught up with them— he had almost succeeded in sending his nephew to join the ranks of his ancestors. And slipping silently between the night-shrouded trees to their sleeping place, to take a stick in hand and gently lead the fire to Maeve's dry bed; had not that attempt, too, nearly taken one of them?

Someday, he thought, someday soon. I will kill them, however many guards they set, however light they sleep.

He picked up the pack and began a slow, near-silent descent down the back side of the hill. This path neither Cormac nor Connal had seen; it was barely a path at all, invisible to the naked eye from any distance. He moved down between the stunted trees toward the wide fields below. No cover for a horse, perhaps, but for a single man on foot there was cover enough.

What he had overheard had alarmed him. It was bad enough that their numbers had increased; sure, and it was no part of his plan to raise the slightest suspicion that the fire, the boulders, were anything other than accidental. As much as he might hate his brother's brat, it would not do to underestimate him. That could be fatal.

He moved quietly around the base of the cliff, peering through the waving reeds that grew, this close to the sea, so tall that they completely covered him. He heard hoof-beats, a burst of distant conversation, a spurt of laughter, and his mouth tightened with hatred.

They were going north. Well, and so would he go north. It would be harder now to get close to them as they slept; with two more of them, they could set a guard to watch while the others slept. That meant that his attempts must follow the one that had only just failed, boulders falling, trees. . . .

An idea stirred in his mind. North. If they went north, following the coast road, they would come into Connacht, to the wide forests that banded the borders between Kieran's realm and Maeve's. And the only good road led straight through those forests.

What was an advantage in on situation might be a disadvantage in another; though they might outnumber him in bodies, he had the advantage over them when it came to speed, encumbered as they were.

He cut off to the hunter's track that ran parallel to the main coast road and began his journey north. With any luck at all, he would be there a full day before them.

14

Borderlands

As Samhain grew near, and with it the snows of winter, four riders pulled their weary mounts to a halt before the scanty palisades of a tuath that was poor by any standards.

It was almost nightfall, and Maeve was cold. She never complained of it, but half a year's sleeping in the open, or with only the rough walls of a cave to keep the wind from her back, had made her aware of how easily she chilled. Today had been mercifully dry, but there was a sharp nip in the air and her ears ached with it. As the horses stopped, they heard the first spasmodic barking of the village curs.

Maeve pulled her fur cloak tight around her shoulders and cast an uneasy glance at Connal. "By all the gods, but this is a sorry place! Poor comfort here, and I'll wager they are hungry with it. So close to the sea, too! What is Kieran about, to let his people starve?"

She caught a razor-sharp glance, both wry and amused, between Connal and Brihainn, and lifted one eyebrow. Connal answered her gently.

"No blame to Kieran for this place of poverty, allana; we came out of Muman late yesterday. If there is blame . . ." The words died, and he shrugged.

It took a moment for his meaning to sink in. When it did, her face paled. "Out of Muman? Can this be Connacht, my own fair province?"

242

"It is that." This came from Cormac, who had come up close behind them on the roan mare Fila. "We are only just into your lands, lady; this is the first of the tuatha. These people live in the borderlands, and suffer for it."

Her face was scarlet with shame and anger intermingled. "I would have none of my people suffer. How is this?"

"No fault of theirs, Maeve," Connal explained. "Raiders love the borderlands; they may sweep down and take what they will, with no one to answer to. If these victims go to Kieran, they must prove that their attackers came from Muman." He saw pain in her face, and recognized outraged justice. "The same can be said for Connacht. No High King—or queen, for that matter—can be expected to comb the mountains in search of thieves that may just as easily have come from the other side of the borders. So these people dare not put their time into rearing cattle, for it will be stolen from them in the end. As for fishing, why, they suffer there as well. Both provinces claim the sea here and use it mightily; it's scarce pickings left for those poor folk. Between leaders and outlaws, they go hungry."

Maeve's mouth was trembling. "When I come to my throne once more, heads will fall, I promise you that. I knew nothing of this, nothing!"

Connal laid a comforting hand on her shoulder. "You were not queen long enough to know." He looked up. "Ah. Poor or no, we must have shelter tonight. Here, if I mistake not, is the village vanguard. But where are the menfolk?"

It was a small group that approached them, women and children only, and they wore all too clearly the signs of poverty, the caution of those who live under constant threat. They carried farming tools, held gingerly as weapons; Maeve saw fear and wariness in the eyes of the children, and quickly made up her mind. With the widest smile she could muster, she slid from Huil's back and turned to face the incongruous group.

"A fair night to you, good people," she said cheerfully. "We are traveling east and hoped for a dry bed and a warm fire. We have food to share with you and can pay nicely for your hospitality."

There was a moment of silence as the ragged women

looked quickly back and forth. With a slight gesture to the men to remain mounted, Maeve waited, easy and smiling, for a response. Finally, one of the women stepped forward.

"Greetings, lady. We have little to offer you, but a dry bed you can have." The woman, tall and thin, with the blackened teeth and lined face of the poor, glanced from Maeve's spears to the weapons the others carried. There was a surprising shrewdness in her glance.

"Warriors, are you? To say truth, we would be glad of some weapons tonight, and gladder still for strong arms to wield them. I am Pera. Will you follow us in, then?"

The voice was gruff, deep for a woman, and surprisingly elegant under it all. A suspicion began to grow in Maeve's mind. As the men dismounted, leading the horses through the gates under the admiring eyes of the children, she continued her conversation with Pera.

"We shall be only too glad to put our arms at your service, lady. But where are your menfolk? What has happened here, that they have left you and the children to fend for yourselves so close to Samhain?"

A pair of black eyes, very reminiscent of Connal's, slid sideways. The look was appraising, as sharp as a knife, and for a moment Maeve felt oddly undressed before it. A moment later the eyes slid away; Maeve had apparently passed whatever unspoken test Pera had set for her, and the woman had decided to confide.

"They have gone east, lady, to the great forest." Pera's mouth, thin with long years of keeping secrets, closed for a moment over the rotted teeth. "There was a rape and a killing, only yesterday. One of our girls, fair as a lark in the morning, was taken and left to lie in her blood. They have gone to seek the man who did it."

Remember Ahnrach and her day of dying. Ice moved up Maeve's spine and settled. Her voice was taut.

"May they find the man who did that thing and unman him for all his days. But surely it will be hard for them, so many together to find a solitary man. Have you thought to send to Cruachain for help, Pera?"

The shrug, the sudden hopelessness on the lined face, told Maeve the story. So Connal had been in the right of it, then; these people believed that no chieftain would bother with such as them. The chill Maeve felt melted away in a rush of bright anger, so that she barely heard Pera's reply.

"Lord Carhainn, him that bides on Queen Maeve's throne, has much to do, lady. All the land knows of the doings at Tara; there was much confusion in Cruachain, and many things to occupy the man's time. We would not worry him with a matter so small."

Maeve's sudden wild desire to tell this woman the truth was forestalled by Connal. He was close behind them, listening to every word. Now he spoke compellingly.

"Not so small, lady. Not small at all, if it has cost you a loved life. We know Lord Carhainn very well. If your men have no luck, we shall willingly send him a token for you, with some few of your men. Carhainn is a good man, just and strong; by all the gods, he is not one to wave you off because you cannot give him gold, lady, and such thinking is unworthy not only of the High Throne, but of you, yourselves."

Maeve stopped and stared up into his face, speechless with surprise. He was white, his lips compressed. In the dimming light of evening she thought she saw sweat glisten on his brow. And Brihainn, at his shoulder, looked odder still. One hand was rubbing at the scar at his mouth, and by the gods, was that a glaze of tears?

Then Brihainn turned his face away, Connal stepped out from under the flickering torches, and the moment passed. Pera was looking at Connal with frank approval.

"A pretty speech, gentle lord. Perhaps, if you are still here when my husband returns, you can put your offer to him; he is chieftain, and I have nothing to say without him."

So, Maeve thought, I was right; despite her ragged clothes, her body gaunt with constant toil and want, she is the chieftain's lady. She glanced over Pera's shoulder to where two children had separated themselves from the rest and come to stand staring, and suddenly broke into laughter.

"By all the gods, Pera, are these yours?"

The harsh face suddenly went soft. With that softening came a complete change; exhaustion was suddenly replaced

with pride, and even her back seemed straighter. "Mine,
yes. Girls! Step up, my lovelies, and greet the warriors."

To those unused to such things, identical twins can be
disconcerting. The girls were no older than two, with hair
the color of corn and wide gray eyes. Now that their
mother had welcomed these strangers, their initial
nervousness had apparently fallen from them. They bobbed
identical bows, the gray eyes casting up at precisely the
same moment. Connal burst out laughing; even Cormac,
no lover of small children, had a look of tender amusement. Brihainn, staring down at this marvel of nature,
spoke genially.

"Why, you are blessed, lady! Not one fair daughter,
but two, and the best of it is that they will never quarrel
over who is the finer to look at." He caught faint smiles,
ghostly imprints of their mother, on the two small faces.
"And have these blessings name, lady?"

"They do." Pera, beaming at compliments so obviously sincere, drew the two children together at her knees.
"Though to be sure, it's a hard enough time we have to
tell one from the other; my husband swears one name
should do for both of them, since they share all else! This
is Maeve, and there on the left, that is Nieve."

In the sudden silence Pera saw the smiles fade. The
warrior woman looked for all the world like someone had
struck her; pale as a spirit, she was, and the men with her.
Now, what was this?

Maeve, her voice trembling, spoke at last. Her discomfort was so obvious that even the children caught it,
caught, too, the way the big man in the heavy armor put
his arms around her, as though for protection. "Maeve and
Nieve. Named for the high ladies of Connacht, I take it.
Well, my girls, may you grow brave and strong. Pera,
where can we tether the horses?"

"This way; there's a paddock, with a roof of sorts."
Pera, glancing over her shoulder at Maeve in puzzlement,
led the way. Slings over her shoulders, she had. And was
that a wisp, a single flyaway tendril, of copper hair peeping
out like a naughty babe from under that fierce helm of
hers? Yes, it was. And a shock at the names.

Realization, when it came, nearly took her breath away. It must be, it must. Slings, each with a spear to fill it. Green eyes, beautiful green eyes, like a stormy winter sea. A tall man in armor, comely and dangerous to look at. Why, the tales that had come through here since the great fight at Tara had been garbled but, to be sure, they had all been concerned with the gallant beauty of the young queen. Could it be, could she be so lucky? And if this were truly the lost queen and her northern chieftain, who were the other two?

Chattering, her mind racing with its own thoughts, she saw the horses tethered and led the way indoors. In the mean stone hut she quickly made a small fire and waved the visitors, and the children too, to come and warm themselves.

The tall one, surely he was the one they called the Victorious, opened his pack and pulled out two fresh-killed hares and an enormous slab of dried mutton. The man with the harp began to carve, and the third man to pour. Within moments they were all eating, passing conversation that was light and meaningless. Only the warrior woman sat silent, a spitted rabbit in her hand, staring into the fire.

The twins were eating rapidly and with such intense concentration that Connal realized how rarely hot food must come their way. He realized something else, as well; Pera had her suspicions. If she had felt none before, the telltale shock on Maeve's face when the girls were presented had certainly raised them. He took a bite of mutton and, on an impulse he could never explain, bent forward to Maeve.

"You should take your helm off, allana, else it will overheat, and you with it."

The green eyes were streaked with firelight. She seemed to be lost in some hinterland of the mind where memory was master and ancient hurts still had the power to wound. Her voice sounded dead.

"My helm? Yes. You are right. I had forgot I was wearing it." She addressed the man with the harp. "Cormac, fila, will you hold the stick?"

She deposited the helmet on the floor beside her and

shook the fiery mane free. It cascaded nearly to her waist, a glowing veil as bright as the embers she stared into.

And Pera, looking up sharply, found the tall one's eyes fixed on her own. There was an approving smile on his face, and his eyes held amusement and confirmation.

"Yes," he told her smoothly. "You are right, and we are exactly who you think we are. Now, Lady Pera, if you would be so kind, tell us about this rape. Your menfolk are not the only ones on the hunt."

Maeve, her attention reclaimed, started. Pera was staring at her, as were the children. Before the chieftain's wife could move, one of the twins moved first. She put out a tiny hand and touched first the bright helmet and then Maeve's hair. Her voice held all the admiration of a tiny child for a distant star.

"Pretty," she said, and went back to her food.

No one spoke. Maeve stared at the child with tears in her eyes, and the others stared at Maeve. When the silence had spun itself out, Pera sighed and pulled the twins close.

"I meant it as an honor, Queen Maeve," she said quietly. "No more than that. So. You wish to know about this rape, Victorious, and I will tell you."

The girls, replete and warm in their mother's arms, were already drowsing. The gruff voice was pitched low and clear.

"She was just a village girl. Fourteen summers she'd seen, and Eilen was her name. A fair lass, she was, but too trusting and too easily pleased." Pera looked at Maeve. "She looked like you, high one. Red hair, pale skin. Not so beautiful as you are, but comely enough. We all liked her. Sure, and none of us thought she would meet such a destiny as that." She shook her head, and the twins settled closer. Her voice was sad. "Seems the druid was wrong."

"Druid."

Pera seemed not to notice the electricity in Connal's voice, or how Brihainn's hand froze with his food halfway to his mouth. "Didn't I say so? A druid, yes. A big man with a voice like a fila's harp. He was through here not three days past." Tears, shockingly unexpected, welled up in her eyes and spilled down her thin cheeks. "He read her destiny for her. Blessed with a special destiny, he said."

"Blessed or cursed. Well, and he should know, this druid." Now the strangeness in Connal's voice caught her. She looked up into his face, her eyes wide with disbelief. "You cannot mean. . . ? No, Victorious. It cannot be. Would a seer do such a thing?"

Maeve, cross-legged and stiff-backed, stared across the fire. The leaping flames turned her face scarlet, their color lost, conquered, by her waterfall of hair.

"Pera. A voice like a harp, you said."

There was an ugly expectancy in the small room, and Pera's arms tightened around her sleeping babes. "Like a harp, dancing, lovely. Ran like water, it did. But—"

"Remember Ahnrach and her day of dying," said Cormac softly. He was staring at Maeve, the harp dangling laxly between his hands. "Ahnrach. Red and gold and white, you said. And a druid with a voice like a harp . . ."

Maeve was breathing heavily now, a picture coming into her mind, sudden, complete, undeniable, the image she had strained for and missed so many times in the months gone by. "Ahnrach," she said, and her voice was deadly, dreaming. Connal shivered suddenly, his eyes caught by her. "Ahnrach, sweet cousin, and her day of dying. Red-haired. A small girl with red hair, to be taken hostage." The pictures were whirling now, an unbearable tapestry of images caught and twisted, bound inextricably together and impossible to separate. "A voice of music. Did he take his hood off, this druid of yours?"

Deep in sleep, one of the children whimpered as Pera's hold tightened to pain. "Yes," she whispered. "Yes. He took it off when he read Eilen's destiny. They were alone together, but I was looking through the hide."

Connal's voice was a whip cracking. "You saw him?"

"I have said it." The story, known by her only as disconnected gossip and fragments of the truth, was coming clear. "A big man, and pale. Pale hair, eyes of a pale blue, pale skin. A man of power."

Maeve made a face at her, a transforming face, the face of a stranger, another person altogether. It was a smile of sorts, a pinching of the lips where they met, and dozens

of tiny lines sprang into being around her tender mouth.
Her green eyes were wide open and staring, and exquisite
cheekbones peaked to form deadly hollows beneath. It
lasted only a moment, this living mask, and only the
chieftain's wife saw it, for the three men were staring at
each other. It was involuntary, and Maeve did not even
know she had done it; certainly she could not have sum-
moned the memory to do so again. Pera, terrified, threw
up one arm, her fingers moving frantically as she warded
off evil.

"That was his image, lady," she moaned. "His very
face, the very picture of him."

"And he read her destiny," Connal whispered. "The
swine, the filthy swine. Let us see if Great Crom will help
him hide from his own destiny when at last we find him."

In the charged atmosphere of the room, where five
adults sat and stared at each other, one of the twins woke
up and began to cry.

In the highest reaches of an ancient oak tree, Covac
sat perfectly still among the concealing foliage and looked
down at an angry mob.

They were a poor lot, he thought, and considered
them dispassionately. He recognized most of the drawn
faces beating uselessly in the undergrowth so far below
him; these were the men of that pathetic tuath, set like a
rotten plum in the bare hollow where the hills of Connacht
met those of Muman, where he had donned his druid robe
and added one more terrified face, fair as a flower, to his
store of memories. The druid robes were once more in the
pack that rested beside him on the stout branch. One
hand, moving with silent ease, slipped into his tunic and
came free with a long strand of curling red hair across its
palm.

That the men of the tuath had given chase was
surprising in itself. The whole day he had scrambled,
keeping just ahead of them as a leaping rabbit might run
with the hounds at its tail. It was not until, panting and
exhausted, he had gained the safety of the first of Connacht's
great forests that the realization had come to him. They
did not suspect the passing holy man, these stupid peas-

ants. They had no idea, in fact, who they were chasing. He had only to find a sturdy tree and wait them out. Sooner or later they would give up the chase, returning baffled and empty-handed to their poor little homes.

And once again the gods had shown him favor. In spite of the irresistible stop, in spite of the precious time he had used in the taking of the village girl, he was still some two days ahead of his prey. Time enough to recoup his strength from the headlong, panic-stricken flight along the eastern road. Time enough to set a trap and then spring it.

Suddenly impatient, he parted the dense branches just enough to afford him a better view. Yes, they were going; already the crowd was smaller, the voices fainter. These superstitious fools had no wish to linger among the tall trees with Samhain so close. Three of them, their clothing torn and their faces scratched from the whipping brambles, were huddled in low-voiced converse directly below his tree.

He felt a stab of contempt so strong that it brought a sour, acrid bile to the back of his throat. Thirty to one, and they had not even enough sense to keep quiet; no wonder, then, that their women starved, if such was the way they hunted! Let them straggle back to their cold beds, and the sooner the better. He had work to do.

He heard a voice raised suddenly, and for a moment he stiffened. But no, they had seen nothing; one of the men was gesturing, a clumsy, expressive movement of the body that eloquently bespoke his tiredness and disappointment. A hushing of voices, and footsteps diminishing over the dead leaves that lay strewn across the forest track like tears.

Covac, his lips pinched into the tight smile that never seemed to fully leave his face, leaned his head back against the bole of the tree and laughed. It was a soft laugh, a low laugh, impossible to hear over the soughing of the wind in the forest canopy above his head. Yet for a startled moment it seemed loud in his own ears, and the wind took it and carried it across the late autumn afternoon, to scatter its echoes like seeds. He bit his lip, flinching, his head tilted. He heard only silence.

The strand of red hair, a shining talisman, moved soft as vair as he pulled it rhythmically between his fingers, the curl flattening under the pressure of his hand, only to magically reappear as he slackened the tension. It was something of the girl, this living hank of color; he wondered, now, why he had not thought to take something from the first of the scarlet beauties he had killed, the first and best, the most beautiful, the highest of his triumphs. Ahnrach, bleached and motionless in her silent cairn on the windy hillside. Ahnrach, with the snakes and the black crows for company. Ahnrach, the queen's chosen . . .

He was growing drowsy, sleepy with remembered pleasure, and he must not descend from the tree until he was certain the rabble had gone. Regretfully, he slipped his trophy back into its hiding place. Methodically, he pulled his cloak fast around him against the cold of the October night. Then, wrapped against whatever waited on the ground below, he lashed himself to the tree with his girdle. With the edge of the cloak for a pillow, he closed his eyes and gave himself up to the smoky, sensual delights of remembrance.

When Covac woke, night had come and gone. The first weak shafts of morning gray fell slanting between the high trees and lay like discarded spears across the forest floor. On the end of his branch a gray squirrel with something between its paws froze, staring at him with wide, inscrutable eyes before it suddenly panicked and leaped to the next tree, fleeing in silence from this strange creature come to threaten the security of its gathering place.

Covac yawned and stretched, trying to shake the stiffness from his joints and muscles. The forest held the vast, living quiet of a place without men; here and there a bird scolded, and something moved through the undergrowth on soft paws, but man had come and gone. Now there was only himself, alone in the woodland.

Still, it would be best to make certain. He reached up to the branch above him and came away with a fistful of acorns. Drawing back his arm, he flung them as far from his tree as he could, and waited.

Nothing. They had given up the chase, defeated by

the black trees and the proximity of the demons of Samhain. He chuckled, long and low, and with cold fingers unbound the girdle that held him safely in the tree. Humming under his breath, he fastened the clasp once more around his waist, took up his pack, and calmly descended to the ground.

It came to him abruptly, although realization, some intimation, had been lurking just under his conscious mind. The pack was very still; no motion, no impatient rustle, no unspoken demand from the deadly occupant to be let out for sun and food. And surely the snake must be growing hungry; it had fed on a fat bird three days ago, with nothing to eat since. The snake was regular in its hunger. Three days . . .

He had begun to tremble. With stiff fingers he fumbled with the closing of the pack, wrenching at the gathered cords. Impatience, not unmixed with black terror, had taken hold of him, and he was cold with it. With none of his usual ginger caution, he plunged a hand into the pack and pulled the snake's sack free.

It hung motionless, dangling from between his fingers. He shook it, and shook it again. Nothing. Laying it gently on the ground, he pulled the sack open and peered in.

It lay there lifeless and cold, the gemstone eyes glazed with death, the vivid scales without sheen. Death had come to take it unawares, perhaps as long as three days ago; Covac could see the small bulge in the limp body, the bulge that was a bird only partially digested.

He stood and trembled, staring at the snake. A cold sweat had sprung up to bead his brow and run scalding down the backs of his legs. His companion, his safety, his surety, his good luck talisman. Dead in the night, gone from him, and all his fortune with it. . . .

He dropped the sack with nerveless fingers, his eyes wide and ugly. A sound, a small choked noise, made him leap wildly and sent one hand to the knife at his belt. Only the quiet woods, the empty woods, met his eye, and it took him a moment before he realized that the noise that had frightened him had come from his own throat.

He stood irresolute, unable to move, unable to think.

This seemed like a direct threat from the gods, this brutal taking of his sacred companion, seemed like a deliberate removal of protection. Only two sunsets to Samhain, the scum of two royal houses on his heels, and his snake gone . . .

Well, he had sneered at superstition all his life, and taken ruthless advantage of it whenever the opportunity came his way. It would not do to succumb to it at this of all moments. Whether the gods stood with him or against him, he would survive. And still he had work to do.

He picked up the sack and its dreadful burden. With the considerable strength of his powerful upper body, he hurled it as far as he could into the undergrowth. He heard it crash through bracken and brush to fall some distance away. Sleep there, Covac thought. Sleep there all your days, and watch these woods for me.

Then, turning his back on the tree, the sack, the entire episode, he began to walk east along the deserted forest road. Somewhere there would be the perfect spot, a spot where old trees sheltered young, smaller ones, where a snare might be set.

The morning of Samhain eve, a sunrise and a sunset after leaving the tuath of the borderland, Maeve woke shivering with fever, to feel the first soft fall of the winter snows against her brow.

There had been no convenient cave for them last night. So far down in the lowlands as this, caves were scarce and isolated huts even scarcer. They had pulled into the partial shelter of the first great trees of Connacht's southern forest and made a small fire to keep off the chill. It had rained here, however, and the wet bracken, the soggy wood, burned only fitfully. The men, more used to hardship, had tacitly backed away from even this inconsiderable warmth, leaving its poor comfort to Maeve.

She had never truly been ill in her life, and for a while after she woke, she simply lay, aching and trembling, wondering at the massive discomfort of this new and disagreeable sensation. In the heavy sheepskins she was wracked with heat and knew a desire to kick the covers off and lay naked in the cold morning air; some instinct, mixed with dim memories of illness in Cruachain during her childhood years, prevented her.

The men still slept, Connal pressed tight against her. The feel of his body beside her, usually so comforting, was unbearable; everywhere their bodies touched she hurt. And something had happened to her eyes during the long night; though no sunshine came to touch them, even the cold, nonreflective gray of a snowy morning hurt them, and she could not seem to bring the soaring treetops above her into proper focus. She closed them gently and pulled herself away from Connal.

The movement, slight as it was, woke him. His eyes popped open and, for the few moments it took for sleep to release its hold on him, lay blinking in the silently falling snow. Then he turned his head to smile at Maeve, and jumped to his feet.

"Allana, what is it? What ails you?"

She opened her mouth to reply, and made a new discovery; her throat was raw, burning, as though she had swallowed the embers of their midnight fire. Wide-eyed and disoriented, she lifted a limp hand to her throat and croaked, "Oh, it hurts. Swallow, or speak—no. It hurts."

She spoke to his back. He had laid an experienced hand on her brow and found it aflame; her skin was wet, flushed to nearly the color of her hair. He was already shaking Brihainn awake; beside him Cormac was already stirring.

Brihainn sat up and stretched. "A new day," he yawned. "High Lugh, Connal, what goes here, then?"

"Maeve is ill. Get up, cela, and look to her." But the urgent request was unnecessary. Brihainn was on his feet and kneeling by the trembling girl. He felt her brow and her wrist, his face set in a worried frown. Lastly he ran a hand across the sheepskins. The hand came away wet. He climbed to his feet and drew Connal apart.

"A fever, brother, and a bad one. No, don't look like that; she should be in no danger if we can get her to warmth. But we must find some place out of this snow, and that quickly, someplace dry, out of the wind, and she must have a roaring fire. Yes, I know she feels like a fire herself, but she must be kept yet warmer." He looked up into a face gone tight with dread and shook Connal's arm. "No danger, if we do this. Trust me for it."

Connal nodded and began to issue a rapid stream of commands to Cormac. The bard nodded, threw a worried glance at Maeve and ran for his horse. In moments he was gone, riding as quickly as was safe down the forest road toward the east. Connal came quickly back to the others.

Maeve had given up the battle to stay awake and aware. She was tossing restlessly and muttering under her breath. Brihainn saw the white horror on Connal's face and spoke quickly and sharply.

"I told you not to worry. You waste time standing here, doing nothing. Since you have sent Cormac off to seek shelter, there are two things for you to do." He held Connal's gaze with his own. "Will you help?"

Connal let his breath out. "Yes, cela. I am sick with fright and worry, and I cannot think for myself; I have no history with illness, and you know it." His voice flattened out as he met Brihainn's eyes. "Command me."

Brihainn nodded decisively. "First, a litter. Go gather some branches, branches of a like length, and bring them back to us; they must be lashed together, you know the way of it. She cannot stand, much less ride, and we must carry her."

Connal nodded. "And the other?"

"She must take some food. It will be difficult to get her to eat; every tooth in her head is alive with the pain of fever, poor sweeting, and she will likely be sick and bring up anything we give her. Since she cannot chew, dried mutton is of no use to us. Take your sling, and your water skin too; there will be partridge and quail nested for the winter on the ground. Bring me back a fowl and as much water as you can carry while I blow up this fire."

He was rummaging through his own pack; after a moment, to Connal's complete astonishment, he exclaimed triumphantly and pulled loose a small, battered cookpot. "The gods protect us yet, my friend; I thought we might need this. She must have liquid, and a fowl will be good for her. I shall make a hot broth, of water and the wing of a bird." He glanced up, found Connal staring at him in amazement, and spoke curtly. "Why do you wait? I said go."

Connal went.

Alone in the tiny clearing, Brihainn went quickly and methodically about his business. He stirred the cold ashes of the previous night's fire and threw fresh branches on the remains; he struck a flint and set the flames licking through the dead branches. He emptied his pack until he found, at the very bottom, his extra tunic. Taking his knife in hand, he slashed it quickly into long strips; when Connal returned with the boughs for a litter, they would have to be tied. He worked quickly, efficiently, one ear always cocked for noise in the woods that surrounded him.

"Snakes."

Maeve's voice, from directly behind him, was so unexpected that he dropped the knife with a cry. He spun around to stare at her.

Her eyes were open, her mouth pinched into that uncanny grin she had shown to Pera. He felt his flesh creep and made a wild, abortive gesture, a sign for magic, for she did not look like Maeve. The fever had taken her and transformed her, and he was looking, he felt, at a changeling, a demon, not Maeve at all. Not Maeve, no. But impossibly familiar...

"A badge, a token, a ring," she said dreamily, and he broke into a cold sweat. Maeve's voice, yes, but not her inflections; this was a musical voice, singing in its very cadences, with no notes, no tune. And the voice, too, touched some long-buried chord in him. He stepped back from her, his lips trembling, casting in desperation for the elusive memory that would identify both voice and face. Her stretched eyes were fixed on some point over his shoulder.

"Two snakes dancing, a circle unbroken," she said, and the thin lips pinched into a face he knew. His jaw was trembling, his hands clenched painfully tight. Where had he seen that face? Where? In his nightmares, maybe. Or in life, somewhere, sometime...

"Spears," she droned, and all the fine hairs on the back of his neck prickled to life. "Spears glittering like sloe plums among the trees. A gray cairn on a lonely hilltop."

"No," he whispered. "Stop. Stop now."

"There was a token. Do what you must!"

"Please, lady," he whispered, and felt tears on his face. "Please, stop now, no more..."

"Brihainn!"

Connal was behind him, a thin quail lying bloody and silent in the fast-gathering snow. He was staring at Maeve, his deep-socketed eyes enormous with shock, the flesh of his face pulled so taut that it seemed the strong bones beneath must thrust through to meet the daylight. As they stared, Maeve's eyes suddenly closed, her head turning to one side in an instinctive search for a cool place to rest. They heard her sigh once, and then a single word that was too low for them to hear. In a moment she was asleep once again.

In a deathly quiet broken only by their uneven breathing, they heard the distant hoofbeats of Cormac's horse returning. Brihainn took Connal's arm and held it hard.

"That face," he whispered. "That voice. I know them, I swear I know them. Connal?"

Ghosts, shades of tormented flesh, the empty laughter of men steeped in cruelty. A woman's shriek, the sound of a blow, men with faces heavy and bestial in the chilly predawn of Samhain day. A woman, regal and dangerous in her contempt, with a man's battered head dangling from her helm. The images flashed and whirled, intolerable in their brightness, and were gone.

Yes, he knew the face. He knew it too well for his own peace of mind.

The chieftain was gray-faced. He put out a hand, a gentle, tentative hand, and with a feather-light finger touched the scar at the corner of Brihainn's mouth.

"Fearghail," he said. "The very mask of my uncle."

15

The Hunt Is Up

Carhainn was dreaming.

It was the same dream, always the same. He rode a white horse, a horse he had never seen before, a horse that obeyed him as though man and mount were a single entity. He rode a straight road, narrow and sharp, and all around him hung the heavy boughs of the six sacred trees. They arched above him in a canopy of green and brown, blotting out the light. The air around him was thick with silent, eddying mist.

Deep in the arms of sleep Carhainn shifted uneasily on his pillow. In the eight months that had passed since he took on the throne of Cruachain, this dream had been a nightly companion, and during that time it had taken on the sly familiarity of an old enemy. Exhausted and spent, his body wanting nothing more than oblivion for a few precious hours, there was no escape from this dream. He knew what followed, and he turned on his bed, restless and grieving.

The white horse, stately and beautiful, cantered at an impossibly slow gait down the glittering road. It seemed lit from within, that stretch of travelers' ground; though no sunlight came through the heavy roof of trees, he could yet see every pebble, every stone, every twig that fell beneath his horse's hooves. Alone, riding to the east . . .

And then alone no longer. In the distance, where the

road met the horizon, another horse appeared, a horse as gray as the northern sea in winter. It carried two figures, a man and a woman.

The white horse reared, pawing the air with forefeet that glittered silver in the mist. Then, lowering its head like a dragon wanting only to spray the sky with flame, it charged, leaping forward to meet the oncoming riders and their galloping gray.

They were going to crash; it was inevitable, they must collide, throwing beasts and riders into a bitter tangle of torn bodies. Carhainn moaned aloud, little pools of sweat forming in the hollows of neck and collarbone. However often he faced this vision of misery in the night, the terror of the impending collision never lessened.

Yet they never collided, and tonight was no different. The horses thundered past each other with inches to spare, coming quite close enough for Carhainn as he was carried in the opposite direction, to clearly see the two figures astride the gray, being borne past him just beyond his reach.

A man, or a demon; either way, a huge, hulking shape, the face hidden behind its white hood, one enormous and beautiful hand steering the gray with iron control and the other wrapped around the girl, the girl, the girl who was Ahnrach, and Maeve too, a young face, an old face, the lovely shifting planes of the blended features tortured and pleading—

He wrenched himself awake, as he had almost nightly since the dream first took hold of him, and lay shivering in the winter morning.

As always, the first few minutes of waking after the dream were wretched indeed. As always, he shuddered against the pull of the night behind him, let his breath out with caution, felt the cold sweat on him and knew the simple gratitude that he was, at last, truly awake and free of this nightmare for another span of waking life. At length the shivering passed, the hideous forms of the dream faded, and he could face the living world of Connacht again.

He pulled himself from his bed and dressed hastily; the land was deep in winter, there was a dusting of snow on the trees, and the air in the small house was bitterly cold. Though he could with propriety have taken Maeve's house as his own during his tenure as shadow, he had decided against it; this, had he but known it, had gone a long way to stilling the mutterings of the few malcontents who whispered in corners that Carhainn had plotted to come at Maeve's throne by marriage, by murder, in any way he could.

He was taken, as he was every morning, by a sense of hopeless urgency. In less than four full moons it would be Imbolc once again, the gathering time, the time of reckoning. He had sent his spies out, sent his men to three of the four other provinces, seeking what they might learn of a high-born man with high training in the past, now turned to darkness. The men had returned to Cruachain, singly and in disconsolate little groups. The allotted time was nearly used up and he had learned nothing.

He called for the slave to bring his morning meal, musing as he waited on the messenger that had come yesterday from Kieran, High King of Muman. The man was obviously big with tidings, mysterious news not for the public ear; he had arrived in Cruachain as night was falling, nearly delirious with a fever taken from riding in the snowy valleys of the southwestern borderlands.

Carhainn, in spite of a curiosity that mingled with a prickling sense of intuition, had told Kieran's messenger not to be a fool; sure, and the message would keep until morning, while the messenger himself might not if he did not get himself between warm covers, with a healing draught to bring the fever down.

Well, and it was morning now. The man would be rested, ready to give his master's news. Carhainn ate quitely and, with his slave in attendance, strode across Cruachain to the small, richly-appointed house given to honored visitors.

He found the man among the remnants of what had obviously been a hearty meal. Carhainn waved the slave out of doors and sat cross-legged beside the bed. The messenger swallowed the last of his food and bowed his head.

"Lord Carhainn. My thanks, high one; I was well-nigh dead with cold and hunger."

"Well, and you look better this morning. Last night you had the look of something that walks the world on Samhain night. Are you recovered enough to give me your master's news, then?"

"My thanks, lord, I am. I am Mer the Two-Fisted, younger brother of Kas the Strong-Shouldered, closest of King Kieran's celi. We had a visit at King Kieran's court some months back from a great warrior and his lady, the Woman with Two Spears." He shot a quick look at Carhainn's impassive face. "I need not go too deep into this, lord? You know of whom I speak?"

"Yes." Not a muscle of Carhainn's face had moved, but he was conscious of the sudden construction in his chest. "Continue, Mer of the Two Fists. You interest me."

"Yes, lord. I did not see them at court, as I was out hunting alone in the great forest. But as I was making my way back to court, I was set upon by some outlaws who sought to take my goods and leave me for the ravens. I thought for sure I must join the Sidh when over the crest of the hill came these two warriors, a man and a woman, astride an outlandish great horse. They saw my plight and came to aid me. Between the three of us we made short work of the outlaws and left them for Kieran's men."

"A great outlandish horse?" Through the swelling mix of pain at this reminder of Maeve and the delight of knowing that she and Connal were well, the remark had touched some chord. "They were on foot when last I saw them. What horse was this, then?"

Mer grinned. "Lord, I know not how they came by it. But a great outlandish beast it was, near half again as tall as the fine war stallion I saw tethered outside your house, with huge hindquarters and little manes of hair all about its ankles. They sat astride this beast together, with room for one more on its back, so great a size was it."

Enlightenment dawned. "Ah. We have some few of that breed in our pens here; not great for speed, that strain, but huge and sturdy, nigh impossible to bring down. Give me the rest, Mer."

"Well, lord, King Kieran had sworn to them that

should he perchance come over news about the man they sought, he would send my brother after them. But perhaps a fortnight after they'd departed, a man came pelting into court. He demanded speech with our king, lord, saying he had come from the warriors and asking for Kieran's aid."

Carhainn was stiff, locked into place. "His name?"

"Cormac, lord. Cormac, personal fila to Connal the Victorious, he said, and to his father Sibhainn before him."

"Cormac! But he returned to Emain with Brihainn . . . well, never mind the way of it; I shall know that in the end. What was this news he brought, and what aid did he require?"

The man closed his eyes in an effort of concentration and opened them again. "A strange tale, lord. He said that he and this man Brihainn you spoke of had come up with the others and had entered a poor tuath on the borderlands. They found this tuath, Kahr it is called, undefended, and in begging shelter from the chieftain's lady, they were told that the men had gone hunting a killer."

Something stirred in Carhainn's mind. "A killer, you say. A killer of men?"

"Lord, this bard gave us the tale in private chamber. He said a druid had passed through Kahr, a holy man, and this holy man had read the destiny of a young girl there. He paid this red-haired wench special attention—"

"Red-haired!" Carhainn held a hand out, staring at Mer but not seeing him. "A moment, friend. Let me see if I may guess the rest. She was lured out, this red-haired girl, raped and left to die. Was that the way of it?"

Mer nodded. "Yes, lord. Raped, and left with a slit throat for the night beasts to feed on. But there was more."

"Tell me, and quickly."

"Lord, I was to tell you that this seer kept his hood on, so that he thought none but the girl saw him. But the chieftain's wife spied through his hide and saw his face. Kieran sent men out hunting straightaway, lord, he sent my brother Kas with twenty strong men to the north, to aid the warriors in their search."

He paused a moment and then remembered something. "Lord, I was to tell you these things, that Cormac the fila had gone to Kieran because the road to Cruachain is blocked with snow, that Queen Maeve was ill near to death with the winter fever, that Brihainn—son of Sheilagh, Shadow of Emain—has nursed her back from the Sidh. I was to bring you all good greetings of my lord Kieran and beg you for the love you bear the Queen of Connacht that you send armed men to scour the great forests, that you might aid them."

"It will be done." Jubilation was sweeping through Carhainn, weakening him in every limb. "The queen— you say she was ill?"

"Yes, lord, but though she is still very weak, she is in no danger. Lord, the fila gave me a message for your private ear. He bade me tell you that Queen Maeve, as she lay in the travail of fever, remembered the face of the druid, and that this druid was the same as the seer in Kahr. And he bade me tell you, from the Victorious himself, that he knows who this druid is."

"Thanks, great and undying thanks, to highest Lugh," Carhainn whispered. "Did he name this man?"

"He did. The man we seek is Fearghail mac Bhoru, brother to dead Sibhainn, uncle to the Victorious. Seasons he spent at sanctuary to learn the druid's art, but was deemed unworthy by the master and sent away from that place. Lord, he raped a young girl, he and the leader of a roving band of so-called traders, and was banished by his brother the chieftain. Cormac well remembers him, he said. This man, this Fearghail, could have taken the ring of Bhoru with ease before he was banished from Emain. They had thought he must be dead, lord, and never thought on him."

The pieces were falling into place now, the picture coming clear and full in Carhainn's mind. "Yes. Yes, it fits, all of it. Unless . . . Mer, did Cormac say when this uncle of his was sent away from Ulster?"

"He did, lord. It was Samhain day, he said, in his sixth year."

"And Connal is now eighteen. Twelve years past, and

one year before the first raid. And that first raid reason
enough for hatred of Maeve, after she escaped him. . . ."

"Lord?"

Carhainn pulled himself from his reverie and looked
up. "I muse aloud, Two-Fist, no more than that. Yet my
musings come together to make a scene in my eyes, and I
believe it is a true picture I see." He climbed to his feet.
"Are you rested enough to travel, warrior?"

"I am, but no doubt my horse is not."

"We shall give you a war stallion that will make even
Kieran's eyes bulge, never fear. Now. If the road between
our provinces is closed, how did you come here?"

"Lord, it is only the north road, the road through the
forest, that is impassable. I cut through the hills and came
up the old road to the northeast. The wanderers cannot do
this; Queen Maeve is not yet well enough to travel. And
since they were only a day behind this druid and he cannot
get free of the snow either . . ."

"Then this Fearghail must be there in the forest yet.
Do they hunt him, then?"

"I think not. They have built a small hut as shelter
from the winter, just outside the forest on the great plain
to the northwest. They are greatly hampered in their hunt,
no matter how close this evil one may be, for only one of
them is free to hunt."

Carhainn spoke sharply. "One of four? How is that?"

Mer sounded apologetic. "Well, lord, the lady is too
weak to hunt, and one of the men stays always with her.
With the fila riding to Kieran's court, only one is free."

A vision as clear as the features of the man he stared
at came suddenly to Carhainn. Maeve, sick and weak,
unable to defend herself. The hulking, looming dreamshape
that had haunted him all these nights a doom towering
over her. And with that image came the sudden, sickening
correlation of what it must mean. Ahnrach, this girl he had
raped in Emain, the dead child with the red hair left to rot
in the snow outside Kahr . . .

And Maeve. Maeve, who had thwarted the man,
escaped him, killed three of his men when she was scarce
out of swaddling clothes, fallen in love with the nephew he
had wanted to destroy; what did he have in mind for her?

His gorge rose suddenly in his throat as he remembered Ahnrach thrown across a raider's horse. He swallowed hard, biting back on the hatred that sat like flame in the pit of his stomach. Well, and he had a few scores to settle with this Fearghail himself.

"Get dressed now," he told Mer. "Twenty armed men I will send to bear you escort, with food, with rations, with salves. You will not take the road you came by. Snowed in or no, you must take the road to the south, through the forest; there must be nothing left to chance, and no chance provided for this Fearghail to escape us. Ask my slaves to provide you with whatever you may need; the plain, too, will be under snow and must be dug out. Somehow you will find them, find them and bring them the tokens I send, and together you will hunt for this beast who walks on the legs of a man."

Mer nodded. "We will do this."

"Well and good. You say Kieran has already sent men to the Victorious, to bring him aid. Is the road clear south of the borderlands, then?"

"Indeed. It is only the forest road, the road that runs from the southern borders of Connacht to Cruachain itself, that is blocked by the drifts of snow."

Carhainn's voice held a deep satisfaction. "That is good hearing, man of Muman. If this Fearghail were fleeing north toward Cruachain, he cannot hope to escape by slipping past the Victorious to the south, for he would run straight into your brother and his men. With the gods' help we may yet have him trapped."

"I hope we may." Mer's voice held fervency. "They saved my life for me, the Victorious and the Lady with Two Spears, and it would pleasure me to kill this filth for them. How better to pay my debt?"

Carhainn, his hand on the hide, whipped about. "Kill him? By the gods, man, no! If you kill him, we can bring the druid master no proof, and Connal and my queen are outcasts forever after. He must be taken alive. The man who kills this Fearghail, by chance or by spite, will give me his head to hang on Queen Maeve's girdle. Do I make myself plain, Mer?"

"Very plain." The other seemed disappointed, and Carhainn softened his voice.

"Never worry, warrior. Any death you could give him would be too clean an ending for him. If you feel he may escape without justice, think on what the druid master will do to a man who has defiled the mysteries for his own ends, and your mind should be easy." He saw the color die from Mer's face, saw one hand twist in the gesture for magic, and smiled grimly. "Yes, Mer, the foulest of all deaths. Dress yourself and be ready on my word. My men will be with you within the hour."

Muffled and hidden by a blinding world of white, Connal sat in the rude shelter he had made and for three endless nights watched over Maeve as she slept.

The fever had frightened him more than anything in his life. It had been violent and of long duration; three full days she had lain burning, muttering to herself, showing no recognition of the men who tended her, showing no obvious improvement in spite of Brihainn's assurance that the illness was running its proper course.

Sometimes she would lie weeping in covers rank with perspiration, calling for Connal yet not seeming to know him when he took one hot hand in his own. Sometimes she would speak to people long dead or far from her reach; she called out for Carhainn, for her mother, and sometimes for the girl Ahnrach, whose death had so affected her.

Other times she would lapse into conversation with her dead father. Lying exhausted, eyes closed, she would speak to Flyn as though he stood at her bedhead, asking questions, begging him to send the healer to her. The poignancy of these moments was more than Connal could bear; at such times Brihainn would gesture his friend away, sending him out of doors awhile and seeing to Maeve himself.

Never again, not even when the fever was at its peak and they must hold the thrashing body down to keep her from doing herself an injury, did her features fall into the hellish mask that was an uncanny travesty of Fearghail's face. Never again did her voice move back through the dregs of memory to reproduce the odd musical lilt that was so damning and distinctive. But it was not necessary; once had been enough, and her companions were sure.

On the morning of the fourth day Connal woke to find Maeve awake and staring at him with eyes that held sense and recognition. He struggled up on one elbow and glanced around the tiny hut. Brihainn was gone, hunting for breakfast or scouting, as was his wont as the day broke. He could hear Cormac whistling out of doors as he tended the horses, an eerie sound floating in on the wafts of wet snow that blew across the forest to the great plain on which they had come to rest.

"Connal?"

"Yes, allana. I am here, never worry." He laid a gentle hand across her brow and found it cool to the touch. "May there be praises, the fever is past."

"Fever." Her voice was a thread, no more than a paper-thin shadow of itself. She reached a wondering hand up to her throat and winced. "Oh, my throat! It hurts me to swallow. All my body aches, and I feel so weak. . . . Connal, I think I have been ill."

He swallowed an unaccustomed lump in his throat and closed his hand tightly over hers. "Ill near to death, darling girl, but you are better now." He looked up as Cormac entered the hut. "A new day, fila, and the best of days. Here is my lady, herself again."

"Give thanks to the three Mothers who keep watch on the sick," Cormac said gladly. "Lady, you are a poor, thin bird. I will make you a broth to drink. Connal, I have been thinking, and would speak with you."

He had curled up beside Maeve and was holding her with careful gentleness. "You have my attention."

"Lord, this morning I scouted to the south, the way we came. Past the forest to the south the road is clear. I would take Lhiam and ride with haste to Kieran's court to tell him what we know, if you will permit."

Maeve, moving her head with some effort between the two men, saw grim purpose and was bewildered. With the querulous ill temper of the convalescent, she spoke peevishly. "I cannot understand you. What do you know? What has happened while I lay ill?"

Connal, already warned by Brihainn that Maeve would be temperamental and inclined to crying fits for some days after the fever had passed, kissed the nape of her neck. "A moment, allana, and you will have the whole tale. Go, fila. Take Lhiam and enough provisions to get you safe to Kieran's court, and go at once. Take my spear, if you wish; you remember my uncle even as I do, and he is a deadly fighter and dirty with it."

Cormac looked steadily at him. "A spear I will take, be sure of it. But I have little expectation of meeting Fearghail. Your pardon, chieftain, but you have not reasoned this thing out."

Connal stared at him, brows knit, saying nothing. After a moment Cormac continued.

"The road north is buried deep, and if we cannot pass, why then, neither may anyone else. And he would be mad indeed to turn back toward the south, for if he went that way, he would run straight into Kahr and its angry people. Nor do I think he would take the risk of losing you."

As the hard common sense of Cormac's words came clear to Connal, he jerked his head up to stare. "Gods protect us, fila, are you saying he is trapped here with us? That he is within reach of my hand?" He shook his head incredulously. "I would not stay, did I but stand in his place."

"You are not thinking," Cormac repeated patiently. "Above all else, he must know your whereabouts. And he dare not put himself within reach of the people of Kahr again, for fear of his life." He grew persuasive. "Lord, listen to me. Why should he fear to stay close to us? He can have no reason to think you a danger to him, for he cannot know that we have discovered him. What fear from you?"

Connal shook his head slowly. "You speak truth, fila, and I am a fool. Go now. I will make a broth for my lady to eat and give her the tale of our doings. Go."

"Farewell, then. I will ask Kieran to send men back with me." He swung his cloak over his shoulder and hesitated. "Connal . . ."

"Yes?"

"Have a care to yourselves." The quiet voice held a dark note. "Because he cannot share our knowledge, he must believe he can still come at you, at all of you, in safety. He may try another trap, or set a fire. Have a care."

Connal opened his mouth to reply, but Cormac had gone.

"Well," said Maeve, and the weak voice held a distinct note of pettishness, "if it is not too much of a burden on you, perhaps you will tell me what you spoke of. I would be thankful for that, for I understood not a word of it! Who is your uncle? Why does Cormac ride for the southlands?"

"It's a long tale, allana; will you not take some hot broth first? No? Oh, very well, then. This may take a while, for the roots of this twisted tree go back to when I was scarce more than a babe and when you were likely still in your swaddling clothes." And Connal, lying down beside her once more, gave her the full story, a concise, unemotional encapsulation that omitted nothing. When he was done, Maeve stirred against him.

"Your uncle," she said softly. "Connal, that man Machlan you spoke of—what of his men?"

Connal pulled himself upright and stared down at her. "What do mean you, allana?"

"If your uncle was to survive, he must have found himself a place of resting. Why, if you are right when you say that this Fearghail was the man who led the two raids against my people, then you must answer a question in yourself. Where came he by those raiders?" She gave him no time to answer, rushing into speech. "And this girl he raped, this cousin of Brihainn's. What was she like?"

"Alhauna? Young, fair as a flower. Silly, as are too many young girls, silly and credulous." He looked down at Maeve, not seeing her, seeing instead shadowy figures moving in a complicated dance around a tortured girl, a lake, a warrior woman on horseback with a man's head dangling from her girdle. "She looked a bit as you do. Hair of flame, skin like snow."

"Yes." Maeve, her eyes closed with exhaustion, lay back against her pillows. "Even as Ahnrach had hair of flame, and the girl he killed at Kahr. Even as does this warrior woman of yours, this Sheilagh, whom he has cause to hate. Even as I do."

In a forest clearing not a mile from Connal's hut, Covac had made himself a shelter where he might sit and think.

Though the snow might be a problem, the lack of wind was a blessing. On the morning Cormac set Lhiam to the southern road, Covac came quietly to the forest's edge.

He had already guessed that Maeve was ill. For two days the men had taken turns gathering wood, tending to the horses, hunting whatever small game might be found in the heart of this vast endless winter. Maeve he had not seen at all. The erstwhile queen was sick, then, and from the look of it, seriously enough.

With this information to his hand, Covac would not have hesitated to slip indoors and kill her as she lay. Most likely she had succumbed to a winter ague; helpless and delirious, she would have had no defense against him. But Maeve was never left alone, and the constant vigilance of her menfolk had defeated him.

Morever, Cormac was not the only one who had scouted the roads out of the forest. Covac had done the same and reached the same conclusions; to go north was difficult if not impossible, to go south was madness. To the east the forest stretched vast and impenetrable, and to the west it continued again on the far edges of the great plain; a man might wander a lifetime in either direction and never come clear of the trees again.

Well, there were virtues in staying still. If he could not travel, why, neither could they; too, it would give him time to plan, time to think, and time was growing short enough for worry.

He stood behind an enormous oak, staring at the empty clearing and thinking.

Maeve was ill. Sane enough, then, that the men would never leave her side, but that could not last, and when she came to her senses once again, the opportunity must offer. People were slow to recover from the ague, and as they did so, they needed much sleep. He had learned the intricacies of illness well enough in his tenure at sanctuary; this gift of healing was something men prized the druids for. Yes, people recovered slowly, they tended toward testiness, and weakness, and the desire for solitude. It would be no difficult thing to wait for the three men to go together for the hunt. If he could but come at Maeve alone, he could take her as she lay and leave a floor drenched in his lady's blood as a gift for Connal to find.

He was pulled from his musing by the dropping of the hide. Cormac came out with a sack at his side; as Covac watched, the bard strapped his provisions to Lhiam and mounted. Wheeling the horse, he turned south toward the forest. Covac drew back until he was hidden by the snow-covered bushes and watched until Cormac was out of sight.

When the muffled hoofbeats had died in the distance, Covac emerged to stand thinking. A journey of some length, and to the south? What would send the bard on a hard ride of some distance? Perhaps the lady suffered from something worse than the ague. Perhaps she lay dying. . . .

Hatred trickled through Covac and was pushed away. Her mother had escaped him by her own hand, her cousin had spat in his face. By the watching gods, but she would not do so! She would die, yes, but it would be at his hand in his own time. Not even death would cheat him this time.

He ran back to his watching place. He had seen Brihainn, snare in hand, go out before it was full light; the falling snow had since covered his tracks, and the single line of prints that led from the hut to the horses told it own tale. Brihainn had not returned, Cormac was gone and Connal bided indoors with his lady love.

For a moment, as a sudden impossible urge to take his great knife in hand and confront the pair of them together swept through him, everything hung in the balance. Maeve, weakened by fever, would be no match for him; Connal, tall and strong as he was, lacked Covac' great bulk and the years of experience behind him. The bard was gone, and the bastard was out on the hunt, deep in the forest. One against two. Perhaps. . .

He took an irresolute step forward, his hand sliding

toward his knife. The sudden crashing in the undergrowth behind him brought his head up, sharp as a hunting fox. He whipped around, dropping low, and pulled back behind the tree, waiting, cradling his knife.

Brihainn, a rabbit at his belt, pushed the bushes aside not ten feet from where he crouched. As Covac watched, the rabbit, improperly tied, slipped with a soft thud to the forest floor. Brihainn, with a muttered curse, bent to retrieve it.

Covac's heart was pounding, the blood rushing to his loins in the old, familiar burn of pleasure. His fingers, cold and stiff, slipped down the knife with a lover's touch. His shoulder drew back, tensed and waiting, his eye on the narrow back so suddenly and miraculously vulnerable.

Something, a premonition of danger or perhaps an inner awareness of some tiny sound, suddenly hit Brihainn. He flung himself face forward down in the snow, desperately trying to roll to one side, reaching for his weapons.

The movement was enough, just enough, to keep him alive. It may have been that the falling snow, thick and wet, deflected Covac's aim. As it was, the great knife, thrown with deadly skill, caught Brihainn high in the back of the left arm. Had he not fallen forward when he did, it would have taken him through the heart, killing him soundlessly.

The scream of pain, intolerable in that hushed silence, rang across the forest and out to the plain beyond. Covac saw immediately that the knife had missed its chosen mark. Abandoning the knife in favor of safety, he crashed through the bushes to the north, leading any possible pursuers away from his own shelter. Behind him Brihainn lay screaming, the sounds of pain fading as Covac moved farther away.

In the little clearing hut, Connal was dozing. The ghastly echo jerked him awake and brought him to his feet. On the bed Maeve opened her eyes. She rubbed them, shaking her head. "What was that?"

"Stay here," he said tautly, and turned for the hide. A sudden thought made him stop and throw his knife to Maeve. She lay, her eyes wide, staring at him.

"Stay," he repeated, and shot through the door.

The screams had died, replaced by a moaning that turned his stomach over. With one of Maeve's spears in hand he pushed his way through the trees and bushes, calling for Brihainn. He had recognized the voice of pain. Standing alone in the forest, he threw his head back and shouted.

"Connal..."

It came from the left, weak and barely audible. Lashing the branches and brambles away from his face, he followed the call and nearly tripped over his fallen brother, lying in an ever widening pool of bloody snow.

"Brihainn." He dropped to his knees, and gently pulled away the hands that clutched the wound. Deep, and ugly; much salve would be needed, and some stitching, if it were to heal. But the blood still flowed, and it must be stopped. Brihainn would bleed to death before his eyes if it was not.

He pulled the thong from one of his sheepskin boots and knotted it around the damaged arm. As he pulled it tight, he spared a glance for the other's face. It was blue and drawn with pain.

Something glittered in the snow near Brihainn's head. When the thong was tied and the wound had stopped pumping the bright blood, he took off his cloak and laid it under Brihainn's head. Then, the immediate danger over, he reached out and took it up.

A knife, old, the hilt worn but the blade honed to a killing edge. And wrapped around it, brightly visible against the yellowed bone handle, was a long curling lock of red hair.

For a long moment he squatted motionless on the forest floor, the knife in the snow at his feet, the gleaming tress dangling between his fingers. At his feet Brihainn had moved from the pain of the waking world to the mercy of a deep faint.

Dropping knife and hair alike into one boot, Connal picked his friend up in both arms and carried him, gentle as a mother with a newborn babe, back to the hut.

16

Be Silent, Be Secret

"Yes, my darling one, I swear to you that I am well enough to tend him. Please, Connal. You must go back and hide that bloodstained snow."

Brihainn, his arm covered in salve and tightly wrapped, slept heavily. His breathing was rough, and Maeve knew that he dreamed by the rapid flutters of his eyelids, the stifled muttering, the occasional twitch of his body under its heavy coverings. Maeve, shivering with cold and light-headed, sat huddled by the fire, stirring hot broth and trying to talk sense into the worried man who paced the shelter beside her.

He stopped his pacing long enough to lay a light hand on Brihainn's brow. "He is feverish," Connal said tersely. "Well enough to tend him? I can see from here how your legs are well-nigh too weak to carry you. Suppose he becomes wild in his fever and begins to thrash? What then, allana?"

"I can soothe him and give him drink, if need be." She got unsteadily to her feet and crossed to stand beside Connal. "That snow," she said. "There are beasts in the forest, Connal; these are Connacht's own tracts, these trees, and I know much of them. Wolves there are, perhaps bears too. If such a beast comes upon that blood in the snow, they will hunt the forest round until they find us." She grasped his arm and stared up into his face, her eyes pleading. "I am strong enough to deal with a fevered man, but not with a bear or a wolf maddened by the smell of blood. If you will not go, then I must. Do not force this on me, I beg you."

He was silent, his eyes hooded and unreadable. Her hand slid down the sleeve of her jerkin to rest in his. "What is it, my only one? Why do you not wish to go?"

"I am feared to leave you!" The words burst from Connal as he dropped her hand, only to pull her roughly into his arms. "Wolves and bears, what care I for such things? Do you think a beast walks these forests on four legs that I would fear to fight? No, Maeve. There is a greater beast than these stalking us, a walker on two legs, secret and deadly. And he would like no greater prize than you."

"Ah. Your uncle, this Fearghail." Maeve leaned her face against Connal's chest as a sudden, dizzying rush of fever and weakness rippled through her. He heard the tiny sigh, felt the tremor of a weakened body forced by the unexpected to assume its duties before it was ready, and tightened his hold. On the bed beside them Brihainn muttered something and turned, restless and fretful, in his stifling bedding. Maeve pulled herself upright and together they stood, looking down at the slumbering man.

"Perhaps you are right, love. For me to say I was full enough mended to fight a trained killer alone would be to play the fool and dishonor the gods with a lie. I shall do neither. Stay with me, then; as for the wolves and the bears, why, let them come, and we will deal with them."

She moved back to the broth and gingerly tested its heat against her tongue. "Connal, tell me. If your uncle wants us dead, wants me dead, why did he not slay me all those months ago, when he stood alone with me in Cruachain? He could have slain me then, and that with ease enough; it was only us two, and myself unarmed, suspecting nothing. Why did he let me live then? What did he gain?"

The shelter rattled and shook under a fierce gust of wind. Connal, with a shudder, threw some kindling onto the fire and stood staring into the dancing sparks as if Maeve's answer might lie there.

"I cannot be certain, allana. It is true he could have killed you, but you had men outside your door—what chieftain ever did not? He might not have gained even the gates of Cruachain before the hue and cry was given. Perhaps he was unsure of your strength—sure, and he must have heard the stories, the legends of your fighting ability. He could not have felt sure that you might not have some deadly skill of which he knew nothing. And there is another reason . . ." His voice trailed off.

She ladled hot broth into a small wooden bowl and brought it to him. "What was that, love?"

The black eyes glittered oddly across the top of the bowl. "I think he wanted more than only your death. Did he not put Bhoru's ring there for you to find? Myself he hated, only for being born. You he hated for escaping him, for thwarting him. He wanted both your flesh and your blood, and you gave him neither."

She tilted her head at him, puzzling it out. "So. You think he dreamed a pretty revenge, to set our people against each other, not caring who won and who lost, so long as our blood was shed?"

"I do. And the sentence of Tara, that we fight one another to the death on the great plain of Bregia, east of Tara? What of that, my queen? The master is a fair man, too fair. He would never come to such a thing without counsel, though he might well have agreed to it if the auguries fell that way."

Her breath shortened. "Do you . . . are you saying that he was at Tara, this uncle of yours? At Tara in druids' robes, poisoning the ear of the master? Connal, how would he dare such a thing? If he should be discovered . . ." Shaking her head in disbelief, she let the words die.

He drank off the rest of his broth and wiped his sleeve across his mouth. "How might he not?" he asked impatiently. "What daring would it be to him, after he had murdered your father and walked into your house in Cruachain and bent you to his will?" He looked down at her wide eyes and spoke slowly. "Maeve, my only one, make no mistake here, for a mistake may kill you. Did you think my uncle a coward or a fool? He was neither when I knew him last; daring, cold, taking what he wanted, with courage of steel and wits to match."

"He is a bad man," she whispered. "Bad and deadly, tainted throughout with lust and ambition, caring for nothing and no one. He killed my cousin, raped her and left her to rot in the hot sun." Unconsciously her hand moved to her shoulder and tightened on the hilt of one spear.

"Your cousin? More than that. There was a girl in my own tuath; I have not forgotten her bruises and how her wits never came back to her. Brihainn still bears the scar of that morning's work." His eyes bright with danger, he glanced at the figure on the bed. "Today he has given me yet another debt to pay. And he left another girl dead beneath the trees, as Pera told us." He looked at her somberly. "And forget not your father and mother, Queen of Connacht. If there is to be a vengeance taken, a price exacted—"

"I will kill him." It was a queen's voice, cold, old, flat with decision and passion. "For my father's head, for my mother's shame, I will kill him." She pulled the spear free and shifted it to fighting grip. Connal saw the flaming color in her face, the sweat on her cheeks, and knew the fever had come back to her. He pushed her gently down.

"Rest awhile, Maeve. Rest, and think on what you have said here. You cannot kill him; take his blood and we wander this land until the Sidh calls for us. If Fearghail dies, our proof of treachery dies with him."

She shivered and laid her head suddenly against Brihainn's bedside. "Then we must take him alive."

"Alive," Connal agreed, and closed his eyes wearily. "Only two of us now against his one, and he possessed of a cunning and strength such as I have never known. No wonder that he still lives; doubtless he frightened off even the fomori when they came for him. It will be a difficult and bitter thing to take him; I have faced no harder task."

She watched him, aching and giddy. The burst of strength that rage had given her faded and was gone, leaving her limp with reaction. Her voice was the merest thread. "Can we do this thing?"

"We can try," he replied, and suddenly yawned, his

jaws gaping. Outside the wind eased, and the snow covered the footprints and the drops of blood he had left there. "We can try. We must try. We will try."

Be silent, be secret...

Brihainn, on the edge of the waking world, turned his hot face, shifting on his pillow. His mind, edged in fever and an oddly distant pain, had caught snatches of their conversation. Things were clear, very clear, in the unreal way of a fevered brain; though he was not truly awake, he was aware of the low-voiced conversation, the butterfly touch of Connal's hand against his brow, the tantalizing aroma of the broth steaming in the cookpot.

He was aware, too, of things that followed; Maeve's sudden fit of weeping, Connal's hasty movement to her side, the clank of falling armor and whispering cloth sliding to the floor. Though his eyes were closed and sightless, his senses were heightened; in his mind he watched them coupling, saw Connal's hands, warmed over the fire, slide from the smooth shoulders and down the arched back, coming to rest on small perfect breasts on which the downy hair stood up in the cold air. He heard Connal's heavy breathing and Maeve's stifled cry with the mixture of envy and tenderness he had come to live with since the night they had slipped between the cracks of Connacht's army to beard the queen in her own bed.

Be silent, be secret. Lazily, one edge of his mind always on the bitter pain in his arm and shoulder, he began to remember things, to apply them, to understand what he felt. Fearghail, that pale man, held in chains, speaking a curse to him, a fate to Connal, a vengeance to Sheilagh. His own childhood credo, be silent, be secret, and how well Fearghail had taken that credo to himself, how well he had used it!

His mind moved, puzzled and languid, noting and then forgetting the whispered endearments from the fireside, Connal's quiet laughter, the sound of a light slap that was Maeve's reaction to his teasing. Be silent, be secret. He must be taken alive, alive, and it would be a good ten days before any help could be expected.

Nothing would come from Cruachain. It would be

madness to hope that way; the road to the north was lost, buried under the drifting white curse of winter, and with the best will in the world to aid them, Carhainn could not change the weather. If help came, it would come from Kieran, in the south, and in this weather it might take all of a fortnight before anyone came.

He heard Maeve's husky voice, pitched carefully low, say something incomprehensible. Wood clanked against iron, and the smell of broth was suddenly richer on the cool air.

He lay still, a bit closer to full waking, and thought.

Maeve was still weak. Brihainn knew these winter agues of old; she would be subject for weeks to come to spells of sudden, paralyzing weakness. She was in no condition to track a killer under the frozen trees, then, and he himself, wounded as he was, was as useless as the trees themselves. Cormac was gone, their best hope, to the south. That left only Connal, and Connal was afraid to leave her.

As things stand, he thought bitterly, we might as well be three small children hiding from a bear. If Fearghail could but take the courage to attack them where they waited, it would be one on one, uncle and nephew, and Connal would be hampered by his fear for his lover and his brother. Three to one, and there was no doubt to it; the one was the stronger.

Be silent, be secret . . .

An idea was forming, desperate and mad, but an idea nonetheless. His eyelids fluttered for a moment, then eased. Was it possible, then? Could it be done?

Bracing himself mentally against the pain, he flexed the muscles of his right arm. Little pain there, true, but not half of his usual strength either. Carefully, so carefully that the others noticed nothing, he made a fist of his left hand and tried to bend the arm.

The stab of pain, bright and vital, nearly made him cry out. So the left arm was useless. There might well be a severed nerve there; at the very least, there was some damage to the muscles of his shoulder. Well, and he was not left-handed in any event; let him build up some strength in his right arm and it could be possible. But silently, but secretly. Let Connal but get wind of this notion and he would tie Brihainn to the bed to keep him there.

He opened his eyes.

They were standing by the fire, as he had thought. That they had been making love was evident, he thought wryly. Though both were dressed once again, there was a bright edge to Connal, a sharpness and energy that Brihainn remembered perfectly from the nights the chieftain had spent with Annak. Maeve, in contrast, showed a languor in every line of her, and the green eyes were smoky and replete, giving her the look of a cat who had been stroked. It was as though, in some way, Maeve made him a gift of something of her spirit; when they love, Brihainn thought, it seems that his freedom of her flesh comes with some of her power, her mind, whatever it is that makes the woman within.

They stood, touching only at hip and shoulder, staring into the flames. He studied their profiles from beneath lowered lids for a few moments, seeing the pure relaxation of Maeve's posture as the most sensual thing in the world.

Then Maeve, as if she had heard something or sensed his thoughts, turned her face toward him. "Brihainn!"

Connal came to the bedside. "Praise to Lugh, you are awake. How does that shoulder feel, cela?"

"Sore." This was his first attempt at speech, and he was surprised at the rasp in his voice, the sour taste at the back of his throat. "Maeve, as you love me, may I have a bowl of whatever you cook there? It smells of the earth, and my mouth tastes of the stables."

She brought him a half-filled bowl. Crouching at his side, she watched his ravenous drinking with satisfaction. "This gladdens my heart, brother. To wake hungry is a sign of health." She reached a hand out and tested the bandage. "No bleeding, and all is well. You are young, and strong with it. I believe you will heal."

Connal stood with his arms akimbo, frowning down at him. "Brihainn, do you remember what happened?"

"Some, not all." He set the empty bowl down on the floor and sat upright. "I caught a hare—"

"You are eating it; I put it in the broth. Go on."

"Well . . . I had come to a clearing, I remember that much, and—oh, of course. I had not properly fastened the hare to my belt, and it slipped free. I bent to take it up . . ." His voice tailed off. Shaking his head, he looked up at Connal with a puzzled frown. "I am not certain, Connal. Something warned me, but in truth I cannot tell what."

"Did you hear something? See something, perhaps?"

"No." He was remembering it now, his numb feet, his desire to get home and out of the accursed snow, the sudden sensation of eyes on his back. He struggled to explain. "Neither saw nor heard. Felt, rather. Eyes on my back."

"Ah." Maeve nodded with perfect understanding. "Did you turn around and see him?"

"No." The memory was clearer now, so much clearer that he shivered. "There was nothing to tell me what watched me, you see. Bear or wolf or man; I knew only eyes, and the touch of danger on my skin. I threw myself facedown in the snow and something hit me, hard, in the left arm."

Connal reached into his boot and pulled the knife out. Worn and deadly, it lay shining across his palm, six inches of glittering steel. Brihainn looked at it and shuddered, turning his face up to Connal. "That?"

"This, yes. I found it bloodied, in the snow by your head. You screamed out, cela, and I ran for you. He had no time to take it up before he ran." His lips flattened into an ugly smile. "One weapon the less, for him."

Brihainn took the knife. Turning it over in his palm, examining the hilt, his eye was suddenly caught by the glint of red hair. He pulled it free and held it up to the light. "What is this?"

"Red tresses, cut, not torn. A trophy for our uncle." Connal flicked the hair with a deliberate forefinger. His voice was vicious. "He always fancied red hair."

Brihainn turned cold. "May the three Mothers protect us," he whispered, and fought back nausea. "It was Fearghail who threw the knife back in the woods. No doubt of it, then." He swallowed hard. "You think this came from the head of the girl he killed, back there in the borderlands? A trophy for him?"

"From her, or from Ahnrach whom he murdered so many years ago. A trophy, yes. A little memento."

Brihainn pulled the curling hair between his fingers, feeling it as a living thing, moving and breathing. He was fascinated by the flexing and tensing of it, the way it straightened flat, only to curl once more when the tension relaxed. "He must not live, Connal. He must not."

Connal's voice held a dark amusement. "Oh, he will die, never fear it. What the druids will do with him when we take him is so ugly that for anyone else but Fearghail I would hold pity." The voice softened to deadliness, and Maeve's eyes flickered up to his face and away again. "Not for him, though. Never for him."

Horses. Horses, and men to ride them.

Covac, high in the boughs of the holy oak that was split down the middle, sat as still as a nesting bird. With one hand he clutched the tree bole, the knuckles white with the brutal grip. The other hand moved in a continual rhythm, stroking the empty sheath where the knife had been. He was unaware of the stroking.

They were too far down for him, too far. Not all of his careful craning and peering would let him see the badges they wore. Unlikely, most unlikely, that they were outlaws. They were well-dressed, richly cloaked, and their mounts were enormous, healthy, well-fed war stallions. The horses of Connacht, he thought grimly. He had personally supervised the stabling of some head of these same horses, stolen during that last raid, in the paddocks of the hill men.

He pressed his body against the tree bole and watched.

They were clearing the road. If he did not know who they might be, he could not begin to guess their business in a snow-shrouded forest deep in winter. For a moment his scalp prickled; was it possible that the men of that wretched tuath to the south had somehow succeeded in reaching Cruachain, in telling Maeve's shadow their grievances, in gathering help for themselves?

The fear faded in the harsh light of reason. It made no

sense, that answer. He was trapped here in the forest by
the blocked roads to the north, and if he could not get
through, neither could they. No, it was unlikely that their
business was with him, and unlikely, too, that whatever
that business might be was secret or illegal. They were
moving openly enough, sending their men in groups of
eight, it seemed, to clear and mark the road to the south.

The thought, when it came to him, was so unexpected that he jumped a little in his aerie. If they had come
from the north, then they had been clearing the road all
the time they came. And if the road was clear, he could
slip past them, get out of this filthy wood, to freedom. . . .

A sudden commotion directly beneath his tree brought
his eyes downward. They were kneeling, examining the
ground, waving their arms at the tracks he had left there
that very morning. The rustling in the bushes that had
proven to be a lean vixen searching the forest for food had
sent him off the path he had so carefully committed to
memory, leaving him no time to brush his footprints away.
What were they doing now?

Fifteen, sixteen, seventeen . . . twenty-two men all told,
ten of them moving for the cut wood and tanned hides to
build a shelter, a dozen of them now turning their horses
toward the great plain. Covac sat perfectly still and watched
them. His mouth had gone dry.

They were some miles away, it was true, but the
danger was there, and blatant. Connal and Maeve were
there, camped on the plain. Brihainn, too, if he had not
bled to death by now from the knife wound Covac had
given him some ten days ago. For those ten days he
had skulked among these trees like an animal, a frightened
forest creature, not knowing from where danger might
come.

These travelers would find them. And with this troop
of men camped directly across the road, he himself would
be trapped here, perhaps to die of cold in this very
tree. . . .

He knew an insane desire to laugh, and stifled it. This
was no time for panic, no time to submit to the rigors of
terror. Better, far better, to keep one's nerves intact and
concentrate the mind on a means of escape, a way out.

Very gently, keeping a tight grasp on the tree bole, he bounced his weight against the thick branch that supported him. Thick and strong, it would not break under him. He looked down, making certain that the men below were occupied, and began to move in tiny, precise movements toward the edge of the branch.

His sharp eyes had caught, through the snow-hung canopy, the end of another branch, another tree. If he could reach it, swing himself to that tree and perhaps another after that, he might well climb down in safety when darkness fell.

Carefully, an inch at a time, he moved closer. Once, as he neared his goal, his weight dislodged a lump of wet snow from the branch. It fell with a soft plop through the high branches to land gently on the path below. For a moment, his heart stuttering in panic, he thought it had captured the attention of the men, tiny figures so far below him. But no, they had not so much as turned around to see. He sat motionless, letting his breathing steady, and resumed his steady inching toward the waiting branch.

When he had come just close enough for safety, he grasped it. Indeed, it might have been put there expressly for his purpose, for it was slightly heavier than his own and lay across it like a step to safety. With a deep breath, using the considerable strength of his massive shoulders, he swung his body from one tree to the other.

The screaming in his ear, the sudden beating of wings in his face, nearly sent him plunging to the earth below. A bird, its plumage the buffed white of the season, had been so perfectly camouflaged that he had brushed against it. It shot straight up through the trees, calling in panic, seeking its mate and the open skies in its terror at his intrusion. He hugged the tree, trembling, and watched it go. When quiet fell again, he turned to regard the abandoned nest.

Two eggs, speckled and small. Well, if he could get them safe down these accursed trees, they might make a meal. He took them up, putting them carefully in his pack, and peered around to the next tree, an enormous pine. The branches were knobbed with cones and bird droppings, and they were too thin by far to support his weight.

Well, and it would have to be this tree, then. When the interlopers below had camped in the darkness, it should be safe enough. It was cold, bitterly cold, but perhaps the gods had put him into this tree to force him into thought.

His options, with the coming of these travelers, had suddenly shrunk to two. He considered them coldly, wondering what best to do.

It was a simple enough matter; he could take the risk of going back to the shelter on the plain, take the risk of killing them as they lay. That would remove all his danger, and give him great satisfaction too.

But balancing the pleasure of the first choice was the common sense of the second. Their time grew short now, Maeve and Connal, months shrinking to weeks. He had only to make himself scarce for a few short weeks, just long enough for Imbolc to pass, and they were lost, outcast forever, never again queen, never chieftain. They hunted in darkness, and he in light. And their year of grace was almost over. . . .

Yes, he thought, yes. Perhaps a living death, years of wandering the roads, sleeping in wet beds in the cold hills, would be a more fitting thing than the quick death he wanted for his nephew, the slow rape and prolonged misery he had thought to give to Maeve. He could always return to the hill raiders, if he chose.

And what was to stop him, thinking on it, from killing them anyway? Once Imbolc had passed, once the druids had met once more at Tara, all time was in his hand. He could watch them, follow them, lead the raiders after them.

Unaware of his own smile, he closed his eyes and curled his body into the tightest possible knot, waiting for nightfall and his own chance of escape.

Tonight. It would come tonight.

Brihainn, for a week past, had been careful to hide his returning strength. The wound was healing cleanly, and some control of his shoulder muscles had come back to him. He was better, far better, strong enough to put his plan in place.

Let Connal get wind of it, though, or Maeve for that matter, and Connal would simply talk him out of it; he rarely failed to bend his half brother to his will. Should that not succeed, they would likely bind him to his own bed to keep him from it. Be silent, be secret, and he would succeed.

He sat at the fire, his face expressionless, and stirred the broth that would send his friends to sleep.

It was easy enough. Connal had gone for the hunt that morning; in spite of the thin game, he rarely came back empty-handed, and this morning had been no exception. He had come back with a bird, scrawny and tough, obviously too old to escape him, a victim of its own age and the bitter winter. Tough or no, it was good enough for the stew pot. Though it might be hard to chew, it would flavor the broth. And tonight, of all nights, the food must be flavored.

Maeve had grown tired of sitting and watching him cook. Her sudden restlessness took her to the hide, where she stood staring into the oncoming night. Connal, who was rarely ill and resented it furiously when he was, had been fighting off a chill for two days past. He lay curled on his bed, heavy-eyed and irritable, wrapped at Maeve's command in warm covers. They had nearly quarreled at his insistence on hunting this morning, Maeve alternating between fury at his obstinacy and cajolery to soften him, Connal sneezing and light-headed, furious as always at any sign of physical weakness in himself.

Brihainn, stirring the broth, thought that of all Connal's idiosyncrasies, this reaction to sickness was at once the most exasperating and the most endearing. He had nursed Maeve through a dangerous ague, showing nothing but concern. He had nursed Brihainn through an injured arm, waiting upon him hand and foot. When those he loved needed patience and tenderness, he was like a child's wet nurse. Yet with his own body he had no patience and showed no mercy. Sure, and he would drive himself into the ground if he took no rest now.

Well, he would rest. Like it or not, he would rest,

and his lady with him. By the time the drug eased its hold on them, all would be done and the thing resolved.

Maeve still gazed out across the snow-fogged plain, and Connal had closed his eyes. They were paying him no mind. He ladled himself out a bowl of broth. Then, with a quick movement, he slipped a dried leaf, folded small, from the sleeve of his tunic to the pot and flicked it open with one deft forefinger. A yellowed powder swirled for a moment on the golden surface of the simmering liquid. Then it dissolved and was lost in the soup. A quick flick of the hand and a second leaf followed it.

The drug was harmless, even in this amount; his own bowl was untouched, and even if they licked the pot clean between them, it would not harm them. They would sleep deep; deep enough for him to slip into the night on a hunt of his own.

"Brihainn!"

Maeve's voice was so sharp that he jumped guiltily. Could she have seen him? Well, if she had, he would say it was flavoring. "Lady?"

"Lights! I see lights on the plain!"

For a moment he simply stood and stared at her. Then he ran across the room to stand beside her, straining his vision across the darkening expanse.

She was right. There in the distance, to the north, on the plain itself; a ghostly flicker, torches perhaps. The lights were dim, muted by the snow, unearthly in the dying shades of the winter twilight.

An ancient terror moved down the back of his neck. Men rarely moved in the forest by night. And, in any case, how could the holders of those flickering pinpoints be men? The road to the north was still impassable, solid with snow; Connal had gone that way only this morning.

No, they could not be men. But the demons of the night, the fomori, they needed no clear roads for their purpose. They could move on the snow, on the night air itself, lit from within and carrying the lights of hell with them. . . .

He wrenched her back inside and pushed the hide shut. The grip on her arm was so tight that it left livid marks on her skin and brought forth a small cry. Puzzled and hurt, she stood rubbing her bruised arm, staring at him. On the bed Connal opened his eyes and spoke hoarsely.

"What ails you both?"

"Naught. Rest you." Brihainn threw the taut reply over his shoulder and bent his head to Maeve. "Your pardon. I meant no hurt to you. But they are to the north, those lights. I see no way that men could move on that plain."

Her face bleached. He saw the frantic gesture against magic, the comprehension in her eyes, and spoke so low that Maeve, inches away, strained to hear him. "Demons, the fomori perhaps. The plain is no place for such as we, lady; we rest indoors tonight."

But I will not, he thought, and bit back a chill, cramping fear. I feel it; it is for tonight, and whatever walks abroad may bear me company if they choose. He spoke gently. "The broth has cooled enough, lady. Eat now."

She took the bowl from him with hands that trembled and sat beside Connal on the bed. Connal, revived somewhat by the fragrant steam, sat up and sniffed. "A good smell," he said appreciatively. "Perhaps it will restore me."

"Perhaps. We cannot know until you eat."

Be silent, be secret, he thought. The broth, more highly flavored than usual to hide any revealing taste of the drug, disappeared rapidly. Maeve drank two bowls, and with an endearing mixture of tenderness and bullying, induced Connal to finish the rest. And Brihainn, tense and alert, terrified of the wanderers out of doors yet determined to face them if need be, saw their slowly enlarging pupils, their stifled yawns, and settled back to wait for the dead hours to fall.

17

Sacred Snake

It had stopped snowing.

Brihainn, pressed against the trees that flanked the plain on its southeastern edge, lifted his face to the heavens and sucked in deep draughts of air. The air was very cold, a stark piercing cold that penetrated his wrappings, but the wind had died completely and the night was preternaturally still.

A coating of gray rime lay across trees, ground, horizon. Overhead, the dark, oddly luminous masses of clouds drifted apart to show a few stars, stitched bright gold against the darkness. The moon, a few days off the full, was a brilliant glow in the night sky; it was halfway up and climbing, shedding a clear radiance on the snowy ground.

He patted his belt, more from a need to reassure himself that Maeve's sharpened spear still hung there than from any rational reason to suppose it did not. In the shadow of the tall trees he had become a shadow himself; no human eye more than a few feet away could have seen him.

He turned his face to the north and shivered. The lights, muted and lower now, were still visible a few miles off in the distance; if the condition of the northern road did not make such a thing impossible, Brihainn would have sworn that this was a small troop of men, camping on the plain for the night.

Well, he wanted no part of them, whoever or whatever they might be. And if his idea as to Fearghail's place of hiding was right, he could avoid them entirely. He had left Maeve and Connal deeply, thickly asleep; he need fear no interference from them. The only problem now was whether or not the light of that gibbous yellow disk would be potent enough to illuminate the paths between the trees.

He took a deep breath and, grasping in one hand the great knife Connal had found in the snow, slipped like a shade between the trees and into the forest.

Even in his fear, his intense concentration, the scene had a deathly, frozen beauty. Streaks of pale moonlight fell across snow-covered mounds that, in the nacreous light, might have been anything from simple shrubs to crouching bears. Once, he looked up and felt his heart stop as he met a pair of enormous yellow eyes among the branches. Before he could move, it had given its eerie cry and swept past him, wise and quiet on its great speckled wings, in search of a titmouse or a wren awake and vulnerable in this frozen landscape.

He let his breath out, stifling an insane urge to laugh. Sure, and his nerves were in a sorry state, if he could be so frightened by an owl! He wiped his sweating palms against his thighs and moved farther in. The trees seemed to close ranks behind him as he went, sealing him in.

As mad and desperate as this midnight hunt might have seemed, as inexplicable as his companions would have found it, Brihainn was not acting from blind instinct alone. He had thought as he lay recuperating, his mind working constantly, mapping and remapping the forest he had learned and come to hate before he was wounded. Fearghail must be here, and close by; he could not have gone to the north, he dared not have gone to the south, to the east lay even denser woodland for many unexplored miles, and had he gone west across the great plain, they must have seen him.

So he was still about, trapped even as they were by the harsh grip of the winter months. And he knew where they were; that he could have attacked Brihainn so close to home spoke of a man keeping a wary, constant watch. That being so, he must have made himself shelter someplace close by.

Brihainn himself had explored most of the forest paths in and around the part of the woods and plain where their shelter lay. And he had found nothing. But there were a few smaller tracks, barely discernible to the naked eye, that he had not yet followed. That was for tonight.

He stopped to orient himself, feeling for a bad moment lost and claustrophobic. He had forgotten, and he cursed himself now for a fool, that everything would look very different under moonlight. But there were signs, an abandoned fox's earth here, an oddly distorted bush there, that would point the way. He had only to find them, and he would know which way to go.

And there, after all, was the empty lair, partially fallen in, partially covered over with weeds, where a vixen had once raised her cubs. He stood a moment looking down at it, wondering idly what had driven her away. Another fox, stronger and fiercer, who had stolen this safe cover and then abandoned it in her turn? The hand of man hunting, or the frosts of winter claiming a forest life? The owl, perhaps, sweeping down and over to come away triumphant, a piteously squealing cub dangling from the cruel beak?

Ten paces to the left, an ancient elm tree. Beyond that elm tree, what seemed a solid wall of shrubbery, thick with dead branches and thorns. He moved to the elm and stepped around it. The bushes parted under the weight of his hand, scratching him. But his attention had been caught, and he did not notice.

Something dangled from the back side of those bushes, something soft and glinting pale in the deadened moonlight. For a shuddering moment he thought the owl had dropped its prey here, that the object was a dead creature, perhaps a badger or smaller bird thrust upon these vicious thorns by a shrike. Swallowing his disgust, he reached out and touched it, light and careful, with a fastidious hand, and as he did so he caught the muted glint of gold. It flapped against his fingers, soft and limp.

A sack. Now, what would a sack do here, in th

middle of the forest, snagged on this thorn bush as if thrown here? He took it up and rubbed it between his fingers, testing its strength, seeing its supple beauty, knowing that this costly thing had never seen the inside of a peasant's hovel. It was not empty; he felt the light weight of its burden. Sure that whatever dwelt within no longer lived, he carefully slipped his hand inside.

Something cold and light and curiously limp fell into his palm. He drew his hand out, sweating, shivering with a fear that he could not himself have named. Hidden and silent under the protective boughs of the elm, he looked down at what he held.

The snake had been dead some time. It was rotting, decaying, but in this cold weather there was no way to tell how long ago the thing had died. The scales, falling away and uniformly gray, were light and insubstantial, the moonlight glowing through them to his palm.

He thought of the druids, the elders who carried these fine bags with their sacred and lethal occupants. He thought of his companions, lying in a drugged stupor on the plain. Without reaching for them, he took a mental tally of the things that he carried; the coil of strong hemp, the sleeping drug, the spear, the torch.

He stood a while longer, weighing the sack in his hand, considering. Coming to a decision, he dropped the druid's plaything back into its silken tomb and fastened it securely at his belt. Then he pushed the bushes aside and began to move, slow and careful, down the narrow, pitted path.

The track was a bad one, fit only for the creatures who came here by right. It was darker here, too, the thickness of the canopy overhead screening out much of the moon's glow, and with the increased darkness came a resulting decrease in his pace. The sack, the hemp, bounced together at his hip. Their feel was oddly reassuring. But where, in this white tangle of trees and shrubbery, was the clearing that must be Fearghail's sanctuary?

He found it so suddenly that, had the deadly occupant been at home, Brihainn would have stood no chance. One moment he was squeezing his body between two thick trees which, over the years, had entwined their roots and grown uncomfortably close together. The next, and he was standing at the edge of a tiny clearing, the barest possible space among these dense guardians of the wild. In the center of the clearing was a rough shelter, no more than a pile of branches lashed together with vines and covered with rotting sheepskins, its back edge up against the trees. It was barely large enough for a man to stand in.

He stood in the moonlight, looking at the dark hovel and the carefully doused remains of what had been a small fire. The place was empty, the resident not at home. Still, it would not do to take unnecessary risks. With the great knife held for the killing strike, he moved round the clearing's edge until he stood at the rear of the shelter.

For a few moments he stood listening, his ears cocked to the night air. Silence, total and deep. He pushed the flap aside and went inside.

Any lingering doubts that this might, after all, be the hut of some forest dweller were immediately laid to rest. He picked up the heavy pack and pulled out the white robes, banded in gold. They lay across his hands, smooth, luxurious, the final proof that here was the man he sought.

He knew, now, what he would do. Pushing the robe back into its resting place, he dropped the pack where it had lain. Then he went quickly back into the night air and pressed himself between the trees, the knife ready in his hands, to wait.

Thwarted. Thwarted yet again.

Covac, blue with cold, sat huddled in his tree. They had fanned out, the men below; the interlopers, fanned out across the road, guarding it, blocking it. He could not slip past them, and the miraculously cleared north road was as closed to him by the watching men as it had been by the snow.

His teeth grinding with frustration and discomfort, Covac clutched the tree bole and watched the moon rise. The clouds eddied and shook, drifting apart at last to reveal an indigo sky peppered with frosty stars. Enough light, it was true, to safely and quietly descend the tree by. But enough light, too, to keep him in the forest, penned here, a prisoner still.

When he knew he could no longer bear the cold, the moon had risen completely. It rode the black horizon like a yellow ghost. He had been in the canopy nearly a full day, and he knew a curious lightness of the mind that was nearly giddiness; so, to his frustration and physical misery was added the terror that he might pass momentarily into unconsciousness, toppling to his death from his lofty seat. Feeling his way, willing his chilled body to silence and grace, he began to descend the tree.

He inched his way carefully, feeling with caution for the solid ground, biting back a sigh of relief when at last his feet came to rest. Still no movement, no sound; they had heard nothing, and his hidden shelter could certainly not be seen from this far through the trees. Silent as the owl who, unbeknownst to him, watched him under hooded eyes from the very tree he had just abandoned, he moved like a wraith to the southwest, searching with staring eyes for the signs that would point out the hidden track that led to safety.

As he moved even farther from the men in the road, his confidence grew. He might be a little quicker now, less worried that they might hear his progress. Even if they did hear him, he thought, how were they to track him in the blackness of an unknown forest? He scrabbled and climbed, his pale head twisting from side to side as he searched for the markers that would show him the way.

The circle carved lightly on the tree bough, yes, there it was. A sharp left here, another ten paces forward, and a careful squeeze through a bush that prickled with thorns the length of a man's finger. And then that almost invisible curve of the track. Almost there, now.

For a long moment he stood framed, his massive body hunched under the protecting tree limbs, listening. It was quiet, very quiet. The hut was dark, and no footprints showed. Still inviolate, then. Still sanctuary.

Had he been less eager for warmth, less desperate for food, less exhausted from the long hours spent high in the oak tree, he might have sensed the watcher in the dark.

Since the day of his exile he had lived and thrived by heeding the slightest touch of intuition.

But tiredness and cold can dull even the sharpest edge, and no small, passionless voice came to warn him. He ducked his head sharply, avoiding the low-hanging boughs, and hurried across the unmarked snow of the tiny clearing to his own private haven.

Maeve woke slowly, aware of the moonlight falling through the cracks in the hide and the familiar discomfort that comes when one takes too much liquid before sleep.

For a few moments she simply lay on her back, eyes closed, head swimming. The bed was warm, so warm and soft. The room was very cold, little fringes of night air licking with sly hunger at her face, insinuating their way between the covers and the bed itself, adding to her unwillingness to get out of bed.

Fool, she thought groggily, fool to have been so greedy with the broth just before bed! Fool, not to have realized that a full bladder, with all its attendant discomfort, would be the result! And now she would have to pull herself from the warmth and go out into the snow!

She lay inert, her eyes closed, willing the pressure away. But her body would not be denied; it raised an insistent clamor. If she did not get herself up now and pass water, she would have bitter cramps to show for it.

She listened to Connal, running her tongue over a mouth that was oddly dry. Deep in sleep, he was breathing raggedly, close to snoring. Fortunate one, she thought, greedy one, this is simply unfair; you had as much broth as I did, so how do you sleep so deep? Well, there was little point in prolonging this agony. Face it, she told herself, face the cold air against you now and you will be wrapped up warm again shortly. . . .

The wave of dizziness that hit her as she lifted her head was as unexpected as it was unpleasant. She let her head drop hurriedly, feeling her gorge rise, and sucked in lungfuls of air.

By the three Mothers, what was this? Not even the fever had left her so giddy! Her eyes were burning, her head swimming unpleasantly. She let the nausea subside and slowly, gingerly, pulled herself upright. The dizziness hit her again and she dropped her face into her hands, trying desperately not to retch.

Drugged, she thought. She remembered this sensation well enough from a rare childhood illness, the feeling of sickness, the light head, the dry mouth. This was no fever, no natural sickness, and Connal's thick, rasping breathing was not natural either. Brihainn made the broth, no one else touched it. We laughed about it being so highly flavored. But why? And where has he gone? She listened, trying to place Brihainn by his breathing, but heard only Connal. Brihainn was not in the room.

Her bare skin electric in the cold air, she moved on unsteady legs across the hut. Brihainn's bed was empty. He was not in his bed, nor had he been. The covers showed smooth and unwrinkled in the moonlight.

Breathing heavily, she ran to the hide and thrust it open, gasping in the sudden onslaught as the cold night came in. No one, nothing. But the line of footprints showed clearly, blackly, against the crusted snow, leading off into the forest.

She stood shivering, willing away the waves of vertigo, wondering what to do. Wake Connal? Yes, but he had taken even more of the broth, the broth that Brihainn had so obviously and unaccountably drugged, than she had. He was breathing like a man in a drunken stupor. She knew from her own experience how hard it was to rouse a drunken man.

Moreover, he had been fighting a chill. If she woke him now, he would likely be even sicker than she was.

Her naked body was turning blue from the cold, but she ignored it. The misery of the cold might help to rouse her from this lethargy, might help to clear her addled wits. She looked at the prints, and with a sickening feeling of certainty, suddenly knew where Brihainn must have gone. Turning on her heel, she ran back inside and fumbled among their carefully hoarded supplies.

The great coil of rope, gone. And the knife that Connal had found, the ugly knife with the red hair wrapped so lovingly around its hilt, that was gone too.

Hunting. Brihainn, alone, still weak, had gone into the night to find their enemy.

She wasted no more time. She pulled her leather tunic on and her armor after it, and stuffed her feet into the soft, thick boots which were mercifully dry. No time to spend in coiling the mass of hair away from her neck; she dropped her crested war helm on over it, letting it hang in a molten river down her back. With a last look at Connal, she reached for her spears.

One, only one. So Brihainn had taken the other.

For a moment, as common sense took hold, she knew a sudden panic. To go out alone into the forest at night, with those lights to the north that might be the fomori or worse, hunting a killer who wanted nothing better than her head at his belt and the worst of her agony along the way—no, she could not. She would wake him, tell him the whole tale. Let him decide what best to do. . . .

He snorted, turned over on his side, one bare arm covered with black hair curving around his cheek. He looked very young suddenly, the long lashes making sweet shadows across a face unlined and unworried in slumber.

No, she could not wake him. There was no time. It might take half the night to rouse him from this drugged coma, and Brihainn might be in danger even as she stood here undecided, wondering what best to do.

There was no help for it; it was for her and her alone.

Maeve slipped the single spear into its sheath and slung it across her right shoulder. It was not enough, and not good enough; if she found herself in hand-to-hand combat, the spear was worse than useless. She hesitated a moment, knowing that he might be angry with her, but the hesitation was swallowed up in the larger sense of urgency, and she took Connal's knife from its place at his bedhead. Let him rage, if he was so minded; the knife might mean the difference between life and death, Brihainn's death, her death.

For a moment she stood looking down at him as he slept. She was very frightened, and very calm; never had she felt her youth, her inexperience, more strongly or with greater resignation. It came to her with a sense of detachment that she might not live to return to this hut, this bed, this man.

He had turned his face into the pillow, away from her. She knelt and kissed the palm of his open hand, very lightly, as if offering a benediction. He did not stir.

She breathed a short prayer, to Crom of the battles, to Cernunnos who might protect her from his beasts if he chose, to Danu who was her patron, her own. Then, without a backward glance, she flung her heavy cloak over her shoulders and went quickly through the hide to face whatever awaited her in the night.

Once her eyes had grown accustomed to the peculiarities of the light, she found the going easy enough. Brihainn's tracks, very fresh in the snow, were a clear line and simple for her to read. She followed them to the forest's edge, noted the confusion and scuffing where he had paused, and followed them in.

She was aware of an odd sense of security, a feeling that she was protected. One corner of her mind picked at this sensation even as the rest of her concentration was focused on the line of prints, weaving through and between unlikely places, dense bushes, finding tracks where it seemed impossible that a track might be. She traced the feeling to its source just as she came to the abandoned fox's lair. It came from the knife she held, not from its size or strength, but from the fact that she carried something of Connal with her, something he had held, honed, used. She held it tightly, a talisman against fear.

Brihainn had paused here; the footprints were deeper, more defined, the signs of a man who had stood awhile, as though getting his bearings. Then he had veered sharply to the left; the footprints led straight to a huge elm tree, gnarled with age.

Something rustled in the bushes. A wolf, a bear, a man with power and weapons? She froze in place, instinctively using the weapons of the wild beasts—camouflage, silence, stillness.

The fox, small and lean, slipped past her without a second glance, disappearing between the trees. Something small and bloody, a bird or a hare, dangled from its jaws.

Maeve let her breath out raggedly, feeling the harsh pain of terror and relief as her constricted heart relaxed. Only a fox, she told herself, and tried to still the trembling in her hands, the paralyzing weakness of her knees.

She leaned against the elm tree, panting in small sobbing breaths, trying desperately to calm herself. *No man, and no wolf, and no threat to you.* The hilt of Connal's knife was slick with her sweat, and the forest seemed living, threatening, a huge alien creature from the world of light that had swallowed her whole and watched her now with cold amusement, waiting for her to move, waiting to see what she might do next, playing with her. . . .

Stop, she thought lucidly, *stop this at once. You are a fool, and a queen, and you have a task ahead of you.* She forced herself to think of Brihainn, of Connal sleeping in their warm bed, of the pale face and cornflower-blue eyes of the druid. The panic eased.

Sweet Crom, what had happened here? The prints led to a solid bank of shrubbery, and surely he could not have gone through that! She reached out a tentative finger and pulled it back hurriedly as the vicious thorn went home. Bright blood from her pricked finger welled up, glossy and warm.

She sucked her punctured finger, staring in frustration at the thornbushes. The prints ended here, showing scuffed and blurred where Brihainn had scrambled for a firm footing. Could there truly be a path beyond this brutal barrier?

Well, she could but try. As carefully as she could, wincing as an errant branch whipped across her cheek and left a long scratch, she pushed the thick shrubbery aside and pushed her way through.

And there was a path, poor and pitted but a clear track nevertheless. The prints began to vary here, the imprint of the ball of the feet deeper and the heel prints lighter. He had gone on tiptoe here. Why? A sense of danger, or a true knowledge of it?

Whatever the reason, it would be folly or worse to ignore the example. Light as air, she tiptoed down the winding track, her eyes wide and staring, alert to any hint of life, of danger.

The flicker of light came and went so quickly that for a moment she thought she had imagined it. Then it came again, and a third time; a tiny pinpoint of firelight, red and gold. Someone on the other side of these old and twisted trees had lit a small fire.

Her heart was pounding and she had the uncomfortable feeling that the noise it made in her own ears must be audible across the forest. She tightened her fingers around the knife and moved quietly forward, her eyes fixed on the dance of flame ahead.

It happened so quickly that she had no time to react, no time even for fear. The tree at her left side suddenly moved, resolving itself into a dim shape, and an arm wrapped itself with brutal efficiency around her throat.

Maeve reacted instinctively. She lifted the knife, twisting, thrusting back with her elbow, searching for the soft groin, praying incoherently that she might hear the expected grunt of pain, that the vicious grip around her throat would ease, give her air, give her a precious moment of time to adjust. Her head was swimming and the dark outlines of the forest came through a red haze.

Her arm met only air. There was a soft chuckle of genuine amusement and a brutal twist of her right arm. The knife clattered to the earth and lay there, useless. A hand hard as iron took her by the wrist, twisting her arm behind her back. The grip was agonizing, impossible to break; the hand that held her had only to add a bit more pressure and her arm would snap like dry wood.

The arm that lay like a tree trunk beneath her chin shifted and became a man's hand, huge and deadly. Struggling madly and uselessly in the iron grip that was tightening around her neck, she heard a voice, soft and musical, in her ear. Brihainn, she thought madly, are you dead, then? Have I walked into my own ending, and all for nothing? Connal, oh Connal, oh please . . .

"Silly little bird," it said, and the singsong lilt that had haunted her nightmares ran through her blood like ice. "Such a foolish little forest bird, to visit the wolf in its own lair. Enough now, pretty bird. Time to sleep awhile."

Thumb met index finger on the great artery that pulsed just behind her ear. The forest exploded into fire and light, and then into a soft, velvet blackness that rushed up to meet her, as if in welcome.

For a moment he stood, staring down at the crumpled body on the path at his feet. The night was very quiet, punctuated only by his heavy breathing. Picking Maeve up, he carried her back to the clearing and into the hut.

"Connal? Connal!"

The voice was familiar. It came again with greater urgency, seemingly from miles away, a fuzzy, teasing touch against his sleeping mind. Yet he had no wish to wake; this sleep was deep, deeper than he had known since Sibhainn was still alive, and he would hold to it. . . .

"Connal! Gods love us all, can you not wake!"

Would it give him no peace, this infernal noise? He groaned and snorted, moving unwillingly a step closer to waking. A hand took him by the shoulder and wrenched, hard.

"Connal! *Where are Brihainn and Maeve?*"

He opened his eyes.

For the first few moments of waking, his dazed mind took note of facts with no recognition of their meaning. It was night, and cold. The hide was open and the room alive with men and torchlight. There were faces, faces he had never before seen, and the night air carried with it the jingling of bridles, the snorting and stamping of many horses. And Cormac, who had ridden off to beg help from Kieran in the south so many days ago, was standing over him like a fury, disheveled and filthy, his eyes starting in his head.

Connal's own eyes seemed crusted with stickiness. He rubbed them, yawning widely, noting with some surprise the ugly and metallic taste at the back of his throat.

He tried his voice. "What . . ."

Cormac spoke with desperation in his voice. "Wake, chieftain. You must wake. I have twenty of Kieran's best warriors with me. We have ridden nearly without pause since we left Muman, and more men have gone to Cruachain for help from Carhainn. He cannot escape us now, the roads are blocked in all directions. But where are the others?"

Connal made no answer. He had lifted a hand to his brow and was sitting with his eyes closed. Cormac saw the groggy incomprehension in his face and knew a moment of black panic. Drawing back his hand, he slapped Connal across one cheek, as hard as he could.

The blow rocked Connal backward in his bed, snapping his head to one side with a sickening sound. Behind them one of the southern warriors drew in his breath. For a moment they stared at each other, and Cormac saw the livid weal rising on Connal's face. Then the chieftain pulled himself unsteadily upright, rubbing his mouth.

"My thanks, fila. I think I am sickening, for I feel as though drugged, my head is so thick. It is unlike me to sleep so deep." He looked about him, his brows snapping together. "Who are all these men, Cormac? And where are Maeve and Brihainn?"

Cormac's pleasant voice held an edge of steel. "That is what I asked you. We rode up not ten minutes ago. As we pulled the horses to the rear, I saw two lines of footprints leading from here into the forest. I thought it strage that you would sleep and set no guard, so I kept the men and the horses from despoiling the prints; they are there still. When I came in I found you sleeping as though dead, and alone. I have brought the help we need, chieftain; the net will close now, and for the prey there is no hope of escape. Where have the others gone?"

But Connal did not hear him. He jumped from his bed and, not even pausing to reach for a cloak, ran naked to the hide and looked out. There they were, two sets of footprints, disappearing toward the forest. They were gone.

His gorge rose. Unable to resist it, he fell to his knees in the snow and was wrackingly sick.

His head was throbbing, and high on one cheekbone a tic leaped and fluttered. When the spasm was past, he felt better. His mind moving quickly, he came swiftly back indoors and reached for his armor.

"They are gone, gone into the forest. Brihainn first, I think; the smaller prints look fresher. I suppose Maeve woke and found him gone. It seems she went after him."

His fingers never pausing in the fastening and securing of his armor, he looked to where she kept her weapons. "Yes. Both spears gone, and all her armor. My knife too."

He stood up and reached for his helm. His voice was shaking with a suppressed rage that Cormac had not heard since Connal's youth.

"Help me with these things, as you love me. By all the gods, I will take the skin off them both for this folly! I was drugged, no doubt of it. Brihainn made the supper, and I drank it. That he would do such a thing to me! Oh, I shall pay him out. The fool, the fool!"

Cormac had come up behind him, throwing warning glances at the silently respectful men of the south. "Why would your gentle brother drug you, lord?"

Connal laughed bitterly. "Why? Because he had made some plan in his head, no doubt, and he knew I would never let him go wounded after my uncle." He felt the hands on his cloak tighten, and added, "Wounded, yes. It happened after you left. A knife in the arm, thrown from the trees."

Panic, a hot violent taste, rose in his chest. His voice lifted with, filling the small room. "And my lady is alone under the tall trees, searching for him. If my uncle should find her, either of them..." It burst from him in an anguished wail that raised the hair on their arms. "Why? Why did she not wake me, if she woke to find him gone?"

"She may have tried," Cormac said quietly. "If you were drugged, she might have shaken you to no purpose. It took me five minutes and a blow to the face to do it. Be not angry with them, lord, for I will not believe that they acted from anything but their love for you." He saw a glaze of tears across the black eyes, and said quietly, "Lord, we must go quickly. We can follow the prints. Will you give these men your orders now? We have no time to waste."

"Truth." He swung to face the others, towering over them like an avenging spirit, taller by a head than any man in the room.

"My thanks to you, and to Kieran your lord. I will show my thanks when the time is with me. Six of you, the six deadliest fighters, accompany us. The rest will remain here. The man we seek is a big man and a very dangerou fighter. He is not to be killed, do you understand me? Wound him if you need, but not to the death. The druids want him alive, and they will have him. One of you who will remain, give me your knife. My lady has taken mine." His voice shook. "May it keep her safe."

With no argument among them, six men promptly stepped forward. Connal reached for his sling and took the proffered knife. With the others following behind him in a tight line, he ran out into the night.

Cold, and something prickling against her cheek. A brush of firelight across her closed lids.

Maeve opened her eyes, and remembered.

She was lying on her side a few feet from the fire, facing him. Her arms, tied fast behind her, ached with lack of blood. The firelight glinted on her armor, neatly piled in the doorway of the shelter. She lay in her soft shift, barefoot, bareheaded, bare-armed, and the rising wind obscured his face, sending eddies of smoke across her eyes.

She closed her eyes once more, identifying and exploring each of her individual hurts. The rope that bound her wrists was the most painful, a vindictive, personal agony, biting deep into her skin. Her mouth throbbed as well; I must have bitten my tongue, she thought in vague surprise, and never noticed. Where the agonizing pressure had been put on her neck, there was no pain at all.

Above all the places where her body hurt, she was conscious of a deep sense of shame. She had come like a silly chit into the bear's jaws, thinking herself invincible, with no one to know where she had gone and no one to know what had become of her. This Fearghail, this master of all their troubles, had manhandled her unconscious body, stripping her of her armor, trussing her like a skinny fowl and meeting about as much resistance, leaving her to wake to the bitter knowledge of her own failure, her own stupidity.

And there was another pain, a burning ugliness between her thighs, that told its own tale. Her faint had been merciful; the gods had shown her that much favor, then. But the knowledge that he had taken her as she slept was too much to bear. She moaned, a cold, angry sound. He lifted his head.

"Ah." He rose and regarded her, his even and beautiful teeth glinting across the small space that separated them. Yes, she thought savagely, he had enjoyed what he had done. There was a lazy pleasure to his movements, disconcertingly reminiscent of her own reactions to Connal. "So the bird wakes. Good, very good."

She heard the laughter in his voice with a terror too black for expression. He sounded very gentle and very mad. "I have been waiting for you, queen. You have a debt to pay me, you see."

Somehow she controlled her voice. It sounded very flat. "A debt, false druid? Surely not. It is you who owe me, for my cousin, for my father, for my mother." A sudden gust of anger shook her, and she stared up into the wide blue eyes. "For my throne, Fearghail."

She had shaken him; even with her nerves stretched to breaking point, she saw the pinched mouth, the suddenly fixed stare. "So you know who I am. Well, and I am Fearghail no longer, pretty one. It has been long years since I was Fearghail. I am Covac now, and will remain."

"Hidden."

He raised his brows and took a step toward her. The smile was back in place, fixed and terrifying. "So the bird was well-taught, was she? Hidden, yes. Hidden I have been these many seasons, allana, and hidden I shall be after you are dead."

The words, a flat statement of fact, turned her to ice. She stared up into that smiling face and, for the first time, truly understood that she would die, that he would kill her, that it would not be a clean death or an easy one. Blue eyes held green, seeing the fear in them, knowing pleasure. He walked around the fire to her side and knelt, and with one hand took a handful of hair in a painful grip. In his other hand he held a knife.

She wrenched her face away, keeping her chin down, knowing through her terror that she must keep her throat protected as best she could. She heard him chuckle.

"Useless, and unnecessary. Do you think I would kill you so clean, so quick?" The hand twined, pulling hard, jerking her head back. She saw the knife come down and closed her eyes, waiting, despite his words, for death.

He stood up, his eyes alight, a hank of bright hair held triumphantly in one hand. "Look and see what I have here, flame-hair. A piece of you, and all for my pleasure."

She lay motionless, eyes closed. He stood a moment, looking down consideringly. Then, with a shrug, he drew his foot back and kicked her in the side.

The cry of pain was quickly bitten back. She opened her eyes and stared up at him, hating him, her voice scathing with contempt.

"You like red hair, do you, filth? The hair you wrapped like a talisman around the knife you threw at Brihainn, whose hair was that? My cousin Ahnrach, perhaps? The girl who trusted you, the girl you murdered at Kahr?"

"Hers, yes." He knelt at her side and laid a light hand on one breast. It lay there, alive, potentially killing.

Ignore him, she thought concretely. Ignore him, show no hurt, no fear, no shame, no pain. Talk to him, make him talk to you. You have no hope else.

Even to her own ears, her voice sounded remarkably normal. "Why, Fearghail? What hate had you for my people, that you tried to send us into war with Ulster? Your hatred for Connal I can understand. But why Connacht?"

The hand moved casually down, finding the line of bruised ribs, the hollow of her belly. She gritted her teeth to keep from screaming. But she could not break her eyes from the blue ones. They held her as surely as the ropes around her wrists.

His voice held a dark music. "You thwarted me, you see. So very small you were, tiny and perfect, the two cranes flying. Three of my men you killed that day, with your little spears." The hand suddenly tweaked viciously, and the cry this time would not be stifled. He laughed, a sound of enjoyment. "Your cousin paid forfeit for you that day."

Remember Ahnrach and her day of dying . . . the hand had moved back up on its slow journey, and rested across her face. And suddenly, through her choking terror of him, the smell of his madness and his need, hatred boiled in her, a hot sustaining draught. Moving so quickly that he had no time to react, she twisted her face and sank her teeth as hard as she could into his hand.

The raking, flailing blow knocked her sideways with its force. He was straddling her now, a huge figure, towering and potent. Too late, she remembered that her legs were unbound; her attempt at a kick was stifled as he put his full weight against her thighs. For the first time she saw the rage and hatred in his eyes. He bent and took the front of her shift in one hand, lifting her up to him.

"Now," he said softly, and ripped the soft cloth away. She pulled back against the pressure, and his other hand reached forward to catch her by the hair, pulling her face to his, his kiss cutting off breath. "Now."

She was breathless and panting, sickened by the kisses, by his proximity, by her own panic. She wrenched her face away from him and managed to say, "Connal will come. He will come, and you will die."

"I don't think so," he said through his grin. "He would not let you wander the forests alone, had he known. My guess is that you left him sleeping, drugged perhaps. By the time he wakes there will be only a ruined body and I—"

"Fearghail."

The voice was quiet, calm, deadly. It froze them into place, killer and victim, an ugly tableau. Then Covac let go of her and whirled to meet that voice. She fell painfully back to the ground, crying, unaware of her own tears.

Brihainn, a knife in one hand and a small white sack in the other, stepped out from behind the fire.

"Greetings, chieftain's brother, outcast, slayer. It has been many years since we last met."

The big man said nothing. He stood as if carved from stone, unblinking, the knife held cocked and ready. His eyes were fixed on the bag in Brihainn's hand.

Maeve lay still, catching her breath, trying to believe in the sudden reprieve, forcing her confused mind to understand. So Brihainn had come here, had come to wait, to beard the enemy on his own ground. Why, then had he not come sooner to her aid? And what was that he held, and why did Fearghail stare with such fascination?

The clearing was alive with shadows, Brihainn's shadow, Fearghail's shadow, dancing and twisting like spirit lovers in a mad embrace. She saw Brihainn's hand rise, not the hand that held the knife, but the other.

The sack dangled, the firelight turning its whiteness to blood. Even from behind him she saw Fearghail's head move to follow the motion of the sack. The heavy shoulders were hunched and tight.

Brihainn's voice was uninflected, nearly a chant; it had a familiarity that raised the flesh on Maeve's bare arms. Suddenly she placed it, and closed her eyes against the memory. It was the cadence of the druids, the toneless, passionless drone of the seers condemning her to fight Connal to the death, back there at Tara.

"Your talisman," Brihainn said. "Dead and discarded, and all your fortune with it. Come and take your fortune back from me, chieftain's brother."

He flipped his wrist and the sack bounced. Fearghail made a noise deep in his throat, a harsh rasp as ugly as it was eloquent. "I hold your fortune in my hand, betrayer. I have found the gods' favor, that you lost." The voice was soft and taunting. "Will you leave it to me, then? Are you so afraid?"

Covac took a step forward, the great sinews of his arm tensing as he gripped the knife tighter. As he lifted his arm for the throw, Maeve suddenly realized what was happening and understood Brihainn's peril. Without conscious thought, she moved.

Her legs, left unbound for Covac's pleasure, swung out with all the strength she could muster. The vicious kick caught Covac just behind the knees, one foot hooking him by the leg, toppling him forward toward the fire. As he threw out a hand to save himself, she kicked once more. This time her flying foot connected with his hand. The knife spun from his fingers to fall to the snow at her side. With a wriggle of her hips, she rolled her body to cover it.

The blue eyes were bulging with fury; they had gone so pale that they looked white, and the thin lips were drawn back into a snarl that turned his face from human to demon. There was no sanity left there, and no humanity either. As he drew his foot back to kick her away, Brihainn dropped his knife and jumped for him.

He landed on Covac's back, his free hand taking the big man around the throat. Together they crashed to the ground, inches from Maeve's side. Brihainn's other hand, still clutching the sack, moved up to press the white bag against Covac's face.

"Your luck, your fortune," Brihainn said, and his voice was low and breathless. "Here it is for you. Do you not wish for it, Fearghail?"

Covac's scream rang across the clearing and echoed across the night. The heavy body began to thrash, the face pulling desperately away from the soft fabric, a steady babble of imprecations pouring into Maeve's ear.

Both men, to Maeve, appeared to have gone mad. Fearghail—no, Covac—had two free hands to Brihainn's one, and by far the greater weight and strength; it would have been the work of a moment to snap the other's neck. Yet he made no attempt to do so. He seemed to have no control over his muscles; all his attention seemed concentrated on escaping the mysterious white sack pressed against his face, while Brihainn was obviously putting every ounce of strength he possessed into holding it there.

This was no normal battle of strength against strength, but something darker and deeper.

Maeve's mystification grew. He had only to reach up both hands, one hand, and snatch the sack from Brihainn's hand. But he seemed afraid to touch it. She could not even guess what the bag might contain. Whatever it was, it was something, perhaps the only thing, that this man feared.

But fear or no, let the big man regain his wits, and Brihainn was a dead man. He could not hope to withstand the other's strength for long; the moment the sack was dropped, he would reach up and break Brihainn like a dried twig. And there was nothing she could do.

She had forgotten her hurts and her shame, forgotten everything in the overwhelming need to do something. The two men, locked in their strange combat, seemed

oblivious to her existence. Straining her face away from
the rigid bodies only inches from her, she turned her face
to the trees and began to scream.

She had never before screamed in all her life. It was
not for a child who would be queen to shame herself in
such a way; Flyn had allowed her tears to ease a childhood
hurt or a sudden fear, but from the time of her birth she
had been trained as a warrior and not as a woman.

But she screamed now and, with the sobbing breath
of the men beside her loud in her ears, the screams grew
wild and uncontrolled, pounding against the cold air,
sending nesting birds in the high branches shrieking their
alarm into the night sky. The screams died to whimpers.

"Take it away," Covac said, and his voice was as high
as a girl's. The sack was pressed against his cheek, wet
with sweat. "Take it back from me, king's bastard."

"Take it yourself," Brihainn replied. He was grinning
now, a death's head rictus as terrible as Covac's own and
nearly as mad. "A sacred snake for you, false elder, your
own sacred snake. A druid came to Emain to tell us how
two elders had gone missing. Did you find them, Fearghail?
Did you find their holy robes, their pretty bag banded in
gold?"

His right hand, twined in Covac's hair, suddenly
lashed out to wrench the sack open. The snake, its
death-whitened eyes open and its opalescent scales ver-
milion in the firelight, slipped with a whispering rustle
from the opening to lay like a scar across Covac's eyes.

"No." The huge body had gone very still, and Covac's
glazed eyes were fixed on Brihainn's. He began to wail, a
high babbling keening. "No. Take it back, take it—"

"Move it, if you dare." Brihainn pulled himself upright, sitting on the other's chest, his shoulders shaking
with exhaustion. From the pouch at his belt he took a leaf
folded small. The powder, gray and gritty, fell into his
palm. "I knew it for yours when I found it cast aside in the
horns. You hurled it from you in fear, did you not? No
escape for you once your fortune had gone, and all your
life come back to you again. I knew it. I knew."

He was grinding the powder to paste now, the end of
one forefinger thickly covered with it. He ran the finger

across Covac's lips in a teasing, gentle motion. "You are parched, chieftain's brother. Your lips are dry, cracked with the cold and with your own fear. You dare not move for fear the god's fire will strike you. It waits in the body of your ruined talisman."

"You dare not poison me." Covac giggled suddenly, a crazed little laugh. "You dare not."

"Oh, I would dare. But perhaps it is not poison. Perhaps it is something to give you courage, something to give you sleep. You have two choices only, betrayer. You can find the courage to touch your fortune, or you can chance my kind of vengeance. Lick my gift from your lips and see."

He spoke without turning his head. "Maeve. I could not reach you before he took you. I failed in that. I was behind the shelter on the wrong side of the clearing when I heard you cry out." His face was gray. "I saw but could not stop him. My life is forfeit."

"Behind the shelter."

"Yes." His voice was limp, nearly uncaring. "I came here before him and waited there, in the trees. I saw him carry you indoors."

"And you did nothing?"

He turned his face at that. "What could I do? He had you, he had a knife; you were insensible. A wrong move would have meant your death for while you slept you could not struggle, defend yourself, twist away from him. I was helpless." He looked at her and repeated dully, "You came to harm through my agency. My life is forfeit."

Bound and bruised, she was still a queen. Her voice, through the cracked and swollen lips, sounded rusty. "I give you back your life again, my brother. The fault was my own. How could I demand your life from you?"

There was pain in his voice now. "It makes no odds, lady. Even if you pardon me, Connal will not. I drugged you both to keep you safe at home. You came for me, and were shamed in the doing of it." He laughed without mirth. "Do you think my brother will forgive that? Why, why did you not sleep, stay indoors? No, you will find no clemency for me under Connal's hand. He will take my head for it. I die either way."

"Then we will not tell him." She shifted her head, not knowing whether the cold on her cheek was snow or tears. "That is a command, cela. You will say nothing."

The body under his had gone limp. Moving like an old man, Brihainn climbed to his feet and stood staring down. Covac's eyes were heavy and sightless, his breathing even. The powder lay thick across his mouth, like a white shadow of the snake that banded his brow.

"So I did not need the drug, the mandragora and the poppy that I mixed," Brihainn said aloud. "It is as I thought; he has succumbed to himself, to his own terrors." He bent to Maeve and began to untie her wrists.

Covac lay immobile, his mind drifting, lost in the annihilation of a lifetime. He was barely conscious of the man and woman beside him; he was wandering through a grove of the sacred eight trees, wandering there as he had once before. Once again he carved the stick; once again the snake bent its gemstone eyes on him and crawled into his stolen pouch. His luck and his fortune gone into the night wind, only to return to him as the curse of his own blood. The snake lay weightlessly across his cool brow, and somehow it was right and fitting that it should come home to him.

Covac thought of Ahnal, Ahnal who had been his teacher and friend, thought of him as he had been in his last moments of life, his arms stretched toward the west. He saw a pretty girl, her red hair streaming out behind her, her mouth distorted with her last consuming fear, but he could not give this phantom a name; she might have been Ahnrach, or Alhauna, or the girl whose hair he had so lovingly wrapped around his knife. And still the snake lay across his brow, holding him there as securely as his own memory.

His mind was gone. He was a million miles from this clearing, this night, this ending, alone in a wilderness populated by ghosts, and they would not let him rise.

Maeve sat in the snow, rubbing her arms, wincing at the welcome bite of circulation restored. Reaction had set in, bringing a detached exhaustion in its wake. "What do you mean, succumbed to himself? Is he dead, then?"

"Not dead, no. But his mind has gone into the world of the Sidh, though his body has not. Help me bind him."

"No!" She stood shuddering, and backed away. "I—Brihainn, I ask your forgiveness. I am a coward, a coward and a weak fool, but I cannot bring myself to touch him."

"All right." He dropped his cloak across her shoulders. "Get you warm while I tie him. Once he is bound—" His head whipped around. "Maeve!"

Crashing in the undergrowth, shouts, torches flickering through the trees. Maeve jumped for her spear and stood shoulder to shoulder with Brihainn, waiting. And suddenly the small clearing was full of men, Connal and Cormac and six others, and Connal had Maeve in his arms and was crushing her against his chest, weeping his relief into her hair.

Epilogue

At the dawning of Imbolc, the festival of lovers, men once again gathered on the great plain of Bregia.

Their numbers this time were thinner. War had once again broken out between Ulster and Des-Gabair, and the men of the north, led by Sheilagh, were largely absent from this gathering; she had sent her blessings, her relief, and ten of Connal's own celi to represent her. Many of the petty chieftains, too, had stayed away; the bitter winter had laid a curse on the fields, and crops would be slow to grow in the ruined ground this season.

But the druids were present in force, led by the small, enigmatic man with his horned snake's mask. Kieran had come from Muman with all his train, and Carhainn, with all the nobly born of Cruachain, had ridden as escort for Connal and Maeve from the southlands.

On a gray and misty morning they gathered, one and all, around the rath-na-riogh, listening to the judgment.

Brihainn, at Maeve's shoulder, kept his eyes fixed on the master and was silent. He had changed since the night in the forest, changed in ways that Connal found subtle and disturbing. Never talkative, he had grown even more quiet. He was quicker to anger, short bursts of bad temper which invariably led to muttered apologies and sudden, crushing hugs. He had taken to solitary rides in the forests.

Yet his loyalty, if anything, was stronger than ever. He was as attentive to Connal as he had ever been; it was his attitude to Maeve that had altered. Shy admiration had become fierce partisanship, and there were times when he seemed unwilling to let her out of his sight.

He stood, his cloak whipping behind him in the wind, with one hand on her back. She saw Connal's glance, the look of puzzlement on his face, and felt again the weight of the secret she shared with the chieftain's brother.

Brihainn had obeyed her. When the men had carried Covac's unresisting body from the clearing, Connal's first words had been of concern. Was she hurt? What had become of her shift and her armor? Had he laid hands on her?

The urge to tell him the truth, to weep out her anger and shame against him, had been almost unbearable. But Brihainn had spoken the truth, and she knew it. Let Connal have the sum of it and, brother or no, Brihainn would die. Though she had gone of her own free will into the snare, Brihainn had led her there, and it had been his sleeping draught that had kept Connal from holding her safe. Though she blamed Brihainn for neither the rape nor her own stupidity in walking into it, Connal would not see it her way.

So she had cast a warning glance at the stone-faced Brihainn and made her answer. No, and no, and no. No, she was not hurt, no, he had not laid hands on her, no, no, no. She had reassured him, hiding the physical pain, smiling, playing a part, and with her silence had entered into a complicity that weighed on her as only a secret kept from a lover could.

Carhainn, too, had changed. The year of rule had left an indelible mark on him, imprinting an already strong man with a calm dignity. He had been at the head of the party of oinach that welcomed Maeve and Connal back to Cruachain, but only Maeve noticed that he was not wearing her crown. She learned later that for the year of her banishment it had sat in her own house, wrapped and covered, untouched but for cleaning; she could not know, for there was no one to tell her, of the times Carhainn had woken in the night and gone to sit before that crown, thinking and remembering.

He had stood between the two leaders on Cruachain's rath-na-riogh, raising their hands to the roaring crowd smiling with relief that was obvious to all. Somehow he had come to terms with his gains and his losses and learned to accept them; the anguished lover fretting at his loss, railing against the fates, had gone for good. Carhainn was a man at peace.

Now, at Connal's left hand, he looked at Maeve and felt no pain. This was not the girl he had loved, nor the hot-tempered, impetuous young queen either. She had aged, grown, during her year in the hills; the green eyes were wiser, the mouth sadder, the slim back that had once arched beneath him was straight and serene. Even the red hair hanging loose down her black robe could not reduce her to perfect youth again. It came to him that this new, calm maturity fitted Connal's stern, dark beauty as a perfect foil. They were no longer young lovers, but man and woman together.

While they watched each other, covertly or openly, most other eyes were fixed on the hill. Behind the ranked druids was a single stake, heaped high with dry bracken and kindling. There was a man lashed to that stake, a huge man in white, his face covered by a hood that had no eyes. He was blinded and ready, his passions gone from him, with nothing left to do but wait.

The master raised his hands above his head. The high voice was sharp and clear.

"Chieftains, rulers, oinach all. At last Imbolc a quest was given and a day set. The conditions have been met, the transgressor taken. Connacht and Ulster, I give your kingdoms back to you once more. By Crom, by Cernunnos of the beasts, I give them back to you, by highest Lugh I give them back to you. Connacht!"

Maeve stepped forward, calm and quiet. "Holy one."

He laid a gentle hand across her face, covering it. "Queen you are again, outcast no longer. Will you take your birthright back from me?"

"I will."

"It is well done, and will be done again. Ulster!"

Connal came forward slowly. His face was set and dark, inscrutable. "Holy one."

Again the hand was laid, light as a leaf on water,

across Connal's face. "Chieftain you are again, outcast no longer. Will you take your birthright back from me?"

"I will not."

For the space of a heartbeat those on the plain simply gaped. The silence was ghastly, palpable. Yet the master showed no surprise.

"You will not?"

"I will not." Connal turned, not toward the expectant crowd, but to Maeve. "Hear me."

The snake mask shifted. "We hear. Speak, then."

Connal's voice was calm, assured. "At Imbolc last we fought at your behest. A quest was set, a quest was met. My uncle was taken, and meets his end this day. By your own law, master, I may take my throne again. But, in truth, I do not want it."

Though every man on the plain heard him, he spoke directly to Maeve. She stood very still, smiling up into his face, saying nothing. He spoke again.

"My people have no love for me, master, nor I for them. They hate me when times are calm, flock to me to beg the power of my protection in war or sickness or trouble. In Emain are only those who love me in foul weather; my heart is where my lady is, for her love is constant. In truth, master, I would rather be regent in Connacht than High Chieftain in Ulster."

The snake mask turned to Maeve. "And you, queen. How do you stand in this matter? Would you take this man from his crown and his people, to shadow you?"

She laughed suddenly, a joyous gurgle that cut through the stunned silence. "Take him? Holy one, I would settle for nothing less."

"Then let him name a chieftain, here and now, before us all, and it is done. Ulster?"

They had discussed it, argued over it, worried the question like dogs snarling over a bone. Brihainn stepped forward, cool and watchful. "Master."

The mask traveled from boots to face and stopped there. Behind the slits Brihainn saw shrewd hazel eyes that held knowledge and some humor. "You are to rule?"

"I am to rule." Years of bastard shame, shame that had lain so heavy on him, and all for what? A throne, and days of peace. He shrugged suddenly. So, it will shock them; let it, then, and have done with it! He lifted his voice.

"Seers, rulers, gentle people all. I am Brihainn mac Sibhainn, son of Sheilagh, shadow of Connacht and Sibhainn that was High Chieftain of Ulster. I am half brother to Connal, chosen by him to rule in his stead." He swallowed once, the man who would one day be called the fairest warrior in Hibernia, and spoke simply. "I have the right."

"Truth, master." Connal stepped forward and laid his hands on his brother's shoulders. "I have known this since my father's day of dying. I name him chieftain of Ulster, I name myself shadow of Connacht." He turned to Maeve, smiling through a glaze of tears. "If Queen Maeve will have me."

Her lips were trembling. "I have said it."

Behind the cheers of the watching crowd, two elders bent to their task. The flames caught, running through the bracken and the kindling, catching the hem of the white robe, sending a pall of greasy, foul-smelling smoke to catch at lung and breath. The fire crackled, then roared, as the stake and the man merged, blended, ran together to blow, in the end, as handfuls of gray ash across Tara. It settled in the long grasses, on the shoulders of the watchers, to be brushed clean of Maeve's hair with a single sweep of the hand as the rulers of Connacht turned their horses toward home.

ABOUT THE AUTHOR

DEBORAH GRABIEN is a historian with a passion for mythology in any shape or form. After living in London for several years, she relocated to San Francisco, where she now lives with her husband and daughter. She is especially fond of cooking, music, and Stonehenge at sunrise.

DON'T MISS
THESE CURRENT
Bantam Bestsellers

☐	27814	**THIS FAR FROM PARADISE** Philip Shelby	$4.95
☐	27811	**DOCTORS** Erich Segal	$5.95
☐	28179	**TREVAYNE** Robert Ludlum	$5.95
☐	27807	**PARTNERS** John Martel	$4.95
☐	28058	**EVA LUNA** Isabel Allende	$4.95
☐	27597	**THE BONFIRE OF THE VANITIES** Tom Wolfe	$5.95
☐	27456	**TIME AND TIDE** Thomas Fleming	$4.95
☐	27510	**THE BUTCHER'S THEATER** Jonathan Kellerman	$4.95
☐	27800	**THE ICARUS AGENDA** Robert Ludlum	$5.95
☐	27891	**PEOPLE LIKE US** Dominick Dunne	$4.95
☐	27953	**TO BE THE BEST** Barbara Taylor Bradford	$5.95
☐	26554	**HOLD THE DREAM** Barbara Taylor Bradford	$5.95
☐	26253	**VOICE OF THE HEART** Barbara Taylor Bradford	$5.95
☐	26888	**THE PRINCE OF TIDES** Pat Conroy	$4.95
☐	26892	**THE GREAT SANTINI** Pat Conroy	$4.95
☐	26574	**SACRED SINS** Nora Roberts	$3.95
☐	27018	**DESTINY** Sally Beauman	$4.95

Buy them at your local bookstore or use this page to order.

Bantam Books, Dept. FB, 414 East Golf Road, Des Plaines, IL 60016

Please send me the items I have checked above. I am enclosing $_____
(please add $2.00 to cover postage and handling). Send check or money
order, no cash or C.O.D.s please.

Mr/Ms _____

Address _____

City/State _____ Zip_____

FB–11/89

Please allow four to six weeks for delivery.
Prices and availability subject to change without notice.